THE FORT AT RIVER'S BEND

Forge Books by Jack Whyte

THE CAMULOD CHRONICLES

The Skystone

The Singing Sword

The Eagles' Brood

The Saxon Shore

The Fort at River's Bend

THE FORT AT RIVER'S BEND

THE CAMULOD CHRONICLES

JACK WHYTE

A TOM DOHERTY ASSOCIATES BOOK

NEW YORK

To my wife, Beverley

and to my grandson, David Michael Johns, who finally got old enough to read his Grandpa's books

This is a work of fiction. All the characters and events portrayed in this novel are either fictitious or are used fictitiously.

THE FORT AT RIVER'S BEND

Map by Ellisa H. Mitchell

This book is printed on acid-free paper.

A Forge Book
Published by Tom Doherty Associates, Inc.
175 Fifth Avenue
New York, NY 10010

Forge® is a trademark of Tom Doherty Associates, Inc.

Library of Congress Cataloging-in-Publication Data

Whyte, Jack.
The fort at River's Bend / Jack Whyte. — 1st ed.
p. cm. — (The Camulod chronicles)
"A Tom Doherty Associates book."
ISBN 0-312-86597-X
1. Arthurian romances—Adaptations. 2. Merlin (Legendary character)—Fiction. 3. Britons—Kings and rulers—Fiction. 4. Arthur, King—Fiction. I. Title. II. Series: Whyte, Jack. Camulod chronicles ; 5.
PR9199.3.W4589F6 1999
813'.54—dc21 98-44007
CIP

First Edition: April 1999

Printed in the United States of America

0 9 8 7 6 5 4 3 2 1

AUTHOR'S NOTE

THE TASK OF acknowledging contributions to my work and to my research has always been a daunting one. I am grateful to so many people for encouragement and assistance that it would be impossible to name all of them. On this occasion, however, three contributions tower above all others in my recollection, since, lacking any of them, this story would not have emerged as it has.

The diagram of a pattern-welded sword that appears on page 217 was developed by John Anstee of Great Britain, who actually made such a sword, using ancient materials and techniques that he had researched over the course of decades. I found the diagram, and a vast range of other, equally useful information, in Hilda Ellis Davidson's excellent book *The Sword in Anglo-Saxon England.* Although first printed in 1962 by the Boydell Press of Woodbridge, Suffolk, I did not discover it until 1995. Had I made the discovery even a decade earlier, my life would have been much simpler and less racked by doubts. I spent years struggling with my own conception of Excalibur, knowing approximately what I envisioned, yet uncertain of the practicality of the ideas I had so crudely developed from my peripatetic research. Between them, these two people provided both enlightenment and gratifying confirmation.

It was my brother Michael who first introduced me to the setting for *The Fort at River's Bend.* In May 1993 he was on holiday in the Lake District with his wife, Kate, when Beverley and I, on a visit to Britain, joined them for a few days in the middle of a glorious early heat wave. When Mike learned that I was fundamentally unhappy with the east-coast location I had chosen for this stage in Arthur's education, he drove me up into the Fells for about ten minutes, along the wildest and most frighteningly narrow, precipitous road I had ever seen, and showed me the site I have since come to know so well.

The Fort at River's Bend is still there today and has become one of the most famous surviving Roman auxiliary forts, thanks to its magnificent and isolated siting, high in Britain's beautiful Lake District. Today's visitors know it as the Fort at Hardknott Pass, but Hardknott Pass is a modern name. The fort's original name—something of a jawbreaker to non-Latin speakers—was Mediobogdum, which translates into English as "situated in the curve (of the river)." The name itself was probably pronounced "Media-BOG-d'm," with the emphasis on the third syllable.

The fort lies nine miles north-east of Ravenglass, an ancient coastal town whose name (Yr-afon-[g]las) predates the Romans and means "the blue harbour" in the Celtic tongue of the local inhabitants the Romans called the Brigantes, a fiercely independent people who never were successfully Romanized. The Roman name for Ravenglass was Glannaventa. The Romans built a supply road from there to the inland town of Ambleside on Lake Windermere, threading it through the two bleak passes of Hardknott and Wrynose. The road was a mere thirty miles long, but it was the only route of its kind from the north-west coast south of Carlyle into the hinterland, its importance underscored by the three forts built to guard it: Glannaventa on the coast, Mediobogdum at the highest point and Galava (Ambleside) at the inland terminus. Towns grew up around Glannaventa and Galava, and survived. No such growth occurred in the magnificent but inhospitable and infertile Hardknott Pass. The garrison there was on its own.

The most astonishing thing about the Hardknott Pass fort is that it sat abandoned, undisturbed and unvandalized for almost fifteen hundred years. Only in the seventeenth century, when the oak forests of Eskdale were plundered to build ships for the Royal Navy's wars, did the fort come to light. Land clearance followed the destruction of the forests, bringing in more and more farmers, who began to strip the sandstone blocks from the great gateways to build houses for their families. In the early nineteenth century, William Wordsworth alluded to the fort, in one of his Duddon Sonnets, as "that lone Camp on Hardknott's heights / Whose guardians bent the knee to Jove and Mars."

Since then, in the past century, hordes of souvenir-hunting visitors have stripped away all the magnificent red tiles that decorated the underground hypocausts, or central heating pillars, that served the bathhouse outside the walls of the fort, and there is no way of knowing how much else has vanished into the same abyss.

The site, maintained now by a local society dedicated to its preservation, is a fascinating place, where history reaches out and grabs you by the throat. I returned to spend a period of weeks there in 1995, living in the delightful Bridge Inn at Santon Bridge, Wasdale, and passed many hours each day absorbing the atmosphere of the fort and the countryside around it, grateful for the support and encouragement of local residents, many of whom were highly knowledgeable about the fort and its environs. The original garrison who built and occupied the fort were Dalmatians—from the region that today is Croatia and Serbia—and I wanted to acquire some impressions of how they must have felt in their isolated post up among the misty, rain-soaked peaks so many hundreds of years ago, with no welcoming little inn awaiting them on the valley floor. All of those impressions, and most of what I discovered about Mediobogdum and its history, will be found in this story. The descriptions of the fort and the details of its construction are accurate. The road it guarded—identified only recently as the famous Tenth Iter of the Antonine Itinerary—climbs from the valley floor to the summit of Hardknott Pass at a gradient of 1 in 3 and presents astonishing challenges even to modern vehicles. The river in whose bend the fort nestles—although far below—is the Esk.

Some aspects of my description may raise quizzical eyebrows among my readers, but even the most surprising of these details are factual. The Romans used concrete, and the domed roofs of the fort's warehouses were made of that material, so that each lateral wall had five buttresses to support the weight of the concrete. Those roofs endured for centuries, perhaps even for a millennium. The barrack-houses were floored with mortar. The garrison also boasted a sophisticated, running-water latrine exactly as described herein. The inscribed plaque above the main gate has been recovered and restored. The bathhouse was as described and was sixty-six feet long and twenty feet wide, its waters tapped from the nearby stream known today as the Campsike. Since the place sat intact for fifteen hundred years after its abandonment, it seems reasonable to postulate that it would have been refurbishable and habitable when Merlyn had need of it a mere two hundred years after the garrison had departed.

Jack Whyte
Kelowna, British Columbia,
June 1997

MAP LEGEND

1. Glannaventa (Ravenglass)
2. Mediobogdum (The Fort)
3. Galava (Ambleside)
4. Manx (Isle of Man)
5. Brocavum (Brougham)
6. Mamucium (Manchester)
7. Deva (Chester)
8. Lindum (Lincoln)
9. Londinium (London)
10. Verulamium (St. Albans)
11. Corinium (Cirencester)
12. Glevum (Gloucester)
13. Aquae Sulis (Bath)
14. Lindinis (Ilchester)
15. Camulod (Camelot)
16. Venta Silurum (Caerwent)
17. Isca Silurum (Caerleon)
18. (Cardiff)
19. Nidum (Neath)
20. Moridunum (Carmarthen)
21. Cicutio (Y Gaer)
22. (Castel Collen)

Key: Roman place names (English/Welsh in parentheses)

THE LEGEND OF THE SKYSTONE

Out of the night sky there will fall a stone
That hides a maiden born of murky deeps,
A maid whose fire-fed, female mysteries
Shall give life to lambent, gleaming blade,
A blazing, shining sword whose potency
Breeds warriors. More than that,
This weapon will contain a woman's wiles
And draw dire deeds of men: shall name an age;
Shall crown a king, called of a mountain clan
Who dream of being drawn from dragon's seed;
Fell, forceful men, heroic, proud and strong,
With greatness in their souls.
This king, this monarch, mighty beyond ken,
Fashioned of glory, singing a song of swords,
Misting with magic madness mortal men,
Shall sire a legend, yet leave none to lead
His host to triumph after he be lost.
But death shall ne'er demean his destiny who,
Dying not, shall ever live and wait to be recalled.

PROLOGUE

I CAN REMEMBER the first time Arthur Pendragon ever called me by my name. He was not yet two years old and he could not pronounce it properly, but neither he nor I was displeased by the result. "Mellin," he called me, crowing with delight at his achievement, and "Mellin" I remained until sufficient time had passed for him to master the new sound my proper name required, the letter "r."

I can also remember the last time he called me by my name, starting up from the pallet where he lay and clutching at my arm, his startled eyes filled with dismay at the wrenching finality of the sudden internal rupture that tore away his life. "Merlyn—?" he gasped, and he died there, with my name upon his lips.

Years have passed since that raw day, and I am still here, the sole survivor of the place men knew as Camulod, the sole repository, in all this land of Britain, of the knowledge that once flourished here and of the dreams a people dreamed of being free.

Solitude, of its essence, is a curse, for man was never meant to live alone, forced to shout out aloud from time to time merely to hear a human voice. I have been thinking about that for two days now, recalling conversations, arguments, debates and songs sung loud and sweet, and all my memories have shrunk to one word and two occasions: the first and last times that the King uttered my name.

Today, I believe, my name is unknown to men and women in this land. In other lands, I hope and pray, some few might yet live who think of me with fondness, in Eire and in Gaul, the land now of the Burgundians and the incoming hordes men call the Franks. Here in Britain, however, if any recall my name, it must be with fear and awe, for I was Merlyn, Sorcerer and Warlock, familiar of dark gods and darker mysteries. None lives today in all of this sad land who might think otherwise. They are all dead, those few who knew me well enough to see beyond the fear, all of my friends, all whom I loved.

And yet, self-pity set aside as being impotent and more of an indulgence than a vice in my life nowadays, I feel much gratitude that I am left alone and free to tend my task without hindrance. I have my tale to tell, and it is not yet done. And my tale has much to do with my name, for in the changes to my name have run the chapters of my life, and those of the King, Arthur.

When one is always alone, what else is there to study, save oneself? I thought to have long since abandoned the self-analysis that claimed so many of my younger years as vanity of the most egregious kind. One's past deeds cannot be undone—their consequences are unalterable.

Throughout my life I sought to be decisive. Better a decision firmly made in error than an opportunity lost forever through vacillation, my father said, and I believed him. He taught me to weigh the evidence, to align it with hard, cold circumstance and then to base a firm decision on the weight of probability. That I have always done, or tried to do.

Even now, in recording my tale, I have asked myself how I could have been so blind, so callow, so at fault or so unquestioning at times. Yet in all the things I did, I was young, still learning, still full of hope and the vigour of youth. I knew what I desired and what this world required of me, for Arthur and for Camulod and for my own self. I saw the end, I firmly believed, and though I lacked the full means of achieving it I trusted yet in God, in life and in the rightness of my task to grant me time and trust and guidance in bringing our Dream to completion. At times, I erred, but seldom grievously.

My goals were simple, their realization complex: I had to bring a boy to manhood, teaching him to perform a task the like of which had never been set for any man before. I had to breed a kingdom from a single colony. I had to lead a people into a new age of hope and wonder. And I had to guard my life close-held to make all these things possible.

I knew none of this consciously while it was happening. I sought merely to offer counsel, to lead from one thing to another. I had no true awareness then of what I was about. I sought to do my duty, and my duty ruled my life. Overall I was successful. I blundered and I hesitated, but I learned with every step. In the end I saw my great success, then watched it vanish, wiped away by the heedless hand of God, and that of man. And I survived it all. For what? To write my tale for eyes that may never read my words? I will shun such despair and continue my chronicle.

On the day when this chapter of my story began—a day approached in trepidation and uncertainty—Merlyn the Sorcerer did not exist. The man who bore my name in those times was yet young, barely approaching his rich, middle years. I was Caius Merlyn Britannicus, Councillor and Legate Commander of the Forces of Camulod; Merlyn to all, and Cay or Caius to my intimate friends and family. My family had almost disappeared by then, reduced with the death of my aged aunt Luceiia Britannicus to one young child, both nephew and cousin, and one half-brother, Ambrose, the son of my father by another woman and a bare six months my junior. I had cousins, in Cambria, but they were distant, in all senses of the term. My friends and intimates were few, as most men's are, but all of them were close by me that day . . .

PART ONE

RAVENGLASS

I

WE STOOD TOGETHER on the forward deck of a galley that moved slowly forward through a bright, still September morning, mere months after the murderous incident that had almost taken the life of one of our number and had subsequently forced us to flee from Camulod in search of the safety we ought to have enjoyed at home. The large, square sail sagged limp in the languid, early-morning breeze that wafted the fog softly from the surface of the bay into which we drew, dispersing its drifting wreaths into nothingness. The oarsmen who propelled the vessel did so cautiously, their eyes intent upon the boatmaster, Tearlach, who directed them with arm and hand movements, his own eyes fixed on the wharf that stretched to meet us.

I stood on the stern deck with the galley's captain, Connor Mac Athol—Connor, Son of Athol, Son of Iain. Connor's father was the King of the Scots of Eire, the people whom the Romans had called the Scotii of Hibernia, and Connor of the Wooden Leg, as his men called him, was the king's admiral in the Southern Seas. I followed his gaze now to where two other galleys, one of them dwarfing its consort, lay already moored at the long wooden pier, on the side farther from us. They were unmistakable—warships like the one in which we rode, sleek and deadly in their aggressive lines—and I could tell from Connor's face that they were not his. They seemed to be deserted, their massive booms angled at the tops of their masts and their sails furled and bound. Beside them, the score or so of fishing boats that shared the anchorage, at that main wharf and at the smaller pier built to the south, seemed tiny. I glanced back to Connor.

"Whose are they?"

His face betrayed nothing of what he thought, but his tone betrayed tension. "They are Liam's. The Sons of Condran."

"What will you do?"

"Nothing. Ignore them. Then leave before they do."

"That one is huge, larger than this."

"Aye, it ships forty-eight oars to our thirty-six. That's Liam's own galley."

"And? Will you fight them?"

His features creased in a wintry little smile. "Probably, but not here. Not in Ravenglass. This is neutral ground."

"Forgive me, I don't understand. What does that mean?"

He turned his head now to look at me. "Simply what it says. This is the only harbour in the entire north-west where ships can call and provision themselves in safety. It has always been that way, since the day the Romans built the fort. All warfare ceases once a ship enters this bay, otherwise it is denied entry. The fort, there, as you can see, is walled and occupied. It can't be taken from the sea, nor can it be surprised from overland, so it sits inviolate and inviolable, and all men use it as a base for gathering provender. We'll rub shoulders with Liam's men inside the town, but we'll ignore them, as they will ignore us. If any trouble does break out, the party causing it will be denied reentry in the future. No trouble ever surfaces within the town." He smiled again. "Of course, when two groups such as ours meet here, it creates a certain tension when the time arrives to leave."

"How? You mean there's an advantage to being the first to leave?"

"Aye, there is. The same advantage that the smith has over the iron he works. He may swing his hammer as hard as he wishes, and the iron is pressed flat against the anvil. The coast becomes the anvil when you are the last ship out."

"But you have three ships to their two."

"I do, and that may make the difference. We'll see."

He turned his head now, his eye seeking Tearlach, and then he nodded and returned to the side rail, where he leaned forward, his attention focused closely on the spot we would occupy here in the harbour called Ravenglass. It was clear to me he had dismissed me from his mind for the time being, absorbed now in the berthing of his long, sleek craft, which had borne us swiftly and effortlessly northward. We had skimmed around the coast of Cambria from the estuary south of it by Glevum, skirting Anglesey, the sacred Isle of the Druids, to seaward before swooping back to the coastline, driving north-east again to where the rugged coast of the region known as Cumbria waited to receive us, across from the humped shape on the horizon that Connor called the Isle of Man.

Accepting that other priorities had claim on him, I turned away and looked towards the prow, where my own party stood gazing forward as raptly as Connor to the new land ahead of them. These were my friends, my family and all my world, now that we had left Camulod behind us in the distant south. Others there were who had set out with us, and those were split between the two galleys that rode as escorts at our rear, but these eleven were my special ones.

The youngest of the men, a giant who towered a hand's width over even me, was twenty-four years old and brother to the galley's captain, Connor, although no stranger would ever have taken them for such. Where Connor was black-haired, blue-eyed and dark of skin in the pure Celtic way, his younger brother Donuil was fair-skinned and light-haired.

His face was clean-shaven in the Roman style, like my own, and his eyes seemed to change from brown to green, depending on the light.

Connor was no small man. He was above average height, huge in the shoulders and deep through the chest. Great, sweeping moustaches drooped below his chin, emphasizing the thickness of his neck, a solid pillar of muscle, and directing attention to the heavy torc, an ornate, intricately worked chieftain's collar of solid gold, that encircled it. Yet even Connor appeared small when seen beside his younger brother. Donuil's great height—he stood a full head taller than most full-grown men—combined with the graceful proportions of his physique to belie the true bulk of the man. His shoulders were broader than his brother Connor's, yet seemed slighter; his chest was larger, yet seemed not so deep; and he seemed slender where his brother appeared broad and bulky—all due to his height.

Looking at Donuil now, and seeing the ease with which he stood, one arm about the waist of his wife, Shelagh, as they gazed together at the scene ahead of them, I wondered again, as I had a hundred times, about the influence this clan of aliens, this single family of Scots, had exerted upon my life.

Athol Mac Iain had not lacked progeny. All of them had, however, been born in Eire, far from where I had grown up in Camulod, ignorant of their existence. One of them, his youngest daughter, Deirdre, had become my wife and had been killed while pregnant with my child. Long before her death, however, her brother Donuil had become my hostage, captured in war and held against his father's promise of non-intervention in our ongoing conflict with the warlord Gulrhys Lot of Cornwall. None of us knew of the link that bound us until I eventually brought my wife home to Camulod and Deirdre and Donuil were reunited, each stunned by the other's reappearance.

Another sister, Ygraine, had been wedded to my archenemy, Gulrhys Lot, to bind the early alliance between her father's people and Cornwall. Angry and disgruntled at the treatment she had endured from her inhuman spouse, she willingly fled with my cousin Uther Pendragon during a long campaign, and the two became enamoured of each other, producing a bastard son. It was I who later found Ygraine on a lonely beach on the Cornish coast, being violated by a man who was wearing my cousin's armour, stripped from Uther's corpse. I held her as she died, and I barely managed to rescue her infant son, Uther's son. I leaped aboard the boat where he lay crying and drifted with it, helpless, out to sea, where we were found by yet another brother, Connor, dispatched by his father the king to meet Ygraine and bring her safely home to Eire. That same boy, Arthur Pendragon, my lifetime charge, now stood by his Uncle Donuil's side, peering towards the land.

Remembering, I shook my head again at such a host of wild improbabilities. But I no longer thought or sought to question them. I am a Christian, by birth and upbringing, but I am also a Druidic Celt, trained by my mother's people, the Pendragon of Cambria. The Celtic half of me has always believed in fate and the inevitability of things decreed by minds greater than human. The Christian, Roman-British half of me, thanks to my great-aunt Luceiia Britannicus has come to believe the same: some things are meant to be and will come to pass, despite the blinking disbelief of humankind. That thought brought a smile and a stirring of goose-flesh as I stared forward now to the wooden wharf that drew closer with every gentle stroke of the oars, for there stood the crowning proof of what I had been thinking.

The man who slew Uther Pendragon and stripped him of his armour was a man I had met before—an enemy, but not a mortal foe. I believed him when he told me he had not known Uther's identity when he killed him. His surprise at learning he had slain Uther Pendragon was too genuine to doubt. And so, sickened by the carnage I had seen throughout the final battles of the campaign in Cornwall, I made no effort either to fight him or to detain him that day. I simply watched him ride away unscathed. His name was Derek, and he called himself the king of Ravenglass. Now, many years later, I recognized him easily among the crowd thronging the wharf.

The great galley slid smoothly to the side of the long, wooden pier, propelled by one last sweep of its thirty-six oars. The oarsmen brought their long sweeps up in unison, scattering drops of water inboard as they held the oars briefly at the vertical then brought them down, blades forward, lowering them hand over hand with the skill of long usage and dropping them in overlapping rows along the sides of the craft, atop the rows of benches. Two men crouched at prow and stern, poised to throw mooring ropes to eager hands waiting on the wharf. Four others hung far overboard, positioning great pads of hempen cushions to protect the vessel's side against damage from the barnacle-encrusted timbers of the pier. The galley slowed, its forward motion bleeding away with the dying impetus of that final thrust until it barely moved through the water, and a stillness fell as everyone waited. Then came a gentle nudge as ship met moorings. Ropes flew outwards and were seized by willing hands, and an involuntary roar of approval came from the watching crowd, which surged forward in welcome. Crewmen leaped down onto the dock to secure the heavy gangplank, which was already rearing high above the galley's side, hoisted by ropes and pulleys from the recessed well in the central causeway that housed it. Momentously, ponderously, one end swung outward over the rail and was lowered gently to the dock where, in moments, it was safely grounded and secured by the waiting crewmen.

Satisfied that his vessel was securely berthed, Connor turned away from the rail and moved towards me, walking effortlessly despite the carved and tapered wooden cylinder that had replaced his right leg from the knee down. He was smiling, taking no notice now of the crowd bustling on the wharf.

"Well, Yellow Head," he said to me, "I'm first ashore, by custom, so you have a few moments to collect your thoughts." His smile broadened. "This is the worst part for me—the transition from ship to shore, from sea legs to land legs. It's bad enough on two feet." He stamped his peg leg against the decking. "I've ended up on my arse more than a few times. You'll notice that my men take care not to look at me until I call to them." He shook his head, his smile now one of self-deprecation. "I'll see you over there."

As he spoke, a rope came swinging, apparently out of nowhere, and he raised his hand to seize it, almost without looking. I spun to see whence it had come, and almost before I'd had time to realize that it dangled from the same pole that had hoisted the gangplank out from the ship, Connor had grasped the rope in both hands and quickly placed his foot in the loop at the end of it. Immediately, he was snatched upward, swinging smoothly out and over the side to be lowered gently to the dock. There he removed his foot from the loop and stood slightly spread-legged, retaining his hold on the rope, which remained taut, until he had achieved balance.

I glanced around me, and it was true: none of his fierce-looking crew was watching him. A moment longer he stood there, swaying slightly, and then he released the rope.

"Take it, Sean!" he roared, and it swung inboard again as the captain turned towards the onlookers on the shore, who had watched all of this with curiosity. He threw his arms wide in a gesture of triumph and greeting and was immediately engulfed in a crowd of welcomers.

Now the galley was suddenly filled with the moving bodies of the oarsmen, who normally sat in serried, disciplined ranks for hours on end, working or resting. Released from their oars, they appeared to fill the ship beyond its capacity as they crowded towards the gangplank in a noisy, undisciplined tide. I could see there was no point in attempting then to walk the length of the vessel to my own party on the foredeck, so I resolved to wait and go ashore with my people at the end of the exodus and with a modicum of dignity. As the thought occurred to me, I heard Tearlach, the boatmaster, call to me.

"Merlyn! Come you forward now and we'll clear a way for you."

I shook my head, smiling at him and holding up my hand. "No, Tearlach, not yet. Let the men go first. I have to talk with the boy before we leave the ship."

Tearlach shrugged and shook his head. "Please yourself," he muttered, and he swung away to start shouting more orders.

I turned my eyes back to the crowded wharf, seeking the man who called me "Yellow Head," but my view of him was obscured by the oarsmen filing down the gangplank, their brightly coloured Celtic clothing ablaze in the early-morning sunlight and their weapons and armour glittering and gleaming where they caught the light. These men were warriors, with a wildness in their looks and in their bearing that boded ill for any who might seek to bar their way. And yet it was evident from their demeanour that they were at ease, that this was not their first time here. None sought to flee their presence, and there were many, indeed, who greeted individuals by name and bade them welcome.

As the crowd swirled upon itself, Connor's head came into view again and I found him looking at me. He nodded, raising one hand to me casually, unseen by his companion, Derek of Ravenglass himself, who stood with his back to me. Another group moved down the gangplank and my view was obscured again. I glanced to my left, into the body of the ship, and saw that fully half the men had gone ashore and that I could now begin to make my way towards the prow. I set off, moving slowly along the central causeway, pausing occasionally to allow crewmen to pass in front of me from one side of the vessel to the other.

Ahead of me, the oldest member of our group, my closest friend, Lucanus, watched me and nodded, one eyebrow raised sardonically in an amused half-smile as I approached.

"Well," he murmured as I reached him, "Derek of Ravenglass has weathered the years well since Verulamium. A bit stouter, much greyer, but I recognized him instantly. Has he seen you yet?"

"No. Connor has managed thus far to keep him from looking up here, but he will not be able to for much longer. I had best get down there."

"Hmm. Are you sure you would not like me to come with you?"

"Quite sure, but thank you. I must go alone. Whatever comes of this visit must take place between him and me. I want no other eyes or ears there in the first few moments."

"So be it, then." Luke's eyes were on the crowded scene below. "But bear in mind, my friend, that if he refuses it will be a setback we are already prepared to take in stride. The arrangements are in place for us to travel onward if we must."

"Aye, but let's hope we need not travel so far, Luke. Arthur!"

At my call, the boy stopped what he was doing and turned towards me instantly, his large, wide-set eyes reflecting golden in the low-angled, early-morning sun. I beckoned, and as he reached my side I nodded towards the wharf. "I'm going ashore to speak with the man talking to your Uncle Connor. He is the king I told you about, and he may wish to meet you, since he met your father once. In the meantime, whether he does or not, I want you to wait here patiently and behave like a grown man. Will you do that for me?"

The boy smiled at me, showing far more maturity than his eight years might indicate. He said nothing, merely nodding his head.

"Good lad!" I ruffled his hair and made my way directly to the gangplank, aware of all their eyes watching me. I was aware, too, of the spring of the down-sloping passageway beneath my feet, and of the fact that the press of bodies on the wharf had thinned out greatly. But with all of my being I was aware of the broad shoulders and imposing height of the man Derek, who stood with his back to me, waving an arm to emphasize what he was saying to Connor.

As I drew near them, Connor grinned at me over Derek's shoulder, then stretched out a hand to grasp the other's arm. silencing him.

"Your pardon, Derek," he said, smiling still. "I have brought a good friend with me, whom I believe you know already."

Arrested in mid-word, Derek of Ravenglass swung around to face me, and I watched as a series of expressions swept rapidly across his face: puzzlement, followed quickly by recognition, surprise and finally a close-guarded look I could not define. I saw suspicion there, and a hint of fear or defiance.

"The Dreamer," he said, frowning.

I nodded. "Merlyn Britannicus."

"Aye, I remember. Cornwall, by way of Camulod. The first time we met, you used another name."

"I did. Ambrose of Lindum."

"That was it. You're Roman."

"No," I shook my head. "No more than half, and that in name alone. I'm British."

"British, what's that?" The scorn in his question made it plain that Derek was far from intimidated by my sudden reappearance.

I shrugged. "The other half of me is Celt, like you. The combination makes me British, since I am neither one nor the other, yet was born here in Britain."

"You're a talker, I recall that from our first meeting, when we were on the road to join Lot's army."

"You were on the road for that purpose. We merely rode along with you."

"Aye, you did, then disappeared." He paused. "Your physician paid me gold to take your wounded through the meeting place that time, to safety beyond Lot's army."

That was true. He had taken the gold, but then had failed to fulfil his end of the bargain in entirety. That no ill had befallen our people had been due only to Lucanus's quick thinking on that occasion. I knew I would have to speak with care here if I were to avoid aggravating the situation by stirring up feelings of guilt on his part.

"What was his name, that physician of yours?"

"Lucanus."

"Aye, Lucanus. Did he survive?"

"He did, with all his men and wagons."

"Ah, he did. Good, that pleases me. I've often wondered about that."

This was not what I had expected. I had been attempting to analyse his tone, listening for signs of truculence or real hostility.

"What do you mean?" I asked.

He looked me straight in the eye, then sniffed, glancing sideways at Connor.

"It was a foul-up, all around." He cleared his throat. "We came to Lot's gathering place without problems, but instead of proceeding clear through, we had to stop when I was summoned to a meeting of commanders. Some fool had seen us coming and passed the word that I had arrived. We left your people on the outskirts of the encampment—couldn't very well take them with us, right into Lot's camp, could I? Anyway, the gathering was enormous, and I rode on in with my men to find the rest of our contingent, most of whom had come down the coast by water, ferried by Lot's galleys.

"As things turned out, Lot wasn't there and never did appear, and one thing led to another and I couldn't get back that night—held in a so-called planning session all night long. A dog-fight was what it was, more than anything else. With Lot away, everyone wanted to be a general, even though most of them couldn't find a latrine if they were standing in it. Later that evening, when I finally realized how things were going to be, I sent some of my people back to find yours and lead them on through, but by the time they reached the spot where we had left them, your people were all gone. No sign of them at all. My own men thought nothing more of it, and I didn't hear of it until the following day. Didn't know what to do then. I asked some questions but found no answers, and I didn't want to be too specific. I heard nothing about any disturbance or fighting or disagreements over wagons, and so I let it go. But I've often wondered what happened to them, how they got away."

I was smiling by this time, feeling much relieved. "Why don't you ask Lucanus how he did it? He's here, on the galley." I nodded towards where Lucanus stood on the foredeck, watching us. When he saw the astonishment on Derek's face, Luke smiled and nodded a greeting.

"Well I'm damned," Derek muttered. "And there's that other one, too, the one who rode with you. The big Scot."

"That is my brother Donuil," Connor said.

"Is it, by all the gods?" Derek turned back to us, his eyes moving from me to Connor and back to me. "Why are you here, Merlyn the Dreamer? What do you want from me?"

"Nothing that may not be within your power to grant or to withhold,"

I responded, smiling and shrugging my shoulders. "Food and lodgings, for the night at least, for me and mine, and perhaps sanctuary."

"*Sanctuary?*" He frowned as he repeated the alien sounds. "I don't know that word."

"It means shelter, respite."

"Respite from what? Or from whom?" He glowered now at Connor, his face clouded with suspicion. "There will be no trouble here. You know Liam, Condran's admiral, is here?"

Connor nodded. "Coincidence," he said. "Nothing to do with anything. Liam has never seen or heard of Merlyn, and is no part of his cares. The rules apply, as always."

"Hmm." Apparently mollified, Derek looked back at me. "So? Respite from whom?"

I shrugged. "It is a long story—not long in the telling, but complex. I would be happy to tell it to you."

"Hmmph." He looked away again, towards the galley. "You have women with you, and children. How many?"

"Twelve, counting myself, aboard the galley."

"Aboard the galley . . . and elsewhere?"

I indicated the two escort galleys that held their place outside the harbour. "Six more, split between the other vessels."

"Why do they stand off like that, Mac Athol? Afeared of the Sons of Condran?"

Connor smiled and shrugged his great shoulders. "Not since they learned to stand on two legs. Simple courtesy, my friend. We had no knowledge of the enemy's presence until we arrived, but it makes no difference here. They merely wait to be invited to enter. Three galleys at one time might have seemed too much like an invasion."

"Aye, well, signal them in. They are yours, and therefore welcome. Feargus, is it?"

"Aye, and Logan."

Derek spoke again to me. "The hospitality, for a night at least, presents no difficulty. It would have been extended anyway. Further, I'll not commit. But your story should be interesting." He paused. "Tell me, do you still dream?"

"From time to time," I answered, smiling. "I dreamed of you less than four weeks ago. That is why we are here."

He sighed deeply. "I was afraid you would say something like that."

"I saw you wearing Uther's armour," I said. "Do you still have it?"

"I do." His voice was level.

"When did you last wear it?"

"Not since I returned home, after we last met. I had my belly filled with war, and I thank the gods I've not had to take a sword in my hand since then. Why do you ask?"

"Is it in good condition?"

"Aye, perfect. I could strap it on again today if the need arose. Is that likely?"

My smile widened to a grin and I shook my head. "No, but I might like to buy it back from you some day, were you willing to sell it."

He gazed at me for some time, sucking on the inside of one cheek, before he responded. When he did, his voice was thoughtful. "Some day, you say? And how far off might that day be? I warn you, it could make a difference to my decision and to my price." He glanced back towards the galley and then nodded to me. "Bring your people ashore and come you with me. One of my men will conduct them to a place where they can rest and clean themselves. We have a Roman bathhouse here, if they would like to use it."

"You mean a working bathhouse?"

"You think I'd offer you a broken one?" The big man was glaring at me from beneath lowered brows, but I saw the glint of humour in his eyes. "Should I be thinking now you are surprised to find we might be clean, or clever enough to maintain a furnace, even though its Roman owners are long gone?"

"No, by all the old gods," I demurred, straight-faced. "Such thoughts would never have occurred to me."

"Hmm. Well, bring your people off."

I beckoned to my party on the galley and they gathered together immediately, moving towards the landing planks, already prepared to disembark. Connor cupped his hands and called to Tearlach, bidding him summon Feargus and Logan inshore. As men began moving about, preparing the signal to the waiting galleys, the first of my group, Dedalus and Lucanus, stepped onto the wharf together and made their way to us, followed by the others.

"Lucanus," I greeted him. "Derek remembers you from the road to Aquae."

"As I do him," Luke answered, smiling slightly. "You look well, Derek, little changed in twelve years. Who would have thought you and I would ever meet again?"

"Not I, but you are welcome here, Physician. Merlyn tells me you brought all your people home, that time, even without my help." His eyes moved from Lucanus to Dedalus. "Derek of Ravenglass," he said, nodding.

"Dedalus," the other answered, nodding in return. "I am a friend of Merlyn's."

"Aye, from Camulod. I can see that. *You're* no physician."

Ded's mouth quirked into a half-smile. "No, I'm a centurion, but not from Rome."

The others had joined us by that time and I introduced each of them, including the boys, to the king, their host at least for the night, and told them that arrangements would be made for all of us. Derek had been joined by a man whom he introduced to us as Blundyl before instructing him on the housing and distribution of our group. When he had finished, Derek took me by the arm.

"Come. You and me. Blundyl will see to the others for now. I want to talk to you."

He walked away immediately and I followed him, exchanging expressionless looks with Lucanus and Shelagh as I went. We walked the full length of the wharf, apparently ignored by all, except that I was conscious of a curiosity in many of the people, who took pains to show no awareness of our passing.

Once through the portals in the central gate-tower of the western wall, I found myself in a Roman fort the like of which I had never before seen. It was a standard cohortal fort, built to house and maintain a garrison of five to six hundred men. I had been in several similar places over the years, all of which had been in varying stages of ruin and decay. Most of them had been abandoned and deserted many years before the start of the legions' withdrawals from Britain, during my father's boyhood. Compelled by harsh economies, thanks to a total lack of reinforcements from beyond their shores, the central garrisons of the province were being remanned and reinforced at the expense of lesser, more outlying forts. Such had not been the case, though, with Glannaventa, as this fort had been called. A garrison had occupied this place right up until the final days of the withdrawals, during my own boyhood, and because of the importance of the natural harbour, the place had been reoccupied by the local folk the moment the legionary garrison abandoned it. It was like stepping backwards into the time when, in forts like this all over Britain, the life of the country was maintained and closely governed in good order.

All of the barracks buildings that had housed the garrison were still in use and still in good repair, their log walls tightly mortared and their tiled roofs free of moss, betraying no sign of rot or sagging. A number of new doors in the long walls indicated that they were occupied today by families, rather than by military squads. These buildings, six of them, each constructed to accommodate close to a hundred men plus their centurions, were laid out laterally in two blocks of three. Behind each block, looking very similar to the barracks buildings but serving another purpose altogether, were two more long, low buildings, dedicated to the service of the troops and housing smithies, tanneries and a variety of other manufactories. One block of four of these buildings lay on each side of the wide central road that joined the main gate behind us to the east gate in the opposite wall more than three hundred paces distant, and the eight of them completely filled the front half of the fort, the *Praetentura*, the section that lay closest to the main source of enemy attack. In the case of Glannaventa, that source had been the western sea.

Now, as we walked swiftly along the straight, wide avenue towards the stone-built central buildings that had once housed the garrison's administrative centre, I stared about me avidly, curious to learn all that I could about the life Derek's people lived here in this ordered place. Derek himself was striding ahead of me, immersed in his own thoughts. As he drew abreast of the end of the last barracks block, I lengthened my stride to catch up to him.

"I'm impressed," I said. "You modified the barracks into family units."

He looked at me and then beyond me to the building on my right. "Aye," he growled. "That was a nuisance at first, until it became clear we had to do it properly. At first it was a haphazard thing, people doing what they wanted to do, whether they were capable or not. Then others started carping because some people had more space than they had, and that was true, but it seemed there was nothing to be done by then. And then one fool ripped out a wall and brought down an entire building—killed four people. That's when I decided something had to change, and the changes had to be according to a plan."

He stopped, abruptly, and turned to look back the way we had come. "That one there," he said, indicating the second building on our right. "That's the one that collapsed. Never know it now, would you?" He did not wait for an answer. "After that, I put every builder in the place to work, systematically. Some of them, most of them in fact, had worked for the Romans, so they knew what was required and how to do what needed to be done. We gutted the interiors, divided them equally with new walls, cut doors in the outside walls and turned each building into housing units for twelve families. No more problems after that."

"All the units are the same size? What about the centurions' quarters, on the ends here? They look larger."

"They are. What of that?"

I shrugged. "You said you had no problems. How did people decide who lived where?"

He spat into the road. "They didn't. I decided, and no one argued. I'm king here." He turned on his heel and began to walk again. "Most of the people who live in these buildings are our best artisans and their families. Their workshops are here, too, in these last two buildings, courtesy of Roman efficiency—smithy and foundry, cobblery, barrel-maker's cooperage, carpenter's yard, pottery and tilemaker, stonemason's yard. All in one location, everything the garrison needed. Clever whoresons, the Romans. I could see no point in not using these places for ourselves."

We had now arrived at the central rectangular space containing the three main buildings of this and every other Roman military installation:

the commandant's house, the headquarters building and the central granaries and storage warehouses known as the *Horrea.* These stone buildings sat apart from all others, isolated by the main lateral roadway, the Via Principalis, which crossed in front of them, and the second-largest street, the Via Quintana, at the rear. Since time immemorial, these two lateral streets had divided the interior of every Roman military camp, regardless of size, into the front half, the Praetentura, and the rear half, the *Retentura.* "That where I live." Derek pointed his thumb towards the massive commandant's house.

"The Praetorium? You live there?"

"It is my house."

"Aye, I suppose it is. You are the king."

I examined the Praetorium as we approached it, but could see little to indicate that it was a king's house now rather than a Roman commander's. High walls surrounded it, pierced by one large, central double portal, the doors of which stood open but were cloaked in shadow. I could see no guards anywhere and reflected that this king must have no need of such.

We cut diagonally across the main road in front of the king's house and he led me into the building flanking it, the former *Principia,* or garrison headquarters block. This had changed greatly since the legions left. It had been built originally around an open quadrangle containing a fountain, with the main entrance facing the cross-street. The principal part of the building, at the rear, occupied more than a third of the total area of the block and had once housed the garrison's most precious properties: the regimental chapel where the standards, colours and battle honours were stored, the regimental paymaster's vaults and the personnel records office of the regimental clerk. This part of the headquarters block also contained the tribunal briefing room where the officer commanding, down through the centuries, traditionally received his staff at formal meetings, addressing the assembly from the rostrum of the tribunal at the far right of the long room.

The building's open quadrangle had once been the off-duty domain of the garrison's officers. Wide colonnaded walkways on both sides and on either side of the main entrance gave access to a series of lesser offices around the building's exterior. Some time within the past three decades, after the departure of the Romans, the open space of the quadrangle had been roofed, leaving only a large rectangular hole in the centre to vent the smoke from the enormous firepit that had replaced the obligatory ornamental fountain in the open yard. Great beams of handhewn oak now spanned the space, supporting a second framework, less massive, that reared above them to hold a peaked and gabled roof of heavy thatch, open around the overhanging eaves to permit the passage of air among the rafters. This roof was intricately built, evidently engineered and erected by a master carpenter, but I thought it a pity that it should shut out much of the light along with most of the bad weather. Gazing up at it, it struck me as the local equivalent of King Athol's Great Hall in Eire.

All of this I saw as I strode at Derek's heels, for he made no attempt to play the guide for me. Matching him step for step, I followed him as he swung right, up to the colonnaded walk, and proceeded to the first door on his left. The bottom half of this door was closed, a hinged flap on its back raised to form a broad counter behind which stood a man evidently on duty of some kind. As Derek spoke with him, exchanging muttered greetings, I edged forward curiously to peer into the dim room at his back. It was a spartan place, bare of furnishings, with high, deep shelves lining every wall.

"Weapons," Derek grunted. I stared at him blankly. "Your weapons, take them off. They stay here until you leave."

"What, all of them? Am I to go unarmed among strangers?"

"Aye, along with everyone else, so you won't be lonely. That's the law in Ravenglass—no weapons. This room is for your people. Condran's crowd left theirs in a room on the other side. If someone else arrives while you are here, there's place for their things, too."

I had already loosened my swordbelt, catching it up and wrapping the loose ends around the scabbards of my long sword and my dagger. "How long has that law been in place?"

"Ever since this port was opened up to passing ships after the Romans left. It saves a lot of strife and bloodshed."

"I'm sure it does, but don't you find enforcing it to be a little . . . hazardous?"

His teeth flashed in a tiny, swift grin. "No, not at all. You don't want to comply, you leave, assisted or otherwise, and you don't come back."

I could only shake my head as I passed my bundled weapons over the counter to the custodian. "Different," I muttered.

"Healthy," the king responded. "Come on, then."

He led me once more through the courtyard to the main entrance, where he turned sharply and made his way between the walls bordering his own house on our left and the headquarters building on our right. We emerged on the other cross-street, the old Via Quintana, which we crossed to continue moving towards the eastern gate now visible ahead of us. In this portion of the fort, too, most of the buildings had been converted into living quarters, although I could smell fresh-baked bread and other delicious aromas which spoke of the enterprises being pursued here. I noticed another stone building, close by the rear wall.

"Is that a hospital over there?"

"It was, but there's no need of it now, and no surgeons to use it. It's more living quarters."

"What about the stables? What happened to them?"

"Outside the walls, now. We needed the living space."

We were close to the rear wall now, and I looked up to the empty parapet walk between the turrets. "You don't post guards up there?"

"Against what? My people are farmers. They have their fields to tend, beyond the walls, and the only threat to us would come from the sea." He nodded towards the distant mountain peaks that reared up inland. "We have the Fells, there, at our back, and only one road through them, impassable in winter and easily held, if need be, in the summer. We have no need of guards. I told you, I have not had a sword in my hand since I came home, seven years ago."

"Seven? It was eight years ago we parted, and you were homeward bound then."

"Aye, I was, and it took me the better part of a year to walk from there to here. I lost my horse soon after you and I parted company."

We passed through the double gates in the eastern tower, and I stopped dead in my tracks.

"What's wrong?" Derek had stopped, too, and was staring questioningly at me over his shoulder, shouting above the noise that had suddenly engulfed us.

I shook my head. "Nothing," I cried. "I'm surprised, that's all. I did not expect this. . . . It's bigger, far bigger than I would have thought."

He looked around him. "It may be," he shouted back, "but it's still too small. We have no room to build, and no good stone to build with."

Somehow, arriving from the sea and entering the bustling confines of the high-walled fort, my mind had formed the notion that the fort was all there was. I had expected to emerge into open farmland beyond the walls. Instead, I found myself at the edge of a thriving vicus, the township that had grown around the fort for hundreds of years until it stretched farther than the eye could see, in the shape of a large funnel, its narrow spout blocked by the eastern wall of the fort itself and its swelling shape defined by the steep, tree-clad hillsides stretching up and away on either side.

We were standing at the edge of a congested marketplace, the tables of the closest vendors placed against the walls flanking the gates at our back, and chaos swirled about us. The air was filled with the sounds and smells of animals and poultry, the voices of the crowd that thronged around and between the stalls and the cries of the vendors whose wares were everywhere in evidence, in an enviable display of prosperity and wealth. There was fresh produce of all descriptions, from onions and fat leeks to green-leafed clumps of growth that I had never seen before. The smell of fresh-baked bread came from my left now to mingle with the odour of fish from somewhere ahead of me. I smelled the heavy musk of frying garlic, and saw a stall with deep, metal dishes and a stone-framed fire on which a woman fried fresh shrimp, stirring the mass of them with a large, heavy wooden ladle. Saliva spurted from beneath my tongue, reminding me that I had not eaten since the previous night.

"Market day," Derek grunted, needlessly. "Come on."

I stayed close to him as he picked his way among the crowds, nodding from time to time and sometimes returning a spoken greeting to those who called him by name. Ahead of us on our left and towering above the intervening stalls, I saw the sandstone walls and arched roof of yet another Roman building. I caught his arm.

"What's that place over there?"

"The bathhouse. That's where we're going."

Moments later, I heard my own name shouted. Sean the navigator grinned at me from behind a baker's stall, where he stood clutching a steaming pasty. I waved to him then had to hasten to catch up with Derek, whose height alone had prevented me from losing sight of him among the press of bodies.

I now began to notice others of our crew among the crowd, but few of them saw me, and those who did ignored me, apart from an occasional cool nod. The Sons of Condran were there, too, I saw, but neither group paid the slightest attention to the other, and when I jostled one of Liam's men by accident, he passed me by with no more than a grunt and a surly look. From then on, I concentrated only on keeping Derek in sight.

II

THE CROWD THINNED out as we approached the bathhouse, the densely packed stalls giving way to pens and larger, open spaces containing livestock: cattle, swine, goats, horses of the local mountain breed known as garrons and unkempt, brown-wooled sheep, as well as flocks of hens and geese and ducks and one gathering of regal swans, their wings evidently clipped to prevent them from flying.

"Over here." Derek made his way directly to a dreary-looking collection of flimsy buildings. The bathhouse's western and southern wings defined a bare, open, L-shaped space that sheltered a herd of shaggy garrons. A humpbacked little man with violently crossed eyes, working among the horses, saw me and came scuttling to meet me, scowling as he weaved between the bodies of the animals that prevented him from seeing my companion. As soon as he recognized Derek, however, he stopped, then turned about and disappeared again among the horses.

I glanced at the king. "Do many people react to you that way?"

He almost smiled. "That's Ulf. He never speaks."

"Never? Is he mute?"

Now he did smile. "Only when he's sober. He has a tongue like a pike's jaws when he decides to use it. Most of the time, thank the gods, he chooses to be silent." He said no more, turning away to look about him, and I began idly counting the horses, but I lost track of the milling bodies before I reached twenty.

"Are these all his? For sale?"

Derek grunted. "They're mine. He tends them for me." As he spoke, the little man re-emerged from the depths of the herd, leading two bridled garrons. He handed one set of reins to each of us—flat-braided ropes attached to simple head stalls with metal bits—and vanished silently again.

Derek led his horse to a nearby block of wood and used it to mount, swinging his leg easily over the horse's back from the top of the block. I followed his example. It had been too many years since I had vaulted to the bare back of a horse, and I had no wish to make the attempt here and fail. I dug my heels in gently and the animal beneath me twitched his ears, plainly wondering if the stranger on his back could be ignored or should be heeded. I reined him sharply, pulling his head down as I kicked again, letting him feel the strength of my legs, and he moved forward contentedly, leaping ahead to catch up with his companion.

At one point, as we rode past a long, low building almost on the farthest edge of the town, I saw something that caught my attention. A man had suddenly stopped moving, on the point of entering the building. I looked directly at him but saw only a dirty, yellow tunic and a full beard before he pushed the door open and went in. Nevertheless, I knew he had been staring at me, not at Derek.

"That place over there on our left, what is it?"

Derek glanced where I was pointing. "An alehouse."

"You mean a tavern?"

"That's what I mean."

Moments later we had passed beyond the limits of the town and were riding among dense trees that grew right to the edges of the road on either side. Derek kicked his garron to a canter and mine stayed with him without urging. Soon we passed out of the trees into an area of open fields through which the road ran arrow straight. The few buildings I could see on either side were evidently storage sheds and shelters, and the borders between individual fields were difficult to define, consisting mainly of slightly differing patterns of growth. In the continuing silence from my companion I looked about me curiously.

The valley through which we now rode was perhaps a mile in width at this place, and had obviously been reclaimed over a span of ages from the forest that wooded the steep hillsides to left and right. Ahead of us, on either side, the hills rose higher as they marched inland, until the highest I could see, in the far distance, were crowned with crags and rearing cliffs, some of them shrouded in what was either cloud or snow.

"How far does the valley extend, Derek?"

He glanced at me, frowning slightly at my interruption of his thoughts. "About six miles. To the edge of the mere."

"The mere? What mere is that?" I asked from pure contrariness.

"The mere. It has no name. It's just a mere like any other."

"Six miles. And the farmland extends all that way?"

"No, only as far as the soil permits. The land rises and the rock breaks through about four miles from here."

We had reached a division in the fields on our left. Ripening grain gave way abruptly to a crop of coarse-leafed plants I recognized as being some form of kale. Derek swung his mount off the road, leading us along a narrow, well-beaten path between the two crops, heading directly for the treed hillside about half a mile distant.

"Where are you taking me?"

"To a place where I can think and we can talk."

We rode thereafter in silence broken only by the plodding of hooves and the song of birds, until the narrow track reached the end of the field at the entrance to a V-shaped notch in what I had assumed, from the moment I first saw it in the distance, to be a chest-high wall of stone running the entire length of the valley. As we approached, however, it became apparent that what we were facing now was not so much a wall as an accretion—I can think of no other word—of stones, some of them barely larger than pebbles, others that looked large enough to defy the powers of a single man to move them. All of them had been piled haphazardly to form a barrier I now realized was no less than twenty paces thick. As I stared, my mind numbed by the enormity of this rock pile, Derek's horse entered the passage that pierced the middle of the heap, and mine ambled contentedly after him.

"Where did all these come from?"

"From the ground, the fields." Derek drew rein and hitched himself around to look back at me. "We have a local jest that we grow more, and bigger, stones than we do crops. They work their way up to the surface every winter. Our people spend months each year clearing them out and dragging them over here, and the next year there's a brand-new crop of them. It never ends. It's been going on since before the Romans came."

I looked at the stones piled on my right, some of which reached higher than my head. "I can see that, but that's more than four hundred years!"

"Far more. Our people were farming here a long time before that."

"Is it the same on the other side of the valley?"

"It's the same everywhere."

"I don't understand—you said you had no stone for building."

Derek threw me a scornful look. "I said no *good* stone. I meant sandstone, stone that can be quarried, cut and dressed. Most of what you see here is useless for building. It's too small, too loose, too brittle and too much trouble. Hurry."

The trees began again on the other side of the barrier, and our path took us up and beyond the crest of the hill to where, just below the summit, the hillside terminated in a high cliff. Beyond it lay another valley, this one still choked with trees, and on our left stretched the sea.

Derek sat still for a few moments, admiring the view, then dismounted and tethered his horse, nodding for me to accompany him as he led the way to a shallow, grass-floored shelf above the cliff's edge, where he seated himself comfortably, his back against the bole of a tree. I found a spot by his side, wedging my back comfortably between two thick clumps of grass on the hillside behind us. Thereafter, we sat in companionable silence for a spell, gazing out across the valley and squinting against the glare of the sparkling sea in the distance, each of us composing in his own mind, I had no doubt, the words that he would use to frame his ideas most persuasively. We had come here to think and talk, after all, not merely to enjoy the vista. Derek's voice broke in on my thoughts.

"*Sang . . . Sank* . . . What was that word you used?"

"Sanctuary."

"Sanctuary, aye . . . You said it meant shelter or respite, and I asked you from what. Now I'm asking you again. No one will interrupt us here." He looked sharply at me. "Why are you smiling?"

I shook my head. "It occurs to me that we are totally unable—any of us—to anticipate what's going to happen next at any time. Last night, when we dropped anchor outside your harbour . . . even this morning as we approached your wharf . . . I had no idea in my head about what kind of reaction the sight of me might provoke in you. I was trying to prepare myself for anything—from outright violence, to disinterest, to a refusal of permission to land."

He had been plucking at the end of his moustache, eyes narrowed in concentration, lips pursed as he watched me speak.

"Why would you expect violence? You and I have never quarrelled."

"No, but neither have we shared a common cause. Nominally, on the two occasions when we met, we did so in enmity as warriors of Cornwall and Camulod."

"Aye, well, that was one-sided on the first occasion. I thought then that you were with us. It was not until we met the second time that I knew otherwise. Frankly, you didn't cross my mind between those times. I thought about you often after our second encounter, though. I was damned glad to get away from you on that beach."

"How so?"

"I thought you would kill me."

"Kill you? You threatened to kill me, if I fought you."

"I did. And I'd have tried. But I'm a mere man, no match against a warlock." There was absolute sincerity in his voice and in his eyes.

"Warlock? I am no warlock, Derek. I'm an ordinary man like you."

"Hmm. An ordinary man who sees his friends die in his dreams and knows the timing and the exact style of it, describing the scene and the weapon used long afterward, when he was nowhere near the place. That's far from ordinary in my mind. I told you that day on the beach you'd been touched by the gods and I wanted no dealings with you. And here you are again, except that this time you come seeking *me* after a dream. I warn you, others have dreamed of me, ere now—enemies who dreamed and schemed while they were yet awake. They are all dead. Why should I regard your dreams as different from theirs? It takes no great intelligence to see that you have schemes in mind, as well as dreams, since you are here."

"My presence here bears no menace for you, Derek. You'll take no harm from my arrival. I come as a supplicant, seeking assistance that I think lies within your power to grant."

"My power . . ." He shifted his body and dug a pebble from beneath his hip, flicking it out and away and watching as it fell into the abyss in front of us. "You know, a wise man once told me that the most vicious enemies a king can make are those he once contrived to help. That sounds strange, eh? It did to me, at the time, for I was young. I asked him what he meant, and I've never forgotten his answer. He said that kindness frequently breeds hatred . . . that there is a type of man—and woman, too—in whom resentment simmers all the time, like an evil brew, and nothing brings it to a fiercer boil than feeling obligation." He waited, watching me closely for a reaction.

"I can see some of what you mean," I began, "but not, I think, the depth of it. Judging from your words, it seems you would apply the measure to everyone you meet, whereas I see its application in only a few. Wherein lies the difference?"

He sniffed, then made a clicking noise with his tongue. "We are wandering from our track, but perhaps it's worth it. Tell me, Merlyn Britannicus, how often do you dream these wondrous dreams of yours?"

"Not often. Once every year or so, perhaps even less."

"They always involve people?"

I had to think about that. "I don't really know. I think so."

"Do you like people?"

"*Like* people? You mean people in general?"

"That's what I mean, people in the mass."

"I've never really thought about that, but I suppose I do."

"Well, I don't. I like my friends, I like my family—some of them, anyway—and I like a number of people I have come to know casually without befriending them, if you know what I mean. But I find the mass of people, the faceless, impersonal herd, to be unlikable. They are generally mean-spirited, envious, grasping, untrustworthy, unclean and vicious."

I listened in amazement, recalling the last time I had met this man and watched him violate and slaughter an injured woman, my own wife's sister, Ygraine, on a beach littered with corpses. I knew, however, that this was no suitable time to recall the incident to his attention.

He had fallen silent, his eyes on my face, searching. "What are you thinking?"

I shrugged elaborately, but I knew I had to respond honestly. The king of Ravenglass was no man's fool, and I knew I had not yet begun to penetrate the depths of him.

"I'm surprised to hear you say the words you've spoken. The image they suggest does not fit with what I saw in Ravenglass today."

"I don't follow you."

"Well, I'm not sure where I'm leading, but it seems to me that if you truly feel the way you say you do, if your dislike of others is as deep as you describe, then that would inevitably be reflected in the way you govern your people. And yet I saw no signs of fear of you, or of dislike, among the people I saw today."

He grunted deep in his chest. "That simply proves my point. They are untrustworthy."

I looked him straight in the eye. "That's not true, and you don't even expect me to believe it. Do you?"

When he answered, I detected a glint of humour in his eyes. "Go back to what I said before," he said. "I like some people I have come to know casually without befriending them."

"A whole town full of them?" He shrugged and I continued. "Perhaps a kingdom full?"

"No! Stay with the town, for now. Those who live there are those with whom I can live."

"And the others, beyond the town?"

"In the farms, you mean? Those too."

"So? That would make you a good king, Derek, not a cynic or a misanthrope."

"A what?"

"Someone who hates everyone."

"Aye, well, Fortune has made me a king, and so I can have those people I dislike stay far away, as long as I possess the strength to hold them off."

"And the seven years?" I saw from his expression that he had not understood me. "You told me you have not had a sword in your hand for seven years. That indicates a lack of need for harshness."

"Does it? I think not. I said I had not held a sword. I didn't say I've lost the ability to swing one."

I smiled and raised my hands in surrender. "So be it. You said at the start that we were drifting off topic. Now we've done it again. Why did you ask me about liking people?"

"Because we were talking about resentment. I was seeking it in you. I choose to believe that the majority of people are ruthlessly self-centred. That ruthlessness is all-important to a man in my position, to be ignored at his peril. People like those I'm speaking of, the resentful ones, see kindness in others—or call it tolerance, compassion or forbearance, what you will—as a weakness to be exploited. Yet at the same time—and here is where it made no sense at all to me at first—they perceive that acceptance of any kindness indicates a weakness in themselves. That means the wise man should be wary of those to whom he has shown favour in the past, because such people will convince themselves that, in preferring them, he has somehow demeaned them."

I sat staring at him, greatly impressed by wisdom I had never thought to find in such as he, but before I could respond in any way he spoke again.

"And that brings me back to you, and the request you have not made. What will you ask of me, and how will I respond, and how will this new word . . . this 'sanctuary' . . . affect my life in time to come?"

I made no move to respond. He had more to add.

"You and I don't know each other, Merlyn the Dreamer, but I find myself wondering what you must think of me, and I'm concerned. . . . And that surprises me, because I seldom think about such things. Why should I bother with what others, strangers, think of me? We've met but twice before, and each time then I was my warrior self. My other self, the man who rules and governs his people, you have never met. I know you are Roman, in background at least, and that leads me to suspect you might think you have some advantage over me, a plain, untutored Celt. If that is true, then be aware of this: the word you spoke to me today is new to me, but the application of it exists already, here in Ravenglass. Liam, the son of Condran, will eat and drink and sleep tonight with all his men, cheek by jowl with Connor, son of Athol, and all his. In Ravenglass alone and nowhere else I know of in all these lands could such a thing occur without blood being shed. That, I believe, is a form of sanctuary. But it is one they may enjoy only by obeying my laws: no weaponry, no fighting and no harm to me or mine. Transgression earns immediate banishment with forfeiture of privilege, and there is no appeal or possibility of leniency."

I nodded my head, more and more impressed with each observation I heard from this man's lips.

"That is exactly as it should be," I said, soft-voiced. "I have been thinking of it ever since surrendering my own weapons, and I can see no other means of ensuring your own safety. You offer a privilege, as you have said, and privilege entails an obligation to the privileged. Abuse of it is, by definition, unforgivable. The fact that your community should benefit from it is incidental, yet part and parcel of the arrangement."

"Good. So you are a man of sense, as well as dreams. You accept, then, that you would be bound by my laws in return for whatever privilege it is that you seek."

"Of course."

"Of course? Without knowing those laws?"

I shrugged. "I've heard enough of your ideas to know that whatever laws you impose would be sane and, in all probability, sensible."

"Hmm," he grunted. "Seek, then. What is it that you want?"

I pondered my answer, then spoke briefly.

"A place to rear a child in safety."

He made no immediate response. Instead, he turned his gaze away from me to stare out across the valley where, at a level only slightly above our heads, a bird of prey made lazy circles against the clear blue sky, planing on rigid wings that caught the air and bent it to the creature's will. Three times we watched it circle in widening loops until, without warning, it tucked in its wings and fell like a stone. After it had vanished, lost to view beneath the lip of the cliff, my companion remained motionless for moments longer, and when he spoke he did not look at me.

"What kind of child requires the shelter of an unknown land to grow in safety?" I knew immediately that I had phrased my plea as badly as was possible, but he was still speaking. "Don't tell me, for I have no wish to know. I think the knowledge might be perilous."

I grimaced, knowing he could not see me, and tried to keep my voice calm. "How so?"

"How so?" He turned back slowly towards me as he repeated my question. "Well, let's suppose—let me suggest—some ways in which that might be so. . . .

"Suppose a child lives in the care of a man like yourself, a man of substance, wealth and influence who is concerned for him. And let's suppose this man to be a friend of someone like your friend Connor Mac Athol, who has lands in Eire, and even newer lands far to the north in Alba—that land you call Caledonia. Would it not seem reasonable that this friend might undertake to offer shelter to the child, in either place? Ample space in each to raise a single child, you'd think. . . . Unless the child's own parentage might imperil his very life among Connor's folk. That makes the child a threat, dangerous to others.

"But more than that, suppose this child is unsafe in his home . . . in Camulod. . . . He must be, else why the need to shelter him elsewhere? Now, were I you and had to hide a child for any reason, I would hide him close to home. A child's a tiny thing, beneath most people's notice, so I would spirit him away, perhaps far away, but into some neighbouring region. Not east or south, for fear of Saxons and the like. More probably to the south-west, to Cornwall perhaps, now Lot is dead. Most of all, however, were I you I would be tempted to the north and west, to Cambria, to the Pendragon lands, among my own allies. There I could I find some safety for the child. . . . Unless, of course, his parentage—and hence the very threat of his existence—were such that he might meet his death there, too."

The silence grew long before I broke it.

"How much do you know?"

"Among all these suppositions? I know nothing. I did not even know you were alive until I saw your face this morning, and I suspected none of this before you told me what you want." He shook his head and puffed his breath out through swollen cheeks.

"Merlyn, I did not become king of this place by being stupid. Who is this child? It must be a boy, a son and heir, but whose? It's the distance that concerns me. Surely you see that."

"What distance?"

"From Camulod to here! Why not Cornwall? You never fought there. You have no enemies in Cornwall, or had none when I met you there. Has that changed?"

"Indirectly."

Derek frowned. "What kind of an answer is that? Do you or don't you?"

I shrugged. "I do, but that is not the problem. The child has."

"So I was right. The child is endangered because of who he is. Who is this prodigy? And why should I imperil any of my own to succour him? Are you surprised that I should ask? If he has enemies swarming in such numbers and in so many places while he's but a brat, what will the future hold for him as he begins to grow?"

I pushed myself to my feet and moved away from him, presenting him with my back as I leaned against a tree close by the edge of the abyss. I was shaken by the accuracy of his conjecture and by the ease with which he had recognized and grasped the difficulties facing me. From my single statement, which I had foolishly thought to be innocuous, he had instantly inferred the essential truth of all that my presence in his lands implied. I had come to Ravenglass in response to the promptings of a dream, expecting, I now realized for the first time, to gull a man I had assessed to be a lumbering, untutored, semi-savage oaf. Instead I had found myself assessed and accurately classified by a clever and subtle mind at least the equal of my own.

One thing I saw clearly: Derek's knowledge, incomplete as it was, now constituted a grave threat to my designs. I would have to defray the damage done so far, and without lying.

"I'm impressed," I said, turning to him and attempting a smile. "From one comment you have built a remarkable structure. Within that, your suppositions are close to the mark in some respects—far off in others. Overall, nevertheless, they are entirely misdirected. The dangers you divined from Connor's folk do not exist. Refused a lodging here, we are prepared to go with him to Eire. I was born here in Britain, however, as you know, and would prefer to stay here if possible. The same holds true for the new lands of which you spoke in Caledonia. But the holdings there, I'm told, are small and new—primitive islands in the western sea. I prefer comfort.

"As for the south-west, you have the gist of it, but not the whole. I have an enemy there now, a man I banished into exile, one Peter Ironhair." I went on to tell him of Ironhair, his eviction from Camulod, his flight and his unsuccessful bid for power in Cambria as champion of the demented prince Carthac Pendragon, and his subsequent alliance with the new ruler in Cornwall. I did not lie, but I confined my truths to my own dealings with Ironhair, making no mention of the boy.

Derek listened in silence, and when I had finished, he sat watching me, gnawing on the inside of his cheek.

"So this Ironhair seeks vengeance on the boy?"

"No, he seeks revenge on me. He knows my feelings for the boy and knows the duty I have undertaken to see him into manhood and into his inheritance. The boy will rule in Camulod one day. He's my only heir, though not my son. Ironhair knows he could damage me more by harming the lad than ever he could by killing me, in any fashion."

"And he has already made an attempt obviously, a strong one, since you are here on my threshold, seeking your sang . . ." He wiggled his fingers, to indicate the ending of the alien word.

"Sanctuary. Aye, he has. He came nigh on succeeding, with murderers sent in among my own people to kill the boy. They failed only because they didn't know the boy himself, but they killed one of the women who was tending him that day."

"They killed a woman? Was she violated?"

"Aye, then slaughtered."

"Hmm. And you are convinced this Ironhair was behind the attack? It could not have been an accidental thing, a simple matter of her having been in the wrong place at the wrong moment?"

I could see his eyes, narrowed and speculative, as he awaited my reaction to his question. First things first, he was suggesting, according to his way of thinking, and I closed my mind to the image that came to me unbidden, of him rising from the rape of Arthur's mother, Ygraine of Cornwall. I jerked my head in an abrupt negative, letting him see my conviction. "No, it could not. It was her violation that was incidental—not accidental. They were there to kill the boy, and Ironhair sent them. They named his name, and I was unsurprised. The worst of it was, however, that to be successful in penetrating our defences as deeply as he did, Ironhair must have suborned some of my own folk, and I had no way of knowing who those people were. That meant I could trust no one, and I felt unsafe and vulnerable among my own kinfolk. It was intolerable, and we had to leave, because the boy's life would have been in constant danger until we could identify the serpents in our midst. And so here we are."

"Who is he, then, this boy?"

"My cousin Uther's son, Arthur Pendragon."

Derek had been scratching his beard, but his fingers stilled as I spoke and his eyes grew wide. "Uther Pendragon, the man I killed?"

"Aye. The boy is heir to Pendragon, thus this Ironhair perceives him as a threat to his own power, his eventual kingship there. The man is mad. You could become king of the Pendragon before Ironhair could."

Derek had been shaking his head as I said the last words, barely listening to me, but now he looked back at me in outrage.

"You say this Ironhair is mad, and yet you ask me to give shelter to a boy whose father died at my hand? What does that make you? Or me, were I fool enough to listen? You would expect me to spend the remainder of my life waiting for him to grow up and claim the blood price?"

"Not true! Of course not! That would never happen, and the boy will never know."

"Never?" Derek's voice was swelling with scorn and an anger born, I felt sure, of guilt. "How not? You know, I know, the gods know! And who else might know, only the gods can tell! But one of them—someone—will tell him, soon or late."

"I would not, nor would you. And no other knows."

"Pah! And I should accept your oath on that?"

"You should, it's freely given."

"You take me for as big a fool as you. Why should I?"

"Perhaps because you owe him a life, in return for his father's."

He sat gaping at me, speechless, then grunted explosively and hauled himself to his feet.

"You leave tomorrow," he growled, and he made his way directly to his horse.

I followed Derek in a curious frame of mind, in part disappointed by my failure to enlist his aid, but also greatly relieved at my success in diverting his attention from the truth he had come so close to grasping. The very last thing I needed, I believed, was any possibility of this man perceiving that the boy in my charge had sufficient blood ties and family connections to enable him to control vast areas of Britain when he became a man. That danger, I now felt, was safely past, and with its passing my own task of finding safety for the boy had been simplified. The very name of Pendragon of Cambria, son of the ravager of Cornwall, was proof enough for him, I knew, of my need to hide the child. I could live easily with Derek's knowledge of that portion of the truth, since it entailed sufficient complexity to satisfy his curiosity, and that, in turn, satisfied me. I knew he would seek no other explanation and that the secret of the rest of the boy's parentage and his claim, through his mother, to Cornwall and to Eire would be safe.

As I rode down the narrow hillside track behind him, I found myself wondering how angry Derek really was, for I could discern no stiffness in his posture. He rode easily, slouched on the garron's back, his weight inclined towards me and against the slope, allowing the horse to pick his own route downward. I made no attempt to speak to him, contenting myself with going over all that had been said and wondering how I might have presented my petition more effectively. And in thinking of that, I began to imagine his reaction could he have known the true danger I might represent to his people—a danger that had nothing to do with the boy, or with who I was, but far more with *what* I suspected I was.

I had a skin disease of some kind, and I had come to believe, despite the derisive guffaws of my good friend Lucanus, our beloved and much respected physician and surgeon, that it was leprosy. Lucanus had thought me mad and deluded, initially, upon hearing of my suspicions, and had been predisposed to make light of what he called my fanciful imaginings, until he realized how deeply concerned and afraid I was. Once he had seen my fear, he set out to calm and reassure me. He had worked among lepers all his life, he told me, gazing deeply into my eyes, and in the space of decades at the work had never known a single person to become afflicted after only a short exposure to the disease. My exposure to it, and to lepers, he insisted, had been less than one day, and I had had no physical contact with any of them.

I listened to him despairingly, yearning for comfort, but I remained unconvinced, because my affliction, whatever it might be, evinced itself incontrovertibly in the form of a dry lesion, a single blemish—on the right-upper quadrant of my breast—that bore all the classic signs of being leprous, according to Lucanus's own description. It was an area of deadness on my chest, less than the size of the ball of my thumb, white in the centre and reddish around the edges. It was impervious to pain, or to any sensation at all, and the hairs that grew within its borders were white, too. Peering closely at this phenomenon, Lucanus agreed that it might, indeed, be a leprous lesion, but then he sat back on his heels and blithely rattled off a long and reassuring list of other things it might have been, ticking each off on his fingers as he named it.

At that point, relieved beyond description, I told him dispassionately about my unsuccessful attempt to rescue his friend Mordechai Emancipatus, a physician who had contracted leprosy from his own work with lepers, from the hillside crevasse into which he had fallen. I told him about my own injuries and my useless attempts to save Mordechai's life, and about how I had finally emerged from that place, covered in his blood and my own, leaving Mordechai's body behind me. In telling this story, I saw the first flicker of doubt on my friend's face. He asked me again how much blood had been spilled there, in the crevasse. How much of mine and how much of Mordechai's? How much of Mordechai's had spilled on me?

I had no way of answering his questions accurately, for the night had been dark and wet and cold and I had been unaware, much of the time, that we were even bleeding, but I could see that the awareness of what I had described was troubling my listener. He confessed to me that the mingling of tainted blood with healthy caused him some concern, although he could not be certain why. He had once found and purchased an ancient treatise on this very topic, he said, a scroll written many years earlier by a noted physician and scholar, but he had never studied it, or even taken the time to really read it thoroughly. The mention I had made of mixing my blood with Mordechai's had recalled it to his mind. He would make shift to find the scroll, he promised me, and to master its contents, but he had been searching for it fruitlessly ever since our conversation, unable to recall what he had done with it or when he had last seen it. Until he found it, Lucanus would withhold his final diagnosis and judgment on my condition, and the threat of leprosy would hang over my head like Damocles's sword.

The illness—the leprosy, in my stubborn conviction—was not fatal in or of itself as I had always, in my ignorance, believed. It was a disfiguring disease, and horribly so, involving as it did the gradual disintegration of the digits and limbs and the facial features, but it did not cause death, save in the bleakest cases, when people died of hunger through an inability to feed themselves.

Leprosy! In spite of my revulsion at the thought of it, I found myself, incredibly, smothering a smile at the thought of what Derek's reaction to such knowledge might have been had I mentioned the matter during our discussion.

Derek and I had reached the edge of the trees and were now on the point of entering the pathway through the piled-up stones bounding the cultivated fields. Derek grunted and straightened up to his full height, abruptly reining his horse to a halt and craning his neck to gaze along to the left of the line of stones. My own mount stopped when he was nose to tail with the other, but Derek was already moving again, turning his horse off the track and into the boulder-strewn ground among the trees. Curious, I followed him, our progress slow as our garrons ventured forward delicately and with great care on the uneven, treacherous ground.

"By the light of Lud," Derek growled. "Look at the size of that whoreson."

On the lower edge of the miles-long pile of stones, concealed from me until now by Derek's bulk and the bole of a silver birch, a great, gaunt wolf lay sprawled in death, its back arched violently against nature in the extremity of its last convulsion. Its enormous front toes were spread wide like the fingers of some hairy giant's hand, and its entire hindquarters, including its heavy tail, were stiff with blackened blood. The air was filled with the hum of the thousands of green and blue flies that swarmed upon the carcass.

Derek had already swung down from his horse, and I watched as he made his way cautiously over the loose-piled stones to where he could reach the dead beast. Ignoring the swarming flies, he bent his knees and grasped the front and hind legs closest to the ground, then straightened with a grunting heave, throwing the carcass onto its other side. The cause of death came into view at once: a flighted, blood-encrusted arrow protruding from the right side of the belly, its smooth shaft slashed and gouged by the frantic creature's snapping teeth. The wolf, a full-grown male, was larger than any I had seen in the southern regions, and it was grey, with whitish tinges in its coat. Standing on its hind legs, I thought, this thing could have rested its elbows on my shoulders and its maw would have engulfed my face.

"Gut shot," Derek said. "Owen was right." He stretched a hand to run his fingers through the ruff of fur beneath the massive neck. "Fine pelt. A shame to lose it. This one was in his prime. Look at that."

"That" was the creature's canine teeth, bared in its dying snarl. They were long and shining white, unmarred by stains. Derek straightened up and moved back to his horse.

"Who's Owen?" I asked him. He kicked his horse into motion, leading the way back to the track again.

"My son, my first-born. Shot at this thing last night, just at dusk, about two miles from here, along the valley. He was in the fields. It was running along the wall there, on the other side. Couldn't tell whether he had hit it or not—grey light, grey wolf, grey stones. Couldn't find his arrow afterwards, of course, but that meant nothing. He shot into the stones, so it could have deflected in any direction. He'll be glad to know he shot the beast, but he'll be sick when I tell him how big it was. A good robe wasted, that's all he'll think of."

We rode clear of the stones and his garron broke into a loping gallop, challenging my own to keep up with him, and for a space we let them run. When they finally slowed their pace, I rode up alongside the king again.

"How many sons do you have, Derek?"

We were close to the road by this time, and he did not respond until we had reached it and turned right, towards the town.

"Eleven," he said eventually. "And many daughters."

I was amazed, for I had guessed his age to be no more than six or seven years greater than my own. He must have noticed my reaction. "Out of five wives," he added.

"Five? You have had four wives die?"

He looked at me then as though he thought me mad, and then he laughed. "No, Christian," he said. "I have had five wives pregnant much of the time."

I winced at my own clumsiness. Polygamy was not uncommon among the pagan people in the isolated parts of Britain.

"How old is Owen?" I asked, attempting to gloss over my gaffe.

"Seventeen."

"And your youngest son, how old is he?"

"Nine."

"Just slightly older than young Arthur." He threw me a sidewise look and I hurried on. "How many daughters have you?"

"Too many. Which one is Arthur? There were three with you."

"Four. Arthur is the oldest, the one with the gold-coloured eyes. He's eight."

"That one. I thought it would be him. I saw the eyes, like a young kestrel's. Is the woman his mother? The good-looking one with the face of a hawk?"

"Shelagh, you mean. No, she is Donuil's wife. Donuil is—"

"Aye, Connor's brother. I recalled him from our first meeting. What of the other woman?"

"That's Turga, the boy's nurse."

"Nurse? At eight he requires a nurse?"

"No, of course not, but he is all she has, and they are close."

"Where is his mother, then?"

"Dead, long since." I tried to shut out the image of her death on the beach in far-off Cornwall, and the sight of Derek rising to face me from his interrupted rape of her, his moist, erect phallus gleaming in the afternoon light. He had no idea who she was, or that his horse had crushed her skull thereafter.

"Hmm . . . So you are father and mother both. You feel responsible for him?"

I looked at him, wondering at the question, unsure where it was leading.

"Yes," I said, nodding. "I am . . . aware of a responsibility."

"Try being a king some day, my friend, then talk to me of responsibility. It pains me, I'll admit it, to refuse what you have asked of me, but I see no other choice. Danger to myself I could accept, but to endanger my people needlessly by taking on the risk you represent would be unforgivable. . . . If there were even half a chance the child might escape detection I might consider otherwise. But the son of Pendragon, escorted by Merlyn of Camulod? No, I cannot take that risk."

I nodded once again, recognizing and accepting the finality of his decision. "So be it," I replied. "I understand your situation."

For the remainder of our ride back into Ravenglass my mind was busy with logistics. I suspected that Connor's crew might already have unloaded our possessions and supplies from his galley, at least, and perhaps from one of the other two. If that were the case, we would have to stand guard by them overnight and reload them come morning.

We returned the garrons to Ulf, their keeper. I thanked Derek for his time and took my leave of him, promising to join him that night for dinner. I then set out to find Connor immediately, making my way directly through the still-bustling marketplace, and thence through the fort to the gate leading onto the wharf.

Connor was in conference with the two captains of his other galleys when I arrived, the tiny Feargus, who was not much taller than the boy Arthur, and his incongruous companion Logan, a giant as grotesquely tall as Feargus was small. Feargus's galley, with the reddish sail that distinguished it even when furled, lay prow to stern with Connor's, filling the length of the wharf. Logan's had been lashed alongside it, so that his crew must cross Feargus's deck to reach the land. All three men turned at my approach, alerted by Logan, who had seen me emerging from the town gate, and when we had exchanged greetings the two captains left me alone with Connor. I came to the point at once, telling him all that had transpired between me and Derek. He took the information philosophically, even smiling in admiration of Derek's acuity, and when I had fallen quiet again he grinned and slapped me on the upper arm.

"Eire it is, then, my friend—or the northern isles, if you find them more to your liking. I had a feeling Derek might not take to your ideas, so I decided not to unload any of your cargo before you returned. We'll rest here tonight and leave with the morning tide. Don't look so doleful, Yellow Head. You'll see, everything will work out for the best."

I grimaced. "Aye, no doubt you're right, but sometimes I wish life could be more simple. Have you seen Donuil since I left?"

Connor nodded. "Aye, he was here a short time ago. You must have passed him on the way. Said he was going to meet Shelagh and the children in the marketplace."

I thanked him and retraced my steps through the fort to the rear gate, still going over in my mind the changes and the difficulties we faced now that we would have no base in Britain. As the crow flies, there was little difference in the distances from Camulod to Cumbria or to Athol's kingdom in Eire. But the Eirish distance was across the high seas, and thus fraught with hazards that did not pertain to the Cumbrian passage. Travel between Eire and Camulod could not be lightly undertaken. But that was not my main concern. The foreignness of Eire depressed me more. Arthur's future prospects, I was convinced, would suffer were he removed from Britain, from his home.

As I approached the double portal in the rear wall of the fort, I was roused from my musings when a man emerged from the shadowed entrance and then stopped and turned away abruptly, hurrying back the way he had come. Had he not done so I would have passed him by without noticing, but the speed with which he whirled and made off caught my eye, and the sight of his retreating yellow tunic reminded me of the man who had stopped to watch me from the tavern doorway earlier in the day.

Curious, I lengthened my stride slightly and passed through the portal, looking idly for him as I broke into the sunlight of the marketplace beyond, but he was nowhere to be seen. Puzzled now, I grasped a pole supporting the awning of a stall and stepped up onto an empty wooden crate, peering over the heads of the crowd until I saw the fellow scuttling hurriedly off to my right, about four stalls away. As I saw him, he looked back over his shoulder at me, and his alarm was instantaneous. He broke into a lurching run, dodging to his left out of my sight beyond the corner of another stall, and suddenly I found myself giving chase, thrusting people aside as I ran after him, fully aware now of the absent weight of my swordbelt at my waist.

As I swung around the corner he came into sight again, still running, and I lengthened my stride again to close on him. Once more he swung out of sight and again I plunged around a corner after him, nearly sprawling over a pile of empty poultry baskets. Now I heard voices raised in angry protest, but all at once I was beyond the confining stalls and into an open, widening space where a well-trodden path led between tall banks of grass towards a stand of trees. There my quarry vanished. Running flat out now, I passed between the first two trees and had to leap immediately to avoid a narrow, steep-sided ditch that traversed the path. I landed safely on rising ground and several steps later found myself at the top of a shallow incline that sloped down to where I could hear the sound of hard-running feet. Pausing only to collect myself and make sure there was only one way down, I launched myself after him again, completely unconcerned by now that I knew not who the fellow was or why he was fleeing from me. His flight alone was reason for pursuit. I dashed headlong downhill, swerved around a tree and was sent sprawling by a foot that hooked my ankle as I passed.

I landed hard, the impact driving all the air from my body so that I writhed helplessly on the ground, blinded by pain and gasping as I fought to draw a breath. Above me, to my right I thought, someone laughed quietly and the sound chilled me. I tried to tense myself against further violence, but nothing happened and the sound was not repeated.

When I began to breathe again, I sucked air into my outraged chest with great, painful whoops. I already knew from the ripping, lesser pains in my face and hands that I had landed among brambles, and I kept my eyes squeezed shut as I waited for strength to come back to me. Somehow, I managed to struggle to my knees, my head bowed and my arms clutched protectively about my ribs, my ears straining to hear any sound of movement around me. Silence.

Soon I straightened up, uncrossing my arms and opening my eyes, and as I did so, someone kicked me violently in the midriff, knocking me backwards into the thorns again. I found myself seated this time, my back and shoulders supported by the thickness and springy strength of the weave of stems behind me.

The man who had kicked me loomed over me, moving closer, and I saw two others behind him, one on each side. All of them were grinning at the prospect of what they would do to me now, three against one. But I was already moving again, thrusting myself up into a kneeling posture, ignoring the ferocious barbs that cut against my hands as I hauled and pushed myself upright. I saw surprise on my assailant's face as he noted the speed of my recovery, and then he moved more quickly, taking a long step closer and aiming another kick, this time at my head.

He was too slow, despite his advantages, and I managed to avoid his flailing foot. I twisted my head forward and to his right and threw up my arms to cross my wrists above his ankle, pulling his heel down hard against my right shoulder and throwing myself to my left and down towards him. Off balance and caught unawares, he fell heavily beside me on his back. I heard the breath whooshing from his lungs and a satisfying grunt of pain. Releasing my hold on him immediately, I swung my left fist over, driving it hard against his nose, and felt the gristle flatten beneath the overarm swipe. Then I stretched and stiffened my hand, chopping its rigid edge against his stretched throat. It was clumsy, and my strength was hampered by the position I lay in, but the blow had its effect. I rolled away from him as quickly as I could then to deal with his companions, who had been slow to adjust to my surprise.

As I came upright again on one knee, my left foot finally firm beneath me, one of the two caught me high on the left cheekbone with a long, raking swing. I heard the distinctive sound of bone snapping as I went asprawl again, my eyes shut tight against the stunning ferocity of the impact. I rolled quickly, expecting at least another kick from the third man, but instead I heard a keening howl and the sound of other blows, none of them close to me.

Scrambling to my knees again and shaking my head to clear my vision, I saw a sight that would have made me laugh at any other time. The second man, the one who had punched me, was the source of the howling. He was hopping wildly around in a circle, his face screwed up ludicrously in pain, his left wrist clamped tightly beneath his armpit and the first finger of his left hand tilted grotesquely backward. The bone I had heard breaking was his. Beside him, flat on his back, legs scissoring weakly while his hands clutched at his throat, lay my first assailant. Beyond both of them, the third man was being systematically punished by Donuil Mac Athol, who towered above him, maintaining a judicious distance from his victim as he pounded him deliberately with his hands and feet. I watched, unable to make a sound, as the man's knees finally gave way and he toppled slowly to lie face down.

Donuil turned away from him to the second man who was still prancing about, clutching his injured hand. He walked towards the man, seized him by the hair and jerked the fellow's head backward to smite him with an awesome, straight-armed blow to the forehead with his clenched fist, swung overhead from his full height. The man fell like a slaughtered bullock. Donuil then turned to where I stood swaying, watching him.

"*Dia!*" he said, conversationally. "Look at you, then. Flayed alive and like to drown in your own blood! Lucky for you I saw you running by. Who are these?"

I shook my head, looking at my attackers closely now and seeing no yellow tunic among them. "I don't know. I was chasing someone else. I've never seen these three."

He was frowning at me. "Who were you chasing?"

"I don't know, but whoever he was, he knows me. He saw me twice today and obviously didn't want me to see him. The second time I caught his eye he ran, and I followed him."

"Aye, and he led you right to these beauties. Liam's cattle."

"How do you know they're Liam's?"

"By their clothing, and they're carrying no weapons, which means they're visitors like us."

"Thank God for that!"

"Thank Derek."

The man whose throat I had chopped began to recover now and pulled himself up until he was sitting, his hands still at his throat. He hawked painfully and spat, and Donuil walked towards him. Before he could speak to the man, however, another voice intruded.

"Well, what have we here? Bloodshed in Ravenglass?"

We spun to find ourselves surrounded by five men, all of them with drawn swords and wearing metal breastplates. I recognized the one who had spoken as Blundyl, the lieutenant whom Derek had entrusted to find lodgings for us. I was still reeling, and now I sat down, resting my back against the bole of a tree. Donuil had not moved. Blundyl's eyes moved around the clearing, taking note of everything.

"Don't you people know the law in these parts?" There was no acrimony in Blundyl's tone, but neither was there any hint of warmth.

I cleared my throat and answered him. "Aye, Blundyl, we do. Weapons are banned in Ravenglass, among visitors at least, as is bloodshed. Failure to keep the peace earns banishment."

"*Instant* banishment," he added, frowning at me. "Who are you?"

"We met earlier," I told him. "I was with Derek. But there has been no breaking of the law here. No blood has been shed, and no weapons drawn."

"No *blood?* Look at yourself, man!"

I looked down at my hands and winced. They were ripped to shreds, torn front and back by the vicious barbs of the bramble briars. I knew my face was in the same condition, for every scratch seemed to burn with its own separate fire and my eyelids were sticky with blood.

"This is blood drawn, not spilt," was all I could think to say. "I am not wounded, only scratched where I fell into the brambles there. My name's Britannicus and we arrived today with Connor Mac Athol. This is Connor's brother, Donuil. Since our arrival I have been with your king, Derek. After I left Derek, I met a man who recognized me and ran away. I ran after him to find out who he was."

"We know you ran," Blundyl said, his voice heavy with sarcasm. "You demolished half the market in passing." He looked at the three downed men. "Which one were you following?"

"None of these. I told you, I don't know them. The man I chased was wearing a yellow tunic of some kind. He ran past here too quickly, I imagine, for these three to stop him, and I came close behind. They stopped me. We had an altercation and Donuil, here, arrived in time to help me end it."

"Hmm." He turned to Donuil. "They're not yours then, these three?" Donuil merely shook his head, his lips pursed. "Then they must belong to the other bunch. Only two lots in port." He moved quickly beyond the sitting man to the nearest of the two bodies, where he knelt and felt beneath the jawline for a pulse. Satisfied that the man was alive, he turned him over on his back and searched him, one-handed, for weapons. That done, he moved to the last of the men and did the same, heaving this one over onto his face. Finally he straightened up and approached me.

"Show me your hands."

I held out my hands and he sheathed his sword before taking hold of my wrists, turning them over and scanning the long scratches on both sides.

"You're going to have fun, bathing those." He squinted at my face. "Not going to be too pretty for a day or two, and you're not going to be seeing too much, either." He reached up and touched my left cheekbone. I winced involuntarily, hissing and pulling my head away. "Aye, that's a beauty." He turned away and scanned the clearing again, clearly deliberating, and then he turned back to me. "I'll be reporting this to the lord Derek as a marginal incident, barely within the law. A brawl, rather than a fight. But I am stretching a point here, you understand me? You are fortunate that there was no damage done in the marketplace. You have used up your credit. Do you understand what I am saying? No more leeway. Behave yourself in Ravenglass from this time on, or suffer the consequences. Now get out of here."

I glanced at the three others. "But what about—?"

"Leave them to us. They're for a night in custody. On your way!"

I limped away at Donuil's heels. Neither of us spoke until we had crossed the transverse ditch at the top of the rise, just inside the trees, where we could see the marketplace beyond.

Donuil broke the silence. "How do you feel?"

"Chastened, like a schoolboy chidden by his master."

"Aye, but I meant bodily aches and pains."

"I have only one, but it's all over me. I feel as though I've been to war."

He grinned. "You have, and look it. I don't think I've ever seen a worse black eye. Can you see out of it?"

I covered my right eye with one hand and tried to see him with my left, but it was swollen shut and throbbing painfully. I shook my head.

Donuil grunted. "Well, we had better find Lucanus right away. As for the other business, with Blundyl, forget it. He did his duty and did it leniently, for we were in the wrong. Connor has told me about this place, and no fighting means no fighting, just as it does in Camulod. Blundyl did, as he said, stretch a point for us. I was surprised."

We spoke no more of the affair until after we had found Lucanus and my scratches had been washed and salved. Blundyl had quartered all of us in the same building, one of the residential blocks in the Via Decumana at the rear of the central administrative block, and we did not lack for space in spite of the overcrowding Derek had mentioned to me. None of my abrasions was deep enough to warrant stitches, but they all stung abominably, and I spent a most uncomfortable afternoon. My left eye was swollen completely shut and more than simply tender to the touch. It had already turned a deep and glowing black, with red and yellow edges. The four boys gazed at me wide-eyed with wonder, but none of them dared ask me what had happened. Derek himself came by late in the afternoon and, upon being shown to the room in which I sat before a brazier, stood facing me without speaking, his face troubled.

"What was the cause?" he asked eventually. I shook my head and told him of the man in the yellow tunic, reminding him of my question about the alehouse when we had passed it that morning. He listened in silence until I had finished.

"And this entrapment, it was deliberate, you think?"

"No, it couldn't possibly have been. The fellow didn't know he would meet me. How could he? I arrived there at the gateway by chance as he came through. It was only his reaction that caught my eye. After that, everything happened quickly—he had no time to arrange anything. My explanation to Blundyl must have been correct. He flashed by those three, angering them, and I came after him. There is no other explanation that makes sense."

"Unless he already knew they were there and led you right to them, calling for help as he passed."

"Then why didn't he come back and join them afterward, once they had me down?"

Derek shrugged. "I don't know. You said he didn't want you to notice him. Perhaps that hasn't changed. Did you recognize him?"

"No, I didn't manage to get close enough to see him clearly. But he didn't look familiar, even from what I saw."

"And yet he knew you."

"Aye, it would seem so."

Derek sighed and scratched at his ear. "You make my point for me, Merlyn, confirming my judgment. Here you are, less than a day in Ravenglass, and already trouble follows you. Will you still be able to dine with us tonight?"

"Aye, where?"

"In my house, beneath the thatch." He saw my blank expression. "I roofed the central space in there, too, just like the court of the administration building. It's not as high a roof, or as big as the one next door, but it keeps the rain and snow out of the house and provides me with high storage and drying racks. And it's mine alone, not a public space."

"I'll be there. Put your mind at ease, Derek. We have made arrangements to sail come morning."

"I know. Connor told me. I'll see you at dinner."

Derek had barely left the room when Shelagh entered, her face twisted in a scowl of concern. I had not seen her since leaving the dock with Derek earlier that day. Now she stopped on the threshold and stared at me. I glanced down at the bandages that swathed my hands and waited for her to speak.

"Why?" she asked. "Who was it?"

I raised my head to meet her gaze. "Didn't Donuil tell you? I don't know who they were. Nor do I know why they chose to attack me."

She stepped into the room, looked around to find a chair, then dragged it to where I sat by the brazier. She leaned close, assessing the extent of my injuries.

"Lucanus told me what happened. I haven't seen Donuil since I got back. We waited for him at the market, and when it finally became clear he was not coming, I sent the children home with Turga. Since then I've been with Logan, down at the wharf. Tell me about it."

I told her, omitting nothing, and when I had done she frowned and reached out to touch the tips of her fingers gently to the swelling on my cheek, wincing in sympathy with me as I flinched. "Is it that bad?"

"No," I admitted, "but it is painful. It'll mend."

"You really don't know who these people were, or why they attacked you?"

I shook my head. "Donuil told me they were Liam's men, because he recognized their clothing. It was obvious they were outsiders, since, like us, they had no weapons. Other than that, I have no idea who they were, or why they were there at that time."

"Hmm." She stood up. "Here, take this." She reached behind her back to the waistline of her skirt and pulled out one of her throwing-knives, a wickedly sharp weapon with a heavy blade a handspan long. I gasped at the sight of it. "Take it," she insisted.

"How—? What—?"

"Oh, for the love of Lud, man, will you take it? Hide it behind your waist, the way I did. No one will know it's there but you, and if you need it you'll be glad of it."

"Shelagh, it's against Derek's law to carry weapons in Ravenglass, and we are his guests."

"We are, but we are also responsible for the safety of others, some of them children. You would not dream of crossing Camulod without a sword. Are you really stupid enough to think you might not have need of a blade in Ravenglass, swarming as it is with strangers, some of whom have already attacked you? Take it!"

I took the knife and weighed it in my hand. "How come you to have this?"

"Because it takes more than the threats of a foolish man to make me part with it, or any of the others," she snapped, her eyes flashing. Then she smiled. "Appearances, Merlyn—everything in the world of men is concerned with appearances. You're far worse than women. When Connor told me of this damnable requirement to surrender our weapons, I removed my belt and strapped it about my waist, covering it with a shawl. Then I bared my breasts a little more. No one here sees me as a warrior, and no one thought to ask me for my knives."

I shook my head in admiration, but I held the knife out to her again, hilt first. "My thanks, Shelagh, but I can't take this. There is honour involved."

"Och, a curse on you strutting men and your stupid notions of honour. I am telling you there's danger involved, too, Merlyn! Why won't you believe me? I can feel it, smell it, in the air of the place."

I nodded, my eyes on the knife I yet held. "I believe you, Shelagh, but this knife would change nothing, even could I accept it. It's a throwing-knife and I lack the skill to throw it. Nevertheless, if it will make you happier, I'll keep it here in my room, beside me when I sleep. I won't carry it abroad, but the only time I won't be here between now and tomorrow morning will be while I'm at dinner beneath Derek's thatch tonight. There I'll have a dagger at table, as will everyone else. Nothing will happen there, and we'll be leaving in the morning."

I stood up and crossed to my cot, slipping the knife beneath my pillow. She watched me, pink-faced with suppressed anger and scorn, then turned and left. I returned to sit by the brazier, fingering my scratches gently and smiling to myself at the temper of the woman Donuil had wed.

III

THERE WERE ALMOST a hundred people beneath Derek's thatch that night for dinner, some twenty of them women, the wives and sweethearts of the senior men of Ravenglass, and all of them had been fed by the time trouble broke out. This was no banquet, but an ordinary meal, although on a large scale. Drink had been flowing freely for hours, however, and many of the guests were already sprawled head down across the littered tables. My swollen eye was causing me difficulties, watering annoyingly and smarting painfully from the drifting smoke that filled the hall, much of it blown downward by the contrary winds that were supposed to vent the upper roof space. As Derek himself had told me, his roof was neither as high nor as large as the one in the administrative building next door, and the reduction in scale seemed to me to have entailed a reduction in the efficiency of the ventilating system, trapping and re-circulating much of the smoke that should have been dispersed high above the diners. The place, as it functioned now, provided an object lesson in why the Romans had left their central courtyards open to the skies.

It had been an uncomfortable dinner for me, involving much twisting about, since my injury made it impossible for me to see any of the people seated on my left without turning my head completely around. I was sitting on Derek's left, however, so I could see him clearly, and Blundyl sat next to me on my left. I had found him to be a pleasant companion during the meal, akin in temperament and outlook to our own Dedalus.

Lucanus sat on Blundyl's left, between him and Derek's eldest son, Owen, with whom he had been deep in discussion since sitting down. On Derek's right sat Connor, flanked by another of Derek's people whom I did not know, and next to him sat Tearlach, Connor's boatmaster. Donuil and Shelagh sat at the closest table in front of us, to my right and beneath the level of our table on its dais, and with them were Feargus and Logan, Dedalus and Rufio, Sean the navigator and several others of Connor's senior crewmen.

Others of our following sat scattered throughout the hall, although not all were present. The ordinary crewmen were abroad, finding their own pleasure in the hostelries. Those who were here, however, senior crewmen and minor officers, mingled with Derek's own. Liam, son of

Condran, was not present, nor were any of his people. They had shared the hall with Derek after their arrival the previous night, according to custom, and now fended for themselves.

We had discussed my misadventure of the early afternoon, dealing with it briefly. Blundyl and his men had questioned my attackers after releasing me, without discovering anything about the reasons underlying the attack on me, and had then thrown them into the cells where they would be held overnight. From there, the conversation had gone on to talk about fighting and brawling in general, with Blundyl admitting that, even in a rigidly controlled location such as Ravenglass, there were times when a brawling fist-fight could not be avoided. From there, Derek had drifted into detailing his experiences in what he called Lot's wars, eating mightily throughout and talking much of the time with a full mouth. I had stopped eating long before, and sat watching him in awe as he consumed enough to last me for a week. He bent forward again, digging into the depths of the heavy, black iron skillet that had been used to roast an enormous rack of ribs with herbs and vegetables and had been brought to our table for his personal consumption. He pulled out the last remaining piece and ripped it in half, one thick, meat-covered rib in each hand.

"Here, eat the last one." He dropped one rib back into the pot and pushed it in front of me before sinking his teeth into the dripping meat and ripping a mouthful from the bone.

As I grasped the handle of the pot, shaking my head and smiling to myself, the main doors burst open and a struggling knot of men spilled in. Blundyl was immediately on his feet, frowning with incomprehension, his eyes squinting as he tried to pierce the smoky gloom to see what was amiss. I heard a loud, anguished voice calling Connor's name urgently and looked in time to see the man who had shouted slaughtered from behind, the point of a sword blade emerging suddenly from beneath his chin, violently thrust by one of the newcomers surging through the doorway. Some people at the rearmost tables, closest to the open doors, began to cry out and several sprang erect, but as each rose to his feet he was shot down by arrows fired from lethally close range. Six or seven men died thus in moments.

All noise and movement at the tables ceased and everyone sat watching in stunned disbelief as Liam Condranson strode into view, teeth gleaming whitely in a wide smile beneath his moustache as his men moved swiftly behind him, spreading out along the walls flanking the doorway at his back. Most of these men held drawn bows, menacing the assembly. Liam carried a broad-bladed sword easily in his right hand, and a round shield covered his breast. He walked forward boldly, his eyes on Derek, glancing neither right nor left as he made his way down the length of the hall between the two central banks of tables. At his back came a wedge of armed and armoured men, twelve of them, who upended the tables as they passed, throwing them aside to widen the aisle and herding the former occupants to either side of the hall. Beside me, Blundyl, clearly seeing the value of discretion, since he was weaponless like us, subsided slowly into his chair.

Liam came to a halt when less than one third of the length of the room remained between him and the dais. As he stopped, two of his retainers flanked him, drawn bows levelled at Derek, who stood rigid, half crouched, his fists clenched in impotent fury. Somewhere at the back, a woman began to wail; then came the sound of a chopping blow, and the voice was cut off. Now the stillness beneath the high thatched roof was absolute. I felt the tension in myself, half crouched, half seated, half blind, clutching the heavy iron pot, and I willed myself to relax.

Liam's voice was pitched so that every ear in the crowd could hear him.

"The trouble with good ideas and good intentions, Derek, is that they encourage smugness. Do you know what I mean?" Derek made no response. "I mean, if you are going to take the weapons away from your visitors, then you had better be aware that some of them, at least, might want to have those weapons back, d'you follow me? Now, I'm prepared to believe you might have been aware of that, at one time, but you've fallen into evil ways since then. Eight guards, indeed! They were dead, all of them, before they knew we had come calling."

Now Derek drew himself up to his full height. "You are a dead man, Condranson."

Liam Condranson checked himself dramatically, raising his sword arm high and half turning to appeal to one of the bowmen who flanked him, taking care to keep his voice raised so that it remained audible to everyone in the hall. "Ah, would you listen to that? I am the dead man and him with arrows slavering for his heart's blood! Sit down, King Derek, and shut your mouth. Sit, sit, sit, sit. *Sit!*" He bent forward and almost barked the last word and, aware of his helplessness to do anything else, the king sat, bidden like a mongrel dog.

The Erse admiral looked about him then, eyeing everyone, beginning with the group at the dais table. His gaze lingered on Connor, who glared back at him, aware that one of Liam's hulking guards had passed behind him and now stood with a bared blade right at his back, covering him and Tearlach. Another stood behind me and Blundyl. Liam sneered, and his eyes moved on to big Tearlach, who also sat rigid. But the insult proved too much for another of Connor's men, who leaped to his feet with an oath and died there, his throat shattered by an arrow before his words were fully formed. Liam ignored the interruption and continued his perusal of the room, turning now slowly and completely until he faced the dais again, where his gaze fastened upon me.

"That's a wondrous eye you have there, big fellow. You must be the one who debated with my men this afternoon. Merlyn, from Camulod. I'd welcome you to my new stronghold, to my new kingdom, since it seems to be the king's own duty to welcome guests, but I would be lying. You have the stink of Athol's Gaels about you, for all your yellow hair, so you're bound for the fire with the rest of his carrion." He broke off suddenly at a sound from Derek and turned to face him. "What is it? You have something that you wish to say? Your last pronouncement as a king?"

"You are mad," Derek growled. "My people will eat you."

"Eat me?" Liam whooped with delight, but then his expression hardened into a hateful mask. "What people? You ruled a flock of sheep, old man, a herd of cattle! Or have I overlooked your thousands hiding in the forests? I have taken your stronghold with one half of the crew of my own galley. Three quarters of my men are still unarmed, playing the fool with yours, getting them drunk and legless. Later tonight, when they have all passed out—your men, not mine—we will complete the . . . conversion. My fleet arrives the day after tomorrow. You may blame your swinish friends, Mac Athol and his vermin, for cutting short your kingship by one day. Had they not come, you could have reigned until tomorrow night. Their presence, all unarmed while rooting at your tables, is a mere windfall, unlooked for and unplanned but very welcome." He stopped, and his face and voice underwent a startling transformation, assuming once again a specious goodwill.

"Now, here's what will happen next. Some friends of mine are waiting with the children and one of the women brought today by your new guests. I see the other woman here, so there's nothing lost of that encirclement." He nodded pleasantly to Shelagh, who sat wide-eyed beside her husband, gazing back at Liam in loathing, and then he continued, addressing Derek again. "Now, you have to understand the mettle of my men. I've been affronted by their bad behaviour often in the past, and they're not good with children at all—I think it might be better if we all remain aware of that. So, after you, the former king, are dead, your guests—by all the gods, man, have you no sense of shame at all, to sit with such as these? Your guests will come with me, as hostages, in silence. Is that not right, Connor Mac Athol?"

Connor said nothing and merely glared his defiance until a smashing blow from the man behind him sent him reeling and his face hit the table top. Liam waited until Connor straightened up again, shaking his head to clear it.

"I said, is that not right, Connor Mac Athol?" Another silence and another blow, this one heavy enough to shake the table when Connor's body fell against it. Another pause, and then, "I said, *is that not right, Connor Mac Athol?*"

"In the name of Lud, Connor, answer him!" This was from Shelagh. Connor gazed down at her for long moments, his eyes glazed, and then nodded his head in Liam's direction.

"What was that? I didn't hear you?"

Connor mumbled something and another smashing blow sent him reeling again. This time it took him longer to recover, but when he did, now bleeding from the nose, he spoke.

"Aye, it is right, Liam Condranson."

"Good! Good, good, good, good, good. D'you see, Derek? I knew I was right." He turned his back on us now, addressing the crowd. "All Mac Athol vermin will accompany us, their willing presence ensuring the lives of their beloved leaders. The rest of you will remain here, to keep some of my fellows company and to make sure no one's sleep is disturbed before morning. Tomorrow will be time enough for you to think of how you may welcome me as your new king."

Now he turned slowly back towards us, pausing to point his sword at Donuil.

"You, the big one. Get up there by your peg-legged brother. Move!" Threatened by tight-drawn arrows, Donuil stood and moved to obey, his passage to the dais followed by the watchful eyes and aimed weapons of several bowmen, one of them the man on Liam's left who had previously been aiming at Derek.

Liam's eyes moved to Shelagh. "You, the whore, come here." Shelagh, too, rose to her feet, then made her way slowly to stand in the aisle, some ten paces in front of him. "Closer." She took another step, almost hesitantly, and as she did so I felt my heart leap into my throat, sensing what was coming. Her hesitancy was a sham, I knew. "That's far enough. Kneel."

Slowly, gracefully, her back to us, shoulders square and head held high, Shelagh sank to her knees. Liam looked at her appreciatively.

"You're a comely bitch, aren't you? Lift up your skirts, let's have a look at what you've got between your legs." He flicked a glance towards Donuil and Connor on the dais. "Watch those two," he said, and looked back to Shelagh. "Well? Will you keep me waiting?"

Shelagh bent her head and began to shift from knee to knee, gathering her skirts from beneath them in both hands, then raising them, slowly and deliberately, to her waist and bringing her hands behind her, stretching the stuff of her skirts tightly across her belly. Liam's were not the only eyes that followed her movements—even the aiming bowmen looked away from their targets in slit-eyed lechery. I watched Donuil, saw him brace himself and grind his jaw at the outrage being perpetrated upon his wife. Surprisingly, however, it was Derek who broke first and bounded to his feet. "Animal!" he roared.

Liam's eyes flickered to the dais and he jerked one hand in a signal to the ready bowman poised on his right, who released his shaft immediately. As the arrow sliced towards Derek's breast, I braced my wrist and thrust the heavy black iron skillet against the king's chest, aware only of the thought that I was grateful not to be defending against a Pendragon longbow. The brutal, clanging concussion of the hard-shot missile against the iron pot ripped the handle from my hand and sent the vessel clattering to the floor. Derek was knocked sprawling backwards, over his chair and off the dais, but alive.

Liam's eyes went wide. He threw out his arms in a crazed shout of laughter just as Shelagh's knife, thrown with blurring speed as her arm whipped up from behind her waist then down again, took him full in the neck. He shuddered spastically, arms and legs jerking like a man in a convulsion, and his chin snapped down against the hilt that suddenly protruded from his throat. The sword fell from his hand and Shelagh dove to snatch it up, stabbing upward with it at the man closest to Liam, a bowman who had not had time to notch another shaft and was now staring in uncomprehending horror at his stricken chief. The man went down, clutching uselessly at the blade that pierced him, but Liam himself refused to die. Stiff-legged, and gurgling loudly through a froth of bloody bubbles, he teetered on his heels, eyes bulging, tongue protruding from his open mouth, his arms waving, fighting for balance as he fought for life. He swung himself around, turning like a puppet to face the crowd behind him, arms spread-eagled and his shoulders swaying almost comically in his struggle to remain erect. And then he fell, face down.

His men stood appalled, gaping, stunned and incredulous at the speed with which their chief had been destroyed. Not so us.

Donuil, Connor, Feargus and Logan had all known what was to come when Shelagh walked forward, and they had exploded into violent action before the shock she caused had even registered. Connor whirled to sink his table dagger into the breast of the guard who had abused him. Donuil surged forward to grasp the edge of the heavy dais table and heave it forward and down to the floor, clearing the way for him to leap forward, his fingers spread like talons for the throat of the nearest of Liam's bowmen. I snatched the iron skillet up again from where it lay behind me and swung it to crush the skull of the other dais guard, with whom Blundyl was already grappling.

Logan, Feargus, Dedalus, Rufio and Sean had thrown themselves against the enemy, too, and as they moved, others stirred to life and moved with them, angry and vengeful now, brandishing the knives with which they had earlier fed themselves. Liam's men, their superiority supreme mere moments earlier, now found themselves assailed and overwhelmed from every side, hampered by lack of space, their bows and swords instantly useless. Chaos was the only word to describe the scene, but it was over in a matter of moments, so that when the guards outside threw open the doors to enter, they were hauled in, engulfed and slaughtered as quickly as their fellows, slain by their own weapons.

Derek was sitting up already, breathing hard and rubbing at his chest. Donuil meanwhile was involved with Shelagh, his arms about her, hugging her as if he would crush her to death, and she bent backwards over his encircling arm. It was Connor who reached the main doors first and closed them, calling for order at the top of his voice. By the time I turned around, he was standing on a table, overlooking everyone. Silence fell quickly and I felt the intensity of Connor's gaze as he glanced from Derek to me.

"How is he, Merlyn?" I knew exactly what he was asking me. This was Derek's Hall, and he it was who should be making the decisions and dispositions. I looked down again at the king, and he saw me look at him and read the expression in my eyes. Derek swallowed, grimacing against the pain in his chest, and waved one hand at me in a peremptory signal that he knew what was happening and what must be done.

"He's not ready yet," I called to Connor. "You organize things. There's no time to waste."

He wasted none. Six of his people were sent running to make sure no more of Liam's kerns remained beyond the door. They were warned to be careful and to allow no one to escape to raise the alarm, but equally to be quiet and attract no attention to themselves. Then, speaking quickly, and telling off his points on the fingers of one hand, Connor outlined our situation to the rest of us.

The short-term chances favoured us, he said, if we moved quickly and quietly to take advantage of this development. He pointed out that we were probably alone within the fort, save for a few of Liam's other men, like those who held the children and the weapons rooms in the next building. Everyone else in Liam's force was likely to be outside the walls, in the outer town, doing their part to cover up their master's treachery inside, and by Liam's own admission, he reminded us, those men were still unarmed. They were now leaderless, as well, and would remain so until such time as Liam's death had been clearly established. We could and must use that time to our advantage.

The dead men's weapons were collected and distributed among the Mac Athol warriors and the fighting men of Derek's folk, and Connor detailed twenty men, under Donuil and Shelagh, whose sons were being held, to seek the children and take them to safety aboard his galley and to seize Liam's two galleys at the same time. As those chosen left the hall, twenty more, commanded by Tearlach, were selected to make their way quietly and in stealth to secure the room that held our own weapons. These, too, Connor sent out at once, bidding them be quiet and cautious, and emphasizing the importance of alerting the rest of us—the unarmed mass of us—soon as the way was clear for us to come and collect our weapons.

When these parties had gone, Connor spoke urgently to those of us who remained. Clearly and precisely, drawing upon his knowledge of the outer town from previous visits, he made incisive dispositions of our remaining forces, delegating authority to men whose local knowledge matched his own. Those of us from Camulod, being strangers here, would follow their leadership. As soon as we could reach the weapons store, he told us, each of us must arm himself with at least three swords, one for each hand and another to be sheathed by his side. We would then spread out, in four large groups led by Connor himself, Derek, Blundyl and Owen. We would move throughout the recognized quadrants of the outer town, passing out weapons to our own as we encountered them. Tearlach and his score of guards, soon to be reinforced to fifty, would remain in place in the administrative building, guarding against any new attempt by Liam's men to seize the place and facilitating the distribution of weaponry to our own people.

Connor had barely finished outlining his strategy when a runner arrived from Tearlach with the word that his men had won their skirmish and now held the armoury. They had found fourteen of Liam's men in place there and had lost seven of their own in recapturing the building. Liam's people had fought hard. Moments later, word arrived from Shelagh that the children were safe and had been rescued unharmed.

I attached myself to Derek's group and spent the next period of hours embroiled in the grim struggle to recapture Derek's autonomy in his own town. It was bitter, dirty work, but having seized the initiative, we pursued it grimly, and by the end of the first hour there was no question of our victory. The Sons of Condran showed themselves doughty fighters, despite their awareness that their plot had failed and that their admiral prince had gone down in death at the outset. They fought with the suicidal madness of desperation, refusing to surrender and often grappling barehanded in total darkness with the baleful, outraged men who swung their swords mercilessly, seeking vengeance for treachery.

Late in the proceedings, we found ourselves on the outskirts of the town, close to the tavern where I had first seen the man in the yellow tunic. Someone had overturned a lamp at some stage of the fighting and the burning oil had set the entire tavern ablaze, so that its hectic glare lit up the night. As we approached, a knot of running men broke from the space between two buildings and came pouring towards us, seeing us only when they were almost upon us, and then veering to attack us immediately. They were five against our four, although others of our group were close behind. One of them came for me directly, his teeth bared in a scream, swinging a heavy-headed axe. Checking my instinctual urge to jump aside, I stood still and waited for him to swing his weapon. Still running, he chopped at me two-handed, aiming to cleave me from left shoulder to breastbone. I avoided his stroke by leaping forward to my left, beneath his axe. Then I thrust my sword point beneath his exposed shoulder, bracing my left knee to check my momentum and throwing my weight backwards, leaning deep into my thrust. The weight of his falling body dragged me around with him, and as I struggled to free my sword, pushing him off the blade with my foot, I saw Derek rolling on the ground beneath another of the men, clutching the fellow's wrist in both hands as he fought to keep the point of a long, sharp knife away from his throat. I reached them in one long stride and swung my foot, kicking the knife-wielder beneath the chin and knocking him backwards. I finished him with a hacking, overhead slash. And then we were alone in the street, Derek and I, both of us panting for breath as we looked around us.

I heard a commotion in the shadows of a neighbouring passageway and started to head towards it, but I stopped to make sure that Derek, who had regained his feet, was unhurt. He was more winded than I was and bent over, gasping for breath, but he waved me away, indicating that he was well enough. I ran towards the noises and heard him begin to follow me, but we were to fight no more that night. Silence had fallen by the time we reached the end of the passageway, and we found some of our companions collecting themselves and congratulating each other.

We returned immediately to the burning tavern. Derek was fearful that the flames might spread to other buildings, but there were no other buildings close enough, and as we stood there looking at the flames and counting the bodies visible in the firelight, a heavy rain began to fall. We regrouped and set out to search elsewhere, but the rain, at first refreshing, soon became a curse. We were relieved to find that the fighting was over and order was being restored everywhere. Ours had, apparently, been the last skirmish, and no Sons of Condran remained in Ravenglass.

Next we organized work parties to help with our wounded and to begin collecting corpses, transporting them, in what had become torrential rain, to a designated area close to the bathhouse. While we were doing that, Rufio brought word from Lucanus that he had established a temporary infirmary in the central court of the administrative building, the largest single space he could find that was uninhabited. Derek immediately passed the word to tell our walking wounded to make their way there for assistance, and he sent runners to the other three quadrant commanders, to pass on the information and instruct each of them to appoint litter-bearers to carry their more gravely wounded to the new field hospital. There were no walking wounded among Liam's people. Those few who had survived the conflict were all gravely injured and close to death.

At length, satisfied that everything that might be done was being done, the king and I went looking for Connor. We found him where I had expected to find him: outside the western wall on the wharf, in conference again with his captains, Tearlach, Feargus and Logan. He dismissed them as he saw us approach, resettled his sodden cape about his shoulders and sniffed loudly in disgust at the weather.

"Is there any place in this town that is dry?" he asked as we arrived.

"Aye, there is, and we were just about to go there," Derek answered. "My house. The place should have been cleaned up by this time, but even if it hasn't, there are some rooms where carnage was shut out. Come with us, we have much to talk about."

A short time later, pleased to see that the space beneath the thatch had been cleared of bodies, and the blood cleaned up and covered with fresh straw, Derek led us into a pleasant room in his own living quarters, where a fire burned brightly in an open grate. Once we had shed our soaked outer clothing and settled by the fire, clutching mugs of mead, he wasted no time in coming to the point.

"You will not be leaving in the morning now, I hope?"

Connor, seated in the middle, looked at me and winked surreptitiously before he turned to face the king. "Why not? There's nothing to stop us now, is there?"

Derek had the grace to flush with discomfort. "No, I suppose not. . . ." Neither Connor nor I made a sound. "But . . . I hope you'll stay."

"For at least two days more, you mean, until Liam's fleet arrives?"

"Aye. They are your enemies as much as mine."

"True, but self-serving, Derek." Connor's nod was judicious. "They have been my enemies for years and I know how to deal with them on my own terms. They have only been your enemies, openly, for hours. It's fortunate for you and yours that we were here at all, today, and you'll admit you've given us little encouragement to remain ere this. Besides that, they are a fleet—thirty of them at least, where I have but three galleys. If I leave with the tide tomorrow as you originally suggested, I'll be well clear of the threat of them by the time they arrive."

"Five, if you'll stay."

"What?"

"Five galleys. Liam's two are now mine, by forfeit. I'll give them to you if you'll stay to help us."

Connor nodded again. "That is appealing, I will admit, although in truth it was my men who took them. But still . . . five galleys, manned by the crews of only three, against thirty . . ." He grimaced and shook his head.

Derek stood up and began to pace. "Look you, it's not your galleys I need, it's your men, up on my walls, to stand them off."

"I don't follow you." Connor was frowning. "You want me to place my men on your walls, and leave my galleys floating empty in the harbour to be burned?"

"They won't be burned!"

"How so?" Connor's tone became scornful. "They are made of wood, dry and well seasoned. Have you never seen what burning, pitch-wrapped arrows, shot from afar, can do to a floating hulk? No, Derek, that's too much to ask. I'll not desert my ships. Mine is a naval force, it functions well only at sea."

"We'll hide them! We have all day tomorrow to conceal them, and I know a perfect place, an inlet, completely hidden from the sea and sheltered from the winds, with a shelving beach and a high tide. Your galleys will lie safe there for as long as must be and none will know they're there."

"Hmm . . ." Connor thought for a long moment, considering that, then sucked a tiny breath between his teeth. It was a gesture he shared with his father, Athol, one that both men used when they were thinking deeply. "How close is this place? Can I go there tomorrow, to see it for myself? I take no man's word at face value where my galleys are concerned."

"Aye, you can go and look. It is close by. Less than two miles along the coast to the south, but cunningly disguised and invisible from offshore. I know, for I have tried to see it for myself, and I would never have found it had I not known where to look."

Connor was still unsure. "That's as may be, Derek, but I mislike the thought of simply going off and leaving my craft lying there untended. It takes long years to build a galley, but only moments to burn one." He stopped, evidently having come to a decision. "If I agree, how would my men get back from there to here?"

"We'll ferry them, in our fishing boats."

Connor turned to me. "Merlyn, what do you think?"

I shrugged my shoulders. "One thought came to me immediately. Suppose we drive these Ersemen off, convinced they cannot take this place from the sea. What might they do then? Sail straight for home? The probability is that they would, knowing their leader Liam to be dead. But would they know that?" Both men were staring at me, their faces blank. "Think of it! Liam is dead. You know that and so does everyone here. But you are discussing the removal of Liam's galleys, the only sign his fleet will have that he is here. By removing them, you are also removing the proof of his presence, and of his failure. The men in his fleet, believing him—as he himself believed—to be immortal, will merely guess, when they arrive to find his galleys absent, that he has changed his plans for some reason and postponed his attack. They're bound to have at least one able captain among them, someone clever enough to see that, since his plans involve treachery, the postponement of them must entail continued amity between themselves and Ravenglass. They'll have no reason to approach us at all, and every reason not to. So they will sail off again to look for him elsewhere, believing him to be close by, and they'll search the coastline to the north and south carefully, seeking a hiding place such as you describe. They'll find your galleys."

"Aye, they will." Connor was gazing at me narrow-eyed. "You have a subtle way of thinking, Yellow Head. I'm glad you're not my enemy. I can't argue with your logic, so that means Liam's galleys must stay here and take their chances of being destroyed or recaptured. They are the bait to draw the animals in close. Hmm . . ." He scratched his chin. "I'm glad I asked, but that wasn't the reason for my asking what you think. You have your own responsibilities, and my sworn duty to my father commits me to your needs before all else. That is why we're here, when all is said and done." He raised his hand now from his chin to scratch his temple gently with a middle fingertip, winking at me again from behind its shelter. "I think this whole affair of Liam's fleet too dangerous and certainly not your concern. What say you?"

"Wait!" Both of us turned to Derek, who was red-faced and looking ill at ease. "Before you respond, Merlyn, hear what I have to say."

I looked back at Connor, raising my eyebrow, and then nodded, gesturing to Derek to continue. He cleared his throat, his thoughts evidently racing with each other as he sought the words to sway me.

"I was at pains to explain my reasons for refusing your request today, and I believed you understood them, at the time."

"I did."

"Aye, well they have all changed, thanks to this treachery of Condranson." I waited. He flexed his shoulders, glancing again at Connor. "You spoke of duty to your father and its binding you to Merlyn, here. I was unaware of that. How is Athol Mac Iain beholden to Camulod?"

Connor looked blank, and I answered for him. "He is not. He has . . . an interest in the welfare of the boy who is in my care."

"What kind of interest?" Derek's sudden frown was speculative, his eyes glinting with curiosity.

"An abiding one, let us say."

"Abiding . . . you mean ongoing? Active?"

"Most assuredly." Connor's voice was dry now, almost ironic. "I think it might be better if you spoke your mind, rather than attempting to be circumspect. What is it that you want to know?"

Derek braced his shoulders, facing Connor squarely. "I want to know if Athol extends real protection to the boy, or merely friendly interest. There's no point in my denying it, this thing with the Sons of Condran spells disaster for my people and my town. This was unknown to me when you arrived, and it changes everything. I need an ally now, a strong one, with a fleet of galleys. If I offer sanctuary to Merlyn and the boy, as I was asked to do, then may I rely on you and yours to extend protection to my folk as part of the agreement? That is what I need to know."

"That's plain enough. You mean afterwards, in time to come. Not merely when Liam's fleet arrives the day after tomorrow. You still need help with that."

"Yes."

"Hmm." Connor snatched a deep breath and blew it out through pursed lips. "I have the feeling, Ravenglass, that you would make me earn those two galleys."

Derek almost smiled. "They're Condran's best. His admiral's own ships. And they're undamaged."

"No thanks to you." Connor looked at me. "There was a holding crew aboard each one. They tried to fire them when they saw us coming. Almost succeeded, too." He turned back to Derek. "The bargain—especially this latest element you've added, of ongoing help—still weighs too heavily in your favour, my friend. Where will you lodge Merlyn and his people now if I accede? Because if all things are changed in your condition, so, too, are the requirements for their safety."

"I know that." Derek turned to me. "How many people are there in your group? In total."

"Eighteen."

He looked at me for a long time, nodding slowly. "I have the perfect place, I think."

When it became clear that he would say no more without prompting, Connor supplied it. "Another perfect place? Where? You have a suitable house?"

"No, I have a suitable fort." He rose to throw some fuel on the fire, leaving us to wonder. When he was satisfied that the fire would burn well, Derek returned to his chair.

"The road out of our town is the Tenth Iter. Does that mean anything to you?" Both of us shook our heads, and he grinned at me. "Well, you once told me you knew your Britain—at least the Roman part of it—but now I can tell you something you didn't know. The Tenth Iter is the only road in all this region that penetrates the heartland from the coast. Very important road, it was, to the Romans, built during the period after they abandoned the other wall they built, up in Caledonia."

"The Antonine Wall."

"Aye, that's the one. Anyway, they built this road, the Tenth Iter, to transport supplies from Ravenglass, here, which they called Glannaventa, traversing the passes through the Fells to the garrison at Galava, which means "by the side of the vigorous stream." We call the stream the Amble. Anyway, the road's more than thirty Roman miles long, and it had three forts, the two at each end and another they called Mediobogdum—don't ask me what that means—in the middle, on a plateau at the top of the highest pass through the Fells."

"It means 'in the river's bend.' Isn't it on a river?"

"No, it's on a mountaintop, but there's a river in the valley below, the Esk, and it bends around the fort, right enough. The fort was a camp for summer garrisons, never occupied in winter, since the road was impassable." He looked from one to the other of us. "That means no town ever grew up around it. Who would want to live up there year-round? You, for all of that, might find it appropriate for your own reasons, but you'll be the first ones in nearly two hundred years, according to our Druids. It lies something over ten miles from here, and it's been abandoned for longer than anyone's ever been able to recall. I think, though, with a little hard work and willingness, it could be made habitable, even now. I was there last summer and spent two nights. The walls are sound—they're built mostly of local stone—and some of the buildings are strongly roofed. There's water and wood in abundance and even a bathhouse, though what condition that's in is something I can't guess at. The site itself is protected by high peaks and by thick forest, and few people use the road nowadays. Those who do come from inland. No one uses it from here, except in the summer, when we post lookouts in the pass up there to guard against intrusion from inland. But we've had no trouble now for more than twenty years."

Connor was looking at me, his lips pressed together. "What think you?"

I shrugged. "I'd like to see it. It might serve."

"Hmm." Connor sat silent for a spell, plucking at his pursed lips as he stared into the fire, and I sat motionless, watching him and waiting for the outcome of his thoughts. Finally he straightened up, his eyes seeking mine. "Very well, here's what we'll do. Tomorrow, Derek, you'll supply a man to take me to this place where we can hide our galleys. We'll take only our own three, leaving Liam's here to be seen by his fleet. We'll need only half-crews, and we'll leave the vessels in this inlet you know of, providing that I'm satisfied it's as safe and well hidden as you say it is. Afterwards, your fishing fleet will pick my men up and bring them back here. That means when Liam's vermin come, they'll see their admiral's galleys and be sure he's here. But they will see their accursed admiral, too. . . . I want to be quite certain of that." He drummed his fingertips against his lips, his eyes on me again, his thoughts evidently elsewhere.

"Derek, last time I was here Blundyl took me around the town and showed me all kinds of wondrous things. One of them, I recall distinctly, was an old cargo shed, still sound and weatherproof, sitting all alone beyond the end of the western wall, facing the harbour. It was full of heavy, hand-forged lengths of rusty iron chains, enormous things. Do you know what I'm talking about?"

"Aye, I do. The Romans made them. Used them to fasten great logs together, a floating boom, strung from the mainland to the island in the bay to seal the harbour against surprise attack. There's one at the other end, too."

"Are they still there?"

"Aye, they've been lying in there for years. We've had no need of them ere now, although we might hereafter." He gazed at Connor, speculatively. "You want to use them? Restring the boom? There's no time. We'd have to cut the logs."

"No. I want to join the lengths together and string them, secured by heavy spikes, along the top of your wall facing the harbour . . . the full length of the wall. Then, using the chains as an anchor, I want to hang the corpses of every one of the Sons of Condran slain last night, with Liam in the centre, so that they'll be the first thing our Erse visitors will see when they arrive. That will give them something to choke over. They will also find the walls well manned, with my hundreds supplementing your own men. They'll be too far away to recognize any of us, and they'll assume us to be your people. If they come too close, we'll throw some fire at them. You still have the Roman catapults up on the walls, I know. Are they serviceable?" Derek nodded. "Good. Make sure they're freshly greased and tightened or whatever has to be done to them, during the day tomorrow. Merlyn will help you. He knows about such things. Liam's fleet will be here with the sun the next day, and they'll expect to find the town already in their possession. They'll choke on their own vomit, but I hope they'll approach close enough to suffer when we open fire on them.

"We should be able to savage them badly and send them home with their tails between their legs, bearing the news of gentle Liam's death. They might return seeking vengeance, or they might not. In either case, they won't be coming back soon, and when they do, they'll find Mac Athol taking interest in their movements. As soon as they've gone, you will take Merlyn and me to see this fort of yours. What did you call it?"

"Mediobogdum."

"Aye, Mediobogdum. An outlandish name, even for Romans. Are we agreed?"

"We are." Each man spat into his hand and we clapped our palms together to seal the bargain.

Some time close to dawn, dirty and weary, I made my way to my own cot and fell across it, hurting my face in the process so that I realized I had completely forgotten my bruised eye and cheekbone. In spite of my exhaustion, or perhaps because of it, I lay awake for a short time, half-consciously recalling sights and incidents from the night's alarums and reflecting on the way things change in life, never remaining constant for any appreciable length of time. I saw Liam die again, spraying blood from his mouth, and the last thing I thought of was Shelagh's other knife, still concealed beneath my pillow.

IV

THE RAIN, WHICH had been diminishing in volume all morning, finally stopped shortly before noon. I pulled back my hood and combed my fingers through my hair, welcoming the cool air about my head. Beside me, Shelagh stood, thoughtful, chewing on the inside of her lip. The two men who had been helping me stood silent, awaiting further instructions.

"He isn't here," Shelagh said.

I turned to her, shaking my head. "How can you know that?"

"I know it."

"How, Shelagh? How can you know it, when I can't? I don't even know who I'm looking for. The single thing I am sure of is that I can't identify him."

Shelagh simply gazed at me, saying nothing more. We were standing by the bathhouse, beside the neatly ordered, rain-soaked rows of the Sons of Condran who had died in the previous night's fighting. I found myself curiously unmoved by the sight of them, even after watching them turned this way and that to expose their faces to my search. Their exposure to the hours of steady, heavy rain had robbed them of all semblance of humanity, leaving them pallid and waxen, their exposed skin cleansed of clotted blood. The casualties from Ravenglass and Connor's crews, by comparison—there were none among the group from Camulod, for which I thanked God—had been sheltered, laid out in a large storage shed behind the bathhouse itself, and their corpses, coated and caked with crusted blood, somehow made them appear more pitiable.

I had examined every corpse, counting involuntarily but losing track among Liam's people somewhere between a hundred and fifty and a hundred and sixty. The first twenty-six had been our men, most of them slain in the opening moments of Liam's treacherous move. I didn't think my man was among them, in either group, but I knew I could be wrong. I shook my head.

"He might have changed his clothes, Shelagh, knowing the yellow tunic made him recognizable. If he did, then any one of these bodies could be him. I told you, I never saw his face clearly. The only time I was close to him, I didn't see him until he turned to scuttle away, and then I only saw the tunic."

"You think that's likely? I don't."

"Why not? It seems logical enough to me."

Shelagh shook her head. "No. No, not at all. You're overrating this man, Merlyn. He's not that clever. He ran, and he drew your attention. A clever man would have passed you by, ignoring you, unnoticed. But he ran because he thought you'd recognize him. Him, not his clothes. Believing that, he'd never think to change his tunic. He'd be convinced that you would know his face no matter what he wore. You don't recognize anyone here, therefore your man, whoever he may be, is not among the dead."

"Which means he's still alive."

"Aye, and could be anywhere within a day's journey from here, by this time. That's very astute of you, Caius Merlyn."

I glanced at her sidelong, half smiling. "Curb your tongue, woman, or I'll have your husband take a switch to you."

She hooted, then smiled demurely and fluttered her long lashes before bowing her head in mock submission, undismayed, like me, by indulging in levity in the presence of so much death.

I had returned her knife to her that morning, congratulating her on her presence of mind and effectiveness the previous night. The children had been present, and I was glad to see they appeared to have taken no ill from their adventures in the hands of Liam's men. Not even Turga had been harmed. Donuil had already gone down to the wharves with Lucanus, Rufio and Dedalus to supervise the unloading of our stores and livestock from Connor's galleys and bring everything into safety behind the walls. Connor's crews were making ready to transport the three Mac Athol craft to safety, out of sight of Liam's fleet when it arrived.

The boys had been agog for the story of the previous night's doings, and Shelagh, who directed them to me as soon as I arrived, had told them nothing. I spent half an hour telling them everything I felt they ought to know, including the threat of Liam's fleet, due to arrive the next day. I exacted a solemn promise from each of them that they would behave themselves, respecting and staying clear of the preparations under way everywhere. Then I released them into Turga's care to visit the wharves where their uncles were working. Gwin and Ghilleadh were the sons of Donuil and Shelagh, and Bedwyr, the third of the constant trio that accompanied Arthur everywhere, was the son of Hector and his late wife, Julia, who had been killed in the attempt on Arthur's life some months earlier.

"What are you two doing?" Donuil had now approached, unseen by either of us.

"Attempting to become as thoroughly soaked as you are," I answered, turning to greet him. "I've just been talking about you, telling your wife I'd have you take a switch to her if she doesn't learn to bridle her unruly tongue." The two were embracing as I spoke, and the big Celt turned to grin at me over his wife's head.

"A switch? You're supposed to be my friend. I wouldn't try anything like that without a troop of Camulodian cavalry to hold her down, and even then I'd lose."

"We've been looking for Caius's man in the yellow tunic," Shelagh said. "He's gone."

"Gone where?"

"Anywhere," I replied. "But away from Ravenglass, so we may never know who he was."

Donuil looked from me to Shelagh. "Is that important?"

"It could be." Shelagh's response was deliberate. She spoke to me. "What do you think?"

"I'm more interested in what you think. Your thoughts have been more crystalline than mine so far this morning. What's in your mind?"

"Much, and I like little of it. Listen, and see if this strikes you as logical." She glanced about her. "Let's go inside. I'm freezing."

The bathhouse was warm and dry, and we sat together on the stone benches in the deserted changing rooms, close to the furnace vents. Shelagh had said no more as we moved inside, and I knew she was deep in thought. When we had shrugged off our outer garments and were settled, enjoying the warmth, she returned to her topic.

"Here's what I've been thinking. We know Ironhair's intentions about Arthur, and about you, Caius, and he has already shown how dangerous he is. That's why we left Camulod—we do not know who is in his pay among the Colonists, but he clearly owns someone. That someone might be close enough to us—although the gods all know we hope it isn't so—to have found out, right at the outset of our planning, that we were preparing to remove the boy from danger. If that is the case, the word might have gone out to Ironhair as long as a month ago, perhaps even sooner. And yet I think we may safely assume, simply because of the time constraints involved, that he has not yet had time to send out spies to watch for us. Not from Cornwall, or even Cambria, by land to here—"

"He could have come by boat, Shelagh. There were more than a score of fishing craft at the wharf when we arrived yesterday."

"Aye, that's right, there were, but most of those would be local." She looked at me, nodding. "Those that were not would be remarked upon, their coming and going noticed. And if one of them left yesterday, after your altercation in the woods, we should be able to find out about it. That had not occurred to me."

"Not yet. It would have."

"Hmm. Well, until we find that out, the timing part of this is debatable. But let's stay with my first thought, that Ironhair may know we've left Camulod but has not had time to send spies out this far. And bear in mind that we are trying to identify this fugitive of yours. Can you think of anyone, other than one of Ironhair's creatures, who might have reason to fear you enough that he would run to avoid you?"

I shook my head, slowly, thinking about that, and reminding myself forcefully that only Lucanus and myself knew anything of my leprous condition. "No, I can't think of anyone."

"Are you sure about that, Caius? Completely?"

"Yes. Yes, I am."

She heaved a deep sigh and sat up straight before expelling it. "Then we would be wise to assume that Ironhair has spies everywhere, and be on guard. And even if I'm wrong, even if it's not Ironhair, someone already knows you're here, Caius."

I could see where she was headed. "No, not quite, Shelagh. Our fugitive disappeared yesterday in the afternoon and hasn't been seen since, and whether he fled by land or by sea is unimportant beside this: none of us knew until late last night that we'd be staying here. When last this man was seen, Derek had rejected my request. But I had made that request privately, in person, and he had not discussed it with anyone else. Now think about what that means. We arrived aboard Connor's galley and we unloaded no supplies. We would have been seen, by anyone who cared to look, as visitors, in transit, and no more than that. It follows that we would move on with Connor, when he left. If we are to assume this man's a spy, we must also assume that, having seen me the first time, when I rode by the tavern, he would have asked questions and found that out before he left."

Donuil was listening closely to us, his eyes switching from one to the other of us as we spoke. "So you think the word he took away is that we'll be moving on, to Eire?"

"Something like that, but merely moving on with Connor, to Eire, or to Caledonia."

"But what if he spoke to one of our people and learned the truth, that you were to stay here?"

"He couldn't, Donuil, not unless he asked one of us, or Connor himself, or any of the other chieftains. No one else knew our plans, and none of Connor's captains would speak out to strangers."

He nodded. "What about this fort Connor mentioned? Can you tell us about that?"

"Mediobogdum. I can, but not much more than I'm sure Connor has already told you. It's in the mountains, about ten miles from here, abandoned for at least two hundred years, but habitable yet, after some hard work, according to Derek. We're going to look at it, once Liam's fleet has been driven off. You'll see it for yourself then, at the same time I do."

"*Some* hard work, after two hundred years?" Donuil rose to his feet.

"I'd better get back. We have all the stores and crates off-loaded, and the horses, and we're moving them inside the fort. We'll be done within the hour, I expect. I'll find out before then whether any boat set sail after noon yesterday, and if any did, I'll find out who was in it. I'll also find out if anyone, in a yellow tunic or otherwise, was asking questions about you and yours of our men yesterday. What are you going to do now?"

"I'm going up to look at the catapults on the walls, to see if we can use them without killing our own people in the process. Derek says they work well, but they've been there without skilled maintenance—as far as I'm aware—for almost thirty years, and I'll be happier once I've verified their condition for myself. I'll be very surprised not to have to change all the ropes, and I'll be even more surprised if I can find enough people capable of doing it in the time we have."

Shelagh returned to our temporary quarters to oversee the disposition of the goods arriving from the wharf, and I walked back to the wharf gates with Donuil, leaving him there and making my way up to the parapet walk.

I found Derek on one of the defensive towers that projected out towards the harbour, examining one of the great, fixed *ballistae* left behind by the legions when they abandoned the place. The long timber throwing arm stretched vertically, high above him as he crouched at its base, and I approached slowly, my eyes more concerned with the weapon than with the king. The great ropes that bound and propelled the device's moving parts looked sound, their surfaces hard and tight-looking, betraying no signs of the dry, weather-worn fuzziness I had feared to see. Derek heard me coming and looked up.

"Ah, there you are. I was looking for you earlier."

I explained what I had been doing, all the while examining the great torsion-driven throwing device on its solid base. "This thing looks excellent," I said, when I had finished. "It looks as though it could really work." As I said the words, another man straightened up from behind the other side of the machine's base, looking at me as though wondering which pit of Hades I had sprung from and what I could possibly know of artillery.

"Hah!" Derek's laugh was a bark of delight. "You hear that, Longinus? Merlyn of Camulod thinks your ballista might really work."

Longinus had drawn himself to his full height, and now he moved around the base of the machine to where I stood, pulling a tiny splinter from the side of one callused finger as he came. When it was out, he held it up to his eyes and then flicked it away before acknowledging me. He looked me up and down, his eyes moving very slowly, then nodded. "Gaius Longinus," he said. "You know siege machines?"

I shrugged. "I know enough to know this one's been well tended."

He nodded. "They all have."

I looked about me. I could see other installations on the walls, but this seemed to be the only one that was complete. "You have others?" I asked.

"Aye, dismantled. They'll be back in place today."

"How many have you?"

"Five." Longinus was evidently a man of few words.

"All on this wall?" I had seen signs of five installations.

He nodded. "Two overheads like this, three catapults."

"All in working order?" He nodded again. "Windlasses, too?"

Now his eyebrows flicked in annoyance. "You ever see a catapult that would work with a broken windlass?"

"Of course not. Forgive me, I'm simply excited. I didn't expect to find someone here with experience in the use and care of war machines. Where did you learn?"

"Right here."

"How, exactly? Or perhaps I should ask who taught you? The legions have been gone for thirty years and more."

"My father taught me, when I was a boy."

"And how did he know about it?"

"From the army artificers. Then, after the garrison left, he took over the defences for the king. Trained me. I've been doing it since he died, twenty years ago."

"Your father was with the legions?"

"Twentieth Valeria. Thirty years."

"In artillery?"

"The last twenty on artillery."

"My grandfather commanded the Valeria."

"Did he, by God? What name?"

"Britannicus, but that was more than forty years ago, probably before your father's time."

"No, he was serving then. But I don't know the name. Before my time."

I glanced at Derek. He was grinning like a split turnip. I ignored him and spoke again to Longinus, resigned now to this business of specific questions provoking taciturn answers. "You have assistants trained?"

"Two crews for each, one in training."

This was like catching fish by hand without bait. "You mean one crew? Or five crews in training?"

"Five. Six men to a crew."

"I see, so how many men altogether?"

He blinked, computing quickly. "Four and a half score. Ninety."

"Good God! Who trains them?"

"I do."

"All of them? You have no one to help you?"

"Five. Head man on each first crew." He looked away, down into the fort beneath the wall, and I heard someone shouting up to him. Then, without another word, he strode away towards the steps and disappeared down them.

I turned back to Derek. "He's not too talkative, is he?"

"No, but I'd choose him over any other man I know, either for company or competence. Wait till you see his people in action tomorrow. You'll be impressed, I promise you. So will the Ersemen, both on shore and afloat. They've all forgotten the Romans and their heavy catapults. When they see how much damage one well-used machine like this can do, and from how far away it can destroy a ship, they'll spin about like tops and they won't stop rowing till they run their keels up onto their own beaches. . . ." He paused. "The dead men. You still want them hung from the walls?"

"Absolutely, every one of them. I promise you, the sight of them in their armour—with Liam and his chieftains in the middle—will be even more effective than your catapults."

"Aye, it might, but it seems gruesome. There's more than a hundred of them."

"Close to a hundred and fifty. I agree with you, but Connor knows what he is doing. To these Ersemen, that much death, so flagrantly displayed, will scream of punishment and consequences not to be ignored. If we beat them off, in addition, they'll think long and hard before they come back this way again."

Derek deliberated in silence for no more than a few moments before nodding his head in agreement.

"So be it. I'll start Blundyl on the arrangements now. He'll need at least a hundred men, I'd guess. Those chains are heavy. They can start bringing them in immediately and fastening the lengths together. They'll string them as soon as Longinus and his people are finished setting up their machines. The bodies can be hung tonight, after the sun goes down." He hesitated, looking along the parapet from right to left. "I'm glad I won't have to do any of the hanging, it's going to be an unpleasant whoreson of a task."

"The hanging" was, as Derek had predicted, a whoreson of a task, but every able-bodied man in the settlement took part in it and it was completed before midnight, by the light of multiple bonfires kindled on the tops of the walls, in the enclosure beneath and on the earthen wharf outside the gates. Stringing the lengths of chain from the battlements had been the most time-consuming part of the exercise. The chains were heavy and cumbersome and had to be joined, then strung in long, pendant scallops anchored by shorter pieces—each about the length of a tall man—secured to the top of the wall above, so that the chain formed a kind of frieze running the entire length of the western wall facing the sea.

By the time that had been done, arrangements were in hand to display the corpses effectively—a grisly enterprise made even less pleasant by the fact that the bodies had now been dead for more than a day and had begun to decompose. They hung in pairs, each pair slung by a loop of rope secured beneath the shoulders of the two corpses and then draped across the chain by men who also worked in pairs, suspended in seafarers' rope cradles from the walls above. The sole exception to the paired arrangement was the body of Liam Condranson himself, which hung in the centre of the wall by a single rope depending from the walkway above. He hung below the chain, as did his dead companions, but he was not attached to it in any way.

When the array of death was spread out in all its stark and gruesome panoply in preparation for the coming of the dawn and Liam's fleet, I passed the word among my own party to assemble in the central hall beneath Derek's thatch. I had several things to say to them before they went to sleep that night, for I had decided I owed them the right to think about my intentions overnight before committing any of them to the course of action I envisaged. By the time I arrived at the appointed gathering place, having had to stop and talk to Derek and Longinus about some last-moment arrangements, they were all waiting for me, sitting informally on a scattering of seats, benches and tabletops, and all appeared to be as weary as I felt.

"I won't keep you long," I began. "Dawn will come quickly and none of us knows what it will bring us." I looked around at their faces, all watching me intently, none showing anything other than curiosity. I moved closer, positioning myself among them where all could hear without my having to raise my voice.

"We came to Ravenglass seeking sanctuary, a safe place to raise the boy. You all know that. What some of you do not know is that Derek, the king, refused our request shortly after we arrived. Fundamentally, what he said was that our continuing presence here—he meant mine, personally, and young Arthur's—would constitute a threat to the safety and welfare of his own people, since we represent a future threat to powerful factions in several places."

I stopped, expecting a reaction of some kind, but no one spoke. They seemed to sense that I had more to say.

"That, however, was yesterday. Since then, thanks to Liam and the Sons of Condran, everything has changed. Now Derek has a war on his hands. He sees us now—our continuing presence here, I mean—as a guarantee of support from Athol and his fleets in the protection of the king's grandson. He wants us to remain now, and I believe we should, providing we can negotiate the terms of our staying to suit our own needs."

Dedalus spoke up. "And what are those? Have you defined them?"

"Aye, I believe I have, but only in the past few hours." I looked around at my listeners. "We chose this place at the outset because it offers us all that we need: safety from surprise attack, with mountains all around us and at our back; open channels of communication with Athol and his Scots; and a degree of distance between ourselves and the dangers in Cornwall and Cambria."

I paused again, waiting for Dedalus.

"You sound unconvinced, now."

I nodded. "I am unconvinced, even with those safeties I've just mentioned. We had all of those, apart from the mountains directly at our back, in Camulod, our own home, and yet the risks were too great to remain there. Even an enclosed community like Camulod can be infiltrated, as we discovered to our cost. We could not identify our enemies even there, among our own, could not tell who might have been suborned. Now we are here in Ravenglass, an open port, and we are strangers here. The dangers are commensurably greater and therefore unacceptable. . . ."

"So you are saying we should move on?"

"I don't think so, Ded, but I don't know."

Dedalus raised his eyebrows and looked around at the others before his gaze came back to me. He coughed, clearing his throat. "You don't know. . . . Hmm. I, for one, would far rather have heard a blunt 'yes' or a loud 'no' there." He shook his head, thinking that over. The others remained absolutely still, no one as much as fidgeting, all eyes fixed either on me or on Dedalus. Finally Ded spoke again. "Look here, Merlyn, don't misunderstand what I say here . . . I mean, you're more than entitled to have doubts from time to time, although we're not used to you being indecisive. We're accustomed to firm guidance from you—mostly in the form of direct orders—in anything important."

He looked about him again, as though seeking support from his fellows. If that was his intent, he gained nothing by it. Donuil coughed slightly, and apart from that there was utter stillness. He turned back to me. "We're all here because you're here and young Arthur's here. Wherever you two go, we go along. You're the leader, the commander. Tell us what to do and it's done. I don't think I can be plainer than that. Does anyone here think otherwise? Lucanus?" Lucanus merely shook his head, his eyes on mine, and it was apparent that no one else had anything to add. I smiled, grateful once more for Ded's plain, outspoken bluntness.

"I'm hesitant, Ded, that's all, not indecisive. There is another option open to us. I've had no time to look at it, or even to think much about it, but it has many disadvantages attached to it. It also has advantages that could work strongly in our favour. But opting for it would leave us open to a vast amount of work, perhaps more than we might realistically be willing or able to accomplish, and I have decided I will not make that decision without first looking at the reality carefully, or without seeking and receiving opinions from all of you. Your lives will be affected drastically, radically, in ways I suspect you could not begin to imagine, should we adopt this course."

Rufio twitched one hand, a signal he wished to speak. I looked at him invitingly and he grinned. "Worse upheavals than moving to Eire or these northern islands?"

I nodded. "Aye, perhaps much worse."

"How, in the name of God?"

"There is another Roman fort, several miles from here, inland. No one lives there."

Dedalus leaned forward, frowning. "It's in ruins?"

"Apparently not, from what I've been told."

"Then why is it lying empty?"

"It's high up, in the mountains, on a plateau. Who would want to live there when they can live here, by the sea, close to other people, close to the farms?"

"How many miles from here to there?"

"Twelve, perhaps fifteen, I don't really know. It's halfway between here and the main fort at Galava on the other side of the mountains, built to defend the road across the pass."

Ded's eyes lit up. "Then let's go! At least we can look at it, and probably make it habitable. How long has it lain empty, twenty years?" I shook my head. "Forty, then? The Romans have been gone about that long. It's a long time, but the place should be salvageable."

"Two hundred."

"What?"

"Two hundred years. Something like that. It's been empty for a long time."

"Two hundred years?" I laughed aloud at the outraged disbelief in his voice, although the truth of my statement was in fact quite sobering. He watched me as I straightened my face, and when he was sure I would not laugh again, he said, "You are quite serious, aren't you?"

I nodded, shrugging my shoulders at the same time. "Yes, I am. Apparently two hundred years up here is not the same as two hundred years elsewhere. Not according to what I have heard from Derek, at least." I noticed that Lucanus and Hector were both frowning and others were shaking their heads. "No, think about it," I insisted. "The fort is built of local stone, and the roofs, on the granaries at least, are domed concrete. The barracks have cement floors, too, and were built of stout logs. Those may be weakened, perhaps rotted, but Derek tells me they still stand. The difference, my friends, lies in their isolation. Everywhere else we know, people tear down old buildings and use the materials to build new ones. But there are no people up there. The only damage has been caused by weather, which has little real effect on stone and concrete. The logs can be replaced. Derek tells me the forest grows right up to the walls of the place now, on the western side. It was cleared, originally, to build the fort, cut back for hundreds of paces to supply fuel for the bathhouse, but it's grown back now. The amazing truth seems to be that the place may be as salvageable now, after two hundred years, as Ded assumed it would be after forty. We will only know once we have looked and seen for ourselves."

There was a lengthy silence, and then Connor raised his hand. "I know I'm not involved in this directly, but you spoke of hardships and difficulties you might be incapable of overcoming. If it's the amount of work to be done that concerns you, well, you have a group of people here, it seems to me, who might find nothing insuperable in the task. You have smiths, I know, and soldiers, stonemasons and carpenters. You'll need labourers, too—muscles to do the donkey work—but I suppose you'll be able to enlist help from your neighbours here."

"Aye, but would we want to?" This was Hector. "You heard what Merlyn said. We had to leave Camulod because we didn't know whom we could trust among our own. Now we know we can trust ourselves alone—no one else. This new fort offers us a chance to keep our numbers few and trustworthy."

"That's nonsense, Hector." Connor's dismissal was immediate. "I suggested help, not immigration. There's nothing to stop you hiring people from the town to help you complete whatever you undertake. Equally, there's nothing that says you must permit them to remain up there once the work's been done. They've already shown they don't want to live there—nothing up there for them. Build yourselves a place to live in comfort and security, then people it and guard it by yourselves." He grinned. "Even Rome must have been far from anywhere before the first people settled there. Do you want my advice, Merlyn?"

"Of course."

"Let's see how the battle goes in the morning, and if we're all alive after it's over, let's meet again tomorrow. That will give everyone a day to think about what lies ahead. Then some of you can ride out the following day and look at this fort."

"That makes sense. Does anyone have an objection?" No one did, and Donuil spoke up for the first time.

"Does this fort have a name, Commander?"

"Aye, it does. Mediobogdum."

He pursed his lips and nodded. " 'In the bend of the river.' Well, at least that means there must be water there."

"A plenitude, I'm told." I straightened up. "Well, it's late. I don't know about the rest of you, but I could use some sleep."

The gathering disbanded shortly after that, with general good wishes for the following day's activities. No doubt, though, that this would be a purely defensive action with no risk of a pitched battle. Secure behind the walls of Ravenglass, covering the only access from the sea, we believed we would have no great difficulty in repelling Condran's unsuspecting fleet.

I was unable to sleep that night. I lay awake, reviewing the numbers and skills of the small group of people in my party, thinking of the personalities involved and of the ways in which each of them might contribute to our new, small colony. Dedalus, Rufio, Donuil and myself were warriors, first and foremost, but apart from that I was at a loss as to what other, more practical skills we possessed. I knew I could turn my hand to iron-smithing, thanks to the lessons of my Uncle Varrus, but decades had elapsed since I had last tried to apply any of the skills he had taught me, and even then my memories had been faulty. I might be able to assist in a forge, but I knew I would never be a skillful smith. Donuil, I knew, possessed no skills in any kind of work other than the administrative tasks he had performed for me in Camulod. Dedalus and Rufio were soldiers, trained since boyhood in their craft. I doubted deeply whether they could have other more valuable, less warlike gifts apart from the ability to hunt and to carry burdens too heavy for weaker men.

Lucanus would earn his keep, his worth was indisputable. And Hector was a farmer before all else, so his skills would be a major contribution to our future well-being. Shelagh was simply Shelagh, to be valued for her pragmatism and common sense and womanly skills, as well as for her mead-making ability. I remember smiling, thinking that while the ability to make mead might not be definable as a necessity of life, its possession might yet allay much of the tedium that would spring from more genuine necessities. Shelagh would be castellan of any household that we formed, and Turga, Arthur's nurse, had womanly skills of her own, not the least of which was in the tanning of leather to make supple, comfortable clothing. That total, increased by the four boys Arthur, Bedwyr, Gwin and Ghilleadh, came to twelve, two-thirds of our total complement.

I had greater confidence in the remaining six members of our party, who possessed abilities in plenty. They included Lars and Joseph, two of the three surviving sons of Equus, the old friend and partner of Publius Varrus. Joseph had been the senior smith and armourer of Camulod when he chose to accompany us, leaving his duties in the capable hands of his younger brother Carolus, or Carol, as he preferred to be known. His skills would be invaluable to us.

His elder brother, Lars, a former legionary whom I had found keeping a roadhouse north of Isca when I rode off to the wars in Cornwall, had long been believed dead by his brothers, and his arrival in Camulod thereafter had been hailed by them as a miracle. Lars and Joseph had become very close since then, and when Lars had decided to accompany me—or more accurately to accompany Arthur and Bedwyr, in whom he had found substitutes for his own two sons, hanged years before by Uther's army—Joseph had decided to come along, too, seeking adventure for the first time in his life.

Both men had brought their wives, Esmeralda and Brunna. Esmeralda's skills as a weaver were the equal of her husband Joseph's as a smith, and I was glad to have her as part of our group. Brunna's skills outshone her husband's altogether, for although Lars was a magical cook and baker, so, too, was Brunna, and in addition she possessed an astonishing ability in shoe- and boot-making. Lars and Brunna, I knew, would function as our quartermasters.

Two other members of our group each combined the skills of artisans and artists, and both were single men, their names Jonathan and Mark, both bosom friends of Joseph since their boyhood. Jonathan was a stonemason, bred of generations of stonemasons, and the youngest of five brothers, four of whom yet lived in Camulod. Mark was a carpenter, although to say such a thing baldly was like saying Homer was a poet. Mark's genius extended far beyond the simple uses of tools on wood. He could fashion exquisite furnishings as quickly and as easily as he could hew a beam from a log, and his work had been the finest in Camulod, gracing the Colony's best rooms and buildings.

Among these six, I knew, we were blessed with skills, but there was only one of each of them, and life atop a distant mountain might be hard in winter. It would be difficult enough, I thought, in summer. Eighteen souls. Enough, I hoped, perhaps, with God's blessing, to survive for a while under even the bleakest circumstances. And thinking such thoughts I finally drifted into sleep.

V

I WAS SHAKEN awake, it seemed, almost as soon as my eyelids had closed that night. It was an hour short of first light, and I was expected up on the walls, where preparations for the morning's business were already long since under way. I hesitated over donning my armour—I had travelled wearing only leather armour aboard ship and my metal harness was still packed with the rest of our belongings—and finally decided to wear only my toughened hide cuirass and go bareheaded. There would be little danger, I thought, high on the walls, and I could see no benefit in betraying my presence in a Roman helmet.

I noticed the yellow glare of torchlight reflected in mist as I mounted the stairs to the parapet. Before searching for Derek and Longinus, I stopped and gazed out to sea. There was nothing to be seen out there in the bay, nor in the sky above. The entire top of the wall was completely enshrouded in a bank of fog, thick enough to swirl eerily in places as people passed through it. I could barely make out the shapes of the ballistae and the great catapult that lay less than twenty-five paces on either side of me. If Condran's fleet was out there, I thought, we had no way of knowing how close they might have approached. I knew, however, even as I formed the thought, that no single vessel, let alone a fleet, would dare to move through fog so close to shore, and I was comforted by the thought that, if they were masked from us, so were we masked equally from them. The signs of our activities upon the walls would go unseen, and the heavy fog had the effect of dampening and muffling the sounds of our preparations.

I found Derek and Longinus among a small knot of men clustered around the larger of the two ballistae, where they were supervising the attachment of a small-meshed, heavy metal grid over the large wooden pan on the end of the machine's long throwing arm. A gin-pole hoist with a pulley attached stood close by, its cable descending to the courtyard below. I leaned over carefully and looked down into the sullen, angry glare of a brick furnace. Longinus had seen me arrive and now nodded to me.

"Live coals?" I asked him.

"Aye. Won't be the first time they've been used up here, but it'll be the first time they've been used in earnest since the Romans left. Those ovens haven't been lit for years. Nothing better to throw at ships than burning coals, though, once you've got the whoresons within range. Dry timbers, pitch-lined seams and weathered sailcloth. Burn like the fires in Hades. They won't even come close, once they see the first load hiss into the sea in front of them."

I returned Derek's nod of greeting and continued to speak to Longinus. "What then? You can only throw fire for a limited range."

"Aye, but we have no shortage of heavy stones. Those will fly far enough to quell the ardour of invading Ersemen."

"And what about the catapults? You have enough spears?"

"More than enough. Don't expect to fire more than a dozen, for the same reasons. If a man stands up and throws a spear at a galley, the crew keeps rowing. When the spear is a tree trunk as thick as a man's thigh, sharpened to an iron-clad spike on one end and thrown by a machine that's stronger than a thousand men and ten times more accurate, the crew's reaction tends to change, rapidly. First six bolts I shoot will do the damage. They're fixed and pre-aimed, as you know. After that, we'll have to re-sight, but once I find the range, I'll cause real damage. I've a score of the iron bolts, but as I said, I don't expect to have to use them all."

"What if you do?"

"Then we'll go to plain wooden stakes. The people they skewer won't notice the lack of iron cladding."

I turned to Derek. "What about your men and ours?"

"Connor's keeping them below, out of sight, until the sun comes up. No point in having them up here too soon, getting in each other's way. They're all down there, and our captains know what to do and what the signals are. When we bring them up they'll come bowmen first, spears afterwards. They'll present a pretty picture—far more than whoever's in command out there will expect to see."

Longinus snorted. "Aye, and they'll be over the heads of Liam and his dead cattle. That'll take the wind out of their Erse sails."

"It ought to." I glanced up at the sky again, noticing that the fog seemed paler. "How long till daybreak?"

Derek was looking upward too. "It's coming now. The fog won't last long, once the breeze begins to blow. Better start bringing the men up now. We want them all to be in place when the fog lifts." He stepped away and began issuing orders to the small group of men who had been standing close by, awaiting his word.

Longinus looked at me and grinned, picking delicately at his nose. "Where will you watch from?"

"Your station, if you don't mind."

"Come, then. We'd best get into place. I'm aiming the catapult myself."

* * *

Less than half an hour had passed when the wind sprang up, and within moments, it seemed, the fog had been swept aside like a curtain. The sea was still empty, not a sail in sight. I stood side by side with Longinus, peering out at the tranquil waters, and Derek stood some ten paces apart from us, to my left. Apart from we three, only four others stood visible on the top of the walls. The others, almost four hundred of them, crouched beneath the line of the parapet, out of sight from the front. The word spread quickly from the men on guard, and I heard a loud muttering arise along the length of the wall from the concealed men.

Derek's voice held them in silence. "Stay down and stay alert!" he shouted. "What did you expect? Of course there's nothing there! They couldn't come in close when the fog was down, and they'll have someone on the island over there looking to see if Liam's craft are here by the wharf where they ought to be. That will take time, and their ships are lying behind the island. They'll be here presently."

Almost as he said the words, the prow of the first galley appeared beyond the low bank of the island facing us. It moved swiftly, propelled by hard-pulled oars. Others followed, until eighteen craft were fanning out into the bay—an impressive sight—less than a mile from the walls. The men were tense with expectation, but everyone remained hidden behind the parapet wall. Long moments passed and the fleet drew closer quickly. Then came a moment when we heard the swelling roar of voices as they discerned the bodies hanging from our battlements. I spoke to Longinus.

"They think those are our bodies."

"Hmm. They must. They're still approaching."

"Only eighteen of them. Connor had expected more, closer to thirty. You think they're holding others in reserve, behind the island?"

"They might be, Makes no difference. They won't be using them."

On they came, deliberate and menacing, manoeuvring skillfully as they progressed. Soon they formed two lines abreast, the rearward slowing down to float almost stationary within a quarter mile of where we watched, while the foremost line came forward, shifting its shape again to permit the three central vessels of the line to forge ahead. But even watching and listening as carefully as I was, concentrating fiercely on their advance, I missed the point at which they came to see that something was amiss. I saw a flurry of signalling break out and heard some distant shouts, and then all oars were hoisted from the water, held horizontally so that the forward motion of the craft died suddenly away.

Beside me, Longinus was leaning forward, his body tense as he willed the leading vessels to approach closer. "Come on," he hissed. "Are you all gutless? You can't see who it is from there, and no one's threatening you. Those corpses should be ours. Come in!"

As though in response to his urgings, the oars of the leading galley dipped again and it moved forward, cautiously now, followed shortly afterward by the other two. Careful to betray no haste, Longinus backed away from the parapet wall, and I moved with him as he bent low and hurried to his aiming point by the catapult on the far right.

"They're waiting for a signal of some kind to tell them it's safe to approach. Probably wondering why it hasn't come. Ready, lads," he called to his other crews. He had personally sighted his three catapults the previous afternoon, carefully aiming each of them at some abstract point determinable only to his own eyes and gambling, he had admitted to me privately, that the Erse fleet would approach exactly as they were doing, three vessels in the lead, forming an arrowhead. I found myself admiring his professional focus as I watched him lean forward, straining like a leashed hound. Beyond him I could see brazier baskets of bright-burning coals being hoisted from below, the air about them shimmering with the fierce, smokeless heat of them, willing hands waiting to tip them into the baskets of the two tightly wound ballistae that quivered on either side of the central catapult, trembling visibly under the torsion of the mighty ropes that held them in restraint. As I glanced back to Longinus, his hands moved to the lever that controlled the locked windlass restraining the mighty bowstring of the catapult, its massive bolt aimed like a colossal arrow four strides in length, wickedly pointed and barbed with solid iron.

"Now, Derek!" he roared, and Derek's hand flew up in a signal. At the sight of it, four men who had been waiting in the courtyard at our back, holding the end of a long rope, ran behind us for four strides and stopped again. As they did so. Liam's corpse, which dangled at the other end of the long rope, jerked upward, rising almost to the top of the outer wall to dangle, stark and unmistakable, before the eyes of his astounded countrymen below. The oars flew up again as confusion struck among the galleys' crews, and in the momentary chaos Longinus gave his own signal, jerking the lever out of the windlass.

The concussion of the massive catapult's release thrummed in my breast as my eyes followed its huge bolt's swift and awesome flight out and downwards towards the ship on the right. Even before it landed, I heard a similar release on my left and glimpsed the second missile flash outward. Then the first struck home, crashing into the packed mass of oarsmen, destroying men and oars instantly before smashing down to the galley's bottom. Screams floated upwards immediately, and I swung my eyes in time to see the second bolt hit home on the lead ship, striking the central mast with sufficient force to gouge an enormous splinter from its side, and then slewing with vicious, eye-deceiving speed in a murderous pivoting motion, anchored by its barbed point, until it burst asunder with the stress and showered lethal splinters in every direction, so that sprays and gouts of sudden, brilliant blood appeared as if by magic among the mangled crew beneath.

I did not see the impact of the third missile on the remaining ship, for my attention was seized immediately by the amazing spread of arcing plumes of smoke as the two ballistae released their loads of blazing coals. Much of it splashed, hissing, into the water, and as far as I could see none touched the first ship that Longinus's bolt had pierced. The others were less fortunate, and the galley farthest from me must have been sorely hit, for now the bulk of screaming seemed to be coming from it, and already I could see smoke beginning to drift over the central spine of its decking.

I had been aware of Longinus's crew working frantically to my right, swarming about their catapult as they readied it to shoot again, some of them manhandling another heavy, lethal bolt into its place as the sounds of windlasses and straining cables creaked ever higher on the weapon's great bow frame. The target ship had not yet been able to move, other than spinning in a wild circle, since the oars on one side now far outnumbered those left working on the other.

Suddenly all movement ceased at the catapult, indicating that it was ready. Longinus scuttled into position, cast a glance along the shaft, then leaped back and released the lever. Again the tree-trunk shaft flew straight and true, striking like a thunderbolt into the churning chaos of the galley's centre and disappearing downward. And then I saw a sight that took me by surprise and left me gaping. A human body flew into the air from atop our wall, arms and legs spread, whirling like a child's toy as it arced up and then down to land among the men swarming in the waist of the farthest of the three galleys as they scrambled to douse the fires that had sprung up. Even as the shape spun high to the zenith of its arc, I recognized the green and yellow tunic worn by Liam Condranson.

This macabre finale had been pre-arranged, but I had not been told. The sight of the soaring corpse was the signal that brought our men erect, lining the walls and roaring their defiance as the bowmen among them sent their shafts seeking the enemy. Stunned, and feeling slightly sickened, I stepped away from the parapet and looked about me. The roaring intensified as I moved away, and I heard shouts of "Sinking!" and "Going down!" amid the tumult.

I stepped back to the edge and looked downward again to see that Longinus had done well with his two bolts. The galley he had struck was low in the water; its crew was leaping overboard, abandoning the craft, which canted sideways even as I looked, its mast waving wildly. It righted itself again, but sluggishly, and then simply settled in the water, slipping beneath the surface to rest on the shallow bottom, its mast projecting high above the waves. Men swam from it in all directions, but others, unable to swim, simply drowned, their limbs churning in panic as they rose and sank in the agitated waters.

On the far left, the burning galley was fully ablaze now, and it, too, was being quickly abandoned; its warriors—swimmers and non-swimmers alike—evidently preferred the risk of drowning to death by fire. The central, remaining boat was under way again, but very slowly. Though its crew had been decimated, the survivors were struggling to bring it about quickly, as far from the threatening wall as possible. Before they could win clear, however, two more blows shook them: a basket full of blazing coals landed full on top of the furled sail, followed almost immediately by a slashing bolt from the central catapult that struck at a shallow angle among the rowers on the right side of the mast, splintering oars and men and lodging in the vessel's side timbers, a full third of its length projecting through the shattered planking above the surface of the water. Seeing the deadly missile strike home, and recalling the angle at which Longinus's two bolts had disappeared, I found it small wonder that the first craft had sunk so swiftly. The impact of the metal-clad tree trunks must have smashed its hull beneath the water-line like an eggshell.

What followed next was an object lesson in defiance and sheer courage that I have never forgotten. One man, wearing a long blue cloak and a horned helmet, which led me to presume him the commander of the craft, moved purposefully along the central spine of the vessel, blatantly disdaining us and our missiles as he harangued the remaining members of his crew. At his urging, they organized themselves into some semblance of a unit again, bending to their oars in unison as he banged a short-sword against his shield, beating a cadence they could follow. I was not the only one who noted his behaviour, and as awareness of his actions spread along the wall, so, too, did silence, until no sound at all came from our battlements. All men, I think, revere the brave, and the spectacle being played out in front of us was one of extreme bravery. After the silence fell, only one shot was fired towards the Erse captain, and the bowman was shouted down and reviled by his own comrades, so that he stood shamefaced.

Five, six, seven strokes the oarsmen made, and then their captain called for them to stop. A knot of swimming men lay just abreast of them, and we watched as the men in the galley threw ropes to the swimmers. When they were safe aboard, the captain strode to the stern and stared up at us, then shouted more orders. The galley turned and moved slowly towards another group of swimmers, hauling them aboard as well. All of this occurred while they were still within easy range of our catapults, but we made no move to threaten them further, until another vessel from the stationary lines behind them sought to move forward.

Longinus leaped to his catapult, shouting orders, and his men began immediately to elevate the device, aiming it skyward. Longinus sighted and calculated, making swift adjustments until he was satisfied, then jumped back and threw the lever, launching the bolt. We watched it as it soared upward, shortening then lengthening as it began its downward curve. It sliced into the sea mere paces ahead of the oncoming galley, making barely a splash. The message was plain. The vessel sheared away. The rescuers continued with their work throughout, ignoring or unaware of the event. Somehow, without a word being said, the captain of the Erse craft below knew he could complete his task in peace.

At one point, a small boat of some kind was lowered from the galley and three men climbed into it. While one worked the sculls, the other two retrieved a lifeless body. Its clothing was colourless, waterlogged, but I knew they had recovered their admiral. That done, and now fully crewed again, the galley swung away and joined the rest of the fleet, after which all sixteen vessels turned and made their way beyond the island.

The men lining the parapet began to turn away, all strangely subdued, despite the totality of the victory. As they began to file by us, headed towards the stairs and talking quietly among themselves, Longinus turned to me.

"Brave whoreson, that. I wonder who he was."

I shook my head. "I don't know, but Connor might. You think they'll come back?"

He looked me in the eye and pursed his lips, then shook his head. "I doubt it. Would you? My guess is, they'll go home and raise a bigger fleet, then they'll come back, looking for blood." He glanced away, to where Connor's men were pouring rapidly, in disciplined files, down the stairs from their positions on the wall. "Where are those fellows going in such a hurry?"

I noted the serious expressions on the faces of the passing men, and returned a nod to Sean as he hurried by. Wherever they were going, they clearly had a purpose. "I don't know," I responded, "but they might be on their way to Liam's galleys, to take them out, down to the spot where they concealed their own vessels yesterday. Connor will not feel comfortable until he has his own deck back beneath his feet again, and as long as there remains the slightest chance that Condran's fleet might stay around, looking for vengeance for their admiral, Connor won't lie easy on land."

"The Ersemen will be back, with others, looking for revenge," Longinus said darkly, "and this time they'll know what to expect."

I watched the last of Connor's men disappear from view, then turned back to face him. "Not quite, my friend," I said, smiling. "They'll have respect for your weapons, I've no doubt of that, but by the time they decide to return, Connor Mac Athol will have gone home too. Remember, they don't know he's here. When they come back, they might find their passage contested by a fleet to match their own."

His eyes widened, and then he grinned and nodded. "Aye, I'd forgotten that. Let's find something to drink. By all the gods, man, we just defeated an entire fleet of Ersemen." He turned away, roaring for Derek, and we were suddenly surrounded by a throng whose noisy enthusiasm waxed rapidly with the growing realization of what they had achieved.

Connor and his men were noticeably absent from the celebrations that began immediately following the victory. They had, as I had suspected, gone to collect their galleys. Donuil confirmed it when he came looking for me some time later. In spite of the general euphoria of the gathering, however, I found myself vaguely depressed, unable to stop thinking of the sight of Liam's whirling corpse soaring up and outward from the wall to crash down on the galley beneath. It was a common topic of conversation that morning, laughed over and discussed again and again as people mingled and moved about in the thronged space beneath the walls, but I could find nothing humorous in it. The hanging of the Erse dead I could stomach as a gruesome, even necessary warning of the violence that awaited any who might treacherously challenge us. But the deliberate defilement of a corpse—even the corpse of a creature like Liam—offended everything I had been taught concerning the dignity of the dead. Eventually I removed myself and stood apart from the celebrations, ignoring everyone and thinking my own thoughts.

Lucanus materialized by my side after a while but read my mood and remained silent, content to sip at his drink beside me. A short time later Donuil and Hector drifted over to us, talking quietly, and soon after that Rufio and Dedalus emerged from the crowd and joined us as well. Rufio huddled immediately with Donuil and the others and Ded came towards me. I was surprised to notice that he clutched an ale-pot, for Ded never drank intoxicants. He noticed my glance and grinned, toasting me silently before taking a deep gulp that left a white ring around his lips.

"Buttermilk," he said. "Cold. You don't look happy, my friend and commander. What's wrong?"

"Nothing is wrong, Ded. We've just won a bloodless victory. How could anything be wrong?"

"I don't know, but you, from the look of you, evidently do." His eyes hardened. "Should we be concerned?"

"No, not at all." I realized that I was being obscure and shook my head. "I was thinking of Liam Condranson, that's all—about shooting him like that, from the ballista."

Ded's eyes widened now in surprise. "You don't approve of that? I thought it was inspired, the only disappointment being that the whoreson was already dead. It was Connor's idea—brilliant, I thought."

"Brilliant? Why brilliant? I thought—I still think—it was barbarous."

"Barbarous?" He blinked at me, as though wondering if I had lost my wits. "Of course it was barbarous, Merlyn, but so was Liam. And so, for all of his polished charm, is Connor. These people are Ersemen, not Roman-trained aesthetes from Camulod! They fight among themselves constantly and they have different rules from ours. We would never shoot our enemies off castle walls like that, but, by God, perhaps we should! It might make us less vulnerable. Seeing Liam tumbling through the sky towards them like that, his people saw an eloquent statement of Connor's assessment of their best, and of the treacherous whoreson's methods. As I said, too bad he was already dead."

I had no adequate response to that, and so I merely nodded and handed him my empty cup. "Take care of that for me. I'm going for a walk. I've matters on my mind and I must think awhile."

Some time later, I found myself beyond the walls, on the outer fringe of the common marketplace. I was walking towards Shelagh, who sat on a low wall beside Turga with her back to me, both of them watching Arthur and the other three boys at play. A knot of local children stood close by, watching our four but making no attempt to join their game, which was, in fact, a training exercise devised by Rufio to sharpen their slinging skills.

The boys stood roughly twenty paces apart on the four corners of an imaginary square, and their game consisted of hurling a fist-sized pebble from one to the other, the object being for the receiver to catch the flying stone and hurl it to the next. The rules were complex, and accuracy figured highly in the scoring. The stone was almost perfectly spherical, bound in strips of leather that were braided to form a handle two handspans long, and it was thrown with a round-arm sweep, much like a slung stone. One point was won by catching the stone itself, but three points could be scored by catching it by the handle, which permitted the ongoing throw to be carried out without changing grip. The boys could play the game for hours.

The two women heard me approach and turned to greet me, but I motioned to them to stay where they were. I sat on the wall beside Shelagh, and we continued to watch in silence for a while. None of the boys had yet noticed my arrival, so complete was their concentration.

"Who's winning?" I asked, eventually.

Shelagh responded without looking at me. "Bedwyr's in the lead, for the moment, by twelve points. Arthur's not happy. He missed three consecutive catches and threw two fouls, one to the ground and one too far away for Gwin to reach. Those cost him dearly. He had been ahead before that." She paused. "You had quite a successful morning."

"Aye, it went as expected. The surprise was against them. They sailed in and were driven off without casualties to us. Where were you while it was going on?"

"In our quarters. I kept the boys inside until it was all over."

"That must have been difficult."

She turned to look at me. "They were not exactly happy, but they knew there was nothing to be done, so they made the best of it. You sank two galleys?"

"Aye." I told her then about the bravery of the captain of the central galley, and she listened closely.

"A blue cloak, you say, and a horned helmet? Was the cloak bright blue?"

"Aye, it was brighter than any other. Do you know the man? Who was he?"

She shook her head. "There's a captain among them called Modrin, famed as a warrior. It might have been him. He is said to wear a bright blue cloak and a helmet crowned with the tined horns of a stag. Did you see that? Were they antlered?"

"I don't know. I didn't notice. He was quite far away."

Shelagh stood up, saying something I could not hear to Turga, and then turned to me, hitching a large and spacious leather satchel over her shoulder by its carrying strap.

"Come, Merlyn, walk with me. I want to talk to you, and if the boys notice you here, they'll be all over us."

We turned our backs on the boys and their game and began to stroll along the path towards the forest where I had been ambushed. Shelagh moved to walk ahead of me as we reached a short length of pathway that was almost overgrown and hemmed in on both sides by high, rank grasses. As we went, I heard my name called urgently in a high, boyish voice and knew we had been discovered.

Shelagh glanced sidelong at me. "Don't look back. Pretend you didn't hear. I told Turga to tell them we may not be disturbed, and to stop them if they try to follow us."

I shrugged and proceeded as though I were a deaf man. Though I was looking down at my feet, I was aware that I was highly conscious of Shelagh's body today, more so than I had been in a long time, and the awareness disconcerted me. She wore a long, full-skirted gown made of a soft, green material that clung revealingly to hips and breasts. As she threaded her way through the narrow passage, she gathered her skirts casually in one hand to protect them from thorns and snags, unconsciously bringing her swaying hips and buttocks into prominence with the tightening of the soft cloth. Fortunately, the narrowest length of the path was short, and we were able to walk side by side thereafter, where the most prominent thing I had to worry over was the soft upper sweep of her breasts. I solved that problem, temporarily at least, by concentrating on the path ahead of us.

Neither of us felt the need to speak, and we walked in comfortable silence broken only by the liquid song of a blackbird. I helped her across the ditch at the edge of the woods, then led the way as we descended the slope.

"This is where I was attacked, the other day."

She glanced around, eyeing the thick briars that had ripped my hands and face so badly. "Hmm," she murmured. "You should give thanks that Donuil noticed you passing and came after you. You might as well be miles from anywhere, out here. What's up there?"

I looked up along the pathway that mounted the hill beyond the little clearing. "No idea," I said. "I didn't go beyond this point."

"Then let's go and see. Your man in the yellow tunic must have gone up there."

The path led us upward, steepening rapidly, until it became difficult to walk upright and we found ourselves proceeding almost on all fours at several points, leaning forward to obtain purchase as we climbed. The first time that happened, I found myself distracted again by the sight of Shelagh's buttocks ahead of me and the occasional flash of white leg as she pulled herself ahead. We reached a level spot and stood upright, both of us panting.

"Is this worth the effort?" I asked.

She glanced at me, blowing an errant curl from in front of her eyes then looking up and ahead again. "I think so. Look, we're almost at the top."

She was right, and moments later we stood among the few trees that crowned the almost bare hilltop. Looking back, we could see the top of Derek's eastern wall beneath us, surprisingly close beyond a fringe of small trees, the clutter of the town laid out behind it. No one stirred on the wall, and in the distance, on the western parapet, one of Longinus's great catapults still raised its arm vertically above the harbour. The streets of the town were jammed with people.

"It's like looking down on an ant hill," Shelagh said, then she turned to look in the opposite direction. "Look at the mountains!"

The ranks of rising hills stretched into the far, eastern distance to become peaks and ramparts against the sky. "They're called the Fells," I said, admiring the peaceful beauty of them. "Now, what was it you wanted to talk about?"

She turned and inspected the tiny hilltop, looking for some place to sit. There was one small, dead tree, tipped over on its side, the bark stripped and worn away and its upper surface polished by the rumps and feet of visitors. She perched on its narrow seat, and I moved to lean against another tree close by. She drew her top lip back from startlingly white teeth and tapped a fingernail against them, clearly unconcerned that I might find the gesture unattractive.

"I've been thinking about the future," she said, and then she lapsed into silence.

I nodded. "So have I. What have you been thinking about?"

"Your name."

I blinked at her, absorbing that and finding it meaningless. "What about my name?"

"What is it?" She grimaced and shook her head impatiently, dismissing my blank-faced bewilderment. "Oh, never mind, I'll tell you. You have four names."

"No, I have three: Caius, Merlyn and Britannicus."

She graced me with an exaggerated, dimpled smile and tucked her skirts beneath her thighs, limning them clearly and drawing my eyes as targets draw arrows. "No, you have four, and it was hearing the fourth of them last night, during our meeting, that made me think."

"Shelagh," I sighed, "I have no idea what you are talking about."

"Lucanus called you Cay last night."

"Of course, he often does. So do you, from time to time. All my close friends and family call me Cay."

"Exactly!" she crowed, as though she had distinctly won the point. "The fellow in the yellow tunic, do you think he came up here?"

"What?"

"What? Would you *think*, man? *Dia!* This thing's too narrow and lumpy to sit on for long." She moved quickly, half rising to her feet to free her skirts, then swung one leg demurely over the tree trunk to sit astride it like a horse, rearranging her lap impatiently before swinging her head around to face me again. "Look, the man ran away from you because he knew you and he obviously thought you would know him. He knew you were Merlyn of Camulod, and he ran away because he knew that knowledge made him dangerous. To you. Why? It's as plain as your great Roman beak! Because he intended to sell the information that you were here, to someone who would pay well for it.

"Derek knew you, too, when we arrived. Merlyn of Camulod, he called you, and he lost no time in telling you we couldn't stay, because the word that Merlyn was here in Ravenglass would bring destruction swarming about his head from Cornwall and from Cambria and every other place where Merlyn's name is known, because Merlyn of Camulod is guardian of the Pendragon brat! Have you met many others since you've been here? Others who know your name?"

I nodded. "Aye, a few."

"And what do they call you? Merlyn?" I nodded again. "And would King Derek ever call you Caius?"

"No."

"Or Cay?"

"Absolutely not."

"Good! Then that's settled. When are you going to look at this new place, the fort? Tomorrow, still?"

"Yes, tomorrow morning—but I still can't see what's settled, as you say."

She shook her head slowly, half smiling, widening her eyes as she gazed at me. "Oh, Merlyn, Merlyn . . . Here am I talking to you as an equal, and you respond like an ordinary, stupid, sightless man. . . ." Her smile broadened to a grin. "Ah well, I'll be an Erse enchantress, then, and speak mystic secrets to you."

"You *are* an Erse enchantress, and well you know it. But why are you looking so pleased with yourself?"

"Oh, I am, am I?"

For a moment, I was unsure which of my remarks she was referring to, but her next words, and the sudden, wicked mischief in her eye, made everything clear.

"I know it well enough, but I'd begun to think you'd grown immune to my enchantments. I've sensed none of that wicked, friendly lust in you for years."

In the space of a heartbeat, my throat was thick with tension, my heart hammering in my breast. The friendly lust she spoke of had been mutually recognized by us long since, ungratified only because of our shared loyalty to Donuil. We had discussed and dismissed it years before, agreeing amicably, she and I, to be aware of it without pursuing it. Through her two pregnancies and my quest for a celibate existence, we had grown ever more comfortable with each other and become fast friends. The attraction, though still there, had mellowed into a warm, sustained awareness. But now, suddenly, the lust was raging in me again. I swallowed the lump in my throat.

"Oh, it's been there, all along," I said, fighting to keep my tone light. "You're just getting old. Your perception of such things has dulled."

"Hah! Enchantresses do not lose their keen perceptions. Ever."

She began to hum a lovely, haunting melody and rose to her feet, stepping away from her log and holding her hands out to me. I straightened from the tree I had been leaning against, and she led me to the seat she had occupied.

"Now," she said, grinning again, "sit you there and listen to my spells, and I'll summon woman's magic to tell you how loutish, lumbering men may live in safety and rear healthy children in this mountain land. Are you ready?" I nodded, having mastered myself again, and her grin softened to a smile. "Good. Pay attention, now."

She stood for a few moments, facing me, humming again the same lilting, unearthly tune she had used before. Then she reached up and untied the filet that held her hair in place and shook her long tresses free about her shoulders. As I stared, wide-eyed and almost disbelieving, she began to turn very slowly, humming all the time, continuing to face me though her body turned impossibly, it seemed, then whipping her head around just when it seemed her neck must break. Her arms were outstretched at her sides, and very gradually she increased the tempo of her movements until she was spinning rapidly, like a child's top. As she progressed from a slow, deliberate and graceful motion to increasing, whirling speed, I sat truly entranced, watching her face and the way her long, chestnut tresses flew out about her spinning head, barely aware for the longest time, of the gradual emergence of the long clean length of her bare legs beneath her flaring gown. Aware of it eventually, alas, my eyes saw nothing afterward but their nakedness and strong, clean-muscled shape.

She had been watching me, I am sure, as closely as I had been watching her, and when she saw my gaze gone from her face she stopped, suddenly, her voice falling abruptly silent on a high, clear note, her skirts cascading downward like a waving, draped curtain.

As I sat there, blinking, staring at her still-undulating skirts, awareness of how sudden had been her stop flooded me, and I leaped belatedly to my feet to catch her as she fell over from giddiness. But she stood motionless, unruffled, smiling at me, her eyes clear and even her hair tamed.

"Sit," she said. "Enchantresses do not fall down. Now hear."

As I seated myself again, she came and knelt in front of me. My heart was pounding, and I felt a sense of strange anticipation. She was lovely, and in spite of her exertions, her high breasts showed no sign of heaving.

"Close your eyes, and keep them closed." I did, enjoying the brief vision I had had of her bare, whirling legs.

"Think upon this, Merlyn of Camulod. . . ." she said softly, and then she began to speak in a rhythmic, almost singing, cadenced voice that quickly lulled me, compelling me to listen to her words.

"Imagine that a party of strong men, and women, too, came to a seagirt place called Ravenglass, then disappeared from ken, their whereabouts unknown to living men. Imagine that their enemies sought high and low to find them, and sent spies away throughout the land to hunt them down wherever they might be. . . . Imagine that these spies all knew a name, a strong man's name, a leader's name, and knew that in finding him, they would find what they really sought and thought to find. Imagine then, that throughout all this land, through Alba and through Eire, too, it was believed that this strong man was nowhere known where men and women throng. . . ."

Her voice died away, but I sat with my eyes closed for moments longer, hearing and examining the visions she had conjured in my mind. When I looked at her again, she was kneeling still, staring at me, her beautiful hawklike eyes betraying no hint of humour now.

"I saw it," she said. "It's what we've hoped to achieve. Shall I tell you where they vanished to?"

"Yes, if you know where my thoughts are leading now."

"They never left. Their ships left, in the dead of night, but they remained and lived in an abandoned fort. Their leader, Merlyn, changed his name to Cay, and while he led still, in truth, he gave the name of leader to another, not a warrior but a farmer, who would feed them all."

"Hector."

"Aye, Hector. Cay became a simple worker, so that when the spies returned at last, their search frustrated, there was no one called Merlyn known in Ravenglass."

I was staring at her in bemused wonder, amazed by the lucid simplicity of her suggestion and knowing she was absolutely right. Only a few people, to the best of my awareness, knew my real name here in Ravenglass, and for their benefit I could sail away ostentatiously with Connor and young Arthur, to be dropped ashore in some convenient spot a short way along the coast. From there I could make my way back to Mediobogdum, avoiding the town. I would be known simply as Cay. Merlyn would vanish.

"Shelagh! That could work!"

"Of course it will work! Enchantresses are never wrong, you blind man."

She was herself again, swaying lithely to her feet and reaching for her enormous satchel, from which she produced a small skin of wine, a whole cheese, a loaf of bread and a sharp knife. Seeing the knife, I became aware that this was the first time I had seen her without her throwing knives for a long time, but the awareness was dulled by my amazement over the food.

"Good God! How did you—? Did you know we would be coming here today?"

She threw me a wry look. "Don't be foolish, how could I? But I did know I'd be keeping the boys away from the walls all day, first because of the fighting, and later, I sincerely hoped, because of the celebration. I didn't bring a cup. And I left the boys' food with Turga. Here, eat." She handed me half the cheese and half the loaf, and for the next while we ate in companionable silence, sitting together on the ground with our backs against the fallen tree. When we were done, and the rich, red wine had left a satisfying feeling of repletion on my tongue, I turned to her.

"That was quite a dance you performed."

"Enchantment. It was an enchantment. It worked, didn't it?"

"It certainly did. Several ways."

"Hmm. You were not supposed to be gawking beneath my skirts. Could you see my bare bottom?"

I shook my head, smiling, unaccountably comfortable again in this arena. "Unfortunately, no, I could not. But I would have made a greater effort had I known it was bare. Do you know, I was so fascinated by your upper part, your arms and head and hair, that I hardly noticed the other at all?"

"Liar. I saw your mouth fall open."

"How could you have? You were revolving far too quickly."

"Horse turds, my friend. A blink is all it takes to see that look. I stopped at once, for fear you'd have an apoplexy."

"That's unlikely. But my celibacy might have fared badly, had you continued."

She glanced down openly at my lap. "It still works, then? Despite all your single-minded self-denial?" There was no trace of prurience in her voice or her demeanour.

"Of course it does." I shifted position slightly, moving my buttocks in search of more comfort, strangely unfazed now, by this turn of talk. "Mostly in the dead of night, thank God."

"Erotic dreams?"

"Extremely."

"How often?"

"Frequently. Weekly."

"Weekly? After all this time?"

I sniffed. "Perhaps because of all this time. I don't know, and I try not to dwell on it. May we talk about something else?"

She was still gazing at my lap, her expression one of musing. Now she looked me in the eye, straightforwardly.

"Who do you dream about?"

I sighed, shaking my head. "I don't know, most of the time."

Her eyebrows rose in disbelief. "You must know! If a woman is attractive enough to draw your seed without even being there, you must know who she is."

Now I smiled at her incredulity. "It's not a woman, Shelagh, it's a dream, a spectral female form conjured by my body's needs and my sleeping mind's instructions. I don't know how the conjuration works, simply that it does and at some unsought, indeterminate time, by some unconscious means, I avail myself of this spectral presence, an incorporeal vessel into which I spill my seed without volition. Most of the time I am completely unaware of having done so. I only remember afterwards by the evidence in the morning."

She was frowning. "Donuil never has such dreams."

"By the Christus, I should hope not! Nor would I, could I reach out to you at night—" I caught myself, choking the words off, but she was barely listening, her brow furrowed in thought.

"You said 'most of the time.' You don't know most of the time. That means you sometimes do. Who?"

"You, Shelagh. You, my dear. You gave me leave to dream of you, once, to lust after you in my mind. Don't you recall? And so I do, sometimes."

I had surprised her.

"How? I've given you no reason. . . ."

"No, nor encouragement, for several years, so be at peace. Nor have I lusted after you—not consciously, at least—in recent times. It is not a voluntary thing, on either of our parts."

"I know that. But how? I mean, oh, *Dia!* I sound stupid."

"Not at all." I picked up the wine skin and took a deep swallow. "You are a woman. Your body does not feel men's lusts, which seem to be more urgent, and more transitory, than women's are. Seem, I say, seem to be. I have no way of knowing if that's true, nor do you."

"It's true enough, I think. Women are slower to arousal than men are, I know that much. Men are sudden and frequent, unpredictable, except for the predictability of their frequency and unpredictability. They recognize no time as being better, more conducive, than another." She paused.

"Look, I know you want to talk of other things, but you've told me something here I know nothing about, and I'm dying of curiosity. May I ask you something else?"

I shook my head again, smiling ruefully at her tenacity. "Of course. What is it?"

She sat silent for several moments, hesitating at the boldness of her words, then blurted out her question.

"When you . . . when you dream of me like that . . . what do you recall?"

We were staring at each other, our faces close, each of us tight with the fluttery tension of discovery, yet lacking, somehow, any sense of sexual urgency or imperative. When I answered her, my voice was husky and my words slow and deliberate.

"Everything about you, from the feel of your breasts to the clinging depth of you."

"But you've never touched me."

I moved slightly away from her. "I am aware of that, my dear, believe it or not, and looking at your legs and thighs today, I saw more of you than I have ever seen."

"No. I was practically naked that day when Julia died. You saw me then, wearing only that ridiculous flimsy mantle."

"Damnation! So I did. D'you know, I've never even thought of that since then? I had completely forgotten!"

She started to smile, but then her face grew somber. "That would have been an awful thing, Merlyn, to have found physical attraction in that place and at that time."

"Aye, it would. I suppose that's why I was unaware of it."

"Hmm." Her face cleared slowly, the troubled frown giving way to a look of concentration. "So, when you . . . lie with me, in dreams, the dreams seem real? I find that really difficult to comprehend."

"No more than I do, Shelagh, but I thank God, from time to time, that they seem as real as they do, because they bring no guilt, and no disloyalty to Donuil, or to you."

"To me? How could they bring disloyalty to me?"

"Because of how you truly are, a faithful wife. But they could not—they are merely dreams. Purely involuntary. Even Luke says so."

Her eyebrows shot up on her forehead. "You've told Lucanus?"

I laughed aloud. "No, not about you! What do you think of me? We've talked of celibacy, that's all, and nocturnal emissions, as he calls them."

" 'Nocturnal emissions . . .' That sounds very grand."

"They can be grand, sometimes, but they don't approximate the real thing."

"Why not? They sound like it, to me."

"Yes, my dear, except for the absence of one important, crucial element: the actual woman, with her delicious, lubricated friction."

We had been speaking in Latin, which she had picked up with wondrous speed, but now she raised one hand to her lips like a little girl, her eyes dancing, and suddenly her Erse speech was more pronounced. "Crucial? You mean spread out like a cross? 'Loo-oobricated friction . . .' Latin's a wondrous language. You couldn't say things like that in Erse. 'Delicious, lubricated friction . . ." Oh, listen to me! The gods would scream, could they hear us! I never even talk like this with Donuil. Can you imagine the face of him, sitting over there, listening to us?" She fell silent, thinking, then laughed in a girlish way. "So you're sound asleep when this happens? Dead to the world, with no idea at all of what's going on?"

"None at all, consciously. Of course, there's much going on inside your head."

"Aye, and other parts of you."

"Hmm."

She made another tiny sound of mirthful excitement, hitching herself more upright and lapsing back into her native tongue. "Wouldn't I love to see that, though? Wouldn't that be something to behold, the bright seed just springing from it like a ribbon, with no warning at all?"

"Aye," I said, more of a grunt than a word, and began to rise to my feet. "And if we don't leave now, it's going to happen here, in the brightness of the afternoon. Come on, let's go."

I held out my hand to help her rise, but she remained where she was, her eyes fixed on the erection that thrust beneath my clothing at the level of her eyes, which had turned suddenly solemn.

"Merlyn, forgive me. I didn't think. That was stupid of me and unforgivable to taunt you like that."

"Come on, get up. Here, take my hand. It wasn't unforgivable at all. I enjoyed it thoroughly. It simply means I'll do it twice this week." I pulled her to her feet then stepped away, literally turning my back on the temptation to gather her into my arms and kiss her. She would have come to me, I knew. I stood there, staring at the closest tree until her voice came from behind me, small and tentative.

"Merlyn? Is that the truth? You're not angry?"

I turned back to her, smiling. "No, Shelagh, I'm not angry. I swear it."

She was silent for a spell, and then, "Twice this week?" She was smiling again. "Does that mean—"

"Aye, four nights ago, aboard the galley, and it wasn't you."

"The faceless, wanton spectre. . . . Will it be me tonight?"

"Aye, it will, and for several nights to come, I think. But don't expect me to thank you for stirring me up this way."

"I won't, but . . ."

"But what?"

She smiled. "I want you to know, though I shouldn't say it. But I'm just as stirred up now as you are. . . . It was you saying 'twice this week' that did it."

I stared at her for the space of several heartbeats, aware that we were both in grave danger, then began to turn away. "Good fortune for Donuil."

She caught me by the wrist, stopping me. "Don't think of it like that, Merlyn. It's not Donuil who has me swimming, here, and he won't benefit from it. I may not lie with you, but tonight, for you, I won't lie with my husband." She stared at me, eye to eye, but I could only shake my head.

"This is insane. We'd better go."

On the way back down we talked of other things, and by the time we came to the town she had taught me the first lines of the melody she had sung in her enchantment.

VI

THE WALLS OF the main gateway tower reared up above my head to the height of four tall men, and the heavy double doors were made from massive, layered slabs of dense-grained oak, shrunken and dried and cracked with age but serviceable still. These were framed, around and between, by heavy, solid, mason-dressed blocks of red sandstone brought down, Derek had told me, from the quarries to the north, along the coast. I craned my neck to decipher the faded, weather-beaten words on the plaque that had been mounted there on the plinth above the double doors.

"What does it say, Merlyn?"

Young Arthur stood beside me, holding his pony's reins and gazing up at the densely packed lettering of the inscription. "You're the scholar, young man. You tell me."

His brow wrinkled in concentration. "I've been trying to read it, but there are too many words I don't know. They're all at the beginning, there. What do they mean?"

I smiled. "They're names, lad. Names you've never heard before, but in their day, when their owners were alive, the whole world knew and feared them. It says: 'For the Emperor Caesar Trajan Hadrian Augustus, son of the divine Trajan, conqueror of Parthia, grandson of the divine Nerva, Pontifex Maximus and three times Consul, the Fourth Cohort of Dalmatians set this here in the presence of the Emperor's propraetorian governor."

He turned to me, his eyes growing round. "Caesar Augustus?"

"Aye, but not the one you're thinking of. This one was a Caesar, but the 'Augustus' in this instance is simply a way of calling him the Great Caesar. His real name was Hadrian, just as mine is Merlyn. My full name is Caius Merlyn Britannicus, but Caius Britannicus was my grandfather."

"Hadrian's Wall? Was that his?"

"Aye. It was built during his reign."

"It says his father and his grandfather were divine. Were they truly gods?"

I grinned at him and tousled his hair. "No, but they were emperors. The Romans have always liked to turn their emperors into gods, to show that they were greater than ordinary men."

"Were they?"

"No, they were much like the rest of us, and many of them were lesser men. But as emperors they held so much more power than we could ever dream of that it appeared that they *must* be gods."

He thought about that for several moments then turned away, looking along the wall that stretched away to our right: its uneven top climbed upward with the rise of the land to a corner turret, some hundred paces from where we stood. Then he looked back, over his right shoulder to the huddle of low, arch-roofed buildings that housed the garrison baths.

"Are we really going to live here?"

"Perhaps. We have to find some place to live, and this might suit our needs. What do you think?"

Arthur Pendragon took some time to look about him more carefully before answering. I watched him, aware of his height, the breadth of his young shoulders and the way he held his head high as he examined the steep, rocky escarpments that reared above this site to the east and south. He then turned completely around, ignoring the watching, waiting group behind us, to gaze out over the tree-filled valley that fell steeply away, beginning some hundred paces from where we stood, to the west, back towards Ravenglass and the distant coast. Above us, on the southern cliff face, the shadow of a cloud swept along the broken, ragged stone.

"It will be cold up here in winter." I could hear from his tone that he had offered an opinion, not asked a question, so I waited as he completed his inspection, watching his eyes move deliberately along the left-hand section of the wall again and back to the central gateway.

"Can we go inside?"

"Of course, but I don't know what we'll find in there. This place has lain empty for a long time."

"Hundreds of years, Lucanus said."

"That's right. Shall we go in now?"

"In a moment. Is there another gate like this in the northern wall?"

I shrugged. "There must be. It's a Roman fort, so it should have four exits. They might not all be as big as this one."

"Why not?"

"Look about you. This is the main gate, facing the enemy. Up here, there's only one way for enemies to approach, and that's along the road, either from the pass, up there, or from the valley below. If they come from the west below, they would have to leave the road and climb a steep hill over rough ground to attack the western gate—difficult and dangerous. The only alternative, the same open to anyone attacking from the east across the pass there, would be to come around by the road and attack the eastern gate, from above, where there's a parade-ground campus, much like the one below Camulod. I imagine the garrison, when it was here, would have kept the heights above that, on this side of the road, well occupied, posing a threat to the rear of anyone attempting that. On the far side from here, the northern wall runs along the edge of the escarpment. No army could climb that." I paused, gauging the attention with which he had been listening. "So, having heard that, what would you expect to find by way of gates in the walls?"

The boy hesitated, thinking deeply, and then turned to glance towards where the others in our party still sat their horses, waiting for us to finish.

"Never mind them, lad. They'll wait for us, just as I am waiting for you."

He looked back towards me and then down, focusing for a short while on a spot somewhere between him and the ground. Then he raised those startling, golden eyes again to mine.

"The east wall will have double gates, as big as these, because of the parade ground beyond. And they'll be well fortified against attack from that direction. The western wall will have double gates, too, but smaller, for sorties against minor attacks from beneath. The rear wall, to the north along the cliff, requires no gate, unless it be a small one to allow refuse to be tipped over the edge."

"Good lad," I said, feeling an absurd lump swelling in my throat from pride. "That's the exact answer I had formed to my own question, for I've never been here either, you'll recall. Let's go and see if we're right."

"May I ask another question?"

"Of course."

He pointed to the tower ahead of us. "Why are the walls that surround the doors of a different stone from the tower?"

I grinned at him again. "I'm learning many things today, am I not? You teach well, young Arthur. Now look about you again and tell me why. Take your time, the answer's there in front of you."

Once again, the boy required little time to reach his answer. He looked about him, beginning with the dressed sandstone pillar between the heavy doors, then running his eyes around the gate's framework and from there to the turreted walls on either side of the central tower. I watched closely as his eyes, empty at first, grew suddenly acute, and I saw awareness grow in them as he turned to gaze up at the cliffs to the south and east. Then he stepped away and bent to wrestle something from the grass-grown ground: a long, flat slab of local stone, in thickness perhaps the width of his boy's palm. He hefted it, testing its weight, then dropped it flat on the cobbles of the causeway beneath our feet, where it shattered into four pieces.

"It's too soft, and too narrow in its depth. Excellent for building defensive walls, but the other kind of stone was necessary to hold the gates." He was still looking about him, up at the cliffs. "There's none of it here. Where did it come from?" When he realized that I would not respond, he went on again. "They must have brought it in, from some other place. Every single block of it must have been dug up and shaped and then brought here. . . . No wonder there's not more of it." He looked back at me now, smiling again. "Am I right?"

"You are. Full credit, and full lauds." As I turned to wave the others forward I congratulated myself on the impulse that had led me to have them wait behind while the boy and I rode forward alone. We had been travelling eastward on the Tenth Iter, an intact, strongly built road eight paces wide, the latter part of our journey a long climb up a staggeringly inclined hill to the high pass the fort had been built to guard, which now lay above us. There, reaching a small plateau beneath the summit, we had emerged from the dense forest, for the first time since leaving Ravenglass, to see the top of the gate-tower of Mediobogdum on our left, partly concealed from view by a steep crest in the short entrance road. Reaching the crest—no more than a hard-won twenty paces from the road—we had enjoyed our first clear view of the empty, silent fort. It looked impressive, from the distance of a hundred or so paces, as grim and invulnerable as the day it had been built, perched on the edge of an abyss beyond which the slopes of the opposing valley's sides were hazed in distance.

Confronting the view, without forethought and purely on the spur of a momentary urge, I had turned to Lucanus, riding by my left knee.

"Keep the others here for a while, Luke. I want to take the boy forward with me for his first look. He's the one to whom this place is most important, though he doesn't know it yet. I want to share his first reactions to the place."

Lucanus had merely stared at me, raising his eyebrows slightly, then nodded, and I had ridden forward alone, calling the boy to accompany me.

Now, as the others joined us, dismounting and stretching my limbs, I moved forward and pulled on the entrance gate, hoping to be able to open it far enough to allow me to put my shoulder to the task. To my great surprise, it swung towards me with much more ease than I had expected, the massive, thickly rusted metal hinge pins that held it in place squealing loudly, almost unbearably, as they turned, grinding in the holes that had been chiselled in the sandstone above and below to house them, the weight of the gate itself swinging it fully open to rest against the wall. I turned back to my companions, holding up my arms.

"My friends . . ." All of them stopped moving to watch me, their faces showing a broad range of interested, curious expressions. "When we step through this gate, we will be doing more than crossing a mere threshold. We'll be approaching a watershed in our lives. Beyond these gates could lie a new future for all of us. I am moved to make this request of you, and you may think it a strange one.

"We are here because we know we could live here, in this place, for the next space of years, if we so choose. But should we choose, that choice should be born out of deep reflection and consideration. These walls above us are sound, but they are ancient. Within the walls, I do not know, nor do you, what we may find, save that whatever we do find will have lain long untouched by man. And so I would like us to proceed from this point on, each one in solitude, uninfluenced by the comments of others. That will be difficult, I know, because the temptation to look at each other and share your initial reactions will be immense and purely natural. Your first reactions might differ, one from another, from disgust to excitement: I have no idea. But I want us to consider them together, later, not in the first, raw moments of speculation. Do you understand what I mean?"

They did, nodding and muttering in their various ways until Dedalus, as usual, moved matters along.

"So you want us to walk in silence?"

"Aye, Ded, I do. But more than that, I want each of us to walk apart. Go as you wish, where you wish, once inside, but try to stay away from the others. Look and absorb and examine and reflect and be honest with yourself, each one of you, but bear in mind what we seek to achieve here. Ask yourself if you can see this place as a temporary home, a place where you could live for several years if need be, and whether it can be adapted and suited to your own purposes and those we share in common."

Dedalus looked around at his companions and then grinned. "And when may we speak to each other again?"

"As soon as we are done. When you have seen enough, come back outside. We'll build a fire out here and eat together, and then we'll talk. There is no need to hurry. Let each take all the time he needs. You too, Shelagh. Are we agreed?"

Lucanus spoke for everyone. "You first, Merlyn. We'll follow."

I stepped from the shadowed passageway through the portals and into the fort with feelings of trepidation and excitement stirring palpably in my breast, aware of the boy's head at the edge of my vision as he moved to stand beside me just inside the threshold. I wanted him with me, so that I might prompt his thoughts, and perhaps even see things through his eyes. Behind me, I could hear the footsteps of my friends following closely, and I stepped away to clear the way, my eyes rapidly scanning the open spaces and the buildings in front of me—seeking, evaluating, assessing and cataloguing. Someone nudged me from behind, and I moved forward, accompanied by young Arthur. Together we walked to where the Via Praetoria, the main central street on which we stood, reached the first of the long, low barracks buildings that stood on either side of it. I was aware of their construction—heavy logs, dry-mossed, green with age and, I suspected, rot—but even as I began to examine them, I was aware that this was not where I wished to begin my inspection of this place.

Arthur had already passed me and reached the first entrance to the building on the left, leaning his head forward into the darkness beyond the empty space where the door had once hung. I moved to touch him on the shoulder, bringing him back to look up at me.

"Be careful, Arthur. Don't go poking your head into dark places before you make sure they're empty. Remember this place has sat abandoned for many years. There could be bears in any of these buildings."

He jerked his head up, wide eyed. "Bears? D'you really think so?"

He was not afraid, merely excited. I smiled and shook my head. "I doubt it, but unlikely as is, it could be possible. It's always best to be a little cautious. Anyway, this is not where I want to begin our search. Not here, not yet. Let's go the other way."

He glanced again through the open doorway of the building he had wanted to enter.

"The floor's concrete, Merlyn. It's dirty, but it's flat and dry and doesn't look cracked or broken."

"Aye, well, we'll look more closely at that later. Let's head up this way, for now. We'll walk around the intervallum." I led him to the right and together we climbed the short flight of steps that led us onto the narrow perimeter road that hugged the interior, uneven base of the fort's walls.

"Well," I asked him, as soon as we were up there, "what do you think of this for a Roman road?"

He glanced up at the wall that reached above our heads at that point, and then followed the line of it with his eyes for approximately twenty paces, to where it dipped out of sight before beginning to rear up again, to climb steadily towards the tower in the south-east corner. That done, he turned and gazed back to where the others were beginning to spread throughout the grounds of the fort. The ground beneath our feet at this point was a hump of solid rock, bare even of moss, and from where we stood, the plan of the fort, classic as it was, was clearly discernible, with the high, arched concrete roof of the granaries marking the central administrative area unmistakably.

"It's different," he said eventually, his tone speculative.

"Aye, but how is it different? You'll have to be clearer than that, to pass this test."

He grinned at me. "The whole fort is different, and it had to be." I said nothing, waiting for him to expound on that, and after a pause he did, looking all around him as he spoke.

"This fort is built to accommodate itself to the terrain, isn't it? There has been no effort made to level it, as there would be with any ordinary fort. This road goes up and down with the walls and the lie of the land. Bowmen could shoot from down there, beneath the walls on the other side, and pick us off up here, but—" He looked up at the wall again. "But the parapet walk up there is wider at this point, probably to hold more defenders to guard against that. This isn't a road we're on as much as a pathway, smoothed out. Not really built."

"A pathway? For whose convenience?" God, but I was proud of this boy! His eight-year-old mind was fertile and intuitive, showing an awareness and astuteness I would not have looked for in a recruit twice his age. At sixteen, most boys knew nothing militarily useful. He was already answering me.

"The garrison's, of course, to allow them to move to wherever they were needed."

"Why? Wouldn't they do just as well using the parapet walk?"

He looked at me wryly. "In an attack? They'd be falling all over each other, pushing one another off the walls. There's only room for one or two men at a time up there."

"Of course. You're right. Silly of me."

He smiled at me again. "You knew that. You simply wanted to find out if I knew it."

"I did." I ruffled his hair and stepped out again, and we walked in silence until we reached the south-east corner with its square angle-tower. Arthur stopped by the narrow steps leading up to the parapet walk.

"There's no door in the tower. What's in there?"

"Nothing, probably. It would have been used for storage."

"Then how did they get in?"

"From above, by a ladder through a hole in the floor up there."

"Can we go up?"

"Certainly, but be careful of the steps."

He was already halfway up, scampering almost on all fours, and I had to call to him as I followed more slowly while he ran the few steps to the tower's entrance.

"Careful, Arthur, don't go in there! That floor is old and probably unsafe. Fall through it and we'd have a hard time digging you out."

Sure enough, when I caught up with him, he was leaning against the doorway, gazing at where the few remnants of the ancient wooden floor sagged dustily towards the black depths of the lower level. He was making hooting noises like an owl through his cupped hands, his head cocked slightly to one side listening for an echo answering him from the depths beneath. Across the gulf that had been the floor of the room, another entrance, as naked of a door as this one was, offered a glimpse of the eastern parapet walk and the land beyond the wall on the eastern side. The jut of the tower walls on either side, however, prevented us from seeing anything of scope or value.

"D'you think they were ever attacked up here, Merlyn?" His wide, golden eyes were straining to see into the blackness beneath the remnants of the floor.

"They might have been, on occasion, but I doubt the attacks were ever strong or victorious. This place is too well fortified to tempt attackers. So I doubt, too, that there are any human bones down there, if that's what you're looking for."

His eyes swung to meet mine. "Then what happened to the floor?"

"It collapsed, that's all. This fort has been here since the days of the Emperor Hadrian, remember? That was hundreds of years ago . . . hundreds of years before even your Great-grandfather Varrus was born. A wooden floor will last for a long time, if it's cared for and maintained, but it will rot and decay quickly, like anything else, if it's left to the mercy of the weather, as this one was. A tree will fall and rot away to almost nothing in one man's lifetime. A flat, solid wooden floor will dry out and rot in much less time than that, if it's not looked after. The doors would have gone first, fallen off their rusted hinges, and once they were gone, the wind and rain and damp were free to do their damage."

"Oh." His eyes had moved away and he was looking over my shoulder now, to where the southern shoulder of the Fell behind me seemed to scrape against the sky. "Would enemies attack from up there?"

I turned to look where he was pointing. "Why don't you tell me? Would they?"

His brow clouded and he moved to the wall, where he suddenly became a small boy again, lodging a toe awkwardly between two stones and straining to pull himself up to peer over the top of the parapet that barely reached my shoulder. He made the ascent on his second try and hung there, arms clutching the top, his toes pinched inward side by side in a narrow crack in the stonework, his head moving from side to side on its impossibly slender neck as he scanned the ground beyond. The mountaintop he had been looking at was half a mile away from us on the other side of a steep gully, on the far side of the road from Ravenglass. He remained there for a long time, looking out silently, the wind ruffling his dark brown hair with its golden streaks. Finally he grunted and released his hold, dropping backwards to the parapet walk.

"No, they wouldn't. Can we go down now?"

"Lead the way. Why wouldn't they?"

"It's too far away, and too difficult. Anyone stupid enough to come down from there to attack would deserve to be defeated." He was skipping nimbly down the steep, narrow stone steps to the ground; I was following much more carefully. When I reached the bottom, he walked beside me, his eyes on the ground now, looking for anything that might be there waiting to be found.

"Why would they be stupid?"

He had lost interest in the far mountaintop as a source of peril and was totally absorbed in scanning the ground about his feet, so that he answered without looking up at me. "Because they would have to climb up there first. That would be stupid, when there's no need. And they'd be visible for much too long on the way down . . . then they'd have to climb back up from the gully before they could become dangerous to anyone. By then they'd be dead."

The red sandstone columns of the eastern gate-tower were looming in front of us by this time, and he darted ahead of me to disappear into the passageway. By the time I emerged from the portals after him, he was already half a hundred paces ahead of me, running up the long, overgrown but clearly discernible roadway that led to the flattish drilling area beneath the frowning escarpment of the mountainside. In the south-eastern distance, I could see a tiny ribbon of the road that crested the pass between this peak and its neighbour and continued to its end by the town Derek had told me of, by the side of the Great Mere. At the crest of the road the boy stopped running, and stood, looking about him. I lengthened my stride to catch up to him.

"It's flat, Merlyn," he said as I reached him. "Why didn't they build the fort up here?"

He was right. We were standing on the edge of an area that was as flat as the great campus training ground beneath the hill of Camulod, although much smaller.

"It's more than simply flat, Arthur. It's been flattened deliberately, by men. But it's not big enough to hold the fort. You see that ramp over there?" He looked to where a narrow, sloping ramp led up to a slightly higher area that overlooked the space beneath. He nodded, slowly, his face showing puzzlement. "That's been built up, too. Can you guess why?" He shook his head, slowly. "I'll give you a hint. Think of Camulod."

Arthur shook his head, frowning. "I don't know what you mean, Merlyn . . . unless you're talking about the campus. But then it doesn't make sense. Why go to all the trouble to clear just enough ground for a training area? Why not do it properly the first time, and build the camp on the flat area?" He answered his own question immediately, his whole face lighting up in a smile. "Because of time! They couldn't! This was done long after the fort was built, when there was time to do it at leisure. So it is only a training field. And that's the reviewing stand up there, just like the one built into the hillside of Camulod."

He was gone in a moment, his long, slim legs flashing as he ran and climbed to the reviewing stand, from which he looked down at me. Then, seeing that I had turned to look elsewhere, and apparently thinking himself unwatched for the moment, he became the child again, raising his hands formally and throwing himself into an unsuccessful handstand. He could not quite succeed in bringing his feet together, so that for a long, ludicrous moment he teetered there, reversed, his legs scissoring wildly before he toppled, slowly, the wrong way, to land flat on his back at great disadvantage to his dignity. Quick as a flash, he was on his feet again, dusting himself off and glancing at me almost furtively to see if I had noticed his misjudgment. I gave no sign, and he strode to the edge of the reviewing stand closest to me, drawing himself erect and frowning fiercely.

"Attenn-shun! Dress files and form your ranks on the right of line! Wait for it, Britannicus, wait for it! Hutt!"

I drew myself to attention and snapped a punctilious salute, which the boy returned with equal gravity.

"Permission to retire, Commander?" I asked.

"Permission granted. Dismissed."

I saluted again, spun about and began to make my way towards the gates again, hearing his feet flying over the ground to catch up with me.

"Will this place be ours, Merlyn? Will we live here?"

I looked at him. He was walking almost sideways now, gazing up at me with wide, anxious eyes, the full circles of his gold-flecked irises completely visible. His lean rump bore unmistakable traces of his handstanding misadventure.

"It's possible, as I said earlier, but would we wish to? That's what we have to ask ourselves. That's why we're here today . . . to answer that question."

"I would!"

I grinned. "I know you would, but that's only because it's an abandoned fort on a high mountain pass and the weather's still fine. As you said yourself, earlier, it'll be very different up here in the rain and snow. I promise you, you'd be even more aware of that with the cold winds howling through all the cracks in the walls and everything frozen solid, including your hands and feet. The adventures you think you could have here with your friends in the summertime are hardly sufficiently strong grounds for having all of us move up here to live permanently. I hope you will agree with that?"

His face fell and he lowered his head. He remained silent until we had entered the fort again and swung right, following the perimeter walk towards the northern gate. But it was not in his nature to give up without a fight. "We could fill in all the cracks in the walls, could we not?"

I laughed aloud. "Aye, perhaps we could, lad, and mount new doors and spread skins over those to keep the draughts out. All of that we could do, although it would entail months and months of work by every single person among us, including you and your friends. But there would still remain the matter of survival, of living from day to day." I stopped and laid my hand on his shoulder, waiting for him to look up and meet my eyes. "Look, Arthur, I'm not saying we will not stay here. We may well do exactly that. But you heard what I said to the others before we came in here, did you not?" He nodded.

"Well then, you know how important I believe it to be for everyone to form his own opinions on this, since it is a grave matter affecting everyone. We will pool those opinions in the form of a discussion, leading to consensus and only then to a decision. That's the democratic way of doing things."

The boy gazed at me, his eyes narrowing, and then his face creased into a smile. "I know it is, but I heard you say to Dedalus and Connor on the galley, days ago when you were talking of the wars in Cornwall, that democracy works best under an enlightened and determined leader."

He had me flatfooted. I had to glance away quickly, covering my mouth with one hand to conceal my rueful smile, before I could look at him again. "True, I did say that, but I didn't know you were listening. In this instance, however and notwithstanding what I said to Dedalus and Connor, because there are so few of us involved here and all of them my friends, I am determined to allow the will of all the others to prevail."

"Until you decide they're being timid, or going wrong, or they aren't able to make up their minds properly to agree with your opinion." His face was straight now, although his eyes were dancing, and I found myself disbelieving once again that he was only eight, approaching nine years old. If his intellect continued to expand at its present rate, this child, already one to reckon with, would be a most formidable adult.

I nodded, equally straight-faced. "That is extremely impertinent, young man, and none of our group could ever be described as timid. But . . ." I allowed myself a tiny smile. "You're right, of course. Could you think otherwise?"

He giggled, something he rarely did, and ran ahead of me, towards the north gate. As I followed him, I looked about me idly to my left, towards the body of the fort. In the distance, I saw Dedalus emerge and then disappear again behind an intervening wall, and Lucanus came into view from the end of the Via Principalis, the east-west axis of the fort, his hands clasped behind him as he walked, looking up at the walls and roofs of the granaries that towered above him. I caught his eye and waved to him, and he began to make has way towards me.

"Well," he began, offering a sardonic little grin as he approached. "I presume it's safe to speak again?"

"It always was, for you. Unless you've found some compelling reason why we can't live here, from a medical viewpoint. Have you?"

"No, not one. What does the boy think of it?"

"What would you expect? He's a boy. He loves the place. His own personal fortress."

"So you're pleased with his reaction? Good. What were you two talking about for so long before the gates?"

I was scanning the fort again. Dedalus had disappeared and no one else seemed to be moving. "About the construction of the place. The gate-towers and the stone. The child is amazing, Luke. Has everyone else finished already?"

"I doubt it. I heard voices in the granary as I passed, though, so someone's already broken your rule." He was smiling again.

"Were they arguing?"

"No, it sounded as though they were discussing something engrossing."

"Merlyn, come and see what I've found!" Arthur was waving to me from close by the north gate.

I glanced at Luke, who was also watching the boy. "I knew if there was anything at all to find in here, he'd find it. His eyes have been fixed on the ground since we came back in through the eastern gate. Let's go see what he has."

Whatever it was, it was very small. Arthur held it between his fingers and examined it closely, glancing towards the ground between him and the wall from time to time as he waited for us to reach him. As soon as we were close enough to be able to see what it was, he thrust his hand towards me.

"Look, it's gold. I found treasure. I saw it shining in the grass there, beneath the wall. There are black ones, too."

He had found a small cache of coins, one of them gold. I moved to where he pointed and, kneeling down, I peered among some loose stones, where I found several small, black and dark-brown metal tokens. The black ones were silver, long tarnished, and the brown ones copper. I had no doubt the purse some legionary once lost had lain here and rotted completely away. They would never have been found, had not the boy's bright eye been caught by the dull sheen of the only golden piece among them. I gathered them up, eleven of them, and tried to see the likenesses they bore, but they were tarnished beyond recognition. Not so the boy's, however. As I straightened up he thrust it at me, and I took it and held it up to the light.

"Who's the man on the front, Merlyn? Is he an emperor?"

The gold coin was small, and well worn, and I had to squint to decipher the crude lettering around its rim. When I did, I felt a shiver stir the hairs along my neck. "No, Arthur," I murmured, aware of my own wonder, "this is no emperor . . . although he might have been, for he dreamed great dreams." Reverently, I handed the coin to Lucanus, who peered frowning at it, his eyes weaker than mine. "That is Marcus Antonius, Arthur," I continued. "The friend, some say the son, of Julius Caesar himself. Mark Antony, whose concubine was Cleopatra, Queen of Egypt. He must have minted his own coins to pay his legions, in Egypt, and one of them made its way here, to lie in wait for you."

The boy was gazing at the coin Lucanus still held up in front of him. "Mark Antony!" His voice was as hushed as mine had been; he knew of Mark Antony from his lessons. "Did he come to Britain?"

It was Luke who answered him, handing the coin back to the lad.

"No, Arthur, Mark Antony died in Egypt, fighting against his former friend, Julius Caesar's nephew Octavius, who then crowned himself emperor and took the name Caesar Augustus."

"Caesar Augustus? The one above the main gates?"

Luke made a face and looked to me for guidance. "I don't know. I didn't look. Most unobservant of me. Merlyn?"

I grinned at him, but spoke to the boy. "The answer is yes and no. Octavius Caesar Augustus was the first emperor. He was also the first divine emperor. All the others that followed named themselves after him. The one above the gates was Hadrian Caesar Augustus, remember?" He nodded, and I continued. "But think of your find this way, Arthur. In every fight there is a winner and a loser, and the Fates, often at whim, it appears, decree which shall be which. Had they decided otherwise the day Mark Antony fought Octavius Caesar, you might now have been holding a likeness of the first emperor of Rome in your hand."

"Hmm." He closed his fist tightly around the coin. "May I keep this?"

"Of course. You found it."

"I know you said he wasn't a god, Merlyn, but how could they even try to make him one?"

I smiled. "They couldn't. Gods are immortal. That was sheer flattery. They called him a god, but he was only a man, and he proved it by dying like all other men. Have you noticed you were right about the gate, too? There's only one portal." I ignored Lucanus's raised eyebrow.

"I know, I saw it. Let's go and look outside." The boy stepped between us and took hold of our hands, wrapping his fingers around two of mine, and led us out, tugging impatiently, beyond the gates. Just a few paces brought us to the cliff's edge, where we all three stopped in awe, smitten by the spectacle before us.

Beneath our feet, the cliff face fell vertically, bare of vegetation for most of its vertiginous plunge to a shattered ruin of scree and fallen boulders seemingly miles beneath our perch. Its far-flung edges were lost among the forest of trees that stretched from there as far as we could see in every direction. We had been riding through that forest all morning, but seen from above, it was like a thick, green mat covering everything except that tumbled, lethal wasteland directly at our feet. Even the road and the river Esk, which I knew were down there, almost directly beneath us, were concealed by the denseness of the overhanging treetops. Arthur, who had let go of Lucanus to lean closer to the edge, but whose hand still clutched my own, drew back instinctively from the gulf, drawing close to my side even though there was no danger of his falling. When he turned to look up at me, his eyes were enormous.

"How far down is it?"

"I've no idea." I tried to keep my voice light, since I could see there was no need to warn him of the danger here. "But the beautiful part of it is that it's too far up ever to be a threat to this place. No army could climb that, nor any single man I've ever met."

"No." He moved forward again, bending cautiously from the waist. "All those rocks, did they fall from the cliff?"

"Aye, they did, every one of them. That's why there are no trees on the cliff face. But there's grass on many of the ledges down there, and it's thick in places, so nothing has fallen recently."

"Hmm." He sounded far from convinced. But then, after a few more moments' contemplation of the abyss itself, he turned his eyes outward to where the oak- and ash- and beech-covered hills shepherded the valley westward to the sea beneath low, cloudy skies of varying greys. There was nothing there to mar the forest's deep-green mantle. The peaks behind us, to the south and east, were hidden by the walls that reared at our backs. Only to the north-east did the high cliffs of the largest Fells shrug themselves free of timber.

"It's beautiful, isn't it, Merlyn? So different from Camulod."

"Aye, lad, it is. You think it more beautiful?"

"No-o, and yet yes. The mountains . . ."

"You've never seen Cambria, have you?"

He threw me a glance, much more an eighteen-year-old's than an eight-year-old's, that included Lucanus and told both of us that I knew very well he had not. I grinned.

"You will, some day, I promise you, and you'll find that the mountains there, too, are beautiful, and very, very different."

"Different from these? How can that be?"

I shook my head. "As soon as you see them, you'll know. They're higher, for one thing. On some of them, in the highlands, the snow never melts. Their crests are white all year round."

He looked up at me in open disbelief. "That's impossible. The summer sun would melt it."

"Not in Cambria, Arthur, nor anywhere else where the mountains are high enough."

"High enough for what? To escape the sun?"

I shrugged. "I suppose you might put it that way. They don't escape the light, but they do evade the heat. It's a known fact that, no matter where you are, the higher you climb above that level where the land meets the waters of the sea, the colder the air becomes. If you climb high enough, you reach a point where even the summer rain falls as snow." I grinned at him. "It's true! Ask Lucanus. He and I have ridden into summer storms, on uphill journeys in high land, where the rain turned to snow as we rode higher. And we've turned around and ridden down again, out of the swirling snowstorm to where there was no sight of snow and the rain still fell. Didn't you notice how cool it became today, when we started climbing the hill out of the valley to come up here?"

He nodded, remembering. "But why, Merlyn? Why is that?"

"I wish I could tell you, lad, but I can't. Luke, do you know?"

Lucanus shrugged his shoulders slowly. "No, I do not. But I know it is true. Heat seems to be heavier than cold, Arthur, if you can imagine such a thing, because it always grows colder, the higher you climb. And yet heat rises upward from a fire, so that the upper part of a room is always much warmer than the temperature at floor level. Contradictory, in the extreme, but true, nonetheless, and defying explanation."

"Hmm." The complexities of the abstraction were too much for the boy, and he dismissed them. "Does this valley have a name? Do you know?"

"I don't really know," I answered him. "I know the river we crossed down there is called the Esk, so this would be the valley of the Esk."

He was staring towards the western horizon, where it flattened visibly beyond the shoulder of the farthest, mist-hazed hill. "Could we see the sea from here, on a bright day?"

I followed his gaze. "I think we could. That flat part is the line of it, I believe. It's out there somewhere."

He turned to face the wall of the fort. "And what's beyond the crest of the pass where the road goes over?"

"Another valley. I imagine, and another, and then eventually another town like Ravenglass, at the end of the road."

"Was there a fort there, too?"

"Aye, and a vicus. As I said, a town just like Ravenglass."

"Cumbria . . ." He murmured the ancient name of the region surrounding us, drawing it out so that the "m" became a resonant hum. "What's the difference between Cumbria and Cambria?"

I smiled, raising an inquisitive eyebrow towards Luke, who merely shrugged and made a face indicating ignorance of this, too. "They're both ancient names. There was probably no difference, at one time. They might be the same name, differing only in the way the people say them. . . . And before you ask me what it means, I'll tell you I don't know. But *all* of it is Britain, Arthur." And some day it could be yours, I thought. "Come now, we'd better go back into the fort and look at what is there. You'll have questions aplenty then, I'll wager."

My inspection of the fort itself, confined to a cursory examination of the condition of its buildings, was brief, since I knew what I was looking for, although one small construction was a surprise. Lucanus pointed it out to me in passing, and then departed in search of food, leaving me to investigate. It was a stone building, in the north-eastern quadrant of the fort, abutting the outer wall close to the guard tower. I leaned inside and then withdrew again, absurdly pleased.

"What is it, Merlyn?"

"A latrine, and a good one, too. I hadn't expected it."

Arthur approached the door then and leaned in as I had done, sniffing deeply before turning to look at me, his eyebrows raised in puzzlement. "It's tiny. What's good about it?"

I grinned at him, then led him inside, to where the air had been untainted by men for many years, and gestured to the stonework of the floor and the upright, less than knee-high wall that framed it. A handsbreadth-deep channel in the concrete of the floor ran along three sides in front of this wall, and it was evident from the slight slope in the floor that the channel had been fashioned to lead water from the mouth of a pipe that protruded from one corner of the small room towards the drain holes at each end. I recognized the style immediately as being of the kind I had only read about before: the classic, early-Roman garrison latrine. I could see where there had been spaces for nine men to squat; three to a side on three sides. In one corner, close by the end of the front wall, I saw what looked like several dust-covered pebbles and a few short sticks. I crossed and kneeled to pick up one of the "stones," finding it, as I had suspected, completely weightless.

"Here," I grunted. "Look at this. You know what it is?"

The boy examined it, clearly baffled as to its nature, and shook his head. I picked up one of the dry sticks and moved directly to the low wall that ran around the floor, where I inserted the stick into one of the three curious keyholelike slots that pierced each side of it.

"This is very much like our own latrine in Camulod, Arthur, but very old, and even more functional. This place could service three or four hundred men. The pit behind the wall here was covered by wooden bench seats, three holes each, centred on these slots." I held up the weightless pebble. "This is a sponge, more than two hundred years old and probably much smaller than the ones we use today in Camulod. Our sponges are precious now, because they are hard to come by, but when this place was built, they were plentiful, because the Romans ruled the world and had endless access to such things. You've heard Lucanus talk about the need for cleanliness the Romans have always shown, well, here's a perfect example. The sponge was held on one of these sticks. The channel in front, here, was filled with running water. The soldiers wet the sponges in the water, inserted them through the slot in the wall between their legs, and cleaned themselves, then washed the sponge again in the channel. Simple, effective and hygienic. And if we can get the water to run again, we'll have a working, permanent latrine. Should we, of course, decide to stay here."

He wrinkled his nose. "It will stink."

"Aye, but that's the nature of latrines. I suspect, though, that since this place was built against the outer wall, above the gorge, we'll find an outlet leading to the cliff beyond the wall, which means we'll be able to sluice the detritus out regularly. This place was built by an engineer."

"But we have no sponges."

"No, but we have cloth. Come on, let's look at the rest of the place."

By this time, we were the only ones left still exploring. We inspected the Horrea, the building that had housed the granaries and storage warehouses, and I was glad to see that the domed, concrete roof was weathertight and solid, and that the buttresses supporting it on either side were sound, the mortar that bound them largely unaffected by time and weather. The headquarters building and the commander's house were in equally good condition, all lacking serviceable doors but surprisingly undamaged after such a long abandonment. There was nothing wooden remaining at all, anywhere, only the obdurate stone.

When we rejoined our group beyond the main gates, they were clustered around one of three fires. The other two were being used as cooking fires, tended by Lars and Rufio. Only Dedalus was missing, and I wondered if we had passed him by, somehow, inside the fort.

"Where's Dedalus?" People looked at me blank-faced, a few of them shaking their heads, but Shelagh was the only one who answered.

"I was talking to him here a little while ago. The last time I saw him, he was headed over that way, towards the bathhouse."

A few moments later, I entered the bathhouse, noting that it, too, had a sound roof. In one corner, lodged partially upright against one wall of the entranceway, the rotted remnants of a door lay mouldering; the brightly coloured glass that had filled its upper panel was still intact beneath a heavy layer of dirt. Surprised to see anything so valuable here, I looked for its fellow and saw the rectangular shape of it beneath the covering of dirt on the floor of the vestibule. Then, curious, I fell to one knee and dragged the leading edge of my dagger through the dirt on the floor itself, uncovering a bright stripe of multicoloured mosaic tiles.

More curious than ever now, I wondered idly at the temperament of the commanding officer who had overseen the building of this place. Such luxurious appointments could not have been installed without his approval, and such concern for the welfare of garrison grunts was unusual, to say the very least. I moved on to examine the rest of the place. It was not large, but it was large enough for its purpose, and it seemed to have been well designed and appointed. There was a good-sized changing room, beyond which lay the series of pools terminating in the *calidarium*, the hot pool, and then a narrow passageway led off to the right to an ample steam room above the furnace. Apart from the dirt of ages, everything seemed to be in excellent condition, except the floor in the hot room, which had collapsed in one corner into the space beneath, and down there, in the darkness, I heard movement and a muttered, explosive curse.

"Ded? Are you down there?" I crossed to the hole and knelt, bending forward to see into the darkness.

"Aye, and I've broken my gods-cursed head!" I heard the sound of him approaching the opening, and as he came I crouched low to look at the base of the hypocaust pillars I could see through the sagging hole in the floor. Designed to channel the heat from the furnace to where I crouched peering, they were amazingly beautiful, although never meant to be seen, each of them clad with dense-packed, deep-red glazed tiles. Dedalus appeared in the opening, crawling into view, and I reached down to help him climb out. He was filthy, covered with dirt and crusted with ancient soot.

"Whoreson," he spat, ejecting a mouthful of saliva mixed with soot as he heaved himself up to sit on the edge of the hole. "It's blacker than a raven's arse down there."

"What in the name of God were you doing?"

He scratched at his face. "Checking the furnace. That whoreson will work. It's not blocked, and it hasn't given way, except at the front, where you throw the fuel in. That's collapsed, so I couldn't get in that way. Then I remembered this hole. But the aqueduct for the run-off's still intact down there, and the cisterns above ground look good, too. I'll wager I could make this whoreson work, once we re-dig some ditches. They're all blocked and filled in, of course."

"Of course." I was staring at him in wonder. "Dedalus, what do you know about bathhouses?"

"Everything." He gazed at me, the whites of his eyes shocking in the blackness of his face, and then he grinned. "You didn't know, did you? I trained as an engineer in my earliest soldiering days. Had three years of it, before I joined your father. I was just a kid of fourteen, two years under age, but big. I started out as a grunt sapper, but I had a real talent for it. Haven't thought about it in years. . . . Not since I met your father, as a matter of fact. That's when I changed from builder to soldier. But when I saw this place it all came back to me. I built one just like it, in Asia Minor, acting as deputy to my first chief. He was a real engineer, an architect. Knew every damn thing there was to know about building."

My wonder had changed to amazement. "Are you saying you might be able to fix this place? A bathhouse?"

"Easy as taking a piss, Commander." His grin was ferocious, a blend of conviction and enthusiasm. "Providing there's a stream close enough, and providing we can find a clever enough stonemason to build a ditch so we can channel water to the cisterns . . . and providing they don't leak. Couldn't see any cracks in them, but they're long dry, so I could be wrong. Fuel's no problem. There's enough wood within hauling distance to keep a furnace blazing for a thousand years. Given those minor details, yes, I can make this place into a working bath again."

I grinned back at him then, accepting his assurance completely. "Wonderful, Ded. You do that, and I think we can find a home here for all of us, providing the others can see it. Here, let me help you up. We'll join them now, eat something and then find out what they think."

Ded's opinion on the bathhouse was all that was required to convince the doubters, of whom there were very few. Within the space of an hour, we had decided to decamp from Ravenglass, with Derek's blessing clearly understood, and to establish ourselves here, on the highest point of his lands, for as long as we should require to remain. The old fort was far gone in disrepair, and each of the men in the group had his own views on the priorities that must apply in remedying that, but everyone agreed that we had the skills among us to refurbish it to a decent living standard and that it could be done. We needed only time, and an ample supply of parts and services from Ravenglass, supported by mild weather and sufficient determination on the part of every man and woman concerned. Shelagh took no part in the discussion. Her female mind had been made up in favour of the place, for her own reasons, long before she ever saw it.

VII

By the time winter finally began to whisper among the browning foliage in the mountain glens that year, we had made huge inroads into the daunting tasks that had faced us so sternly mere months before. September had smiled upon the land, so balmy and benevolent that the trees had barely thought to begin setting their leaves to dying. October had crept in and gone without a hint of frost, and it was late in November before the morning air began to draw vapours from our mouths, harbinger of the frigid weather to come.

By then, we were well ensconced, and the tang of fresh woodsmoke lay everywhere within the fort, by day and night, redolent of warmth and ease and comfort on the long, autumnal evenings. The raw, sappy smell of new-felled, freshly worked timber was everywhere, as well, and three of the six long barracks-blocks had been rebuilt—torn down and burned, and fresh walls of square-hewn logs raised into place, then weatherproofed with mortar and strongly roofed. The windows, which were large and wide, were shuttered in two fashions: an outer set of solid oak closed like doors and could be barred, and an inner set, made by Mark, our master carpenter, were fashioned of narrow, hand-planed slats of beech wood that swiveled up and down to admit, filter or block out the light. These were hinged on both sides, allowing them to be opened wide on summer days. Solid, double partitions of strong planks, fitted tongue-and-groove and solidly nailed to a central frame, the space between them stuffed with layered straw and wood-shavings to conserve heat and stifle sound, divided the space into capacious, comfortable living units, each with its own entrance and windows. The floors were of the original concrete, still strong and sound, and covered with woven grass matting for comfort.

The forest around us had supplied most of our raw building materials, but Derek and his people had been magnificent in their assistance to us, supplying a minor army of men and women to help with the work and a plenitude of material and supplies with which to build, and live. In return, they had been guaranteed the aid from Eire that was so crucial to them. They had already taken in, on their own behalf as well as ours, the cargoes of three convoys from the west, dispatched by Athol, including livestock, weapons and trade goods captured in his recent wars.

Then, early in the winter, just before the onset of the first snow, came our first grand celebration as a newborn community. Dedalus, grinning a sooty grin of sheer delight, approached me casually around noon on a frosty day and, leading me beyond the walls, pointed wordlessly to the smoke issuing from the chimney of the bathhouse furnace, on which he and his men had been labouring mightily, and utterly without commentary, for months. Their task was now complete: the waters were heating above the hypocausts, and the first wisps of vapour were already beginning to filter through the pipes and into the steam room. After an interval of silent centuries, the baths at Mediobogdum would soon echo again with the sound of voices, songs and laughter.

I went with Dedalus immediately to tour the renewed facility for the first time in months, and I made no effort to restrain the praises that swarmed upon my lips, for him and for all his people. The hole that had sagged in the corner of the floor above the furnace was gone as though it had never been, and every surface in the entire place gleamed with sparkling brightness and vibrant colours. To formalize my extreme pleasure, I declared the following day a holiday and sent word to Derek in Ravenglass to bring his folk to join our celebration—or at least those of his folk brave enough to countenance the risk of being surprised and cut off by an early winter snowstorm.

Lucanus, more than anyone else, was delighted by the news of the bathhouse's completion, for the military-trained physician in him had been concerned for months by the necessarily lessened standard of hygiene within our small community. Cleanliness to Luke meant more than the mere absence of offensive smells; it meant health and fitness. He expanded visibly with Ded's news, when he came outside the walls to see what all the commotion was about, and set about immediately to incorporate a formal opening of the new facility into the following day's holiday activities.

I walked back to Luke's quarters with him, and I enjoyed our august surgeon's uncharacteristic excitement as he prattled non-stop all the way, enthusing over the meticulous detail of the renovations Ded had shown us. Once inside his comfortably furnished and partitioned room, however, I refused the cup of wine he offered me, and his ebullience vanished instantly, his observant eyes narrowing to their normal, analytical keenness.

"What's the matter, Cay? You seem . . . upset over something."

I demurred, shaking my head and shrugging my shoulders at the same time, but he was well used to my every mood and refused to be deflected. "Pardon me," he insisted, enunciating each word clearly and carefully, as though speaking to a small boy, "but am I suddenly aged and infirm, losing my faculties? I can see your distress—it is as evident as the colour of your hair—so I shall ask you again, and I trust you'll honour me by answering truthfully. What is the matter?"

I shrugged again, and rubbed my hands as though washing them. "Nothing, Luke," I protested. "There's nothing wrong. I'm simply envious about the baths, that's all."

His eyes widened and he looked at me as though I had lost my wits and uttered something nonsensical. While he sought the words with which to respond, I became incongruously aware of our hands: mine rubbing themselves together in an extremity of nervousness: his motionless, holding two cups of wine, one of them still partially extended towards me. By the time he spoke again, he was frowning. "Envious? What kind of word is that to use in such a case? What, in the name of Aesculapius, do you have to feel envious about?"

I had been holding my breath, and now I exhaled through my pursed lips, in a controlled hiss. "About the companionship in the bathhouse. Because I'll miss it."

"Caius, what in the world are you talking about?"

"About me, Luke!" Suddenly my tight control was gone, and all my fears and my bitterness came swirling to the surface, clearly astounding my friend, if the expression on his face was anything by which to judge. "I'm talking about me! About my condition . . . about this—this cursed, damnable thing on my chest. I'm talking about leprosy! Leprosy, Luke, and the evil of it! If that's what this thing is, this mark on me, this blemish—and you've said nothing to convince me that it isn't—then I'll never step inside those baths, because to do so would be murder. There's no other word in me to say it better. It would be murderous of me to incur the risk of spreading my contagion on to others. That's what I'm talking about, Lucanus, and I'm amazed that you should take so—"

"You are spewing shit!"

His interruption, loud, vicious and whiplike, robbed me of all impetus, so that I hung there, mouth agape. In all the years I had known Lucanus, I had never heard him utter so much as a mild profanity.

"Listen to yourself, man! Listen, for one moment, to what you are saying, and ask yourself how you dare! Do you really have so little regard for my concern, for my knowledge, for my skills? And do you really think me so uncaring about your condition that I would simply leave you floundering in fear and ignorance?"

Abashed now, and suddenly conscious of how rude and hectoring and condemnatory my angry outburst had been, I shook my head, mumbling, and totally unable to look him in the eye. "I . . . No. No, forgive me, Luke, I had not thought to imply any of that. . . ." I could hear misery and something approaching too close to self-pity in my own tone, and my voice dried up. He moved towards me and thrust the cup of wine he still held into my nerveless fingers.

"You had not thought—you have not yet thought clearly in several respects, my friend. That much I can easily perceive. Here, take this. Now drink. And sit. Sit over there." He pointed to a chair against the wall.

When I was seated, he raised his cup towards me, holding it high until I returned the gesture, and then we both sipped. I had no consciousness of the taste of the wine, but I watched him as he moved to pull another chair out from the table to my left and turn it towards me, standing behind it. He drank again, the tiniest of sips, then leaned forward to place his cup on the chair's seat, after which he stood looking at me, leaning his weight forward onto his hands which gripped the chair's high back. The light in the room settled on the arched plane of his forehead, beneath the pronounced widow's peak that crowned it, making the tight, translucent skin of his high brow gleam and throwing a shadow into the dip of his left temple and the hollow of his cheek, so that I became aware of his age again—aware that Lucanus was no longer young. The silence stretched between us until I could bear it no longer.

"Luke," I began, but he waved me to silence before I had even begun. When he did speak, his voice held all of the detachment of his professional persona. My friend Luke was silent: my other friend, Lucanus the surgeon and physician, was speaking.

"You told me once, Caius, the last time we had words, that there is no need for apologies between us when we spark differences occasionally. That applies now. . . . But I deserved your reaction there, for my own carelessness in failing to be aware how concerned you are, still, about this—condition of yours. I know it frightens you deeply, but you conceal your distress so well that I had lost sight of it. So, we shall address it now. Undo your tunic."

"Why? You looked at the damned thing this morning."

"I did, but now I require you to look at it with me. Humour me. Expose it."

I did as he requested, laying bare my breast so that The Mark, as I had come to think of it, lay open to his scrutiny and my own, foreshortened as that was by the awkward angle from which I had to peer at it.

Lucanus moved close to me and reached out, pinching the flesh of my breast, then stretching it between finger and thumb so that the skin around The Mark whitened almost to the colour of the dead patch at the centre of the blemish itself.

"Does it hurt?" I shook my head. "Can you feel it at all? When I pinch?"

"No."

"Very well, now think carefully, has it changed in any way—shape, colour, sensitivity, anything at all—in recent months?"

I thought about it, stifling the immediate negative that sprang to my tongue. The blemish had not, in fact, increased in size since it had first appeared, so that I still could cover it completely with the pad of my thumb. "No," I said, eventually. "You know it hasn't."

"Correct, I know it has not, but we are conducting this particular examination for your benefit, not mine. So, there has been no change: no proliferation, no spread, no swelling, no soreness, no pus and no breaks in the skin; no leaks of fluid of any kind, and no itching. Correct?" I nodded again. He straightened up. "Good. Now cover yourself up again and listen to what I have to say to you." As I rearranged my tunic he went back to the chair opposite me, picking up his cup and sitting down to face me.

"As you know, I am familiar with what frightens you most: the disease of leprosy, and the very idea of it. I have worked with it, and among lepers, for many years. I believe, utterly and with totality, Cay, that this . . . manifestation, of whatever it is you have, is not a leprous lesion. It could be any one of a hundred other things, some known, some unknown. I'll know more when I lay my hands on that scroll I mentioned. If I'm right, it's in a chest that I once gave to your Aunt Luceiia. I've written to Ambrose and asked him to look for it. If he finds it, he'll send the entire contents of the chest to me by the next vessel of Connor's that calls in there. But!" He stood up again and crossed to stand directly in front of me, looking down at me. "But. Your fears, my friend, those fears that just now spilled from you, are groundless. Listen to me. Even if whatever it is that you now have were to become leprosy at some future date, it is harmless, at this time, to others. Do you understand that, Caius? It is harmless. To cause contagion, of any kind, it would have to be active . . . to be leaking, to be exuding poisons, to be sweating secretions of some kind. That is not the case, with you.

"I have never lied to you, my friend, and I will not begin to do so now, over this. What you have on your skin, this mark, is merely a deadened surface area bearing some slight, arguable resemblance to some forms of leprous lesions. And the important word in all of that is 'lesions' . . . plural. You have only one mark, and it has been unique since it appeared, almost a full year ago. It is my firm opinion, based on a lifetime of medical study and practice, that there is not the slightest possibility that you are capable of presenting any threat, of any kind of contagion, to any person. And that embraces, most specifically, your presence in the bathhouse. Have I made myself clear?"

"Yes."

"And, more important, do you believe me?"

I thought about all he had said, weighing not merely his words and his credibility but his tone and demeanour, and I felt relief and gratitude well up in me, so that a smile came easily to my eyes and lips, and my entire chest expanded with well-being. He was watching me closely as I nodded, very gently at first, then with increasing conviction and gratitude. I raised my cup again, this time anticipating the fullness of the wine.

"Aye, Luke. I believe you. So be it."

Before the following day had run its course, my acceptance of Lucanus's opinion was challenged directly. I was relaxing at the time, sprawled out in company with Lucanus, Donuil and Derek in the quiet of the refurbished steam room after the hustle and bustle of the long, holiday afternoon of athletic events and speechmaking. Conversation had been desultory, all of us lulled and lethargic with the heat and humidity, but Donuil eventually sighed and stood up and left us, having volunteered to go and find out when the evening meal was to be served. Lucanus lay, apparently asleep, on the marble bench along the side of the room to my right, and I was lazily watching the steam eddies, enjoying doing nothing, when Derek suddenly leaned towards me and threw me into a complete panic.

"What's that mark there, on your chest? Some kind of scar?"

I closed my eyes quickly, drawing a great, deep breath, forcing myself not to stiffen and gathering myself to be able to look down casually. The Mark stood out plainly in here, against the natural darkness of my skin, its whiteness emphasized by the additional whiteness of the chest hairs that grew within its borders. Now I gazed down at it again, keenly aware of Luke's unmoving presence against the wall.

"No," I heard myself saying, almost musingly, "it's not a scar. It's some kind of skin ailment. Lucanus is fascinated by it, whatever it is . . . he's forever poking and prodding at it. But it doesn't hurt, doesn't itch and doesn't get any bigger. He expects it simply to disappear some day, like a wart."

"Hmm." Derek, I saw gratefully, was not really interested. His curiosity had been nothing more than momentary notice of an anomaly. "I had a wart, once, that used to bother me. Huge damned thing, it was, with hairs on it, and it was ugly. Can you believe that, on a body like mine? Women didn't like it, I can tell you. Had it for years, right here." He arched his back out from the wall and pointed a fingertip to the area beneath the swell of his great, hairy belly, just above his pubis. There was nothing to be seen there now. "Then one day it was gone, just like that." He tried to snap his wet fingertips. "Don't know how quickly it went, or why, or even when . . . I just looked, one day, and it wasn't there. . . . Hector really succeeds, doesn't he?"

The non sequitur left me floundering. "What are you talking about?" I asked him. "That doesn't make sense. How did you include Hector and warts in the same thought?"

Derek stretched mightily, yawning, and then stood up and began to sweep the streaming moisture from his great frame with the edge of one hand. He saw me glance idly at his genitals and grinned, hitching his belly up with both hands and bending forward to peer down.

"Don't see that too much, nowadays," he drawled. "But I don't use it as much as I used to, either. Must be growing old, but it doesn't seem as important as it used to be." He released his belly and reached behind him for a towel. "I said Hector succeeds, that's all. Nothing to do with warts. I was thinking about how you've managed to disguise yourself, and I'm not even talking about the beard and the hair-colouring."

I had grown a full beard and darkened my hair artificially shortly after moving up into the hills to live in Mediobogdum, and sufficient time had passed since then that I gave the transformation little thought. Derek did not even glance at my hair as he continued.

"You've effaced yourself completely. I really noticed it today, during the celebrations. Everyone here knows who you are, but they all call you Cay, and they all treat Hector as though he's the leader of your group. He even believes it himself, or he seems to. Damnation, *I* even think of you as Cay nowadays, and I know damn well who you are. Three or four months ago, when you first arrived, I would have sworn that was impossible . . . unachievable. But you've done it. Merlyn of Camulod has disappeared."

"Good," I replied. "That's as it should be. And the longer he remains absent, the better it will be for the boy."

I had followed Shelagh's inspired suggestion long since, and arranged my own disappearance, making sure that everyone in Ravenglass had seen Arthur and me sail away with Connor. What no one knew but us, however, was that Connor had landed us again, no more than a few miles farther along the coast, safely out of sight of Ravenglass and its people. We had then returned here and become the childless Master Cay and his young apprentice.

I had not moved from my original position facing him, and now I wiped the heavy perspiration from my face, blinking the sting of it from my eyes and thinking we had almost been in the steam room too long. When I opened my eyes again, Derek was still standing there, gazing down at me, his towel hanging from his hand, and Luke had shrugged himself up into a seated position, bent forward with one elbow on his knee while he wiped his face with the towel he had been using as a pillow.

"What?" I asked. "What's wrong? What are you staring at?"

"May I ask you a question?"

I glanced at Lucanus, surprised that Derek would even think to seek permission before blurting his question out. "Of course."

"Do you trust me? That's not the one, not the question, I mean."

I smiled up at him and then rose to my feet. "Let's get out of here, before we melt. Of course I trust you. How could you even need to ask that, after all this time?"

Lucanus stood aside to allow us to pass him, then followed us out into the dry, cool air of the pool-room suite. All three of us plunged quickly into the cold pool, which had the effect of ice on our overheated bodies, and climbed quickly out to towel ourselves down briskly until our skins were glowing with cleanliness and health. By common consent, none of us spoke until all three were dry, and then we made our way to the changing rooms, where we began to dress. Lucanus was the first to speak, uttering his first words since entering the bathhouse, more than an hour earlier.

"I can't believe we're the only ones here."

Derek glanced at him beneath raised brows. "Believe it, they're all stuffing themselves. We'll be lucky if there's anything left for us to eat by the time we get out there." He began moving towards the door.

I felt at peace, not the slightest pang of hunger gnawing at me, and I ignored their efforts to leave, choosing instead to speak with Derek when there were no other ears about to hear me. "You were going to ask me a question, moments ago. But why did you ask me if I trusted you?"

Derek stopped, with his hand on the door, and then turned about and came back, sitting down squarely on the seat across from me. "Because your answer would decide the form of my next question. I knew you trusted me with this secret . . . the secret of your whereabouts and your identity . . . because you know you're safe there. My existence, and my people's, depends on my good faith in that. But I meant, do you trust me beyond that?"

I could see from his face that he was serious, that he expected me to respond, and that he was watching me closely enough to discern the truth were I to attempt to dissemble in any way. I stared back at him, narrowing my eyes and nibbling at the inside of my lower lip. He waited, staring at me as I sought the words I would use. Finally they came to me.

"Yes, Derek, I trust you, far beyond that. I always have, though for no logical reason. I simply have, and that's all there is to it. That's why we came to Ravenglass in the first place. I came in answer to a dream that told me I might trust you. I'll admit openly to you now that there have been times I have wondered at myself, and debated the wisdom and the folly of my own feelings, but I chose to remain here, for all that, with my people, and in trust, and have never regretted it. We have all found you to be a true and loyal friend, these past few months. Luke, here, agrees with me. We spoke of this only a few nights ago. . . . What's the matter? Did I say something to displease you?"

Unaccountably, his face had darkened into something resembling a perplexed scowl. Now he shook his head. "No, but I find that difficult to accept," he growled. "I mean, your loyalty is all to the boy, and I killed his father. How can you trust me that much, knowing what I said to you when you first came here?"

"Why should I mistrust you? Here, I'll trust you even further, with this knowledge. . . ." I paused, watching his face as keenly as he watched mine. I had been keeping back a truth from Derek. I knew him, now, to be a just and honourable man, and until that moment I had been loath to tell him what I knew about his full role in Arthur's fate: how his passing lust had left the boy not merely fatherless, but motherless. Now, I believed, the time had come to tell him. Perhaps it would bind him further to us and the success of our mission.

"Not only did you kill the lad's father, you killed his mother, too."

He jerked back from me as though I had slapped him across the face, his eyes flaring wide with angry disbelief. I held up my hand to quell his response before it could reach his lips. "It's true, Derek!" He checked himself, then sat as though turned to stone, even the motion of his eyes suspended. I continued, keeping my voice level now. "The woman on the beach—the one you were . . . employed with, when I arrived. Do you recall?"

"The red-haired one . . ." He glanced sideways quickly, guiltily, to where Lucanus stood listening, as though expecting Luke to assail him next.

"Aye, the red-haired one," I confirmed quietly. "That was Ygraine of Cornwall, Lot's wife and Uther's mistress . . . Arthur's mother."

Derek of Ravenglass seemed to shrink as though all the air in him had been released, and as he did, I saw credence growing in his eyes. But then he shook his head, a tiny gesture of bewilderment. "But . . . I didn't kill her. She was alive! I threw her aside when you rode up, but she was unhurt."

I nodded, still speaking gently. "That's true, Derek, she was. But then you mounted your war horse, to meet me man to man, and in the mounting, your horse kicked her or trampled her, I know not which. She lay dying when I found her, her skull crushed. And the child, Arthur, was in the birney."

In the silence that followed, Lucanus moved to Derek's side and placed one hand on his shoulder. "That was an act of God, my friend . . . the killing. . . . We both know that. No blame in it accrues to you. You took the woman as a prize of war, against her will—that's normal in such cases. You had no intent to kill her, did you?"

Derek shook his head, his eyes filled with confusion and a suggestion, at least to my eyes, of regret and even pain. "No," he murmured, his big voice now barely audible. "She was ripe and lush. I wanted her, but I had no thought of killing her. . . . And yet I killed the others. Some of them . . . one of them. She fought me, to keep me from the red-haired one. She seized my dagger and came at me. I turned her wrist and thrust, and pulled her onto the point. . . ."

"Self-defence," Lucanus said. I was startled that he should condone such things, even obliquely, but I saw at once that he was being politic. "Ygraine, the red-haired woman, is the important one here. You had no thought of killing her, of bringing about her death in any way, had you?" Derek shook his head, and Luke went on.

"You had no knowledge of her death, did you, until here and now? You were unaware your horse had kicked or trampled her in your scramble to mount up when Cay, here, arrived to challenge you, thinking you to be Uther, am I correct?" Again, a wordless nod was Derek's sole response. "Good, then. No willful involvement in the young woman's death may be attributable to you. But there is more, so you had better let Cay tell it to you, and listen carefully."

Derek collected himself and straightened with a deep sigh, looking me straight in the eye again. "There's more? Then best to give it to me quickly. How much more can there be?"

"Not much, but it is vital, and only we two, Luke and I, have knowledge of it. You will be the third, and last, to know the full connection . . . how the circle closes. Arthur, I swear, will never know, nor any other, from our lips." I stopped, and glanced at Lucanus, suddenly uneasy. "Luke, if you please, make sure we are alone." He moved immediately to verify that no one was within hearing range, and we waited until he returned, nodding to me that all was clear. I turned again to Derek.

"Ygraine was daughter to your strongest ally, the Eirish king, Athol Mac Iain. She was sister to Connor and to Donuil—sister, too, to my own wife, Deirdre. So you see, the boy is Athol's own grandson, heir to Eire's Scots. He also stands heir to Lot's Cornwall, since Lot acknowledged him and never knew the secret of his true paternity. And he is even heir to my domain in Camulod, in that he is my ward—my nephew and my cousin both. All of Ygraine's kin know that she died in Lot and Uther's war, but none of them, not even Donuil, knows how she died or who killed her. So let it be, and let her rest. Ygraine is dead, she has been mourned, and her son is being protected and well cared for.

"There, if you wish to play the cynic, lies the basis of my trust in you, as yours must lie in me. I've come to know you better since then, and I believe you when you say you'd never do such a thing. But had I so wished, I could long since have used my knowledge to your ruin. You must now believe I never will, and have never contemplated doing so." I paused for a moment to give him a chance to absorb this new information. "And so! Are we at peace with this, we three?"

Once again Derek of Ravenglass heaved a great, long sigh, then stood up slowly, his hand outstretched to me. I rose, too, and shook with him, and felt my own throat clench to see the tears that stood in his fierce eyes. He blinked several times to clear them, and then spoke, gulping air to drive his voice, which came out, nonetheless, sounding infirm and shaky.

"So be it," he whispered. "I swear, on all I hold dear, that the boy will never lack a home, or safety and protection, while I breathe."

Lucanus had placed his hand over both of ours, and now he thrust down, breaking our grip in token of a bargain sealed. "So be it," he grunted, laughing. "Now may we go and eat? I, at least, am famished."

On the third day after that, we awoke before dawn to find the snow holding mastery over our new domain, drifting silently down in the stillness of the dark to lay a mantle of utter quiet upon everything. I had awaited its arrival with trepidation: we all had. Our memories of the recent evil winter were yet undimmed, and so we had prepared ourselves to face all manner of hardships here, so high in the hills. We bought up grain from Derek's people and laid in great stores of food and fuel and fodder for our beasts, all of which were safely housed beneath strong roofs. But that storm was brief, and after it had passed the air grew warm again, and the snow melted, so that we came to midwinter and a new year before we saw another snowfall. This time, however, the snow remained when the storm had passed and the air grew colder, but not lethally so.

The children had a wonderland in which to play, and the boys used the steeply sloping, cobbled surface of the hillside road as a chute. They spent entire days, once Dedalus and Rufio had shown them what to do, hauling heavy, metal shields high up towards the pass above the fort, then sliding down, perched on these precarious chariots, to where a high bank of snow, thrown up by some of the men for that purpose, checked their dangerously swift descent. Turga had been scandalized when she learned what the two men had shown the boys, and Rufio, who spent much time with her, earned the rough edge of her tongue to such an extent that he maintained a wary distance from her for days afterward.

I remember quite clearly that I was of Turga's opinion for a while, since my first sight of the activity had revealed Arthur himself, whirling like a top, his hair flying as he clung fiercely to the edging of a circular, metal-bossed shield within the curve of which he sat cross-legged. His teeth were bared in what I took to be a fearful grimace while the thing spun downward, beyond control, at a speed far greater than any horse could run. As I watched in horrified disbelief, my mouth open in a strangled shout, the thing mounted the snow piled on one side of the narrow road, shot down again and catapulted across to the opposite edge of the road, flying into the air and sending the boy, shrieking, into a snowbank. I began to run towards him, calling for help, but he leaped to his feet and began jumping up and down in glee, screaming to Gwin, Ghilly and Bedwyr, who were still high up at the top of the descent, staring down at him.

Bedwyr, whom I now saw to be holding a rectangular, Roman-style shield, immediately launched himself forward, throwing himself belly down along the thing, and shot down the incline. Feeling distinctly foolish at my own panic, I stopped running and watched the way the boy was controlling his descent, guiding the flying shield with his hands on the two leading corners and throwing his weight from side to side to steer himself at incredible speed around the bends in the road. With a clattering roar, he swept past the point where Arthur had left the road, and no sooner was he gone than Arthur was in pursuit of him, leaping into his circular chariot as soon as its surface touched the snow-packed cobblestones.

A glance upward and to my left showed me Gwin and Ghilly, following both of them at breakneck speed. But where they and Bedwyr rode rectangular shields, and could control them to a degree, Arthur's circular conveyance permitted no such mastery. I watched young Gwin approach rapidly and hurtle by until he was lost to sight, and then, shaking my head, I made my way down the bank in the direction in which they had disappeared, hearing the delight and excitement in their voices as I approached. They were already struggling back up the roadway they had just descended, but now Bedwyr had the circular shield and Arthur the heavy, rectangular scutum. They saw me and called out greetings, and I went down to where they had stopped in the roadway to wait for me.

Their faces were bright red and their eyes sparkling but I had no thought of their being cold. They were obviously much warmer than I was, and I fancied I could even see steam rising from their skins and from their clothing. I greeted them cordially, masking my concern, then asked them where they had found the shields. At the sound of my question the faces of the three younger boys fell, but Arthur answered instantly.

"From Ded and Rufio. They showed us how to use them. The shields are surplus, Ded said. They belong to no one."

I knew the boy had beaten me. I could not forbid them to use the shields now, for to do so would amount to a public chastisement of Dedalus and Rufio, and it was clear to me the young scamp knew it. I nodded towards the circular one, which rested now against Bedwyr's leg. "That one's not Roman, where did it come from?"

"It's Erse," young Gwin answered. "It's one of the ones taken from the Sons of Condran."

"Ah, I see. You trust it, then?" I saw from their blank expressions that they didn't understand my weak attempt at humour. I looked at Arthur. "You rode it down." My glance switched to Bedwyr. "But you're carrying it up, why?"

"It's my turn!" He was adamant, and I was left in no doubt that possession of the round shield was a privilege.

"Your turn? You mean you prefer an Erse shield to a Roman scutum?"

Arthur grinned at me, his eyes dancing. "For this, yes. It's much more fun, far more thrilling. Would you like to try it, Cay? Ded's really good on it."

I had a sudden vision of myself shooting down that snowy road, clutching the spinning thing and spewing vomit, for I recalled that, as a boy of Arthur's years, I had been incapable of swinging on a rope the way the other boys my age had loved to. An old willow tree, hanging above the deep hole in which we swam, had been the anchor for a long, thick, heavy, knotted rope on which all of my friends had soared to let go and plummet to the water beneath. I had never used it after my first few attempts. On horseback, I had been supreme, because I had control, anchored by the grip of my legs; once beyond that control, however, the swooping thrill of undirected motion nauseated me immediately and violently. Just recalling it, my stomach heaved. I grimaced and shook my head.

"No, I think not. I doubt my stomach could handle it. Beside, it looks too dangerous for me." I could not resist one last, pusillanimous remonstration, however, looking at each of them briefly in turn. "But be careful. If you should hit a rock, moving so fast, you could injure yourself badly."

"No." Bedwyr was grinning now. "You can throw yourself off the shield, anytime. Besides, there are no big rocks close to the road—they've all been cleared."

I surrendered and left them to their games.

Less than a month after that, the thaw set in as spring made its arrangements to arrive early that year.

Short and mild as the winter had been, it had nonetheless deprived us of all contact with Derek and his people since the first snowfall, so that by the time the new grasses began to sprout, we were sick and tired of the sight of our own faces. My announcement that we would all ride together, eighteen of us, into Ravenglass, was therefore received with general delight.

On the eve of our departure, in the short evening just before the sun set, I called all our group together before the evening meal and reminded them yet again of the necessity of keeping up our pretenses on arriving in Ravenglass the following day: I must continue to be merely Cay, to all of them, and Hector must be accorded the deference that once had been shown to me, as Caius Merlyn. The warning was unnecessary by that time, I hoped, but well worth reiterating, since our ongoing safety depended heavily upon the conviction of others that Merlyn of Camulod had sailed away the year before, with Connor Mac Athol and the Pendragon brat.

When the meeting had broken up among a chorus of good wishes for a restful night and some excited speculation about the following day's journey, I set out alone to walk back to my quarters. I had barely gone ten paces however, when I found myself flanked by Donuil and Shelagh, each of whom linked an arm through one of mine, so that we arrived outside my door mere moments later as a triple entity joined at the elbows—an unholy Trinity, according to my heathen Erse friends, who had picked up enough of the elements of Christianity to be embarrassing when they wished to be.

I stepped inside and busied myself at the fire-pot, blowing the smouldering embers to life and lighting a taper with which to carry flame to the lamps, for though it was yet but early evening outside, the shadows were far-stretched and it was already almost dark inside the buildings. As I bent to the lamp, holding the flaming taper to the wick, I saw that Shelagh had stopped on the threshold, just inside the door, and was looking about her with an air of exaggerated curiosity.

My living space was more than adequate for me it. It had originally been the quarters of the centurion who ruled the barracks block, but it was enlarged at the time of the refurbishment of the building since, instead of eighty to a hundred legionaries, the block was now required to accommodate fewer than ten people, some of whom lived as couples. The actual living space seemed smaller than in fact it was, because much of the room was occupied by packing crates, containing some of the possessions I had brought with me from Camulod. The majority were in storage in the Horrea, the building that contained the granary and storehouses, warm and secure beneath a strong roof. Only the choicest items were in my personal possession, including, of course, the case that held Excalibur and the weapons I had chosen to bring with me from Publius Varrus's Armoury. These I could not have suffered to be out of my personal domain. Nor could I have slept secure without knowing that my greatest treasures, the books of Camulod, were safely stowed beside me, beneath my hand and eye. I also had the two heavy, iron-bound cases that had belonged to Lot's Egyptian warlocks, Caspar and Memnon, of evil memory. These I kept with me not for any love of their contents but simply because they were too dangerous to be left lying unprotected where people might be tempted, through simple curiosity if nothing else, to open them.

Shelagh was still hovering just inside the door. "Well?" I asked. "Are you not going to enter? Is my house to be feared?"

"No, not feared, but perhaps fretted over. You lack your servant very visibly, Cay."

Donuil, who had been my servant and my adjutant until I refused his services upon our arrival here in the north-west, began to flush and moved to stand up from the seat into which he had subsided on entering. I waved him back into his seat, keeping my eyes on his wife and smiling because I knew she had a point she wished to make.

"Lack my servant? You mean my adjutant, I presume? Not so, then. I have no need of servants here and am more than capable of looking after my own needs."

She threw me a look of bright-eyed scorn, and her Erse temperament flashed at me. "Oh, I don't doubt your capabilities, Caius Merlyn. It's your concentration that I worry about . . . that, and your sense of priorities."

I frowned at her through a grin, mocking her fierceness. "What do you mean, woman? Am I going to have to warn you again that your shrewish tongue is for your husband and that I need never hear it? What is wrong with my sense of priorities?"

She flicked her eyes around the room again, a lightning-quick glance into which she managed to compress a world of disparagement. "Exactly the same thing that is wrong with every other man's priorities: they are male priorities."

I raised my hands and brought them together, applauding slowly, knowing it would exasperate her into laughter. She glared at me with narrowed eyes for several long moments, but then she stepped forward into the room and stooped to run her finger along the top of my main table. A long, glowing line appeared where she had stroked, gleaming richly through the dust.

"There you are, look at that! Have you ever seen the like of that before, in the quarters of Commander Caius Britannicus?"

"No, Shelagh, I have not. But there are no military commanders here. These are the quarters of plain Master Cay, a landless farmer, currently inhabiting an ancient and abandoned Roman fort. Who is this Commander Caius Britannicus?"

"Someone I used to know." She stroked her fingers again through the dust that blanketed the highly polished surface of the table. "But I must say the landless farmer Cay owns some very fine furnishings." She looked about her again, sighing. "You need help, Cay, in your simple day-to-day living, as do most of us here in this little, bustling and much-demanding place we have built for ourselves. You are far from unique. But, since you refuse to accept assistance from either myself or Donuil, or from any of the others, I have a suggestion to make."

I placed the lamp down on the tabletop with exaggerated care and bowed to her, waving my open hand in the direction of an empty chair. "Please, Shelagh, sit down. You'll find you can speak just as clearly from a seat as you can when you are standing, and you will find that I listen with more care when I attend a seated speaker."

She looked at me sidewise, but moved without further protest to sit beside her husband, who sat silent, smiling gently at me. When she was settled, I leaned back in my chair with a smile of my own.

"So, you were saying I need help, as do some others, and you have some suggestions. I would like to hear them."

"Good. Our party needs new blood and new incentives. We are eighteen, here in our high-perched fort: four children, three wedded couples, one unmarried woman and seven single men—you, Lucanus, Hector, Dedalus, Rufio, Jonathan and Mark. Ten men to four women—those proportions are unhealthy. Even removing Rufio, who spends enough time with Turga to be considered wedded, that still leaves six men with requirements that demand attention."

I sat smiling at her. "So, what are you suggesting, Shelagh? That we six who remain should all rush out and find wives for ourselves?"

"Hmm. It would not be a bad idea, were it achievable. But no, that is not what I am suggesting. My suggestion is that when we travel into Ravenglass tomorrow, we make an effort to increase our numbers by judicious recruitment—" She held up one hand to cut me off before I could begin to reply. "I know we decided we've no need of anyone other than ourselves, and that we need to keep our heads low, Cay, but think of this: could there be any better way of hiding among these folk than hiding among these folk?"

I sat staring at her, hearing what she had said but failing to understand it. Finally I squinted at her, to show my incomprehension.

"What?"

"Think, Cay! We are alongside them, separate now, not among them, and they're not among us. I'm saying let's bring some of them up here, men and women, to live and work with us. Derek talks about his town being overcrowded, and we have just discovered, during a mild winter, that we are few and would be glad of others to spend time with us in the short days and the long, dark nights. Here is opportunity to benefit everyone. We could ask Derek to send some of his people up here to live with us, and we could have the right to pick those who would come."

"Hmm." I could see the rightness of what she was saying, and I glanced at Donuil. "It sounds reasonable, put like that. What think you, Donuil?"

Donuil grinned and stretched, yawning elaborately. "I think I'm hungry and I'm glad it's dinner time. I also think my wife is a very clever woman and her suggestion has great merit and I know I couldn't have come up with it."

"Hmm." I looked back at Shelagh, who sat watching me and nodded to her. "I agree with Donuil. I'll talk to Derek when we get to Ravenglass. Have you thought about how many of his people we could use?"

"I have. We need craftsmen, and skilled women. I think couples should be counted as one, provided both halves have usable skills. Then we'll need sawyers and more tanners, and we could use a cooper. We are eighteen, but that is really only fourteen, since four are children. We could be fifty easily. We have no lack of space and accommodation, and there are no problems with feed or water or hunting."

"And you feel sure about being able to select only the kind of people we would require, according to our own criteria?"

"Oh, aye. This place has much to recommend it to folk who live in crowded towns . . . especially in spring, summer and autumn. I think we'll have no shortage of volunteers, and strong young men."

"And strong young women, too, eh?"

She looked at me, a look of wide-eyed innocence. "Of course, strong young women. We've lots of work here for strong young backs. And our own young men, like Jonathan and Mark, need to be challenged."

"Challenged. Aye." I sighed, aware that I'd been bested. "Very well, Shelagh. So be it. But we'd best speak to Hector tonight about it, and not leave it till the morning. He has the right to know this information before anyone else. Now, let's go to dinner. He'll be there already."

There was a festive air about our group as it wound its way along the road to Ravenglass the following day. Some of us—myself, Dedalus, Donuil, Shelagh and Rufio—were mounted singly, the boys rode on their matched, piebald ponies, and the other nine occupied our little train of four horse-drawn wagons, empty on the way down but intended to be laden for our return. The day had dawned bright and sunny, warm with more than a mere intimation of the spring to come, so that our sense of well-being expanded remarkably as we came down from the heights, off the flanks of the hills and into the fertile vale of the Esk amid welling birdsong that seemed to hang over the valley like a fluttering fabric.

I rode to the head of the column and then drew my horse aside to watch the remainder of our group as they passed, shaking my head in discouragement to several who would have stopped to talk with me and waving them on in the understanding that I wished to be alone for a spell. The boys, on their ponies, were on the move constantly, ranging far along the road to the west ahead of the slower, more sedate adult party, but returning continually to check our progress, warned as they had been not to roam too far ahead.

As we emerged from the forest into cultivated fields, the skies grew wide above our heads and the trees fell back and away behind us, so that the spectrum of colours surrounding us changed from the deep greens and tranquil browns of the mossy, silent, light-dappled oak forest to the vibrant new green shoots of young, healthy crops against bright, black earth. The branches of the willow trees along the river's edge to the right of us were limned with the yellowish hint of bursting buds, teasing the eye with the faintest, wordlessly suggested promise of new leaves. And then, as we drew closer to the town, we began to encounter people, in ones and twos, most of them working in the fields that bordered the road. Many waved a greeting on seeing us, and occasionally one would approach us to talk, as hungry as we were ourselves for the sight of familiar but long-unseen faces and agog with curiosity about our winter up on the hills.

Derek, by that form of magical foreknowledge that always seems to accompany arrivals such as ours, came out to meet us before we had even entered the town about the fort. He was in fine fettle that day, boisterous and loud, and he made us noisily welcome, sending some of his people running ahead again to prepare quarters for all of us within the fort. Donuil and Shelagh and Hector and I would stay with Derek, in his own house. The others would be spread among the other buildings. Arthur and the other three boys, along with Turga, their custodian and self-appointed supervisor, would stay with a family who had ten children, among whom four extra faces would be barely noticeable. Dedalus, Rufio and the others would fend for themselves. Before we broke up to go our separate ways, however, Derek insisted on escorting us personally to see to the arrangements for lodging our horses and storing our wagons with his own horsekeeper, the taciturn little man called Ulf.

Ulf's reaction to seeing our big, southern mounts again was as truculent as it had been the very first time. His own beasts were all considerably smaller than ours, and he had dragged our horses away to the back of his enclosures, where they would not be seen by anyone who did not already know them to be there. I would have sworn that first day that he was angry and disgusted with having to accept our horses, but as long as they remained in his care, all of them, including my Germanicus, the biggest of them all, shone like burnished things, their coats groomed to perfection.

I greeted Ulf affectionately, calling him by name, and smiled as he huffed and grunted in disgust, refusing even to acknowledge my presence as he took Germanicus's reins from my hand. Only with the four boys was he less than surly, allowing them to lead their own ponies by their halters as they walked behind him to the rear picket lines where he had decided our horses would be kept.

Late that evening, tired and feeling lazy after a pleasant hour spent listening to the songs of an exceptionally gifted visiting Druid—the man's talent was superb, surpassing excellence—I passed an open doorway and saw Shelagh sitting inside with Donuil and Derek around a glowing brazier. I stopped in the doorway and leaned inside to wish them all a good night's rest, and from the looks on all their faces, I knew they had been discussing me when I chanced by. I said nothing, however, and left immediately, carrying away with me memories of the speculative look in Shelagh's eyes when she turned to me, and the way the fabric of her dress clung to her breasts. I slept heavily that night and did not dream.

VIII

CONNOR'S GALLEYS CAME in with the dawn and were already moored to the wharf by the time I arrived, wiping the last vestiges of sleep from my eyes as I emerged onto the waterfront through the western gate. His arrival, like ours, corresponded with the end of wintry weather and a greater freedom to travel. Though his arrival was thus not entirely surprising, it provided, nevertheless, an unlooked-for and welcome addition to our celebrations.

"Yellow Head!"

I squinted upwards to where he swung through the air in his unique way of disembarking, his foot anchored in a loop slung from the lading hoist, his wooden leg pointing directly towards me, one hand clinging to the rope as his men lowered him swiftly to the timbered wharf. I reached him as he alit, swaying slightly, gauging his balance before releasing his firm grip on the taut rope, and we threw our arms about each other. He thrust me away and held me at arm's length, then, his hands gripping my upper arms as his eyes swept me from head to foot. I watched his face tighten in mock-horror as he allowed himself to examine my face and hair.

"Yellow Head! You're bearded like a Celt! And what happened to your hair? I'm going to have to call you Brownhair, now. Have you been ill?" He was laughing as he spoke, however, and I knew that he was unsurprised to see the changes in me. Before I could answer him he pivoted on his false leg, using his arm about my shoulders to turn me with him, and pointed up towards the stern deck of his galley. "Look you, up there! I bring you guests."

I was completely astonished to see both Ambrose and Ludmilla looking down at me and waving, their faces wreathed in smiles, and I felt my heart leap with pleasure as I waved back, calling a wordless welcome up to them. They moved back from my sight and I knew they would appear in moments on the gangplank, so I swung back to Connor.

"What is Ambrose doing here? How did he manage to get away from Camulod?"

Connor laughed and made an elaborate display of cautioning me, finger to his lips. "Shh! There is no Ambrose here, Brownhair. The man you waved to is Merlyn Britannicus, Commander of the Military Forces of Camulod. Don't you know anything? He has come here to visit with King Derek of Ravenglass. They are allies of old, you know."

I could only shake my head, accepting Connor's foolery "Aye, I know. I've heard tell of their great comradeship from Derek himself. And I can't wait to meet this Merlyn Britannicus. But is it true that he comes all the way here in person solely to greet an old friend?"

"Why not?" Connor was still grinning, but his eyes were moving constantly, checking the activity aboard his galley, which was disgorging nets filled with cargo. "When Ambrose received and read your last letter—the one in which you outlined your plans to drop from sight, he approved completely. So excited was he by the thought of what you proposed to do, as a matter of fact, that he read your letter to me—a task not to be lightly undertaken, as my father would say. Your brother has but little skill with the Erse tongue. We had great fun, though, he and I, guessing and translating from the Latin, which is gibberish to my ears, into the Erse, which is gibberish to his. Thank the gods we can both speak the coastal tongue. Anyway, we did it, and we discussed the entire matter in great detail, agreeing that it made a certitude of the boy's safety.

"A short time after that, I left Camulod again and returned to spend what I thought might be the last winter any of us spends beneath my father's roof in Eire. While I was travelling, it occurred to me that if you were successful in your deception, disappearing completely without going away, then Ambrose himself might be able to further and to strengthen your designs by making an appearance here, as you yourself. No one has ever seen him in this part of the world, or even knows of his existence, but everyone saw you and your yellow head, before you 'sailed away' with the boy, aboard my galley. Now they'll see you again, in Ambrose. The gods know the two of you are as alike as two peas in a pod! They'll see Merlyn Britannicus arrive this morning, and they'll see him leave again within ten days, once more aboard my galley. None will doubt that, but what is even more, much more important, is that no one here, among Derek's people, will ever again think to look at you and see Merlyn Britannicus . . . unless you choose to reveal yourself again at some future date. Here comes your brother now."

I reached the bottom of the gangplank before Ambrose and Ludmilla had negotiated its springy length, and I embraced both of them, suddenly overwhelmed by emotions that left me incapable of speech. Ludmilla was as beautiful as ever, although plumper, more matronly than I had ever seen her; she asked immediately about Shelagh, and then about Lucanus, Turga and the four boys. I answered her as well as I could, but having taken in her appearance of happy prosperity and contentment, I was now preoccupied in examining my brother. He looked magnificent—an obvious leader in every aspect and in every sense of the word—and I wondered what he was thinking about me, since I knew he was scrutinizing me every bit as closely. The crowds thronging the dockside swirled about us in every direction and we stood there, oblivious to them, the three of us content for the moment to share our own company in friendly, intimate, familial silence.

Still smiling, but assuming a more critical demeanour, Ambrose passed judgment at last on my outward appearance.

"The brown hair is . . . nondescript, Brother. I preferred it when you looked much more like me."

"Hah!" I grinned at him and gripped his wife more tightly around her supple waist. "That's merely your opinion, Yellow Head, born of a lifetime of narcissism. Ask a woman who has had a surfeit of blond beauty how she feels about brown-haired and comely men, and I'll warrant you'll receive another answer. Is that not so, Ludmilla?"

She leaned away from me sideways, smiling, and peered back at me down the length of her nose. "We-ell, Caius. I would have to say, speaking advisedly and as your sister in marriage, that had you looked this different, this unlike yourself, when you were younger, I might have taken more notice of you. . . . But then again, I might not. As a brother, however, I will confess that you are unequalled and quite surpassing any other such in all your attributes."

I blinked at her, wide-eyed and solemn, schooling my features into blankness before turning back to my brother. "Did your wife say what I think she said, that I am unique?"

"She may have, Brother, since you are the only brother that she has. I don't know. Then again, I seldom do. Being married to a goddess is a taxing task for ordinary mortals. It places demands upon men they are seldom fit to meet. Like comprehension of their spouses' wondrous wondrousness . . . things like that . . ."

"Yes . . ." I reached out to intercept Ludmilla's fist before she could injure it against his breastplate. "But I think we had best bestir ourselves and go and find the others. Shelagh will be ecstatic to see the two of you. We had no idea you would be coming—" I broke off, my eyes moving from one of them to the other. "Why have you come? Is all well in Camulod?"

Ambrose cut me off again with a smile. "Hush, Cay, think you we would be here if anything were wrong? We came because we could, and for that reason alone. Everything is well, and better than well, at home. We had a rich and bountiful harvest followed by a short, mild winter, and my wife and I have not travelled together beyond Camulod since we were wed. Connor was coming here and had the space, and the time, to bring us with him, and I had messages for you and for Lucanus. So, we came. We will remain until Connor returns to collect us again, which will be, he estimates, within two weeks. Can you bear our company till then?"

"Aye, gladly, and for much longer." I turned to look again at Connor.

"But only two weeks, you say? That is not much time, for a double crossing."

He shrugged, frowning. "Why not? It's more than enough. . . . Particularly since we'll be returning empty."

"Empty? From Eire?"

"Eire? No, we're not going to Eire. I told you, we wintered there, then returned to our holdings near Camulod. Now I am bound for Alba, for our new holdings in the islands of the north-west, with twelve galleys full of Liam Twistback's cattle." He saw my look and laughed, waving towards the sea. "They're out there, safe out of sight where I left them, behind the island! No point in bringing them inshore to cause confusion, was there? Derek would have had an apoplexy to see them coming around the bank, thinking the Condranson fleet about his ears again. Logan and Feargus are riding with them, playing the sheep-herders to both flock and fleet. I must have speech with Derek—the work of an hour or so—and then I'm away again, before the tide turns. Everything I have to off load here will be on the wharf within the half hour."

He glanced up towards his vessel again, checking the level of activity, and then reached out to shake with Ambrose.

"Farewell, Ambrose, and may the gods smile pityingly on you, stuck here as you'll be with these savages until I can return." He bowed over Ludmilla's hand. "My lady Ludmilla, I hope you will pass on my best wishes to my good-sister Shelagh, and I'll see you again soon."

He turned and clapped me a mighty blow on the upper arm with his open hand and then swept me into his embrace before stepping back to look at me with a grin.

"Look after these fine folk, Cay Brownhair, and take care they meet no ill, lest you bring the wrath of Camulod about your colourless head."

Then he was gone, leaving us alone on the wharf, listening to the receding thump of his wooden leg.

Knowing that Connor's men would bring their belongings after us, I led my guests towards the gate in the wall and beyond, into the fort and towards our temporary quarters. There, a squeal of delight from Shelagh told us we had finally been seen. From that moment on, everything degenerated into a chaos that endured through Connor's departure on the evening tide and then on into dinner. I had to resign myself to waiting until all the excitement had died down before I heard a single word of news from the south. Even then, I found I had to delve deeply for it, winkling each separate piece of information individually from my brother, who believed, and rightly so as I felt in the end, that there was nothing of real significance in any of it.

By the time we did manage to achieve sufficient privacy to speak with any kind of leisure about events in Camulod, it had grown late, and most of the household had retired. Lucanus had disappeared even before the evening meal, clutching the precious scrolls that Ambrose had brought for him, among them the one particular text that might shed light upon my condition. I was consciously willing myself not to dwell on that. Shelagh and the other women had gone off somewhere with Derek's chief wife, Jessica, after dinner, and had not returned. We men who remained—some score of us—had been left alone in one of Derek's private rooms, well-lit with lamps, tapers and tallow wicks and brightened and warmed in addition by fires in great, open braziers in chimneyed firepits against the walls.

Now the night had advanced, the general talk had been exhausted, most of the others had gone off to bed—some on their own feet, others assisted by friends—and Ambrose and I were the only two left awake, lounging on Roman couches before the one fire that still burned brightly. We were speaking in Latin, the tongue in which we both were most at ease: The talk earlier had all been in the coastal tongue, a language I thought of as being the Britannic vulgate, a seething broth of varying Celtic dialects and tribal intonations that came close, from time to time, to being indecipherable. The local variants, in particular, had left my brother gaping in bewilderment on several occasions. Derek's people had a way of chewing vowel sounds that was unique in my experience. One of the local men had pronounced, on his departure, that he was "g'yaun 'ame." The expression on my brother's face on hearing that phrase had made me laugh aloud, to my own embarrassment when the speaker turned to gaze at me in curiosity, wishing to share the jest.

Behind me, I knew, young Arthur had slipped in a short time earlier to sit quietly against the far wall, evidently hoping to remain unnoticed. He was sleeping in my chamber this night, permitted, as a special privilege, to remain here in Derek's house with the adults on the first evening of his aunt and uncle's visit. I knew he had been abed for more than four hours already: his excitement had evidently prevented him from sleeping with his usual soundness. He had clung like a shadow to his Uncle Ambrose since the moment that morning when his eyes had first blazed with delight at the unexpected apparition of his hero. Remembering my own boyhood, the excitement of returning expeditions and the stories that were told, I decided not to send him away again, but now motioned him forward instead, waving him into a chair close by the fire. As the boy passed in front of him, smiling shyly, Ambrose reached out and grasped him gently by the upper arm, pulling him close and holding him in the crook of one elbow while pretending to pummel his ribs with his other hand before releasing him to pass on, reluctantly, to the seat I had indicated. Then, once the boy was settled, Ambrose began to answer my questions about Camulod.

Life in the Colony continued to progress smoothly, he told us, existence unfolding from day to day in growing peace and prosperity. As a final benison upon what had been a fruitful year in every sense, including the birth of large numbers of babies to our Colonists, the harvest had been huge the previous year, greater even than the three preceding years, each of which had, in turn, surpassed the years preceding it, so that the Colony's granaries, including six large new ones built to hold the year's surplus, were now filled to overflowing. No raids had occurred, even in the Colony's outlying areas, since our departure. I was glad to hear that, since that extended the period of lasting peace from interference to six years. It was always tempting at such times to believe that peace would be everlasting, but that was a foolish presumption. It was miraculous, I knew, that we had managed to avoid molestation in Camulod for as long as we had. True, the presence of our armed strength—and the awareness of it in the eyes of potential enemies—gave us an advantage, since only a heavily armed force would be able to dismiss the prohibitive cost of meddling with our Colony. But there were such forces out there, and their numbers were increasing as strong men—ambitious, successful warlords—grasped at power and gathered loyal men around them.

As for matters originating beyond Camulod, Ambrose said, inactivity and lack of urgency were the prevailing trends in all endeavours. There had been nothing of moment out of the south-west, he told me, with obvious satisfaction, and all of Cornwall lay silent and apparently at peace, despite Peter Ironhair's reputed presence there. From that quarter, he told me, silence was the greatest gift that could be hoped and prayed for. In Cambria, on the other hand, all seemed to be progressing well. Dergyll ap Gryffyd had been made king there, his rule ratified and consolidated now, and he was busily restoring order and prosperity to his Pendragon people. Pendragon longbows were being made again, in greater numbers than ever before, and the territories to the north and west of Camulod were full of groups of young Pendragon, learning the art of bowmanship.

He had heard nothing, either, from Vortigern's country to the far north-east, and so he expected that nothing there had changed. Vortigern, despite his ever-increasing problems with the Outlanders he had brought in years before to help him protect his people, must still be in control there, Ambrose believed, or we would have heard something to the contrary, and that, in turn, meant that Hengist the Dane was yet hale enough to dominate his fractious son Horsa.

Young Arthur sat quietly, listening to what was being said, his narrowed, tightly focused eyes indicating that his interest in what he was hearing was absolute. I noticed his head come up at the mention of Vortigern's name, and I saw plainly, from the look in his eyes, that he wished to speak, although I knew he would never have dreamed of interrupting us.

"What is it, Arthur? You look as though you have something you wish to say."

The boy stiffened and flushed with embarrassment at being noticed, and he began to shake his head, almost squirming in his sudden discomfort and plainly wishing the floor would open and swallow him. Watching him, I divined the source of his discomfiture immediately, and I found myself biting my lip distractedly, somewhat guiltily aware that the lessons I had been teaching him all winter had sunk home too well.

Ever since he and his companions had boisterously broken in on me on one occasion several months before, interrupting me without warning and distracting me greatly while I was in conference with Derek and his advisers on the terms and conditions that would apply to our tendancy of Derek's lands at Mediobogdum, I had taken considerable pains to convince the lad of the need for decorum in his behaviour around grown-ups. I was furious at the outset, and Arthur was made well aware that he had behaved badly that day, and that I had been much inconvenienced and put out of countenance by his thoughtlessness and irresponsibility.

It occurred to me now, however, upon seeing his reaction to my casual comment, that what I had viewed with so much displeasure had been no more than boyish high spirits finding their own outlet as they always have and always will. I had been too hard on the lad, to such an extent, indeed, that he squirmed now upon merely being addressed.

Ambrose looked, in some astonishment, from Arthur's face to mine, raising his eyebrow as if to ask me what in God's name was going on. Stricken by momentary cowardice, I merely shrugged. Ambrose looked back at the boy, whose head was hanging.

"Arthur? What's wrong with you? Do you have to pee?"

The boy looked up, his face flushed, and met Ambrose's gaze. "No, Uncle Ambrose."

"Then what's wrong with you? Didn't you hear what your Uncle Cay asked you?"

"Yes . . . He asked if I had something I wished to say."

"And? Do you?" Arthur shook his head, very slightly, and not at all convincingly. "What's that? You have nothing to say?"

"No, Uncle."

"Well, there's a novelty! You have been sitting there listening to us for what, an hour? And you have nothing to say, no questions to ask, no comments to make? Are you Arthur Pendragon? Don't sit there staring at me, lad! I asked you a question. I thought you were my nephew, but now there seems to be some doubt. Are you Arthur Pendragon?"

The suggestion of a smile came and went from the boy's mouth. "Yes, Uncle Ambrose, I am."

"You are, by God! I thought you were. Then what's wrong with you? Why have you no questions in your head, for the first time ever since you learned to say a word? Have you been stricken mute? Have ants devoured your brain? Speak to me, boy! Tell me you are still alive, unchanged, unchallenged and unchained!"

Now young Arthur was smiling widely, his eyes dancing at his uncle's wit and ebullience, but he ducked his head again and deferred to me. "Uncle Cay has told me that young boys' opinions have no place in men's discussions."

"No, Arthur, that is not true—" I broke off, seeing the shocked surprise and disbelief in his startled eyes. I rose and moved to where he sat, laying my hand firmly on his shoulder as I sat down beside him. "Your Uncle Ambrose has no idea what we are talking about here, but you and I do, only too well." I then told Ambrose the story of Arthur and his friends interrupting my session with Derek and his counsellors and the lesson I had tried to teach.

I straightened up and sighed, looking only at Arthur, who gazed back, steadfastly now, into my eyes.

"I set out to teach you a lesson: that boys' voices have no place in men's affairs when and if their contributions are mere boyish noises and ill manners. I can see that you have learned that. But I also see now that you may have learned it too well, and incompletely. Can you see why speaking out tonight would be a different matter, and not an offence to your uncle and me? Think, please, as well as I know you are capable of thinking, about what I have just said." Even as I was saying the words I saw his brow clear and he nodded, slowly. "Aha. You see it now, the difference?"

Again he nodded. "Yes, I think so."

"Good. What is it?"

"Boys' voices have no place in men's affairs when and if their contributions are mere loud noises and ill manners. . . ." He arched his eyebrows the way he did in class, before he would articulate some thought that had occurred to him. "If that is true, it follows logically, therefore, that boys' voices may have some place in those affairs if they are serious and well informed." His eyes flicked from me to my brother and back to me. "Is that not so?"

"Aye, it is." I could smile again now, and I laid my hand on his head. "Serious is the key word, meaning sober and attentive and respectful. But a serious boy need not necessarily be well informed. Well intentioned might be a better way of putting it, for well-intentioned questions, well presented at the proper time, can lead to his becoming well informed. . . . Now, if you can remember what you wanted to contribute to this discussion, ask away."

The boy went very still, his gaze sharpening and his brows creasing very slightly as he marshalled his thoughts. Then he rocked from side to side, placing his hands palms down on his seat and anchoring them with his thighs, after which he sat hunched forward, gazing into the middle distance. I looked across his head to where Ambrose sat watching. Our eyes met, and Ambrose raised his eyebrows in a gesture of tolerant amusement, but our boy had now finished his deliberations.

"Not so much a question as a wondering," Arthur said. "I was wondering why it is that every great leader seems to carry the seeds of his own defeat with him, and why some of them manage to avoid having those seeds germinate, while others fail and perish because of them."

It was my turn now to be astonished. From time to time this boy, who lived and functioned as a normal, wild and thoughtless boy from day to day, was capable of coming up with the most astoundingly complex thoughts, observations and conclusions.

"Were we discussing that?"

"No, but you were talking of Vortigern."

"Yes, and where is the relevance to our discussion in your question?"

My tolerant question of the boy drew a disparaging glance and a withering response from the seldom-seen but very impressive man who dwelt inside him. "Isn't that obvious? Vortigern sowed the seeds of his own downfall when he imported Hengist's Danes to stand with him against the other invaders. My great-grandfather, Publius Varrus, wrote about it in his books, and so did Uncle Picus, and so have you, in your writings. In his hope of keeping the foxes away from his ducks, he brought a wolf into his house to live with him. He has committed the same basic error that the Romans did, when they took subject races and trained them in their own way of fighting, teaching them to overthrow the Empire. Alexander the Great, on the other hand, was far more fortunate. His weakness went unperceived."

"Alexander of Macedon?" Ambrose was grinning from ear to ear. "What was his weakness? He conquered the world, so it could not have been an overwhelming one."

"On the contrary, Uncle Ambrose, it could have been—should have been—a fatal one."

My brother frowned as though insulted, then looked at me. I kept my face blank, feeling no need to admit that my ignorance was as great as his. Arthur, in the meantime, was looking from one to the other of us, and I would have sworn he was unaware that neither of us knew what he was talking about. Finally, Ambrose bowed to the inevitable.

"Well, then, I admit you have me. What weakness have you identified in Alexander of Macedon—apart from his cavalry?" He was being facetious, of course, but the boy shook his head.

"No. That was it."

"What are you saying?" Ambrose's expression was ludicrous. "That it was a weakness? His cavalry?"

"No, his Companions."

"His—?" Ambrose threw up his arms in exasperation and looked to me for support. For my part, feeling as bewildered as he was, I schooled my features into calmness and cleared my throat before saying anything else. Arthur looked at me, waiting to hear what I would say.

"Arthur . . . The Companions . . . there are some who would say . . ." I was beginning to feel ridiculous, and I cleared my throat ferociously and began again. "Look, boy, I have no wish to argue with you, but the Companions are generally accepted, by those who know anything about them, as the greatest fighting force of the Ancient World. They were hand-chosen by their king, Philip of Macedon, and they trained with him and rode to battle with him at their own expense, providing all their own horses, armour, weaponry and equipment. Each was an individual champion, a warrior of renown and unimaginable value and when King Philip died, a victim of assassination, they transferred their entire allegiance to his son, the young Alexander, and conquered the world under his leadership, long before Rome had begun to gain any power of her own. How could they be defined, by you or anyone, as a weakness?"

Arthur grimaced. "Only in error. You are correct, Uncle. I've made the same mistake I made before: inexactitude. But, if I may say it without being impertinent, so have you and Uncle Ambrose. What I said at first was that every great leader seems to carry the seeds of his own defeat with him. It is the idea of the seeds that is important. It was Alexander's Companions who carried the seeds."

"What seeds, Arthur?"

"Their primary weapon of attack, the *sarissa.*"

"The sarissa?" I could feel Ambrose's blank amazement and utter incomprehension mirrored on my own countenance. "Forgive me, lad, but I have no idea what you mean. We have been trying to improve upon Alexander's sarissa, in Camulod, ever since we first began to train our soldiers to ride horses."

"I know you have, and Uncle Ambrose is still working with it. But the design has changed. The weapons that the Camulodian troopers use are not sarissas, and therefore they are not so dangerous. Besides, Uncle Ambrose has also developed the means of counterbalancing their threat, even if it were there."

I looked at Ambrose. "My felicitations on that. What did you do?"

Ambrose shook his head and gestured with his hand to Arthur, attracting his attention. When he had it, he stood up and moved close to the fire, speaking down to the boy. "Tell me, Arthur, where have you learned all this about the sarissa?"

"From the books written by Publius Varrus and Caius Britannicus. The books from the Armoury in Camulod. We brought them with us when we came here."

"I know you did, but I thought I had read all of them, and yet I have no recollection of anything being said, in any of the volumes I have read, about the sarissa being a thing of weakness, or even a seed of weakness, which means I have not read all of them."

"Well, no . . ."

"What does that mean?"

The boy shrugged. "That was never said, exactly, in any of the books. It was something that occurred to me while I was reading, and I merely wondered at it, when first I noticed it. I didn't think of it as weakness until much later, about a year ago, when I was thinking about how the Empire collapsed, and the weakness within the system that led to that."

I moved to interrupt him, but Ambrose waved me to silence. "No, Caius, let him finish. This is important, I think. I can see that weakness, Arthur, the Imperial flaw, I mean, but not the Alexandrian one. How—exactly how—did you come to construe the sarissa as a fatal weakness? No one else ever has, to my knowledge. Have you, Cay?"

I merely shook my head. Arthur looked from one to the other of us again, his eyes wide, and then his face split in a wide grin, his lambent, gold-coloured eyes laughing in disbelief.

"You are making fun of me. You know the answer better than I do. That's how you found the solution."

"No, Arthur, I'm not laughing at you, and neither is Caius Merlyn. I cannot see the problem—how then could I have found the solution to it? Tell us, as simply as you can, what you noticed, what made you think of this. We do not know, so you must enlighten us."

"But—"

"No buts! Tell us, simply. Where are these seeds of defeat?"

"In the length of the weapon, and the techniques the Companions used in fighting with it." He stopped again, but neither of us spoke or sought to interrupt him further. "It was a great, long thing, six paces long, heavy and unwieldy. They carried it in their opening charge, the butt end over their shoulders, the metal point angled downwards against the infantry before them. They skewered the front ranks and left the sarissas in the bodies of the men they had killed. . . ." His voice faltered. "Is that not so?"

"Aye, it is," Ambrose said, quietly. "And a terrifying sight they must have been, charging down upon a line of men on foot. A solid wall of men on heavy horses, fronted by that line of downward angled spears. Little wonder they were invincible."

"But think of it, Uncle! Great, heavy spears, each one six paces long. What would have happened had one man, one clever, brave, far-seeing enemy, ever thought to pick up those abandoned spears, or to make similar spears, and arm his foot soldiers with them, arranging the men on foot into a wall as well? Think of that! A wall of warriors, shoulder to shoulder, using those sarissas reversed, so that their butts rested firm on the ground and their points reared upward and out, towards the charging horsemen?"

The silence that followed that amazing insight stretched for a long, long time as Ambrose and I sat stunned, visualizing what the boy had described—a realization that had escaped the eyes of all the world for seven centuries. Alexander's cavalry had won him the world, but young Arthur Pendragon, had he lived at that time, could have devised the great Macedonian conqueror's downfall. Faced with disciplined troops, using their own weapon against them, Alexander's cavalry would have been impotent and ruined. Here was an insight that had evaded every celebrated commentator down the ages, and it had been deduced, without assistance, by one small boy, who sat silent now, waiting timidly for his two towering uncles to ridicule his proposition.

I sat staring into the fire for so long that my eyes teared, but eventually Ambrose made his way to the table that held the ewers of beer and mead. There, deep in thought, he filled a cup for himself before turning back to look at the boy, cradling the cup, his drink untasted.

"We use Alexander's techniques in Camulod."

"Aye, Uncle, we do, but not the sarissa. Our spears are shorter—suited to a man on horseback, but not long enough to be used against him in the fashion I described by a man on foot."

"Aye, but you have put the idea into words now, lad, and once that's done, no matter how quietly it may be done, words have a way of spreading. You said I found the solution. If I have, I've done it blindly. What is it?"

"Our bowmen, of course! If anyone should ever attempt to use such spears against our cavalry, they will have to crowd together in a massed assembly, forming a wall and not merely holding, but bracing their spears, and that would leave them at the mercy of our bows. The concentrated fire of massed bowmen, in conjunction with our cavalry as you advocate its use, Uncle, would destroy any such formation before it could become effective. I thought you were aware of that. I was sure that's why you had been so adamant about combining both groups to back up our infantry."

"Hmm!" Ambrose smiled and shook his head, looking at me in rueful acknowledgment of my pride in my pupil. "Aye . . . Well, I know it now, and be assured I'll never lose sight of it again." He placed his new-filled cup on the table, untouched. "Gentlemen, I am going to sleep . . . I think. I know, at least, that I am going to try to sleep. Whether or not I am successful will depend upon the thoughts you have implanted in my mind this night, young Arthur. It's very late, and you should be abed, too." He glanced at me, his face unreadable. "Much to think about in the meantime, Brother, no?" I nodded, saying nothing. "Aye, much to think about . . . boxes within boxes. We will talk more of this, come morning."

We parted company outside the room and Arthur walked by my side as we made our way to my sleeping quarters. I walked cautiously, my hand cupped protectively around the single candle flame we took with us to light our way. My room lay some distance away, and I was not yet familiar enough with Derek's great house to find my way there confidently in darkness, should we lose the candle's light. So deep in thought was I that the boy's voice startled me when it came. I had almost forgotten he was there, so softly did he walk.

"Uncle, what did Uncle Ambrose mean when he said 'boxes within boxes'?"

I coughed, giving myself time to think, unwilling to lie by saying I did not know. "He was referring to the import of what you have said . . . what you have discovered, I should say. He was paying tribute to your mind's acuity, Arthur, and I concur in his judgment. That you should perceive this weakness of Alexander's at all is amazing—no one else ever has. But that you should have arrived at the knowledge unassisted, and at such a young age, based only upon your own reading and observations, is quite confounding. It makes one wonder what other things might become clear to you, thus casually, things that have confounded older, and supposedly more clever, men for years, or even decades or centuries. Upon but little thought, there seems to be no end to the possibilities. That is what your uncle meant, in speaking of boxes within boxes. Do you understand that?"

"Hmm. I think so."

We had reached my sleeping quarters, where a cot had been installed for the boy beside my own, and moments later, both of us were abed. The boy fell into slumber quickly. I lay awake for a long, long time, planning what I would say to Ambrose when daylight came.

As it turned out, when daylight came I had the chance to say very little to Ambrose on the subject of Arthur and his brilliant deductive powers. Shelagh had not been idle, and after enlisting the assistance of Derek's wife Jessica, she had successfully laid siege to Derek's stubbornness on the matter of permitting us to approach his people with a view to finding extra residents for our hill fort. There was no unwillingness on his part to provide us with assistance on principle; he was more than willing to do that. The thing that stuck in Derek's craw, and which surprised me deeply until I perceived the reasoning behind it, was the matter of leaving the choice of who might join us in our hands.

Derek's contention was that anyone who wished to volunteer should be allowed to join us. Shelagh was adamantly against that. We had room, she maintained, for willing, skilled workers in specific crafts, and she named those skills and crafts. Married couples who shared these skills should be given preference, she asserted. In addition to those, she declared, we required a number of women, unencumbered women, to do women's work and to redress the sexual imbalance in our community. It followed naturally from that, she pointed out, that these women should have a certain calibre of youthfulness, real or apparent, and of basic cleanliness and attractiveness, since their function would be as much social as anything else.

Witnessing—with more than a little detached amusement—the ongoing clash of wills between these two aggressive personalities, I suddenly discerned the true reason for Derek's intractability. Shelagh was declaring and asserting and maintaining and pointing out exactly what followed naturally from what; Jessica was agreeing, silently, but nodding vigorously; and Derek was reacting jealously, feeling outflanked, outmanoeuvred and outgeneraled.

I took Shelagh aside and whispered in her ear. She looked at me haughtily and made a face. Then she dipped her head and went back towards the king, apologizing for her own excessive enthusiasm and deferring belatedly, but charmingly, to his judgment and his wisdom. She played poor Derek like a fisherman playing a large fish, so that he ended up according her everything she had asked for at the outset, totally unaware of having done so. We spent the remainder of that day and night selecting two score new residents for our fort from among more than two hundred applicants who had flocked forward to volunteer their skills and services within the hour that followed Derek's public announcement of our interest.

That we were able to do so with such dispatch was due purely to the fact that everything we sought in this undertaking lay within Derek's own township. Most of the people who lived beyond the town itself were farmers, living close to their fields and crops, and we had no need of such skills on our high, rocky little plateau beneath the mountains' crest. Arable land was something we lacked completely, although plans were already afoot among us to convert some small part of the cleared forest, close to the fort, into something approaching fertile plots for growing vegetables. The people whom we sought were those whose gifts and skills could be adapted to making our seclusion tenable: barrel and pottery makers; shoemakers and bootmakers, to provide protection for our feet on the stony mountainsides; cobblers to maintain those boots in good repair; leather-tanners and goat- and sheep-herders; carpenters and stonemasons and smiths; charcoal-makers to supply the fuel for our forges; fletchers to flight new arrows; grooms and farriers to tend our horses. Each time I thought to end the list, I found some other requirements I had overlooked.

Shelagh had a long list of her own that bore little resemblance to mine. She was concerned with finding bakers and cooks and butchers; flensers to skin and cure the hides from the beasts we killed; beekeepers and brewers and makers of mead to augment her own efforts; women adept at needlecraft and knitting, and at carding and teasing the rough brown wool of the native sheep; spinners of fine thread and coarser yarn; weavers of cloth and people who knew the art of dying those cloths. All of these skills, could we find them, would make our lives much easier in Mediobogdum, for at the present time all of us were having to turn our hands to all the work, and we were poorly equipped to do so.

I chose to take no part in the selection process, content to leave the task to Shelagh and Donuil, Hector and Brunna, Lars's wife, who had long years of experience in the choosing of able workers. Seeing that I was distancing myself from the work in hand, Derek sought me out, in need of some comfort after the savaging he had received at the end of Shelagh's tongue. I commiserated with him shamelessly, agreeing that our Shelagh was a formidable woman with a tongue like a rasp, but pointing out that she was highly thought of by all who knew her well, for reasons he would doubtless soon discover for himself. Mollified by my sympathy and obviously wishing to make amends for his earlier stubbornness, he hesitated only long enough to gain my assurance that his people would remain his people, and that since we would be leaving someday in the foreseeable future, in a matter of short years, he would not only regain their presence but would also inherit the fruits of their labour in the form of a habitable fort here in the mountains. Immediately thereafter, greatly reassured, he threw himself into the task of supervising the selection process, adjudicating ruthlessly whenever there appeared to be a conflict or a choice to make in terms of quality and ability. I derived a great deal of ironic amusement from the fact that Derek immediately became our greatest asset in finding the people who would suit us most. He knew all of his people, of course, and was unblinkered in judging their strengths and weaknesses.

By late afternoon the task was complete, and we had swelled our ranks in Mediobogdum beyond our expectations. Every category we had hoped to fill was filled to Shelagh's satisfaction, many of them with couples who, between them, offered complementary skills. Thirty-eight adults would join us, twenty-six of those being thirteen married couples, including a brewer and his wife, a noted beekeeper. The remaining twelve were nine women, five of them young, and three men. The married couples would bring their families, totalling fourteen children ranging in age from two-year-olds to half-grown boys and girls. Shelagh and the others were delighted. I was well pleased. Derek was relieved to have the task completed, and that night we had a feast to celebrate the day's events.

Shelagh approached me in the course of that evening's celebrations, when I was leaning contentedly against a corner wall, eyeing the festivities. Ambrose had left me moments earlier to talk with Ludmilla, who had beckoned him to where she sat with Derek's Jessica, and Donuil was deep in a discussion with Dedalus on the other side of the room.

"Lucanus and Derek are close-huddled over there. I wonder what they're plotting?"

I had not seen her approach and I straightened up immediately, shrugging myself away from the wall and looking to where she was pointing. I smiled.

"They're an unlikely pair, I'll grant you, but I doubt they are plotting anything. They've known each other a long time, those two."

"Aye." She was already looking elsewhere, her glance sharpening, and I followed her gaze to where the two youngest, single members of our party, Mark and Jonathan, were huddled admiringly about one young woman. Her name, as I recalled, was Tressa, and I had met her earlier in the day when she brought me a mug of icy beer, addressing me as "Mester Cahy." She was a striking young woman, far from classically beautiful but gifted nonetheless with youthful beauty and colour, high, cushioned cheekbones, sparkling eyes and strong white teeth. She smiled naturally and often. I had admired her form. She wore a plain white tunic, modelled on the simply draped, classic Roman stola, which showed off her long, slim, graceful neck and the wide, straight shoulders that bore her high, full breasts with pride and artless magnificence. As she had turned to walk away from me, having bowed her head prettily in response to my thanks for her attentions, I had seen, too, that her buttocks filled the lower part of her garment very nicely. An impressive young woman, I thought at the time, and I was pleased now to see my own impression borne out by the attention our two youthful artisans were showing her. She threw back her head and laughed at something Mark said to her, and even from a distance, over the noise of the crowd, I heard the artless sound of it.

"That's Tressa," Shelagh said.

"I know. I met her earlier." I turned and looked at her. "Are you saying—"

"She's one of ours? Of course. Do you approve?"

I looked back towards the tall young woman. "You don't need my approval. Mark and Jonathan approve. I see that plainly."

"Aye. She's a seamstress, and a very good one. Her talents are spoken of with envy by all the women here. Some of the elder ones are jealous of her gifts and have been making things difficult for her, so she has much incentive to come to us. We will appreciate her skills without resentment. She'll help you."

"Help me? How, and with what? I need no help."

"Oh, don't you?" She reached out and thrust the end of one index finger through a tiny rent in my sleeve. I had never seen it before, but I knew it was new. I vaguely remembered catching it on something I was passing, earlier that day. "No, it's clear you don't, not even from someone who could keep you clad and mended without your noticing."

"I can take care of such things by myself."

She smiled sweetly at me and straightened up to move away. "Of course you can, Caius. We both know your opinions on that—you need nothing. But that is your opinion. I disagree with it."

Before I could find a response, she was gone, gliding towards her husband, who was smiling at her. Disturbed, somehow, I turned to look again at the young woman Tressa, but she had gone as well, and then I realized that she was close beside me, less than a pace from me, smiling.

"Mester Cahy, c'n I fetch thee to drink?"

Flustered by her sudden proximity, I managed to thank her graciously, refusing her offer, raging at myself internally for the damnable redness I could feel flooding my face. She appeared not to notice; instead she kept her eyes fixed on mine, smiling at me as I stammered out my words. When I had done, she nodded pleasantly, and I had to fight against the urge to watch as she walked away.

A short time after that I saw her again across the hall, talking to Jonathan, and as I looked, she raised her head and her eyes looked directly into mine. Before I could avert my gaze she smiled again and dipped her head in the slightest nod before returning her eyes and her attention to Jonathan. A moment later, while I was still watching her, I heard Donuil's voice addressing me and I turned to find his wife gazing at me from beside him, a small, secret smile on her lips. I felt a strange surge of anger towards her but recognized it as being unreasonable and stifled it. Very shortly after that, I went to bed, where I fell asleep with Tressa's good-natured, disconcerting smile hovering in my mind.

The following morning, as dawn was breaking, we prepared to bid farewell to Ravenglass again and turn our steps towards our hilltop home. Those of our new neighbours who were sufficiently free of duties, obligations and other encumbrances—slightly more than half the newcomers—accompanied us. The others would follow within the next few days, as and when they were able to. Ambrose and Ludmilla rode with us too, both of them keen to see what we had made of our own private fortress among the towering Fells.

As I sat watching our assembling party that morning, my thoughts were split in two directions: the greater part of my attention was bent upon organizing our train, which had now swollen from the four wagons we had brought down empty with us—they were now all filled to capacity—to include the transportation for another thirty-some adults and children. This hotchpotch of vehicles ranged from ox-drawn carts, to wagons drawn by horses and mules, to light carts, with high, narrow wheels that were evidently intended to be pulled along by hand. These latter vehicles, and there were four of them, I eyed askance, thinking it would be a major undertaking to push or pull them up the steep, narrow gradient leading from the river vale to our rocky plateau so far above. I knew, however, that it would matter nothing to me, and these people were native to the land, so I assumed they knew the task that lay ahead of them in climbing up to Mediobogdum.

Conflicting with the need to concentrate on preparing for departure, however, was an equal, or perhaps an even greater need to dwell at length upon the brief discussion I had had, an hour or so before, with Lucanus. My mind had not yet adjusted to the news that he had delivered, and as I sat there on Germanicus, high up and securely mounted in my saddle, I felt a surge of giddiness that might have sent me crashing to the ground had I not braced myself and sucked in a mighty, belly-deep breath.

Luke had approached me as I broke my fast on a mess of boiled wheat and oatmeal with milk and honey, in Derek's kitchens. Returning my nod of greeting, he had sat down across from me and helped himself to a slab of heavy, fresh-baked bread, smearing it with some of the thick honey I had been using to sweeten my oatmeal. We both sat silent for a while, absorbed in the task of eating. Finally, however, Luke sat back, rubbing his hands and wiping a smear of honey fastidiously from the corner of his mouth with the tip of a little finger, and he stared at me wordlessly until I grew uncomfortable, sensing that he had something momentous to say.

"What? What is it?"

"That thing on your breast, the mark."

My stomach swooped and I felt goose-flesh break out across my shoulders.

"What about it? What have you discovered?"

"It's what I thought it was, some kind of skin blemish, almost definitely harmless."

"You have read the scroll, then, the one from the wooden chest in Camulod?"

"Of course, and it contained nothing of relevance to what you described about your experience with Mordechai—nothing at all that might confirm your fears. You have a blemish there, not any kind of lesion, and, in my belief, most certainly not leprosy."

I heard a roaring in my ears and the room began to spin about me, so that I had to grip the edge of the table with both hands and breathe deeply. Luke sat watching me, a faint smile playing about his lips. When I had control of myself again, and my breathing had returned to normal, I let go of the table's edge and sat up straighter, expelling one last, deep breath in a great "whoosh" of air. His smile grew broader then and he clapped his hands together.

"I can see you feel better already."

I nodded, not yet prepared to trust my voice to speak without wavering.

"Excellent, now hear what I have to say. In any normal case, I would have prescribed exposure to the sun and air for such a thing. But your fears to date have rendered your affliction abnormal to the point of precluding such treatment, in addition to which it has been winter, too cold to go bare-chested. All of that has changed now and the warm weather is coming. From now on, as much as you are able in fine weather, I want you to go unclothed above the waist. The browning effect of the sun will likely mend what ails you, no matter what it is, and render the thing less conspicuous."

"I may do that?"

"May? Of course you may! There is nothing wrong with you, Caius, nor has there been. My original diagnosis now holds true. The sum of my experience, and that of my colleagues down the ages, tells me that you have never been exposed to contagion for long enough to have contracted leprosy, so will you accept that now, once and for all?"

I nodded again, more slowly now, aware of the incredible sensations of relief and delivery from danger that were surging riotously through my breast and in my mind. "Thank you, my friend," I said, my voice almost inaudible even to me. "You will never know the extent of my gratitude to know that I am clean and unfouled." An image came into my mind, filling my awareness—the image of his lovely, deeply carved and glowing citrus wood chest. For all this time, throughout my agonized imaginings, it had contained the healing balm that would put my mind to rest. And then my curiosity stirred.

"So what did the scroll have to say about blood and contagion?"

"Nothing directly concerned with your condition, as I said." Luke folded his arms and leaned back against the wall behind his bench. "It was written by a physician called Oppius, Quinctilius Oppius, a renowned and celebrated teacher in the diagnosis of disease, at Alexandria during the reign of the Emperor Galerius, a hundred years or so ago. Oppius was a great admirer of the work of Galen—have you heard of him? Well, Galen was the greatest physician who ever lived, greater even than Aesculapius. He was born in Pergamum, where his father was an architect, and he studied anatomy in Alexandria before going to Rome, where he remained for forty years, first as personal physician to the emperor Marcus Aurelius and then, after Marcus's death, to the emperors Lucius Verus, Commodus and Septimius Severus. Galen was a wondrous writer, inscribing all of his findings and theories on the practice of his art. His treatise *On Anatomical Procedure* is the greatest medical text ever written, but he wrote also on healing methods, *De Methodo Medendi*, and on the natural faculties, and on the movement of the muscles.

"Galen had been dead a hundred years before Oppius began his work, following the great physician's methods and procedures. It was while Oppius was engaged in working in Asia Minor, at a time when a military action concurred with an outbreak of plague and the medical facilities were overwhelmed, that he became aware of an anomaly that caused the spread of plague infection, in a military ward, among legionaries whose wounds should never have become infected. Oppius formed a theory that these infections might have been caused by the overuse of bandage wrappings that had previously been used to bind plague victims. The wrappings had been washed between uses, of course, but apparently they had not been boiled, which would have been mandatory in less hectic times. We have known for centuries that boiling water cleanses it of impurities. Anyway, Oppius launched himself upon a program to explore this theory of his, and later wrote the treatise that I found long afterward, contending that the careless application of bloody, pus-stained bandages, improperly washed, to open wounds could spread contagion."

I sat blinking at him. "Does that sound feasible to you?"

He shrugged his shoulders. "I am not prepared to state an opinion. Pus is part of the healing process, formed by the body's natural purging of the toxins that contaminate a wound or a sore. From that position, knowing that it is an effluent full of contaminants, no sane physician would ever dream of introducing pus from one man's wounds into another's."

"Consciously, you mean."

He stared at me. "Aye. That is what I mean. But the bandages Oppius used in his studies were clean and washed."

"Some boiled, but some not?"

"Yes, and I see what you are implying, but we have only the words of Oppius, written a hundred years ago and more, from which we can infer any difference between the two. And let me be explicit: his findings in this case, and his proposal that the application of heat, in the boiling process, may make a material difference to the dressings, seem outlandish to me."

"I accept that, but. . . ." I was perplexed, and totally aware that I was beyond my depth in discussing such matters, and yet a point had occurred to me and I wanted to present it. "We know, Luke, those of us who have any knowledge of the art of smithing championed by Publius Varrus, that the application of heat—extreme heat—invariably has the most salutary effect on iron, the hardest metal known to man. Cold iron is practically impossible to work. Heat it red-hot, however, and you may work your will on it. Heat it white-hot, and you may tie it in knots—" I paused, considering my own words. "I know that cloth bandages, dressings, have nothing akin to metal in their makeup, but heat applied to them is heat in either instance. Is it not, then, conceivable that the link, if there is a link, may lie in the heat, the temperature itself, rather than in the material being heated?"

Lucanus stood up at that point, smiling broadly and tightening his belt. "I have no idea," he answered. "You may be right, my friend, and you may be completely wrong. Neither of us has the means of gauging the truth, in either direction. Nonetheless, I like the way you think. It has a clarity that is all too uncommon among those around us. I promise you that I will think on this, and try to see if I can find some way to investigate this matter further without endangering the health of anyone. In the meantime, I have promised Shelagh that I will wait on her before first light, before she leaves her rooms to join the excursion. I will talk more of this with you later. In the meantime, try to remember that there is nothing wrong with you. You are completely healthy, without flaw, apart from one small blemish that the sun will obliterate. Farewell." He left me then, allowing me to dwell on my reprieve and on my sudden, swift return to health.

Mere moments later, Ded had stormed into the kitchens looking for Rufio, and I had been up and out into the pre-dawn freshness, joining the bustle already long under way in the crowded street in front of the old Praesidium, so that as the sun arose, it shone directly into my new, unblemished outlook on life.

Now I squeezed Germanicus between my spurred heels and brought him backing around to face the road ahead of us. Shelagh and Lucanus were already in motion, riding together slowly, side by side, towards the distant eastern gate. Ahead of them I could see Dedalus and Rufio riding on either side of Ambrose. Ludmilla sat in comfort on the driver's bench of our largest wagon, beside Turga and Hector, who held the reins, and the four boys on their piebald ponies were lost to view, beyond the gate already. I waved a last farewell to Derek, who stood watching from the forecourt of his massive house, then raised my arm above my head and gave the signal to move out. Twelve miles ahead of us and far above our heads lay Mediobogdum.

IX

"VERY WELL, I am going to admit defeat before you even challenge me. I confess you have me beaten, outmanoeuvred and outfoxed. I have no hope of guessing what it might be and so I must ask you, what is it?"

I had stopped moving as soon as I heard Ambrose begin to speak from behind me, and now I continued to stand, bent forward slightly, my arms outstretched, my hands loosely cradling the upper end of the length of wood I had been swinging, still breathing heavily from my exertions. I felt my face creasing into a smile as I visualized my brother's possible reactions to what I would tell him. Then I drew a deep breath and straightened up slowly, turning to face him and throwing the object in question to him, underhand. He caught it easily and held it upright at arm's length in front of him.

"You tell me," I said. "What does it look like?"

"It looks like a heavy stick, a branch torn from some old tree, stripped of its bark and dried, possibly in a kiln, then covered with carving. I am tempted to call it a long, purposeless stick, but then I know my earnest, conscientious brother Merlyn would never waste his time with anything as simple as a stick. So I must ask again—what is it?"

"It's a stick, as you said."

"Aha!" He nodded sagely. "But a solid stick, a formidable stick, would you not agree? A stick of substance, long and heavy."

"Yes, I would agree, on both counts, which is why I was using it."

"I see." He nodded again, his face grave, for all the world as though he knew what I was speaking about and we were having a perfectly rational conversation. "Yes, I can see why a rational man might wish to have such an excellent stick, so solid and substantial, of such evident, straightforward purpose. A man could lean on a stick like that, to aid him as he walked, if he were infirm, or older than you are."

"Aye, and if the thing were longer than it is, but it's too short. It is a stick, after all, not a staff. But then, I had no thought of walking with it."

"Hmm. Yes, I could see that. You were . . . swinging it about your head, were you not?"

"I was."

"Aye, I thought you were. . . . Would it vex you if I asked you why?"

"No, it would not. I was exercising my arms—my shoulders, in fact."

My brother stared at me, allowing no hint of raillery to show upon his face. He was seeking a way to lead this strange conversation further, in the hope, I knew, of discovering what I was up to without having to ask me bluntly again. He was holding the stick awkwardly now, uncertain of how to proceed, and I decided to help him out. I bent quickly, flexing my knees, and retrieved another length of wood, almost identical, from the grass at my feet.

"I have two of them, see? Would you like to learn their use?"

His face cleared immediately and his teeth flashed in a broad smile. "I would," he said.

"Good, then I'll show you, but you'll have to remove that cloak, at least until you learn the knack of what we'll be about."

As he fumbled with the fastening of his cloak, holding the stick beneath his arm to free his hands, I removed my helmet, indicating that he should do the same. Moments later, we stood facing each other, each of us wearing a leather cuirass, front and back, over our pleated, knee-length Roman tunics.

"Now, do as I do. This is very simple." I held my arms outstretched towards him, my stick grasped easily in both hands at its ends. He did the same, and I beckoned him towards me until our fists were touching, knuckle to knuckle. Then I raised my arms vertically over my head, feeling my stomach flatten and the flexor muscles of my shoulders stretch, and I watched Ambrose closely as he copied my movements exactly. This was a flexing movement I found easier now than I had a few months earlier, when I first began these exercises. In the beginning, I had cramped quickly, my muscles unused to the contortions to which I was suddenly subjecting them. Now, after months of practice, I was more supple, much more flexible, and I knew Ambrose would already be feeling the strain in his shoulders.

"Comfortable?"

He nodded, the slightest hint of perplexity in his eyes, and while his head was yet dipping I released my left hand, whipping my long, heavy stick around to the right and down from above my head to whack loudly against the thickened hide of his heavy cuirass, sending him reeling but unhurt, releasing his own left hand from its grip on his stick so that his right waved aimlessly, still clutching his "weapon." Before he could recover, I leaped in close and whacked him again, this time with an upsweeping, backhanded blow from left to right that took him viciously beneath the right shoulder, rattling against the covering over his ribs and once again forcing him to fall back. Even as he went I was on the move again, gripping my stick firmly now in both hands and driving the end of it forward, hard and fast, my weight solidly behind it, to strike him clean above the breastbone so that his balance was undone at last and he fell on his rump. As soon as he was down, I leaped back and crouched, facing him, holding my stick firmly in a two-fisted grip, one end pointed unwaveringly at his head.

He sat sprawling backwards, his hands outthrust behind him. His stick lay on the ground beside him. After a long, silent time, he pursed his lips and began to rise to his feet, his look one of quiet determination as he sought and found the stick he had dropped. Then, holding his weapon like me, in a two-fisted grip, he began to circle me warily, his eyes on mine, waiting for an opportunity to strike a blow of his own.

I moved with him, fading backwards, balanced easily on the balls of my feet, and then I feinted rapidly forward and to my left before snapping back to where I had been. But Ambrose, my wily brother, was not gulled and did not react; he was content to wait. He and I had fought before and he knew many of my patterns, as I knew many of his. In this contest, however, I was confident of winning, for I had been practising this new technique for months, whereas he had never seen it before now. Ambrose was no man's fool, however, and least of all mine . . . we were much too alike. I soon saw that we might circle here all day, but that he was not going to commit himself to any attack without having had some opportunity to study the proper moves. Finally I made a throat-clearing noise and nodded to him, coming to a stop.

"Very well, go ahead. I won't move. Hit me."

He looked at me quizzically, his expression sceptical, eyes twinkling. "You won't move at all?"

"I won't move while you're deciding where to hit me. After that, I'll move. You won't hit me."

"Huh." He straightened up and spun his weapon inward, one-handed, so that the end of it came to rest beneath his armpit, and I knew immediately, instinctively, what his next move would be.

Ambrose routinely wore a long, slender sword, modelled on the Roman cavalry *spatha,* designed purely for stabbing men on foot from the back of a light horse. The spatha was admirable in its originally intended use, but as a fighting sword, for brutal, toe-to-toe conflicts, it was worse than useless. Its blade was overlong and too slight, so that it would bend and even break when used against a better-tempered weapon. In the earliest days of Camulod's conversion to cavalry, Publius Varrus, the Colony's master armourer and my own great-uncle, had designed longer swords than the spatha, with broader, stronger, better-tempered blades. This was the sword Ambrose preferred. Its length and construction almost dictated its use, in terms of technique for a man on foot—hence my foreknowledge of what Ambrose would do next.

Sure enough, Ambrose renewed his stance and his two-handed grip, his knees bent, right foot slightly ahead of the left, his "blade" pointed at my sternum. He froze, his eyes locked in total concentration before he grunted and whipped into a blur of action, his weapon sweeping up and then around above my head and down again in a backhanded slash designed to cut the legs from me. I knew the arc of his sweep, I knew the point at which it would change course and be converted to a stabbing, jabbing lunge before being whipped upward again into an overhand, vertically dropping chop.

Without removing my eyes from his I dropped my "point," sweeping my blade strongly, backhanded, to block his downward slash. Then, before he could reverse into his stab, I grasped my stick in both hands, leaving a space the width of my chest between them, and pushed into his stab, sweeping my hands high and forcing his thrust upward, to graze my face and shoot above my head while I reversed the grip of my right hand, dropped my arms and shoulder and rammed the thick end of my weapon solidly against his ribs, knocking him sprawling for the second time. This time, however, before he stopped rolling, I was above him on one knee, the end of my stick pressed against his neck.

He made no effort to move, content to lie there panting until his breathing had returned to normal, by which time the silence had stretched long. "Shit," he said, eventually, and made to sit up. I heaved myself backwards onto my feet and helped him up, then stood watching him as he dusted himself off and rubbed ruefully at his buttocks.

"Now you know."

"Aye." He looked at me askance. "Practice swords, just like the old Roman ones, but new, and better. When did the idea occur to you, and what occasioned it?"

"Come with me and I'll show you."

I led the way back up the steep hillside towards the west gate of the fort, a distance of little more than thirty paces, and from there we went directly to my quarters. Shelagh and Ludmilla were leaving as we arrived, having delivered, according to Ludmilla, a box of new-made papyrus sent to me from my supplier in Camulod. I politely invited them to stay, but was secretly pleased when they declined. I moved, immediately on their departure, to open a large packing crate that lay against the rear wall, and from it I pulled the smaller case that held Excalibur. I opened the case, withdrew the sword itself and passed it, hilt first, to Ambrose.

"Here. Now I need your help, so swing it a few times. Get used to the weight and the feel of it again, because I'm going to want you to use it in a moment, to demonstrate a point."

As he began to swing the massive weapon, making the light flicker along its long, gleaming blade, I turned again to the larger crate, this time pulling out a long spatha-style sword. It had a boss between the hilt and the blade, in the style of the Roman *gladium* short-sword; there was no hint of a cross-guard of any kind. Beneath a light coating of reddish-brown discoloration too fine to be called rust, it looked like a fine weapon, very slightly curved, the tip of its blade broadened, flared and slightly elongated, keen-edged and almost leaflike. Ambrose stopped what he was doing, holding Excalibur's blade vertically as he stared at me and the sword I now held. I reversed my grip and extended the new sword to him and held my other hand out at the same time for Excalibur. We exchanged weapons and he immediately brought the blade of the new sword up close to his eyes, scanning it minutely, pressing the ball of his thumb against the edge of the blade.

"I've never seen this before. Where did it come from?"

"From the Armoury in Camulod. It's a Varrus sword, one of the original prototypes he made with Equus when he was redesigning the old spatha. Before I was born, and years before they discovered the secret of the stirrups, Caius Britannicus wanted a new weapon, much stronger than the spatha, a cross between a spear and an axe, to be used by a man on horseback against men on foot. A chopping weapon, but he insisted it had to function like a sword."

"This is fine," Ambrose said softly, hefting the thing in his hand and moving his arm slowly through a gliding pass. "A fine weapon."

"I made a discovery about it, later—or, more accurately, about one of its fellows—and now I want you to help me discover if what I suspect is true. If it is, and I do believe it is, then there is something else we must do, you and I, in secrecy."

Ambrose was gazing at me in amusement, a half-smile upon his lips, and now he shook his head. "I do not even wish to ask. I know you'll tell me when the time arrives. In the meantime, how may I help you discover this truth?"

"Take this and give me that." We exchanged swords again, and now I began waving my long, curved blade through the air. I ended up holding it out to my right, inclined slightly upward from the horizontal, clenching the hilt firmly in both fists. Ambrose merely watched, awaiting his instructions.

"This is one of Varrus's best blades, Ambrose. He smelted the metal himself, and tempered it. It's quite superb. But of course, the one you are holding is quite probably the greatest blade ever made by any man, anywhere. Now, I want you to swing your blade as hard as you can and try to knock this one from my grasp. Don't be tempted to use the flat of the blade. It is essential that you use the edge. I have no tricks in mind, I promise you. But strike away from me, because there's no cross-hilt on this sword and Excalibur could take off my arm more cleanly than you could imagine. I will not move, nor will I try to deflect your blade in any way. I am simply going to stand here and hold out this sword, and I'll try to hold onto it when your blow falls. You understand?"

He nodded, stepped back and fell into his fighter's crouch again, concentrating on what he was about to do. When he unfolded again into swooping, powerful motion it was beautiful to behold, and I caught my breath as Excalibur's shining blade painted great, hissing swaths of brightness and glittering colours in the drabness of my quarters. Then Ambrose transferred all of his weight and momentum onto the ball of his left foot and brought that deadly scythe sweeping around to clash against the blade I held extended to my right. I had been awaiting the concussion and was set for it, my muscles braced against the shock that I knew would hammer them, but the thing was dashed from my grip as though I had no hold on it at all. The force of the wrenching impact sent me whirling away backwards and I fell to my knees against one wall as the sword I had held clanged hard against another and clattered to the floor.

Ambrose stood, astonished, as though paralyzed, his face blank with surprise, his eyes shifting between the blade in his hand and the sight of me, sprawling against the wall off to his side. As I moved to regain my footing, bracing myself against the wall with my outstretched left hand and shaking my right arm to banish the numbness, he finally rallied and moved towards me, lowering his sword point to the floor.

"Merlyn, are you hurt? What was that? What happened here?"

I cradled my tingling right arm in my left, holding myself above the elbow, which felt numbed and dead. "I'm well enough, Brother, and unsurprised. What happened here is exactly what I had surmised might happen." I nodded towards the long sword lying on the floor against the other wall. "Look at that."

He glanced downward, and I heard the hiss of his indrawn breath. The long Varrus sword lay bent and broken, its finely wrought blade twisted and misshapen. Before he could say anything, I spoke again.

"Check your blade. Is it damaged?"

He whipped Excalibur up, close to his face, and examined the blade closely, but I knew he would find no blemish. "No," he said, eventually. "It's not even dented."

I stooped and picked up the Varrus sword in my right hand, briefly aware of the painful tingling in my fingers as they closed about the hilt. A great, vee-shaped gouge almost severed the blade, the wounded metal glinting, raw and fresh and new-looking, among the rust that covered the rest of it. Excalibur's keen edge had struck deep, penetrating the metal of the other blade as though it were wood or lead, twisting and wrenching it out of shape with effortless force, then lodging firmly enough for the momentum of Ambrose's swing to rip the weapon from my clutching hands and cast it aside effortlessly, ruined and useless forever thenceforth. I held the broken thing up for Ambrose's inspection. Its long blade was twisted and bent far out of true in two directions: one where it had bent sideways around the impact of Excalibur's smashing bite, and the other in a tortured twisting of the very metal surrounding the point of impact, skewing it like wrought iron twisted in a forge. I dropped the now useless weapon to the floor.

"There is the reason underlying my playing with sticks, Brother. The need for practice swords . . . or for one specific practice sword."

"I don't follow you."

"I know you don't, but you will. What you have just done defines and underlines my problem. There's no blade in the world that can withstand Excalibur. It cuts through other metals, without losing its own edge. It is unique, and that, I have decided, is its tragedy."

"Tragedy!" Ambrose's shout was a scoffing laugh. "What's tragic about it? The thing is magical and utterly unbelievable. No tragedy there, Brother."

"No, I agree, just as there was no weakness in Alexander's sarissas."

That wiped the smile from my brother's face. "What? There's no comparison. Where can the weakness lie in Excalibur? Most ordinary men, seeing what it can do—like cutting that blade in half—would swear it to be magic and live in fear of it. The warrior who carries it will be invincible, and the envy of the world."

"The king, you mean . . . the king who carries it."

"Aye—" he broke off, eyeing me askance. "It is to be young Arthur's, isn't it? You have not changed your mind on that?"

"No, I have not. He is his father's son and heir to the Pendragon lands and kingdom in his own right. I have had no change of heart in any part of that. But I am concerned about training the boy to face the task he must, here in these hills, so far away from Camulod and from others who would bring out the best in him. And if he is to master this new sword of his, Excalibur, instead of merely swinging it, then he must have someone wielding a weapon fit to withstand his, against whom he can practice."

"Well, you will train him, won't you? He'll fight you and Dedalus and Rufio and all the others. No shortage of trainers, I think."

"No, but you are still not hearing me. Excalibur's weakness is its strength, Ambrose! I have nothing with which to train the boy—no Excalibur against which he can swing Excalibur." I nodded towards the broken thing in the corner. "That was a superior sword, a Varrus blade. It was cut almost in half with one blow. How am I to train the boy to use the weapon adequately when there is nothing comparable to it? It won't ever be enough simply to train him with another sword, a lesser weapon, because then he'll be master only of a lesser weapon, lacking the refinement, the edge, the balance and the strength of this sword, this blade, this excellence."

As I spoke the words, I saw comprehension breaking in my brother's eyes. Almost immediately, he started to smile, and then his smile grew into a radiant grin as he subsided into one of my chairs, grounding Excalibur's point between his feet.

"What?" I asked him. "You can find humour in that? Why are you smiling? What is it?"

He swung the point of the sword up from the floor, holding it now above his head so that the weight of the hilt and pommel pressed into his lap and patterns of reflected light raced along the mighty blade that reared between us. "This thing, Excalibur. Did anyone work with Publius Varrus in the making of it?"

"Aye, of course, his friend Equus. They made the sword together, working alternately on it until it was finished."

"And does anyone yet live who might know how they made the blade?"

"Aye. Equus's sons, Joseph and Carol. They had no hand in the making of the sword itself, but they are both smiths, and I know their father taught them the art of folding and beating metal the way he and Varrus did in making Excalibur, tempering ordinary iron into superior swords. They do it now, to this day. And more than that, the use of moulds to shape and bind the hilts of our weapons to the tangs of our blades has become commonplace in Camulod."

"So they could make another Excalibur."

"Aye, they could, either one of them, if it were possible," I agreed, before I realized what he had said, and then I checked myself. "What? Another—?"

"From the Lady, Cay! The half of her that still remains in Camulod. Isn't that what you told me, that Varrus melted the statue down to make the sword, then remade the statue, smaller and lighter, with the remaining metal? The remaining metal, Cay, the metal from the skystone! We can make your training sword—another Excalibur, less ornate, but no less magical in its properties, a plain blade with which to test the other."

"By the Christ!" I was thunderstruck. His solution was so crystalline, so perfect and so obvious that I could not now comprehend my own failure to see it for myself.

"Damnation! Joseph is here with you, isn't he? No matter, we'll have Carol make another sword, in Camulod since that's where the statue is, and we'll pattern it upon this one, but as I said, not so grandly and it will be nowhere near as pretty. Is Carol capable of doing this alone?" I nodded, mute. "Good, then. It should not tax him too greatly. What we need here is not another thing of blinding beauty, but a plain, functional weapon of strength and durability that will stand up to this one here on equal terms. We have all the dimensions—all we need do now is have Carol duplicate them, without regard to decoration. What think you?"

I sat shaking my head, overwhelmed by the beautiful simplicity of his instant solution to a problem that had been plaguing me for months. So close had I been to the source of the solution, I saw now, that my eyes had passed over it mentally a thousand times without seeing it. Ambrose was watching me, his eyes aglow.

"You agree?"

"Agree? Of course I agree. It is a brilliant solution, Ambrose! We'll start working on it immediately by preparing a full set of drawings from Publius Varrus's original notations and sketches—I have all of them here. When you return home, you will be able to take written instructions with you, containing the exact dimensions of Excalibur and whatever else Carol's brother Joseph might wish to add in the way of advice on the treatment and melting of the statue's metal and the forging of it into another blade. Of course, we'll have to show it to Joseph—Excalibur, I mean."

Ambrose frowned at me. "Is that a problem? I hear doubt in your voice."

I shrugged. "Well, not doubt, perhaps, but definite trepidation. I hate to do it. Today, only you, Shelagh, Donuil and I know Excalibur exists. That is already far too many people. Every other person who knows about it increases the odds that the secret will be discovered."

He was silent for a while, digesting that, and then he shrugged. "Well then, why does Joseph have to see the thing? As you said, you have all the dimensions, and Joseph's a smith. He should be able to work from those alone. A sword's a sword, and this will simply be a larger, longer, heavier sword than he and Carol have made before. No need for them to see the real thing, is there?"

I smiled at him. "How is Joseph to visualize the sword's reality and depict it accurately and minutely if he has never seen it?" I shook my head. "No, I don't like it, but I think we must show it to him. He is one of us, true to the bone, and his father helped to make the thing, and we are asking him to help us duplicate it. We'll show it to him tonight and swear him to secrecy. Once he has seen the sword, he'll also see the importance of the task. I wonder how long it will take Carol to make the new one."

Ambrose smiled again and rose to his feet, moving to replace Excalibur in its case. "The only potential problem that occurred to me lay in Carol's capability as a smith, and you have put my mind to rest on that."

"Oh, yes. There is not much to choose between the two brothers in terms of craftsmanship, and Varrus trained both of them himself. If I had to grant an edge to either one, however, it would go to Carol, although I never would say that in Joseph's hearing."

"Good, Carol will be flattered that you should approach him, seeking his help. He'll waste no time and he'll understand the need for secrecy. I would suggest that only Carol be permitted to know the source of the metal, and that he be empowered to make whatever arrangements he requires to melt the statue down in privacy, shaping it into an ingot. Thereafter, the metal will resemble an ordinary piece of iron, save that he alone will work on it. You agree?" I nodded and he continued.

"One truth remains unchanged, Brother. No matter how long it takes to complete the making of this second sword, you'll still have your hands full training our amazing boy. But you have time and to spare. The lad will have to grow considerably before he has the size or the strength to swing such a sword, let alone learn the knack of what you showed me earlier, when you rattled my ribs and set me on my rump. He's a big, strong lad, for his age, and his hands and feet are the largest I've ever seen on a boy. He has the family bulk about him, and he's going to be as big as you and me by the time he's grown, but that time is still far distant." He paused, returning the wooden case that housed Excalibur whence I had produced it. When the lid on the crate was securely closed, he turned back to me again, dusting his hands.

"So, your problem is no longer a problem, but you need not grovel in your gratitude. Now I have to go and find Rufio. He's out in the forest, cutting lumber with Dedalus and Donuil and some others, and I promised him I would come by and soil my noble hands by helping on the ripsaw. Come with me, and as we go you can tell me how the idea for the long sword staves came to you."

I knew that almost all the other men of our party were out on a tree-felling expedition, making a determined assault on a grove of prime oak trees selected and marked for felling by Mark, our master carpenter. Lucanus was an exception; he was still engrossed in his hoard of parchments. And I had opted out of the expedition in order to complete some writings in silence and solitude. Having done what I intended more quickly than I had anticipated, I now found the idea of a spell of good, hard, physical work appealing. I realized it had been too long since I had worked up a sweat. I laughed and clapped my brother on the shoulder, suddenly euphoric, and we made our way to the stables immediately.

Germanicus's winter coat was still long and thick, only beginning to fall away in patches despite Ulf's grooming over the past few days. Mounted, I passed through the main gateway of our fort, following Ambrose and then turning directly to the right, to lead him to where I knew the work party was located that day. It took me several moments to become aware that he had not swung west with me, and when I did I turned around to find him sitting erect in his saddle, staring upwards, to the east, where the high, winding road crested the pass and disappeared beyond the mountain saddle. I turned my horse around and rode back to where he sat.

"What are you looking at?" I asked as I reached him.

"That, up there. Has anyone ever come across there?"

"Not since we have been here, and according to Derek, not for years before that, either."

"What's over there?"

"A valley, like the one below us here, except that it's entirely enclosed. The road winds down from the crest there, along the length of it, and then up the slopes at the far end to another pass."

"A big valley? Have you seen it?"

I grunted, almost but not quite laughing. "Aye, I've seen it, but only from the crest up there. There's nothing to see. It may be three miles long, but no more than that. The whole valley is filled with trees, growing up to the shoulders of the highest Fells, just as they do in the one below us. I didn't go down into it, because if I had, I would only have had to climb back up again. There's nothing down there to see except the road itself and the stream along the bottom of the valley floor."

"So where does the road go? What's the reason for its being there?"

It really surprised me to recognize that my brother knew absolutely nothing of this region or its history, although I was fully aware that I myself had been as ignorant as he mere months earlier. Since that time, however, many things had changed. Our people had quickly come to enjoy living in the old fort and had thrown themselves into making it fit for comfortable living. They had organized themselves thoroughly, into work units and teams, and had been painstaking in identifying and tackling everything that could be classified as a worthwhile work project to be completed before the onslaught of winter. Arable land was simply non-existent, but we had set ourselves immediately to felling the finest of the ancient oak trees that grew up here in the high valleys, and to dressing and curing the lumber, which we would soon be able to trade for grain and other crops to the people of Ravenglass. And, as my own acceptance of our lives within the fort had grown, I had made it my concern to find out as much as was known locally about Mediobogdum and its origins, including the road it guarded.

"Have you ever heard of the Tenth Iter?"

"No, should I have?"

"Not really, but it was widely celebrated once, as the only Roman supply route into the heartland of north-west Britain from the coast. This is it, and it runs for twenty miles, from Ravenglass, up over the pass here and on to the garrison fort at Galava, by the side of the big mere."

"The big mere . . . that's what the people here call a lake, is it not?"

"Aye, it is. And a mountain is a fell. We are standing among the Fells."

"Hmm." Ambrose glanced up at the mountains dismissively, plainly unimpressed, his mind elsewhere. "So you have never been to this Galava place? Then you cannot know if it is abandoned, like this."

"No, I've never been there, but it's not abandoned. People live there yet, just as they do in Ravenglass, in the community the local people and suppliers built up around the fort over the years. The road goes beyond there—another road it is, in fact, built at a different time by different legionaries—but it joins up somewhere beyond there, I'm told, at the old fort called Brocavum, with the main trunk road running down the length of Britain."

"All the way down? You mean you could travel on solid Roman roads all the way from there to Londinium?"

"Aye, that's what they tell me, or to Glevum and Aquae Sulis and thence to Camulod, depending on which fork you take at Brocavum. One road goes almost directly south from there, through Glevum and Aquae all the way to Isca, and another branches east and goes almost directly down the centre of the country to Londinium. You must know it, it passes through Lindum."

"I know two roads converge at Lindum, from the north—one coming directly south, the other from the north-west—but I have never been more than a hundred miles north of Lindum. I did not know the road reached so far into the north-west." Ambrose sounded fascinated, although I could not see why. The water route by which he had come here was faster, more direct and far less dangerous than the overland journey he was now evidently contemplating. Finally my own curiosity overcame me.

"Why are you asking all these questions? Have you a wish to strike out overland from here to Lindum?"

"No, nor to anywhere else, but it's good to know there's a solid, passable route in and out of this place if anything goes wrong at the seaward end."

"What does that mean?" He heard the alarm in my voice and turned towards me quickly, raising a placatory hand.

"Nothing, Caius! I swear it means nothing. I'm but being pessimistic. There is no danger and no catastrophic fate threatening you from the sea. I was merely thinking about a conversation I had with Connor, on my way up here. He told me he has heard nothing of the Sons of Condran since the slaying of Liam and the repulse of their fleet from Ravenglass, and he is intelligent and responsible enough to be concerned over that. Some sort of demonstration of Condran's displeasure should have occurred by now, he thinks, and I agree with him. The fact that nothing has occurred, and that nothing seems to be stirring on or beyond the seas, even to the north by the new lands, is disconcerting. Call me foolish, if you wish, but I have had visions of an enormous fleet of alien Erse sails darkening the horizon, come to burn Derek's halls about his ears. But now I know that if that should occur, and all attempts at succour or rescue fail, you and yours will be able to escape across this pass, and thence to the south and safety."

"I see . . ." I faced him squarely, attempting to mask my unease. "Have you really dreamed of this enormous fleet, Ambrose?"

He grinned at me and reached to slap my shoulder. "No, not as you mean it. Not in the way you dream, Brother—no magical occurrences or spectral loomings. No, I'm simply attempting to see what might, could, lie ahead. . . . And speaking of that, hard labour lies immediately ahead. Where are these carpenters and charcoal-burners?"

"Behind us, about a mile from here." I pulled Germanicus up into a rearing, two-legged turn. It was a move we had practised down through the years and one we both enjoyed, I purely for the skill it demanded and displayed and for the awe it inspired in observers. I noticed Ambrose now sniffing the fresh smell of green woodsmoke borne on a stray eddy of wind. "If we follow our noses, we'll ride them down," I said, and I kicked my horse forward.

It took us the better part of half an hour to cross the distance from the fort's gate to the steep hillside clearing where our men were labouring, and as we went we talked of many things, not least of which was the evident and startling intellect of the boy who was our charge. I mentioned again to Ambrose my recently born fear that the very place I had chosen for his tutoring—this lonely, isolated fort with its tiny and embryonic society—would prove to be inadequate for the task I had set myself. This sanctuary we had found—safe, it appeared, from the eyes and weapons of potential assassins of all stripes—was yet no place in which to train a future king. This conviction I had come to accept only with the greatest reluctance. That had not been my first opinion, when I was flushed with the challenge of escaping danger and establishing ourselves in safety in the ancient fort. Only as the weeks stretched into months had I come to see how small our outpost was, here on the edge of nothingness, and how minuscule a template it provided for any parallel study of building and running a kingdom. The boy would have to come to know the larger world of men.

Ambrose listened closely to all I had to say, and when I had finished he reined in his horse and kicked one foot free of the stirrup, hooking his knee over the front of his saddle as he turned to peer at me.

"You think this place is too isolated for the task you've set yourself? And yet you brought him here precisely because of that, and you have effectively achieved a complete disappearance, from Camulod, from your previous life and from all danger to the boy."

"Damnation, I know that, Ambrose, and for months I believed that I had done the right thing. But as I watch the boy shoot upward, growing like a young tree, I grow increasingly afraid that too much of the time he spends here will be time wasted when he could be learning other things, necessary things, elsewhere, in similar safety."

"How so? What could he learn about better elsewhere that he cannot learn here?"

"Life, and the living of it among men of all kinds, venal and noble!" I realized how that sounded and hurried on to negate the insult implied to my friends. "Our people here are good and fine, noble and gracious enough, God knows, and among Derek's Celts the lad will come to no harm. But he is not a normal boy, and that is the crux of all my concerns. We are not raising Arthur Pendragon to be a normal man, Ambrose. Our purpose is to breed a warrior and an enlightened leader. It sounds grandiose and overstated, phrased thus baldly, but it is, nonetheless, the truth.

"If the lad is to rule, in Camulod or Cambria or Cornwall, he must learn to be a king—a warrior and a leader, greater than a Vortigern and free of such errors as Vortigern has made—and I believe he will not learn such things stuck here in isolation. To learn, he needs examples—of the weaknesses of men as much as of their strengths—and to find those he must look abroad, in the world of men, where ambition and greed and ruthlessness and petty, thieving treachery are daily things, exposed and shown for what they are by nobility and honour and integrity. Only by seeing such things will he learn how to deal with them and rise above them. I learned them by riding on patrols with Uther, keeping the peace in Camulod and dealing with the people beyond our domain. You learned them by riding to war with your guardian uncle, in Lindum, and with Vortigern, keeping the peace and guarding your king's affairs. Arthur may learn the theories behind such things up here, but he will lack the practical aspect of training. We have no venal traitors in our little group—no monsters like Lot of Cornwall or the demented, deformed Carthac. We lack even a Peter Ironhair."

"I think you are overwrought, Cay." The level tone of Ambrose's voice brought home to me the stridency that had been present in my own. "I can see clearly why you are so concerned. This is a lonely life you lead, up here, and I have no doubt its shortcomings loom more starkly in the winter months, but I think you are worrying unnecessarily. Arthur will come home eventually to Camulod, as planned, when he and his friends are old enough to ride with our troopers. That has already been discussed and agreed upon, and should take place within the next three or four years—perhaps even sooner if the lad continues to shoot up the way he's going. In the meantime, our concern must be to keep him safe, to provide him with a stable, wholesome home, and to teach him all he is capable of learning. Although after what he taught us both a few nights ago, it might be more accurate to say we should teach him all that we are capable of teaching, for I suspect he'll learn much more than that, eventually.

"Here in these mountains you can teach him to fight like a warrior, on horseback and on foot, and to live like a man, in self-sufficiency. You can teach him the lessons learned and taught to you by those who learned them years before young Arthur's father saw the light of day. You can give him enlightenment: the power to read and write, both of them sadly lacking in this land today. The people with whom you have surrounded him are the best teachers he could have, and the boy is highly gifted. He will waste nothing learning from such as these. So let him learn from them, but expose him to other sources, too.

"Think about taking him away, to Gaul, to spend some time with your friend Bishop Germanus, and let him see how others live in other climes. Maybe take him to Eire, where there are no roads, and to the northern islands his grandfather holds, and let him see how primitive life is in such remote and hostile places. You could take him abroad in Britain, too . . . not to Cambria or to Cornwall, or even to Camulod, yet. But across the brow of the country, following the Roman roads you spoke of to Vortigern for a certainty, I should think, providing the king's peace lasts there, in the north-east. Why not? The boy has no enemies there, nor do you, and Vortigern is kindly disposed to you, as is Hengist. Remember, you are no longer Merlyn of Camulod; you'll travel as a common traveller, in company with others and a boy or two, perhaps even four. You'll both be better for it. His Uncle Connor would be happy to escort you anywhere by sea, even to Gaul, I would imagine."

Listening, I heard the truth and wisdom of my brother's counsel, and sat straighter in my saddle, the cares caused by my thoughts on this over the past months falling away like leaves in autumn to be replaced by surging enthusiasm for what he had suggested. It would be wonderful, I thought, to see my friend Germanus again after so many years. But then I realized immediately how strange friendship can be. I had met the man Germanus but once, twelve years earlier, and we had had almost nothing in common at the time—certainly no easily apparent reason for us to be attracted to each other—and yet we had become close friends. He was the only person in the world to whom I wrote now with anything approaching frequency, and he was a bishop, the Bishop of Auxerre, in Gaul.

He was also a former legate in the Imperial Armies of the Emperor Honorius, and had won great renown, commanding an entire Army Group in the Rhineland, before his retirement. Always a deeply religious man, he had exchanged the disciplines of military life upon his retirement for the equally restrictive disciplines of theology and had brought to his new ecclesiastical activities the same singleminded dedication and commitment that had set him apart from his fellow soldiers.

I had met Germanus when he came as the Church's Champion to Britain, sent personally by the Pope, the Bishop of the Holy See of Rome, to conduct a great public debate in the large theatre in the town of Verulamium, the proceedings open to all who might wish to attend, upon the entire matter of the teachings of the heretical British lawyer and theologian Pelagius. Opposed to him in this Great Debate was the large number of British bishops who had espoused the teachings of Pelagius and thereafter took pride in calling themselves *Pelagian.* I had travelled far, across the breadth of Britain, to attend, because of my own fears of what might spring from it. My whole family had been greatly influenced, during my childhood and for years before I was born, by a venerable and worthy servant of the fledgling British Church known as Alaric, Bishop of Verulamium. Alaric, the finest of his kind, a simple, Godly man and a shining example of virtue and integrity to all who ever knew him, had, after much thought, espoused the message and the teachings of Pelagius, who taught, in essence, that God, in creating humanity in His own image, had provided each person with a particle of His divine essence. Alaric then taught his flock, as did his friends and associates, that this meant, fundamentally, that each individual person had the ability to communicate with God personally, using that Divine Spark as a conduit for prayer, directly from his mind to God's ear.

The tragedy, for Pelagius and his followers, including Bishop Alaric who knew nothing of the furore that would arise after his death, was that this teaching ultimately negated any need for Churchmen as intermediaries. It effectively removed any need for priests from the lives of ordinary folk and it emerged into public scrutiny at a time when the newly enfranchised Christian Church was beginning to spread its hierarchical wings, having won recognition, under the Emperor Constantine, first as *one* official religion and then as *the* official religion of the Roman Empire. The priests of Rome, revelling in their new-found ability to organize themselves and their activities and beliefs, did not welcome being informed that they were unnecessary . . . they had finally achieved not only recognition, but Imperial rank. The image of the penniless carpenter had been overwhelmed within a few short years by the riches and trappings of the Imperial Court and the Roman Papacy had inherited the grandeur and wealth of the Eternal City.

At the same time that this was going on, the learned Augustine, the prominent Bishop of the See of Hippo in Africa, had begun to promulgate the doctrine he had espoused, which stated that mankind was utterly incapable of achieving salvation on its own, lacking the infusion of the divine grace that flowed as a gift from God to His children through the medium of prayer. Without grace, Augustine preached, mankind was doomed to sin eternally. That argument, reduced to absurdity, stipulated that there was no need for—and no point in having—any kind of human law, since every blameworthy act could be laid at God's door, He having failed to provide sufficient grace to counteract the temptation that led to the transgression. These two arguments, laid out head to head, were destined to collide, for one disputed the need for a Church, while the other decried and denied the need for human, as opposed to divine, Law. They collided in the form of two strong men, Pelagius and Augustine, and

Pelagius, condemned by the joint powers vested in the Church and its Founding Fathers, lost the war. He was outlawed and excommunicated, all his teaching categorized as heretical and declared to be anathema.

My personal fears in all of this had sprung from that anathema. As a soldier I had no knowledge of things theological and no interest in politics, but I was wise enough to be able to discern that this matter had become political, if it had not been so all along. With the excommunication of Pelagius, however, had come word of the excommunication of all his followers, and that had appalled me. The idea that the saintly Bishop Alaric could be excommunicated after his death, declared unholy and denied the right to salvation at the behest of men who had never known him, seemed to me egregious and unforgivable. And it meant, by extension, that all the people of our Colony of Camulod, as nominal Christians adhering to the teachings of our Pelagian bishops, would automatically be excommunicated, too, denied the sacraments of the Church and the possibility of salvation. So when I had heard about this Great Debate to be held in Verulamium, I had ridden to attend it, accompanied by Camulod's finest troops. On the way there, we had met and rescued the bishop himself, finding him assailed by marauding Saxons, and thereafter he and I had become friends and he had sent me home secure in the knowledge that Alaric and the flock he had tended, including my own dear family and friends, were all safe from excommunication.

All of this passed through my mind in far less time than it takes to transcribe, and we had barely progressed ten paces by the time I had finished thinking. Ambrose rode calmly by my side, completely unaware that my mind had been elsewhere since he had finished speaking. I smiled at him then, reflecting that my association with him dated from the same time. He, too, had ridden into Verulamium for Germanus's Great Debate, unaware that his life was about to change forever. He arrived in Verulamium thinking himself to be Ambrose Ambrosianus, but when he and I met, and found ourselves alike as two peas in a pod, it was a simple matter to establish that he was, in fact, Ambrose Britannicus, a half-brother sired unwittingly by my convalescent father almost three decades earlier. My smile grew wider as I recalled that he had been less than delighted by the news, upon first hearing it, although he had adjusted to it rapidly. Now he caught my smile and raised an eyebrow.

"What is it? You look as though something is amusing you."

I shook my head. "No, not really, I was merely remembering Germanus, and how you and I first met, in Verulamium. I like your idea of travel, and I think it might be good to see Germanus again. Thank you for the thought." He nodded wordlessly and kicked his horse forward again, towards the woods that loomed a short distance ahead. From then on, we rode in silence, appreciating the beauty of the day and little considering how the Fates themselves would dictate the tempo of Arthur's progress and education.

Not everyone in the hillside forest clearing to which we eventually came was sawing wood. Long before we reached the spot, we could hear the rapid and unmistakable sound of practice swords hammering at each other with the solid, ringing, concussive authority that bespoke a number of mature men belabouring each other mightily. It soon became clear, however, that others were working. Now we could hear the hollow-sounding *thock* of hard-swung axes and, farther off, the asthmatic rasping of saw blades chewing at green wood.

When we emerged from the woods, we saw that Dedalus and Rufio were the two swordsmen, as I had known they would be, simply from the rattling rhythm of their "blades." Behind them, almost beyond our sight, I could see Mark, our master carpenter, whose skills and knowledge placed him in command of this work group. A team of four harnessed horses was pulling and straining on his right under the urging of one of Derek's men, while the burden with which they were struggling lay somewhere beyond my sight. The man handling the horses turned slightly towards us, and I was surprised to recognize him as Longinus, Derek's artillery commander, who evidently worked as a teamster when not called upon to practise his skills with heavy weaponry.

Off to my left, along the bottom of the slope on which we sat, I could see Joseph and Hector, smith and farmer, working together as a team, driving their axe heads with perfect, flawless rhythm into the solid heartwood of a great oak tree. Lars and Jonathan would be somewhere close by, I knew, working in or around the saw-pit, with a handful of other men, some of them new arrivals, others brought in this morning from Ravenglass to aid with this task of felling and dressing enough trees to keep us supplied with strong, well-seasoned lumber for the next few years.

Dedalus and Rufio had not seen us arrive, so total was their concentration on what they were doing. A moment's carelessness in their pastime could bring great pain. The thick ash dowels from which the wooden practice swords were made were as heavy and unyielding as iron, and both men were wearing only light leather armour. A rap with a hard-swung dowel on an exposed arm could break a bone, so both men were rapt in what they were about. Ambrose sat staring at them in amazement, for there was something here he had never seen before, something completely new that had emerged during the winter past. Neither Dedalus nor Rufio held a shield: instead, each held an ash practice sword in either hand. The swinging, swaying play of the "blades," underlined by the brilliant, rhythmical clattering as they glanced off each other—four sounds instead of two—turned what the two men were doing into an elaborate, bedazzling ritual-like dance.

Dedalus had begun this thing, two summers earlier. He had always been equally gifted with both hands, to the confusion, envy and disgust of his friends, enemies and competitors. After seeing and admiring the dazzling skills of an itinerant juggler in Camulod several years before, Dedalus had developed a game he played by himself, revelling in his mastery of the skills of hand and eye coordination it required. He would control a third sword with the blades of two others, holding it between them and juggling it astoundingly, sending it into great leaps and spinning bounds, throwing it high in the air, spinning end over end, to fall back and be recaptured by the other blades.

Rufio had been impressed, at first, then cynical. But then, never one to lie back and allow another to win all the laurels, he had eventually begun to practise the same game on his own, in secret, until he had become almost as adept at it as was Dedalus. At that point he stepped forward and issued a challenge to Ded. No one could guess how long or how hard Rufio had been working to acquire his skills, but his progress had been astounding. The contest between the two men for championship status was long, close, hard fought and never settled. Many wagers had been won and lost by the time the contest had moved on to its next stage.

Asked about it, afterward, neither man could pinpoint the occasion when the next degree of challenge actually emerged. It simply turned out that one day, instead of spinning their third blades, the two men had begun matching their twin blades against each other, testing each other's defensive and offensive skills. From that time on, they never played three blades again; they pitted their skills against each other, and those skills became formidable. No other would have dreamed of standing against either of them.

Sitting beside Ambrose, I told him how the contest had evolved. "That's what gave me the idea for the new sticks." Ambrose merely glanced at me, wide eyed. "The forward leap," I continued, knowing that he had not understood me. "The leap from one sword to two, then to a third, and then to this. For more than a thousand years, men learned to use those wooden swords to perfection. Their weight—twice that of their real, iron swords—meant that the men's arm muscles were huge and agile. Their real swords felt like feathers in their hands, and with them, they conquered the entire world. Gladium and scutum—short-sword and shield. Nothing in the world withstood them for a thousand years. With your gladium in your right hand, your scutum in your left, defending your squad-mate on your right while the man on your left defended you, you were invincible—a Roman legionary. That lasted for longer than a millennium. And now they're obsolete, within the space of our lifetime. The legions are all gone. Their troops are scattered, their techniques abandoned, and their short-swords useless without that man defending on your left, without the legion's hierarchy, traditions and discipline.

"Now men use longer swords, but they don't use them well, because there is no discipline for using them. There's no way of training to fight consistently with them, because there's no consistency in the swords themselves. They're long, but they're all of different lengths and weights, and even shapes. The old techniques of training—one man facing a wooden post, practising cut, thrust and stab—won't work with these long swords. The longer blades demand a wider swing, and therefore they deliver less precision in attack. There is no organized technique for them, no ritual defence, no skilled, detailed procedure of attack.

"And then one day I saw Ded and Rufio using two swords each, two hands, flashing and displaying skills the like of which had never been seen before, by me or anyone. Two hands, two blades—twice the speed, twice the weight and twice the skill. And in my mind I saw, all at once and without warning, a longer stick—a staff—twice as heavy as Excalibur, requiring twice the effort to control its arc and thrust and stab."

Ambrose was staring at me now, paying no heed to the men below, who had stopped fighting and were laughing now together, bent over and wheezing for breath, still unaware of our presence above them. "And?" he prodded.

"And I spoke of it to Dedalus and Rufio." I shrugged. "We made some practice pieces, from some unseasoned wood, then dried some others in a kiln, experimented with the length and weight, trial and error, and evolved the prototypes you saw and used today."

A shout of raucous greeting from beneath told us our presence had been discovered. Ambrose glanced down and waved, smiling, but then turned back to me. "But you used two hands on the stick. You would not do that with a keen-edged sword, not without losing your fingers."

"No, I would not, but a stick is not a sword. These staves of ours are weapons in their own right, as well as practice swords. And as weapons, they have advantages that swords don't have—weight, heft and bluntness. They are clubs, bludgeons as well as swords. Let's go down. We can talk more of this later, with Ded and Rufio. I promise you, you will find great pleasure and great usefulness in this. The simple fact of working consistently with these new things—we have no name for them, we call them simply staves—improves everything in which a fighting man might seek improvement, afoot or mounted: balance, dexterity, weight distribution, strength of arm and leg and wind."

Much good did come of what Ambrose would learn that day, but that day itself was not the time best suited for the learning of it. Ambrose and I ended up, stripped to our loincloths and "assisted" by a highly jocular quartet of sawyers from Ravenglass, working in the saw-pit, occasioning great merriment to all who came to watch, as everyone made sure to do. The saw-pit, as we princes of Camulod discovered, was a humbling place, constituting a rite of passage all on its own.

I know that saws have been around forever, ever since the first men learned how to shape and sharpen metal and make it do what they required of it. The story of the making of the first saw blade is one long lost to history, but, once discovered, the secret swept across the world. Saws earned their place among the most widely used of tools and implements: first they were used on wood, to shape round tree trunks into straight-sided beams, and then eventually, with the development of stronger metals, they were used for cutting certain kinds of stone. Saws became so commonplace that people who were not sawyers seldom took note of them. It must have been similar, therefore, it seemed to me, with saw-pits: they were common things, but seldom noted and widely ignored. Most men might live their lives in ignorance that such things even existed. I know now, however, from my own experience, that no man who has worked in a saw-pit could ever forget or ignore the existence of such places.

Consider the felling of a tree. It has grown to maturity in its own place, while endless generations of men have lived and died, and its heartwood is sound and solid, the finest, strongest material available to men for building their constructions, from huts to barns to houses and great halls, and from wagons and wains to galleys and the great biremes, triremes and quadriremes of the now vanished Roman trading fleets. The time arrives for the tree to be felled, trimmed and fashioned into lumber, squared and planed and shaped to men's requirements. The axes bite and chew, and after time has passed and sweat and toil and keen-edged blades have done their work, the tree falls crashing to the ground. Now the limbs and branches are removed, and the great tree is sawn into log lengths. That part is easy. The difficulty comes in transforming the logs, which are cylindrical, into squared beams or planks.

Thus was the saw-pit created, and it is among the simplest, most functional workplaces in the world: a pit beneath a system of cradles and pulleys for holding logs. Each log is laid above the pit and sawn lengthwise, by teams of men using long, heavy, double-handed saws. One man stands above the log, the other in the pit beneath, and they change places frequently, since the man on top must work harder than the man beneath, pushing downward on the cutting stroke and pulling up on the return. Nevertheless, the man below spends all his time waiting for the moment when he can climb above, because below, he is constantly enveloped in the sawdust from the cutting above. His entire body is a seething mass of relentless itching caused by the sawdust, and the sap it contains, adhering to his sweat-covered skin, clogging his eyes, ears and nostrils, and clinging densely to every hair on his tortured body.

Sawyers love to see a novice approach the pit, and they take intense delight in pointing out how much less work there is in being beneath, and then in gulling the raw newcomer into a rash commitment to remain below for longer than a normal man can stand. Hence the jocularity of our quartet of assistants and the hilarity with which the others all came to watch as Ambrose and I laboured mightily, and sweatily, beneath the constant, clinging, aromatic cascade that blinded us and blocked our nostrils and our mouths and drove us to our knees, coughing and spluttering among the mounds of yielding, treacherous, foot-fouling and sweet-smelling oaken sawdust.

By the time they relented and allowed us to alternate and work above the pit, as well as in it, my brother and I had learned a new analogy to apply to the high and low fluctuations of life and fortune. The effort of grappling with green wood for one short, but seemingly endless day had bred in us a lasting appreciation of well-seasoned timber. That very night, sitting exhausted by the cooking fire outside the fort's front gates, I found myself gazing at the carving on my two-handed staff with more appreciation than I had ever felt before, and testing its strength and resilience in my hands, trying in vain to make it bend or even flex.

Dedalus and Rufio had talked at length with Ambrose and me, in the bathhouse and afterwards, at dinner, about some of the things they had already discovered about fighting and training with the new staves. Both men were very enthusiastic about the potential of this new form of training—for they saw it as training in a new technique, plain and simple—and had no difficulty visualizing armies being trained using the new method to learn the skills that had to be applied to fighting with long swords.

Ambrose, however, was sceptical of that. He believed that widespread use of the long sword would be curtailed by the technological and logistical difficulties of large-scale production. Iron ore was no longer being widely mined and smelted in Britain, he pointed out. With the legions now gone for more than four decades, the industry of forging swords had dwindled to a local skill. We had forges in Camulod capable of smelting ore, could we but procure it, and of turning out long swords by the hundred, but Camulod was unique in that. Ambrose believed that warriors henceforth would carry motley weapons and armour, garnered, bought or stolen from wherever they could be found. Few of those weapons, he felt, would be swords of any description. He believed that clubs and axes would once again become more common than swords, and that the spears of ordinary men would soon degenerate again into long poles with fire-hardened, wooden points.

I sat silent as I listened to him speak of all of this and then, when he had finished, I pointed out that if what he suspected came to pass, it would be to our great advantage, since nothing would then threaten us and there would be no armies to march against Camulod. He sat staring at me for some time, then smiled and nodded, saying nothing more, and soon after that, worn out from our exertions in the saw-pit, we crawled off to sleep. Ambrose and Dedalus and Rufio would be foregathering in the morning, to come to terms on some of the basics of fighting with the ash staff. I had other things to do.

X

IN THE WEEK since our return from Ravenglass, I had thought long and hard about the letter I wished to write to Germanus in Gaul, and what it should contain. Now I set aside the last of several sheets of notes I had made and sat back, rubbing at my eyes and flexing my shoulders. I wondered how much time had passed since I had sat down to my task after leaping from my bed in the pre-dawn darkness to light a lamp and pace the floor, struggling with my unruly thoughts. Instead of writing a letter, I had found myself deeply engrossed in making notations on the topics with which I wished to deal in the missive.

Idly I counted the sheets and found six of them each covered with densely packed script—too little of it, I knew, touching upon or concerned with the question that plagued me more than any other: the matter of the boy's education. The extent of the boy's potential, his abilities and talents and his astounding, vibrant mind, so far advanced beyond his small sum of years, left me bereft of the words to write of them. On the point of starting to read my copious notations over, I felt a wave of mounting frustration and pushed them away instead, rising up impulsively from my chair and beginning to pace the room as restlessly as I had in the darkness before daybreak, aware of the tension roiling in my chest and tightening the back of my neck.

On one transit of the outer and far larger of my two rooms, I glanced through the open doorway of my sleeping chamber and saw the untidy rumple of my unmade bed, and the sight of it made me stop in mid-step with the realization of how greatly I had changed since coming to Ravenglass and Mediobogdum. Throughout my entire life, raised as I had been with a soldier's discipline, the first thing I had done, every morning, was to straighten, remake or stow away my bed before proceeding to whatever else I had to do that day. It was as natural to me as breathing, something done without consideration or a conscious thought. Now, however, the sight of that unmade bed brought home to me the hugeness of the changes that had swept through my life in recent months and years.

My life, I now realized, was no longer my own in the thoughtless, intimate way it had ever been, even in the days when I lived with the woman I loved as my wife. Now I was living for other people—the most important of them Arthur, but the others claiming my attention and my concern nevertheless. My priorities were theirs; my cares were theirs; and my duties revolved entirely around them. I told myself, as soon as the thought occurred to me, that duties always revolved around others, but the difference was clear and stark in my understanding: the duties I had known before leaving Camulod were structured, military and exact; they were definable and thus predictable; and they entailed a reciprocity in their execution—rewards, in the form of recognition, a sharing of responsibility, and an occasional relief from that responsibility in return for performance. That was no longer true. Nowadays, the responsibility was unrelenting.

Knowing I was being self-indulgent and self-pitying, I stepped resolutely into the bedchamber and reached down to grasp the blanket on my bed, just as someone knocked on the outer door of my quarters.

"Enter, the door is unlocked," I shouted, and then, curious to see who had come calling, I leaned back on my heel, craning my neck. When the door swung open, I was amazed to see Shelagh thrust her head through the opening and call to me.

"Cay? May I come in?"

"Shelagh! Of course you may come in. Since when must you await my bidding?"

The surge of pleasure I felt at the sight of her and the sound of her voice drove every thought of dissatisfaction from my mind, but yet I made no move to go into the outer room. The opportunity to benefit from the fact that I could see her while remaining out of her sight loomed too large for me to ignore, so I remained where I was, watching her through the open door of my darkened bedchamber. She leaned further into the room, keeping her hand on the door handle and looking about her, searching for me, and then, just as her eyes fastened on the doorway beyond which I stood in shadow, I saw that she had someone with her, standing close behind her on the threshold.

I strode out towards her, smiling a welcome, just as she entered, beckoning whoever was behind her to follow. The sight of the newcomer quickly slowed me to a halt, halfway across the intervening space. It was the young woman who had smiled at me the evening of the feast, the one called Tressa, whose high, full breasts and laughing eyes had disturbed me so greatly. Now I found myself confronted by those eyes again, staring at me, wide and alert, as though slightly startled, and I was immediately aware that her breasts were, indeed, high and full and impossible to ignore, causing the clothing that should have concealed them to enhance the sweep of their upper surface instead, and then drape vertically from their points. Shelagh saw none of this exchange of looks, and I was fleetingly aware of feeling grateful for her preoccupation with whatever she was looking at or searching for. She took one last, sweeping look around the room and then straightened, facing me.

"It's dark in here, and even dustier than usual. Merlyn, this is—"

"Tressa. I remember her from Ravenglass. Welcome, Tressa."

The young woman dimpled and flushed with pleasure, buckling one knee and shyly whispering, "Mester Cahy." I turned to face Shelagh squarely, feeling ridiculously aware of the other woman and strangely guilty for that very awareness, as though, in taking notice of her, I had sinned through disloyalty to Shelagh.

"How may I serve you? You must forgive me, I fear I am unused to having women here in my rude quarters."

"Aye, that's obvious." Shelagh was smiling, her eyes twinkling and full of mischief. "I have brought Tressa here to see what she must do. She will be looking after two of you, yourself and Lucanus, keeping your quarters clean and bright and aired, and mending your clothes and whatever else may require looking after."

"But—"

"No, no buts, Cay. That is the law, according to Shelagh, and you will save us all much grief and inconvenience if you will simply accept it as decreed. You men are the great ones for laying down laws, but there are times when women's laws are better and more sensible, and this is one of them. You work on those things that concern you, and Tressa here will keep your surroundings neat and clean enough to make your work as pleasant as may be. Do you understand me?"

"But—"

"But? Pardon us, Cay, but we came here apurpose. Now, if you will stand aside, I wish to show Tressa her duties. Tressa, come."

I stood gape-mouthed and watched them as they examined every vestige of my quarters, talking between themselves and taking note of everything they thought to change or better. My initial annoyance passed, and soon I found myself taking pleasure in the sight of both of them. Tressa was no beauty, but she was young and radiant with health, buxom and sprightly enough to suffer little side by side with Shelagh's older, glowing loveliness. Both women were round and full where women needed to be both, and as they spoke together, both laughed quietly from time to time. Presently they completed their examination and returned to where I stood by the window.

"Well," Shelagh said, "I've shown Tressa what's in store for her. She'll keep out of your way, as much as possible, doing what she has to do during the day while you're about your business. The only reason you will have to know that she's about will be the uncustomary pleasantness with which you will be surrounded from now on. Good day to you."

Tressa bobbed, with her shy smile, and whispered my name again, her soft Cumbrian brogue doing strange things to the vowel sounds, and then they were gone, leaving me feeling as though I had been paraded, inspected and assessed—all of which was true. I stood at the window, watching them as they went out, and after they had gone from sight I remained there, peering out at the weather. Between the top of the fort's outer wall and the line of the overhanging eaves above my window, I could see blue sky and small, white clouds scudding across it at a speed that suggested a high, brisk wind. Suddenly the room seemed dark and cold, unnaturally quiet now that the women's voices had been added, then subtracted. I strode to the door, collecting my cloak from a peg as I went outside into the brightness of the mid-morning sunlight.

I found nothing unusual in the silence that greeted me. Even with the recent growth in our numbers, tripling our presence here, fifty people were barely noticeable in a fort built to house six hundred, and the times when all fifty were present within the fort were few and far between. I knew that the wood-gathering party was in the forest again that day, as it had been for the previous seven, so that took care of at least ten men and probably closer to a score. Ambrose was out with Dedalus and Rufio, practising with the staves that fascinated him nowadays. Shelagh and Tressa had disappeared, presumably to join the other women who would all be indoors at their women's work at this time of day, and the boys would already be out beyond the walls, the morning hours of their tuition long over. Somewhere in the distance I thought I heard the sound of high, girlish voices; many of the newcomers had brought young families along with them, and the place was now bright with children of both sexes, where before there had been only the four boys from Camulod. I saw only one other living soul, one of the newcomers whose name I had not yet learned, as I made my way to the northern postern gate. We exchanged silent nods in passing and then I was outside, walking forward the few paces that took me to the edge of the precipice overlooking the valley at the rear of our perch.

Ahead of me to my right, on the far north-eastern side of the valley, the Fells soared up to tower over me. But it was the valley far beneath my feet that drew my attention, because the entire floor of it seemed to be alive, writhing with movement like woven matting covering a swarm of rats. The carpet, as I well knew, was made of enormous oak trees, and the turbulence that agitated them was caused by massive gale-force winds blowing inland from the western sea, twelve and more miles away along the vale of the Esk. Even here, on the heights above, the power of that wind was undiminished, buffeting me with heavy blows as it surged up the unyielding face of the cliff at my feet.

I stepped even closer to the edge, aware of my own foolishness yet seemingly powerless to resist the urge to look down at the cliff face itself. The pressure of the wind increased, becoming a solid, living thing, so that I had to force myself forward into it, leaning out against its power while listening to my mind screaming at me to step back and stop being a fool. It was a strange sensation, hanging there, leaning my weight into that wind for what seemed a long, long time, knowing that if it died without warning I would, too, falling out into the space that taunted me. For long heartbeats I felt convinced that by merely spreading my arms and diving outward I would find the power of flight and might swoop like a bird, in safety, down to the trees beneath. I even raised my arms, holding them out before me and feeling the pressure of the air beneath them filling the folds of my cloak and lifting it to flap like wings about me, before I blinked and stepped back, dropping my hands to my sides and feeling my cloak subside and the hair settle down on my head again as the direct flow of air from beneath was interrupted by the edge of the cliff. As I stepped back, the wind died, without warning, as I had feared it might mere moments earlier. For a count of four heartbeats the air was utterly still and I shuddered with horror, clearly imagining my own body plunging downward into the abyss over which I had so recently been poised. Then the gale returned with a blustering, muffled roar, and I stepped away resolutely, turned my back on the valley and re-entered the fort, making my way straight to the stable where Germanicus was tethered.

Moments later, I left the fort again through the main, southern gate, waving to Lucanus, whom I had noticed walking the interior perimeter road close against the wall. As I emerged from the gateway and kneed my mount along the approach to the main road, passing the bathhouse and cresting the rise that hid the fort itself from the roadway, I glanced upward to my left, to where the narrow ribbon of the road snaked its way up the final approach to the pass to the next valley, and my eye was arrested by a flash of white. Reining in my horse, I looked more carefully and saw that the whiteness was at least one of the piebald ponies belonging to the four boys, although there was no sign of the boys themselves. Curious, I swung Germanicus eastward when I reached the road and kneed him upward, towards the saddleback of the pass.

I knew the boys came up here often, particularly during the winter months, when they had spent their days sledding down from the heights. I myself had made no attempt to approach the crest of the pass since the first and only time I had been up there, late in the autumn, long before the first snowfall of the winter. I had forgotten how unimaginably steep the incline of the roadway was. As we ascended, Germanicus was forced to lean further and further into each mounting step, battling to force his weight and mine upward, his shod hooves scrabbling and sliding on the hard, slippery, cobbled surface of the roadway as he fought to negotiate each tightly twisting curve on the serpentine slope. I found myself imagining again the agony and grief of the legionaries and wagon drivers who must have sweated and racked themselves struggling to control heavy-laden wagons, drawn by teams of oxen and mules, on such an impossibly pitched surface, only to face even greater difficulties on the downward slope beyond the crest.

As I approached the summit, sheltered now from the buffeting of the wind by the sheer, towering cliffs of the mountainside on my left, I drew rein and dismounted, determined to walk the remainder of the way out of pity for my noble horse. The single pony that had attracted my attention was close by, his reins tethered, I could see, by a heavy stone, and I recognized him as Primus, Arthur's own mount. He looked as though he had been ridden hard, over muddy ground, for all four of his legs, his long tail and the underside of his belly were caked with mud. Of the animal's owner I had yet to see the smallest sign.

Now, however, my eyes were attracted by a suggestion of movement among the short grass on the rocky bank by the side of the road. Only when I took a step closer did I realize that I was looking at the scarcely visible, barely rippling movement of a thin, unbroken sheet of water that was flowing straight down from the last vestiges of snow still melting on the heights far above.

Intrigued, I moved closer still, stepping off the edge of the road into the shallow, pebble-filled ditch and leaning forward to brace my outstretched hand against the rock face, breaking the thin sheet of icy water so that it buckled and surged, shockingly cold against the warm skin of my hand and wrist as I bent forward to peer closely at the vegetation. With a tiny thrill of wonder, I discovered then that what I had thought to be grass was actually an astonishing mixture of delicate, intricately structured mosses of incredible complexity, and tiny, bulbous-leaved plants, many of them bearing minuscule flowers of white, yellow, blue and every colour of red, from pale pink to deep, blood crimson. All of these, in hundreds of thousands, clung tenaciously to the very surface of the stone, rooted in an endless web of minute fissures in what had seemed a wall of solid rock. Between these fissures, beneath the flowing sheen of water, the stone was coated with lichens in a wondrous range of colours from pale yellows and greens, through ochres and umbers and purples and browns deepening all the way to black—a miniaturized vista of hues and textures the like of which I had never seen or imagined. I remained there, lost in the wonder of my discovery, losing all track of the passage of time, until I became aware, gradually at first and then with increasing urgency, of the loss of sensation in my chilled hand. Smiling foolishly then, I straightened up slowly and, chafing my hand dry with the lining of my cloak, found young Arthur Pendragon staring down at me from the cliff face above me and to my left.

"Merlyn, what are you doing? What are you looking for?"

I nodded a greeting. "Arthur. I came looking for you, first, because I saw your pony from below, but when you found me I was looking at the plants on the stone face, here, and the way the running water covers them. What have you been up to?"

"Nothing." He bent his knees and began making his way down towards me, balancing easily with one outstretched hand touching the stone face behind him.

I turned and climbed the short distance back to where Germanicus stood waiting for me. I gathered his reins and stood again for a spell, staring in wonder at the greenery that had assumed again, from this distance, the appearance of short, bright grasses. Germanicus whickered gently and butted my shoulder with his muzzle, and I turned lazily around to gaze back downward to where our fort lay beneath us, to all outward appearances devoid of life, its walls presenting an aspect of impregnability I knew they could not maintain in reality. There was a fire, as always, in the bathhouse, the smoke from the furnace chimney spilling lazily to pool in a freakishly sheltered pocket and billow there for a while like an errant cloud before being sucked upward at one end of the hollow, into the teeth of the wind, where it curled over the wall and scattered rapidly into nothing.

Arthur jumped down onto the edge of the road with a thump and came towards me, but only when he was almost within arm's reach did I see the swollen bruise on his right temple and the encrusted rims of blood that framed his nostrils. I had not noticed it before because I had been looking up at him from beneath, on the wrong side. Now it was evident that his right eye was blackening impressively, its upper lid swollen and sore looking. He saw me notice, and his face flushed with what I took for discomfort. I stepped closer to him and took his chin in my hand, tilting his head back and up.

"Well, your consolation may lie in the fact that, a month from now, there will be no sign of this. For the next few days, however, your face is going to be a sight to behold. I hope you won?"

His headshake and the way his eyes moved off to gaze into the distance told me he had not.

"Who was it? Gwin? Bedwyr?"

"No." He still would not look at me, even though I held him by the chin. I released my grip and stepped back.

"Who, then?" Even as I asked the question I could see it would go unanswered. There was a stubborn cast to his countenance that was highly uncharacteristic of this normally sunny youngster. I shrugged, to show him I was really unconcerned. "I have no intention of pursuing the matter, Arthur. I merely asked out of curiosity. The damage is already done. It's boys' business and no concern of mine—men have no place in such affairs."

"And yet they take an interest, sometimes." The boy's words came out as a truculent mumble, causing me to narrow my eyes at once.

"What was that? Who takes what? What are you talking about?"

"Men. They sometimes take an interest in the wars of boys."

"Arthur, what are you talking about? You're not making sense." He continued to glower, his young face dark with anger. "Are you saying a man hit you, not a boy?"

"No. I fought with Droc and he beat me."

"I'm sure he did." Droc was one of Derek's eldest sons, at least three years older than Arthur and big for his age, so close to being identical to his own elder brother Landroc that the pair were often mistaken for twins and were inseparable. Arthur was a big lad for his age, too, but his bigness was yet but a promise, and his present frame was long and gangling. I estimated, now that I had reason to think of it, that Droc must be at least half again Arthur's weight. I waited, but it was clear no reaction would be forthcoming.

"What in God's name possessed you to fight with Droc? He's almost as big as I am." The boy made no response at all. "Not going to tell me? Well, then, I'll have to believe it was insanity, although I've never seen the slightest hint of that in you before today. But you said something about men interfering in boys' affairs. Did someone stop the fight?"

"No."

"Well, someone should have. Come on, I'll ride down with you to the fort. Where are the others, Bedwyr and Gwin and Ghilleadh?"

Arthur shook his head. "I don't know. I left them behind, after the fight. I didn't want them with me."

"I see. Were they involved at all?"

Another silent headshake was all I received in answer to that question, and I straightened up, all at once impatient with the boy's unusual reticence.

"Very well, let's be away. Bring your pony, but there's no point in trying to ride down, for the first stretch at least. We'll have to walk."

He collected his pony and we began to wind our way downward in silence, concentrating on where we placed our feet, since the iron nails that studded the soles and heels of our sandalled boots could find no purchase on the hard cobblestones that made up the surface of the road, making every step a matter of careful balance and the threat of a painful fall.

We remounted eventually, once we had achieved the gentler slopes at the bottom of the ridge below the crest and rode on without speaking, hunched against the battering of the wind. We had almost reached the junction of the roadway and the approach to the fort before either of us spoke again. It was Arthur who broke the silence.

"Ghilleadh found a Roman short-sword—a gladium."

I glanced at him in surprise. "Did he indeed? Where? And how do you know it was Roman?"

"It was lying in the long grass on the hillside beneath the western gate, and it had been there for a long, long time. Almost rusted away completely, but it was Roman. The hilt was bronze. I've seen dozens just like it in the Armoury at Camulod. Some soldier must have either dropped it or thrown it away, a long time ago. It was probably thrown there, because it was a long way down from the gate and far from any pathway."

"Hmm, I'd like to see that. Will you ask Ghilleadh to show it to me?"

"He can't. Droc took it away from him."

I immediately began to ask myself why a big lad like Droc would be interested in the rusted remnant of an old Roman sword, but then all at once I knew, alerted by the tension radiating from my young companion. Droc had taken it to prove a point of some kind. He had played the bully.

"So that's why you fought Droc. He took the sword away from Ghilleadh."

"Mmm . . ."

This time the silence lasted until we were almost inside the fort again. When I drew rein he stopped, too, looking up at me expectantly. I sat thinking for long moments before I spoke.

"Arthur," I said, finally, "I don't want you to think that I am prying, poking my snout into private affairs that are none of my concern. . . ." He nodded, a slight crease between his brows as I hesitated. "Having said that, however, I will admit to you that I am more than merely curious. You made a reference, back up there on the hilltop, and from it I suspect that some man, somewhere, has interfered in something that concerns you. I think there is more to this whole affair than you are admitting."

Yet again I paused, deliberately, leaving him ample time to say whatever might have been in his mind, but he guarded his silence, his mouth held now in the semblance of a pout, although no other sign of distemper showed itself upon his open face. I sucked in a deep breath and finished what I had to say.

"There are times when I feel that you and I are more than simply master and student, more than mere cousins, man and boy. At such times, I like to think that we are friends, in the true sense of the word—equal creatures of like mind and temperament, with mutual tastes and complementary opinions and the ability to discuss things openly between ourselves without acrimony or evasion. Do you ever feel that way?"

I felt scorn at myself for my shameless manipulation of the boy, who now sat gazing at me, nodding his head slowly in agreement, his face clouded with the naked need to discuss the matters that were troubling him. He coughed, and then glanced about him, his eyes flitting up to look at the top of the gate-tower ahead of us, and then down again to scan the empty pathway on either side.

"Yes," he said, in a voice that was barely more than a whisper. "I'd like to tell you what happened, but . . . not here."

"Of course not. We'll go to my quarters. I have some cold apple juice there, crushed this morning in the kitchens, and some fresh bread. Meet me there as soon as you have unsaddled your pony and rubbed him down. He would benefit from a good grooming."

I stabled Germanicus, unsaddling him without haste and rubbing him down thoroughly with a rough towel, even though he had not even broken a sweat on our short outing. Arthur, I knew, would have a much more difficult task with his own mount, and I knew it was one he would not shirk, for the discipline of caring for their ponies was one that had been painstakingly drilled into each of the boys. Any evidence of carelessness in tending their animals would immediately ensure the dire punishment of forfeiture of riding privileges for anything from a single day to an entire week. When I had finished, ensuring that my horse had both food and drink within reach, I made my way slowly back to my quarters, whistling an old marching tune under my breath and wondering what could possibly have upset the boy so profoundly.

I was still wondering about that, and still struggling against the temptation to think instead of young Tressa and her breasts, when Arthur knocked and entered. About half an hour had passed since we parted, and I saw immediately from his expression that whatever had been troubling him was still paramount in his mind. He accepted the cup of unfermented apple juice I offered him and then sank wordlessly into one of the two large armchairs that flanked the open, stone fireplace against the long wall at the rear of the room. I watched him closely, noting his frowning concentration as I poured myself some wine and went to sit across from him.

Dried kindling and wood shavings were piled carefully in the brazier. The room was cool, almost dark, the slanting light from the mid-day sun pooling on the floor directly beneath the open windows. I stood up again and moved to light a taper from the single lamp burning on my writing table, taking the flame to the brazier. When I was satisfied with the blaze, I straightened up again and moved back to my chair, my feet stretched out towards the leaping flames. Arthur sat staring into the fire.

"So," I began. "What was it that drove you from your friends so early in the day?"

The boy sniffed and his frown deepened, and then he turned to face me, his eyes wide and puzzled. "What gives Droc the right to think he can take Ghilleadh's sword, Merlyn?"

"His size, I should think." I knew the words were ill chosen as they issued from my mouth and immediately wished them unsaid. Here, I knew, was neither the time nor the place for flippancy. To my surprise, though, Arthur did not react to my facetiousness.

"No, that's not enough," he said. "His size gives him the ability to take the sword, but what is it that permits him to think, to believe, completely, that he may take it, as his right?"

I blinked with surprise, and I chose my next words with care.

"Forgive me, Arthur, but I'm not sure I understand you. What are you asking me, exactly?"

"I don't know, not really, but I do know the answer is important. Ghilly found the sword, in the spot where it had lain for years and years. Whoever threw it there has been dead and gone for ages, so it became Ghilly's when he found it. And then Droc saw it and took it away from him. It was an old, dirty thing, all rust, and it was useless, but Droc took it and kept it. Why? Why would he do that?"

I shrugged, mystified. "For the reason I mentioned before, most probably. Because he could. Because he wanted to."

"But why?" The question was almost a shout, the boy's frustration boiling out of him. "Droc has a sword, one of his father's old ones. He has no need of another, especially that old, useless thing of Ghilly's. And yet he took it because he believed he had the right to take it—not because he needed it or wanted it, but because he believed it was his to take. That is wrong, Merlyn. No one should have the right to do that kind of thing. It's . . . it's unjust!"

"Well, I can't see that it's worth getting so worked up about. By your own admission, it's nothing more than an ugly of piece of useless, rusted metal of value to no one."

"Ghilly valued it! It was his. He was the one that found it." The scorn and anger in those flashing young Pendragon eyes almost made me flinch, and I suddenly understood that what I, as a man, could accept as being natural, if deplorable, was a source of deep outrage to the boy's sense of justice. I coughed to cover my confusion.

"Well, what did Droc do with the sword, once he had taken it?"

"I don't know. He took it away with him."

"After you and he had fought . . ."

"Yes."

"And why did you decide to fight him?"

"I didn't decide. I was fighting him before I knew what I was doing. He bent Ghilly over and beat him with the flat of the old sword. Ghilly was crying, and the next thing I knew, I was on the ground and Droc was kicking me."

"I see. Did you blood him?"

A tiny smile flickered on the boy's lips. "I must have, his nose was bleeding."

"What about the others, Bedwyr and Gwin? Didn't they help you?"

"They couldn't. Landroc kept them out of it. So Droc thrashed me and then the two of them walked away, laughing. He did it because he could, and that is all there is to understand, I suppose."

"What, that he's a bully?"

The look he threw me was one of pure pity. "No, that he is the king's son."

I was astounded, unwilling to believe what I had heard.

"What does that have to do with anything? Do you believe King Derek would condone his son's behaviour in this?"

"It has to do with everything, Merlyn, and it began last week." Ignoring the expression on my face, he spoke to me as if I were the boy and he the teacher, and I sat, fascinated by his words and his passion. "Last week, the day after Uncle Ambrose came, I found something, too—something much more valuable than Ghilly's old sword. I found a brooch, in the deep woods outside the town walls, a big, old brooch with a jewelled stone in it like a large piece of yellow glass. It was of silver, I think, but all tarnished green and black with age. Foolishly, I showed it to Kesler when I returned to Ravenglass that day, and he tried to snatch it from me. We fought over it."

Kesler was yet another of Derek's many sons, but he was of an age with Arthur, and smaller in stature.

"Well? You fought, and then what?"

"One of King Derek's captains stopped us and wanted to know what we were fighting about."

"Who was it, do you know? And what did you tell him?"

"It was Longinus, the catapult engineer, and we told him the truth."

"And what happened then?"

"He made me give the brooch to Kesler, because Kesler was the king's son and the brooch was therefore his, found on the king's land."

"I see. And how did you feel about that?"

The boy gnawed on the inside of his cheek, considering his answer.

"I was angry at first, and then I was not . . . or not as much."

"How so?"

"Because I did not really believe the brooch was mine. It never had been mine and had belonged to someone else. Someone had lost it, some time in the past. And it had value—even beneath all the dirt you could see that. The size and colour of the stone, and the scribing on the metal . . . it was the kind of thing not worn by ordinary folk, so it must have belonged to someone of rank, someone from Ravenglass, perhaps the king himself or one of his family. . . ."

"But?"

He grimaced. "But if that were so, I think Longinus should have taken it to give to the king himself, he should not merely have permitted one of the king's sons to take it. That did not become clear to me at the time. I only thought about it afterwards. Was I right to think so?"

I let that one pass, for the moment. "Hmm. And then Droc took the sword today. I see now what concerns you."

"Do you?" The lad's face brightened.

"Of course I do. The injustice of what you witnessed today brought out the anger you've been feeling since the first occasion."

"No!" His voice was suddenly loud again, echoing the lightning change that had swept over his face as I spoke. He caught himself, moderating his tone. "No, it's much more than that, Merlyn. Can't you see what happened? Droc had plainly heard about my finding the brooch and what had happened over that, and when he saw the sword that Ghilly had found, he simply decided it was his, by right, since it had been found in his father's territories. So he puffed up his chest, displayed his muscles and took it, despite the fact that it was worthless to him. That is the injustice."

Abruptly, we had come to the nub of the matter. Now it was clearly evident. This nine-year-old boy had come up against an injustice, clearly delineated in his uncorrupted view, and now he was wrestling with the abstractions of justice and its uneasy relationship to physical power; with the philosophical intangibles of force and power and their influence on morality! I drew a long, deep breath, holding up my hand to give him pause, and tried to marshal my chaotic thoughts. Here, I knew, was a seminal moment in the relationship between my ward and me, a moment I could neither ignore nor defer to another time. But how was I to respond? Watching me closely, waiting for me to speak, he leaned backward in his chair and folded his arms across his chest.

"Look you," I began, then subsided again, rubbing the side of one finger against the stubble on my chin. The boy made no attempt to hurry me but sat watching me, unblinking. I dropped my hand from my face and sat straighter in my chair.

"Arthur, there are some things . . . some aspects of life . . . that appear to change as boys grow into men. They did for me, and they do for all boys. I think you have just come face to face with one of them. In a boy's world, I think, colours are easy to identify—black is black and white is white." I saw his eyes cloud with incomprehension and hurried on to explain myself. "All that means is that, when you're a boy, good is good and bad is bad and there's no difficulty in telling the two apart and then behaving in accordance with your findings. For instance, I believe most boys see men in one of three ways. There are men they like and admire, and they try to stay close to such men, emulating them. Then there are the ruck—the unknown strangers, the common mass of men—to whom they are indifferent, and they go on about their lives as boys always have, ignoring them as insignificant. The third kind of men are those they dislike—the bullies, the misanthropes—unpleasant men. These men wise boys avoid and take great pains to stay away from them. Would you agree?"

Arthur nodded, slowly and deliberately, and I found myself speaking with much solemnity as I continued.

"Good. Well, that ability to avoid such men is one of the things that changes as a boy grows older. While he is still a boy, his avoidance of them is unimportant and unnoticed. He may run and hide from them and spend his days avoiding them and suffer nothing by his flight, because he is a mere boy and hence beneath the notice of grown men. That is his great good fortune, though he is ignorant of all of it.

"When he grows up to man's estate, however, all of that changes. He is still the same boy in his heart, but his body has become a man's body, and his cares a man's concerns. He may no longer run and hide when his old enemies and their kind approach. Flight without dishonour has become impossible with the arrival of manhood. Do you understand what I am saying?"

"I think so. You are saying a man must stand and fight such men, or forfeit his honour."

"No, Arthur, I am not saying that, not exactly. What I am saying is that a man must learn to live among such men, to make allowance for their imperfections, and to strive to live a decent, honourable life in spite of them. He need not—indeed he cannot—always fight them."

"Why not?"

"Because . . . because there are so many of them, if the truth be told."

"So many? D'you mean there are more of them than there are honourable men?"

Did I mean that? I had to think carefully before responding.

"No, Arthur, I did not mean to suggest that at all, but you are forcing me here to think carefully about what I do mean, and I find it difficult to be exact. Let me think about it for a little." He sat gazing at me until I was ready to speak again, and I resumed slowly.

"I suppose the reality is that men—the ruck, that common mass of men I spoke of earlier—are indolent when all boils down to honour and dishonour. They would prefer an easy life, free of complication and the need to think about things whose meaning will elude them. That is not to say they lack honour, you understand? It merely means they are . . ."

"Weak." The single word startled me, encompassing, as it did, so great a revelation of the depths of this strange man-child. I blinked and coughed, attempting to hide my surprise, but I saw little point in disputing the correctness of his choice of word.

"Weak . . . yes, I suppose that is the word that best describes them in this case. The mass of men are weak, content to leave their welfare in the hands of other, more resolute men."

"Stronger, both good and bad."

"Hmm. Yes, but remember where this discussion began, Arthur. You are still seeing things through your own eyes, a boy's eyes, in terms of black and white, while in the world of men—the world in which we must all live most of our lives—those colours are but seldom seen. Your pony, Primus, is beautiful, and his coat is pied—black patches and white patches. Tell me, is he a black horse with white markings, or a white horse with black?"

Arthur smiled. "I've wondered about that before now, many times, and I've never been able to decide which is correct. Which do you think he is?"

"I don't have to think, Arthur, I know. He is neither. He is a black-and-white horse, very rare and extremely valuable. Few instances of such colouring exist in nature. Only a few birds, one kind of cattle, certain swine and very few such ponies. Otherwise, the colours mix and blend, and that leads us back to where we were with boys and men. Black mixed with white produces grey, Arthur, and the world of men is filled with shades of grey. Black and white, in the sense of absolute goodness and badness, godliness and evil in men, are seldom encountered in this world by anyone. In all my life I have met only one man whom I consider to be truly good, and I can think of none but two whom I considered truly evil."

"I think most men must be stupid."

"What?"

"I said they must be stupid, men on the whole as you called them . . . like sheep. It is stupidity to let others rule your life simply because you lack the will or the desire to think, or to make decisions. Are women the same way?"

"Women?" I laughed aloud. "Of course they are, why would you even ask such a question? Women are no different from men in such respects. They are fundamentally the same in matters that concern their lives and the way they lead them. Women can be as strong or as weak as any man, as benevolent or wicked, as gracious and kind, or as cruel, mean and vicious. But by and large, they wish only to lead a simple life, uncluttered by the need to make decisions about matters of which they know but little. As you grow older, you will learn much about women and will come to see that they are little different from men in some respects, and universally different in others. You may even find that there are some of them whose company and friendship you will prefer over that of men."

"Hmm." The boy plainly preferred to defer any judgment on that until a later date. He was frowning slightly, deep in thought, his eyes gazing somewhere into the space between us.

"So then, what you are saying is that most men prefer to be told what to do. Is that correct?"

I shrugged. "That would be one way of putting it. Personally, I would carry it further: most men require to be told what to do, most of the time."

The boy's frown deepened. "Why?" He had made no attempt to deny or dispute what I had said, accepting the truth of it as uttered. I sighed, deeply.

"I don't know, Arthur, but that is the way of the world. There are always leaders and no lack of followers. Men build societies—empires, kingdoms, cities, towns—and in all of them, in every one, the ruck are followers and the few are leaders. Even in your own small group of friends, there is a leader."

"Me."

"Aye, but when you turn your ponies loose to graze, what happens? Do they drift apart?"

He sat up straighter. "No, they stay together. . . ."

"And?"

"They follow Primus. He is their leader."

I nodded. "And so it is with cattle. The herd follows the lead bull, the dominant stag leads the herd of deer, the prime ram leads the flock of sheep."

"Dominance. The strongest dominates, everywhere."

"Among the animals, yes, that is true, the strongest dominates by right of conquest, and holds his leadership purely by strength and fighting prowess. But men are different. Men are rational beings, with the ability to combine their strengths with their intellect and talents for the common good. And when they do that, they develop government, which is no more than a regulated system of behaviour based upon the formal rules that we call law." I waited now, observing the play of thoughts upon the boy's face and fighting my own temptation to say too much by forcing myself to count slowly and await his next words. When they came, they were more or less what I had expected.

"But who is it that lays down those rules, in the beginning?" He answered his own question before I could. "The leaders . . ." He shook his head. "But what if they don't want to? What if they make no laws, but rule only by strength, and the fear their strength inspires in others? Or what if they use their laws solely to foster their own ends? What then, Merlyn?"

"Then, Arthur, you have a cruel society in which no true laws exist and the people are no more than slaves, living at the mercy of their overlords, for leaders such as you describe surround themselves with heartless, vicious men attracted by the promise of the rewards of anarchy."

"Anarchy?" I knew he was familiar with that term, for we had discussed it less than a month earlier. "But anarchy means lack of leadership, you told us that last week."

"It does, but ask yourself this. If the dominant leader is a lawless brigand, existing for his own pleasure without law of any kind, what else can exist under his power but anarchy? And that brings us back to where this all began. Do you remember where that was?"

"Aye." There was not the slightest hesitation in his voice. "The changes from boyhood to manhood. No honourable man can run and hide when faced with enemies."

"Good lad! Now you see what I meant when I said that."

"I begin to, I think. Men of honour must combine their intellects and talents to defeat those who would trample on the lives of other, weaker folk."

"Aye, that they must, but the truth goes higher than that, Arthur. Men who consider themselves to have honour have, in their very being, a duty to improve themselves, their way of life and living, and to extend those improvements to benefit their fellows. They are the men by whom societies are founded and built."

"You mean men like Great-grandfather Varrus and Caius Britannicus, don't you?"

"Aye, I do, and all the others who helped them to build their Colony at Camulod."

"Camulod is a democracy, isn't it?"

"In the Greek sense, meaning a place where the people govern? No, I would not say that. But the people are free to live in Camulod in freedom from fear. They know no one will dispossess them on a passing whim. They know their wives and husbands and children may safely walk abroad without endangerment. They know no one will coerce them or force them to do anything unjust or demeaning. And there is no king there, no single man whose will is paramount and unrestrained—the Council sees to that. And that, I suppose, makes Camulod something of a democracy."

"Not like here. This is a kingdom."

I smiled at him. "True, but not a bad one."

"Hmm. It has a king."

Something in his tone made me crease my brow. "What's this, then? Do you think Derek of Ravenglass an unjust man, or a bad king?"

"No." His tone was grudging. "But no one in Camulod would have taken the brooch I found away from me, or taken the sword from Ghilly."

"Nor did King Derek, Arthur. He did not take your brooch away."

"No, but it was taken in his name, under his law, and the manner of it was unjust."

"How so? You mean the giving of it to Kesler? Well, you may be right, but even so, the fault was not King Derek's. What's the matter? Am I wrong?"

Arthur's face had set, in mere moments, into an expression I took for stubbornness. He sat staring at me for a short time and then spoke out, addressing me formally now with that disconcertingly adult directness I had noticed in him several times before, on those infrequent occasions when he had felt strongly enough about something to weigh his options and opinions and had then decided to speak his mind and suffer the consequences.

"One of us is, Commander. The training I have had in logic, from yourself and from Master Lucanus, indicates that one of us is—must be—gravely in error in our basic beliefs in this."

I sat blinking at him, struggling to maintain a non-committal expression as I waited for him to finish.

"It seems to me that if anyone, and particularly one of King Derek's senior captains, makes a decision, or a judgment on a matter in dispute, and does so in the king's name, then he must do so in the firm belief that the king himself will endorse that judgment and back up the decision. It follows therefore, in logic, that the final responsibility in the matter rests directly with the king, since he permits the use of his name in such things. If he does not, and if he is ignorant about, or indifferent to such a thing, then the use of his name and his authority is really an abuse, and the king is king in name alone. His authority has been taken from him."

I was forced to smile, both in admiration and in delight at the boy's mind, but I sought still to cloak both. "Even if the deed is done without ill will, in the belief that the king's best interests are being served? Longinus is King Derek's loyal follower."

"Yes, and even more so in such a case, for then the subordinate betrays the greatest disrespect and arrogance, in daring to think for the king, as well as speak for him."

The shock of Arthur's words was so great that I found myself on my feet, swinging away from him and moving rapidly to the fireplace, where I crouched with my back to him and busied myself piling fresh, unnecessary logs onto the fire. What a boy this was, and what a mind he had! And what a man he would become in the time ahead. I had to swallow the great lump that swelled in my throat as I battled with the intense emotions that filled my breast: pride, love, admiration and an awed awareness of an intellect more powerful and potent than my own. I felt tears flooding my eyes, and told myself it was the fierce heat of the fire that drew them, and then I realized what I had done, and that the lad was sitting silently behind me, perhaps in fear. I drew a great breath and straightened slowly, turning to face him. He sat gazing at me, his eyes wide and troubled.

"I was too bold. I—"

"No, you were not. You are correct, absolutely and undeniably correct, and I was wrong." I took a step closer to him, clasping my hands behind my back and looking down on him. "Only one thing concerns me, in all you said. Do you know what it is?"

"No . . ." His voice had a rising inflection.

"Your judgment condemns Derek as a weak king. Do you truly believe that is the case?"

He looked away from me to gaze into the heart of the fire, and when he spoke again his voice was quiet. "I do not think King Derek is a weak man. His people, the common people, love him, and his sons have no fear of him. But a king must be above all others. By permitting wrongs to be done in his name, even in ignorance, he betrays weakness, undermining himself and endangering his own authority and therefore the safety of his folk . . . and if a boy like me can see it, so may anyone else who cares to look."

I sighed and sat down heavily in my chair again, picking up my cup of wine and draining it.

"Weaknesses come in many guises, Arthur, but I fear you are right in this. Pray now that no one else has your insight. So far, Derek's rule here is unchallenged, and it is benevolent. We must hope it remains that way."

Arthur grinned, a boy again. "Well, as a man of honour, it is now your duty to make sure that nothing changes, Commander Merlyn."

"Aye, it is . . . though it has taken a mere babe to point that out to me, and I do not thank you for it. Well, have we finished here, or have you more wisdom to impart to me?"

He was grinning still. "No, we have finished. Thank you for listening to me, Merlyn."

"You have barely left me opportunity to speak—what other choice was open to me? Now what are you thinking in that mighty mind of yours?"

"Merlyn, will I ever be a leader?"

"You know you will. You will command the men of Camulod, at least, and those of Cambria, your father's kingdom. But why do you ask that now?"

"Because I must decide how to ensure that no one, ever, will usurp the right to use my name or my authority to his own ends without my knowledge. That will be difficult."

"Aye, it will be that."

"But if I am to lead in Camulod, or to be king in Cambria, then I must lead in fact, as well as in name. I must have laws, and see to it that they are kept, and that the people who depend on me can live, as they do now in Camulod, in the absence of fear."

I was smiling by the time he finished. "I think you may succeed in that, Arthur, providing you have men of worth about you. But do you mean they may also live in the expectation of justice?"

"Of course." There was no trace of a smile on his countenance now.

"Good! Wonderful! I hope to be there to assist you. Now let's go and find some food. That wine has made me hungry."

In the course of the meal that followed, I had difficulty concentrating upon anything other than what Arthur and I had talked about, and towards the end of our repast I became aware that everyone around me had accepted my taciturnity and decided to leave me alone with my thoughts. Even the realization that I was being unfriendly and uncommunicative, however, held no power to divert me from what was in my mind, and I found myself mentally composing a long letter to Bishop Germanus in Gaul, the object of which was to enlist his support in the education of young Arthur.

I remember clearly that, right at the outset, before I had made any decision to write the letter, I came close to convincing myself that it would be both dangerous and irresponsible to write down what I wanted to say to Germanus, since the mere writing of it would enable eyes other than his—inimical eyes—to discover the boy's identity and, far more perilous, his location. Within moments, however, sanity and reality combined to reassure me that my instinct had been correct and that I must write the letter. In the first place, it would be written in Latin, and the Romans had been gone from Britain for almost fifty years. Few people spoke, let alone read and wrote, the language of the Conquerors today in this land. Words written down were not merely indecipherable, they were inconceivable to the illiterate populace of Britain nowadays. The Celtic languages of Britain had no written form, although ironically, such a form existed across the sea, in Eire. Here in Britain, however, where the Roman language had been completely dominant, perhaps one person in ten thousand could read and write, but I felt that might be too conservative and, if pressed, I would have made the ratio much higher. We had a school in Camulod, I knew, where some of our brightest children learned to read and write Latin, but it was run by the anchorites of Glastonbury, and I knew of no other like it in Britain.

It was that notion of writing being inconceivable to most people that finally allowed me to decide to write. The letter would be carried by a travelling priest, who would pass through the places on his route without arousing interest or attention, and it would go with him as a small, flat, insignificant package in the bottom of his scrip. Robbers did not molest penniless wanderers nor did warlords or their minions. Only people who looked wealthy or worth robbing would be robbed, and papers covered with scratchings would appear valueless to anyone illiterate. Peter Ironhair was literate, I knew, and might well love to read my letter, but the odds against anyone who knew Ironhair ever coming into contact with our itinerant priest before he crossed into Gaul were incalculable. And even if such a thing were to occur, it was inconceivable that such a chance meeting would ever involve anyone who could both read the letter and know it would be important to Peter Ironhair in Cornwall. That possibility was the single greatest fear I had, for Ironhair was the only man who had made an attempt on the life of my ward, and he had come close to success, undermining much of my faith in my own friends and associates in Camulod because by all the dictates of logic, he could not have come so close to achieving his aims had he not been assisted by someone within the Colony of Camulod itself, someone whose knowledge of my family was intimate and personal. Now, having thought this entire matter through logically and deliberately, I realized that my fears were largely imaginary. The odds favoured my success hugely. My epistle, I decided, would be safe, and therefore I could compose it safely and with a clear conscience.

Germanus Pontifex
Auxerre, Gaul

From Caius Merlyn Britannicus

Greetings, my neglected friend:
For a long time I have sat here, gazing at the spotless face of this sheet of papyrus, painfully aware of how much time has elapsed since I last took a stylus in my hand to write to you. Nowadays, it seems, the only writing I find time, or make time, to attend to is the task of maintaining my own journal.

I have been intending to write to you for months. I have two reasons: to petition you for advice on a matter that has been troubling me, and to bring you up to date with all the things that have transpired here in Britain, and in our Colony of Camulod, since last you heard from me. Now that I am faced with the task, however, it seems impossible to encapsulate all that I wish to say into one single missive.

We have had great upheavals in our land in recent times, as I know you are aware. When last you wrote you expressed the hope that we had passed unscathed through the wars at that time in Cambria, my cousin Uther's former kingdom. We did, in fact, remain largely uninvolved in that conflict, and it has long since been resolved. However, it has also led to dire complications and a political climate dangerous to the life of young Arthur Pendragon. Raising him to manhood has become my life's prime commitment and responsibility.

As you know, the boy is the son of my cousin Uther Pendragon, who died at the time of the lad's birth. Now nine years old, Arthur is the legitimate Pendragon heir to Cambria, his father's kingdom. He is also, through his mother's claim, the ducal heir to Cornwall, although that is a complex issue, fraught with oblique connections: Gulrhys Lot, the erstwhile Duke and self-styled King of Cornwall, ostensibly the boy's father and unaware of the child's true paternity, acknowledged him publicly as his legitimate heir, and I have Lot's personal Seal in my possession, keeping it safe on the boy's behalf. More legitimately, and still on his mother's side, the boy is also an heir to the kingdom and holdings of his grandfather, Athol Mac Iain, the king of the Hibernian people the Romans called the Scotii and who refer to themselves as Gaels. In addition to everything else, he is both great-grandson to Publius Varrus and great-great-nephew to Caius Britannicus, and therefore successor to the major holdings of Camulod.

For all of those reasons, to safeguard the boy's life against men of overpowering ambition who have already sought his death, I removed him some time ago from Camulod to our present location, high on the north-western coast of Britain, in the mountainous region known locally as Cumbria, close by the western extremity of the great wall built by the Emperor Hadrian to defend his Province of Britain against invasion by the Picti, the Painted People of the Caledonian territories to the north.

When first we came to this place, I thought and sought to disappear from the sight of men. I left our refuge here in the town called Ravenglass, openly, and took ship for Eire, accompanied by young Arthur. None but my own people and a few trusted friends knew that the captain of the ship, Connor Mac Athol, was brother to young Arthur's dead mother. He dropped us back ashore again mere miles north of the harbour at Ravenglass, where friends awaited us with horses. From there we journeyed back overland, in secret, until we had regained our mountain fastness miles behind the town. Thereafter, I altered the colour of my hair, grew a full, Celtic beard and changed my name from Caius Merlyn Britannicus to plain Master Cay, a simple farmer. Another member of our group, Hector, a former Councillor of Camulod and an able man, then assumed the titular control of our new home. Thus we have remained.

Mere days ago, however, another layer was added to this open deception. My brother Ambrose, whom you know to resemble me as closely as one robin's egg does another, sailed into Ravenglass, once more aboard Connor's ship, pretending to be me. All believed him to be Merlyn of Camulod. I stood with him, and thanks to my altered hair and physical appearance, none remarked how similar we look.

Ambrose has assumed full command of our forces in Camulod and complete responsibility for the administration of the Colony's affairs. I encountered him for the first time, you will recall, on the occasion of the great debate which brought you and me together in Verulamium. Shortly thereafter he changed his place and style of living, moving from his erstwhile home in Lindum, where he served as a captain to Vortigern, to live with us in Camulod. He is visiting with us now, soon to return to Camulod, carrying this letter with him. He will convey it to one of the itinerant bishops who pass through the Colony, whence it will make its way to you.

In the interim, everyone who has seen him will know that Merlyn of Camulod came here for several days this spring, then sailed off once again aboard an Erse galley before the month had passed. They will also know, and will report to any who inquire, that he came and went again unaccompanied by any stripling boy.

None who seek the boy with Merlyn would think to look for him in the company of a plain hill farmer such as I have become. He will remain safe, therefore, for the foreseeable future, and my hopes are high that we may continue to pursue his education uninterrupted.

In fact, that education, and in particular the scope of it, is the matter that has been troubling me. It is for this reason that I seek your assistance and guidance now.

I take great pride and ever-growing pleasure in the attributes and accomplishments of my young ward. I firmly believe that he will one day confront a destiny beyond that vouchsafed other boys and men. My mind and my very soul are filled with excitement over his remarkable progress. Mere hours ago, he demonstrated to me again his phenomenal abilities, his mental prowess. This has renewed my determination to instruct him properly and as fully as my own powers will permit, to equip him for whatever tasks lie ahead of him. He has already learned much of what he will need to know, and the process of teaching him continues, shared among myself and my good friends here.

In brief, his grounding in philosophy, logic, rhetoric and polemic has been thorough and painstaking, and the same criteria have governed his teaching in mathematical, engineering and military matters. Discipline, tactics and strategy are real to him now, far removed from mere theory and abstractions.

Despite our successes in all of these endeavours, however, I have strong doubts concerning my own capacity to teach him in one particular area. For this boy to become the man I am convinced he will be required to be, I believe that he must have careful and enlightened tuition in the essentials of Christianity—not merely in its basic tenets. He already possesses and practises those basics. He must acquire a fundamentally solid Christian outlook upon life in all respects. Such learning involves an appreciation of Christian philosophy and morality that I am ill equipped to teach. I remain what I have always been: something of a doubter when it comes to other men's interpretations of the Will of God. Arthur needs more depth and far more enlightenment in such things than I can offer him, and no one else among our number can supply that lack. The strength of Ambrose's beliefs and dedication would make him a wondrous teacher, but his place is in Camulod.

I am convinced that the boy would benefit from anything you could recommend to us to aid in this instruction—text, letter, treatise or philosophical dissertation. If you could send such material to his attention, I would gladly undertake to study it myself, with the intention of providing him with a sympathetic and partially understanding ear into which he can pour his reflections. I see such a focus as crucial to his development.

Soon I must return with him into the world. When that time comes, he must be sufficiently well informed to recognize that world for what it is. He must be able to discern, as a Christian warrior, that goodness, strength and order exist to counteract evil, weaknesses and chaos even in our small world of Britain.

I appreciate whatever consideration you can give this matter. I also trust this finds you in good health and that the duties of your calling leave you leisure, from time to time, to ride abroad. I await your response with pleasure and anticipation.

Merlyn Britannicus

XI

On the day before Ambrose and Ludmilla were to leave, the dawn brought a chilling onslaught of fiercely malevolent sleet, with more snow than rain in the mixture, and high, erratic, gusting winds of such ferocity that the worst of them brought trees and limbs crashing down throughout the morning, endangering the men working in the forest. Hector called a halt to all work, concerned that someone might be injured by a falling branch, and thereafter everyone spent the entire afternoon and evening indoors, attending to all the neglected little chores that could be disposed of without going outside.

Of all places in the fort, the bathhouse was the warmest and most welcoming, and most of us made our way there eventually that day, so that by mid-afternoon it was crowded, resounding with the high, excited voices of the children, who were not normally permitted to share the place with adults, but on this occasion were accorded the rare privilege of playing in the tepid pool, the largest of all the pools.

By the time I made my way into the sudarium, bypassing the most crowded area of the baths, I found that almost every man in the fort had had the same thought as me and had contrived to arrive before me, so that I had to wait until they made sufficient room for me to squeeze myself into a narrow space that verged on being uncomfortably close to the main steam vent from the hypocausts. I looked around me in the gloom and recognized most of my companions as their faces drifted into view and away again, obscured by the banks of swirling, steamy vapour.

Lucanus I had seen immediately on entering, and I guessed that he had been there longest. He sat with his eyes closed and his head tilted back against the wall, the sweat pouring from him, streaming down his face and body, and his now-sparse hair was plastered to his skull. He was flanked to the right by Hector, who smiled and nodded to me, and to the left by Dedalus, who sat hunched forward, dripping sweat onto the floor from his chin and the point of his nose. Elsewhere I saw Rufio, Mark and Ambrose, and then someone broke wind richly in the far corner and earned himself a torrent of abuse from those around him. Those closest to him moved away, setting up enough eddies in the steam to obscure all hope of recognizing anyone. Revelling in the heat, and feeling my skin begin to prickle comfortably with the beginnings of a sweat, I slumped backward between the men on either side of me, the brothers Lars and Joseph, feeling the tiled coolness of the wall against my shoulders and allowing myself to relax as I sucked the hot, moist air deep into my lungs.

Gradually, as men drifted out one after the other, surfeited, the space around me grew less crowded, and eventually I was able to stretch out supine on the stone bench, pillowing my head on a towel. I knew that I ought not to spend much longer in the humid, superheated air, yet I was unable to resist the temptation to relax completely.

I must have dozed, because when I awoke again, spluttering in shock and outrage, gasping in vain for my voice, I had no idea where I was. And then I saw my brother's handsome face laughing down at me in heathen glee. He had crept up and emptied a bucket of icy water onto my defenceless, sweat-soaked belly, and the empty bucket still swung from his outstretched hand. With a massive roar of rage I leaped to my feet and made a lunge for him, intent upon ripping off his head, but he was gone by the time my feet hit the floor, and the cold air from the open door set the billows of steam swirling in chaos.

Bellowing in full roar, I charged after him, throwing the door wide again and sweeping out through the deserted changing room into the open bathhouse, to find myself confronting an entire crowd of people, men and women and even some children, all of them turning to see what the commotion was about and seeing, instead, me in my full nakedness. I skidded to a halt, almost falling in my haste, and then I turned and walked back into the steam room again, holding myself stiffly erect, fighting for dignity but carrying with me the image of Ambrose, fully dressed and still holding the wooden bucket, laughing at my discomfiture from across the tepid pool with the young woman Tressa standing beside him, gazing at my nakedness wide-eyed.

I re-entered the steam room, furious and shivering, and I lowered myself to sit on the bench where I had previously been lying. When I had stopped shaking and my breathing was normal again, I found my mind seething with fantastical images of vengeance on my brother, all of which involved my approaching him while he slept and repeating the outrage on him in a variety of ways. At that point I realized that I was alone in the steam room and that no one had been there since my dousing, and I began to smile, imagining Ambrose gliding quietly in while I slept and shepherding the others out of there in silence, his finger to his lips lest they waken me. Only then, I knew, when everyone else was safe from the wrath he knew would follow his jape, had he come back in with his brimming bucket to perpetrate his crime against my dignity. I had heard reports of my brother's love of practical jokes. Never before, however, had he tried anything of the kind on me. And now a state of war existed between us, with me the loser in the opening stage.

The steam billowed again, announcing the opening of the outer door, and the shape of my tormentor loomed through the mist. He stood looking down at me, his eyes dancing with mirth.

"How are you? Have you cooled down?"

"I'll live," I said, keeping my face expressionless.

"Good, I'm delighted to hear that. But weren't you aware that most men normally put on their clothes before venturing out into the public area, among the women? And the children. Cay . . . the remembered sight of you in all your hairy horror may keep some of them awake at night. You really should be more considerate of others."

I allowed my face to relax into a smile. "Ambrose, you are going to suffer for that little fit of self-indulgence. It will come back to haunt you when you least expect it. This outrageous behaviour of yours today will not go unpunished."

He grinned. "Oh, I think it will. I leave tomorrow, don't forget, and tonight I shall be sleeping in the arms of my wife. Not even you would be cruel enough to punish an innocent woman for my little idiosyncrasy."

"An idiosyncrasy? The shock could have killed me! Bear in mind from now on that, at some time over the coming months, or even years, you will have to sleep, or relax away from your wife. Whenever you do, you had best be careful, because I swear to you, I will have vengeance, brother mine, one way or another. You'll suffer for it, I warrant you."

Ambrose laughed aloud. "Attack? I woke you up, that's all I did. What healthy, virile man lies sleeping in mid-afternoon? We have work to do, you and I, so I wanted you to be alert for it."

"Oh? What work is that?"

All at once his expression sobered. "The duplicate sword. I want to sit down one last time with you and Joseph, to make sure that we have missed nothing and everything is as it should be. I spoke with him here, less than an hour ago. He has been working on the drawings we discussed and they are ready, and he tells me he has spent four days, and two entire nights out of the past three, in the forge. Now he is most insistent that we three meet one more time, to finalize the details of this project, and I agree with him. All very well for you and I to feel the matter's in good hands, but the final responsibility will lie in Carol's jurisdiction, and he will have to deal with it alone. It would be unwise, even unjust of us, not to make sure that we have left nothing to chance that might be remedied and dealt with in detail. This may be the most important undertaking any of us ever assumes. That's why I came back in here, originally, to fetch you. But when I saw you lying there, lolling all naked, with your mouth hanging open, some mischievous urgency took hold of me and I went looking for cold water. And now I come seeking a truce. We really must meet with Joseph."

I stood up and moved towards the door, passing him on my way.

"Truce, then, until our business with Joseph is concluded. After that, beware thy mortified and vengeful brother. Is it still storming outside?"

"Disgustingly."

We sent one of the boys to ask Joseph to meet with us in my quarters, where the light was better than anywhere else that late afternoon, thanks to the wealth of fine wax candles I possessed. A dozen of them were burning in two candelabra on my big table when he came in from the rain, clutching an armload of impedimenta and cursing the weather from beneath the voluminous cloak in which he was swathed.

"Damnation," he spat as soon as the door was closed. "I thought winter was gone."

"So did we all," I answered. "Come over to the fire and warm yourself."

As he stood stamping his booted feet and unwrapping the folds of his cloak, Ambrose relieved him of the heavy burden he clutched awkwardly beneath one arm, protected by his cloak, while I poured him a beaker of the hot, honeyed wine we called "sweet flames," some of which I had prepared as soon as I reached home.

Joseph had brought two things with him, clutching them protectively beneath his cloak to keep them dry: a long, cloth-wrapped bundle containing lengths of iron, judging by the heavy, clanking noises it gave out, and a thick roll of heavy parchments. He thanked me as he took the steaming cup from me and then crossed to stand before the blazing fire in the brazier, cupping the drink in his chilled hands, leaving me and Ambrose to examine the drawings he had brought. As Ambrose set about stretching them out on the tabletop and weighting the ends to prevent them rolling up on themselves again, I took the opportunity to look long and hard at this Joseph who had decided to accompany us from Camulod, leaving behind a lifetime of belonging in one place to seek a new life in the unknown north. I was surprised to realize that I had no idea how old he was, although I knew he was at least a decade older than me. Joseph had been fully grown and already working in his father's smithy when I first began to take notice of the people around me who were not part of my immediate family.

Joseph's father had been known as Equus, the Roman name for a horse, because of his great size and strength; his three sons were all big men, but they lacked the sheer massiveness that had earned Equus his name. Lars, the eldest, having no wish to spend his life as a smith, had run away from his home in Colchester as a boy, to enlist in the legions, and had not been heard of again for more than a score of years until I found him, by sheer accident, operating a road house for travellers on the way to Isca, while I was pursuing my cousin Uther, several years earlier. He had journeyed to Camulod at my urging, and there had been reunited with his surviving brothers, Joseph and Carol, who had become the Colony's senior smiths.

Joseph, I remembered from my boyhood, had once had black, thick-curling hair. Although he was now completely white-headed, his hair remained a thick, healthy-looking mane, and it occurred to me now, for the first time, that he was vain about it, keeping it clean and quite long, in a fashion I had seen in no other smith. Publius Varrus, my beloved uncle, had always worn both hair and beard close-cropped, and I remembered him telling me that long hair is a hazard in a spark-filled smithy. By some miracle, Joseph had managed to retain most of his teeth, at an age when his contemporaries were all toothless, and his skin was dark, almost swarthy, so that in the summer sun he quickly turned a deep, dark brown against which his pale blue Celtic eyes stood out startlingly bright. He was, I realized for the first time, a fine-looking man, with a narrow, intelligent face and a finely chiselled nose with a distinct Romanness to it, despite his Celtic blood. As he stood there, gazing into the fire and oblivious to my inspection, I ran my eyes down from his head to his feet, noting the square, solid strength of him and seeing how the hardship of his craft had kept the signs of his advancing age to a minimum. His forearms were corded with muscle, the lines of them thrown into tension by the way he was holding his cup, and I knew that his upper arms and shoulders held the same, clean-cut definition.

Joseph wore only a plain, dark-grey, knee-length tunic of heavy, coarse wool devoid of decorations, a functional garment, tightly belted at the waist, designed and intended to disguise the ravages of working among smoke and charcoal all day, every day. On his feet and legs he wore heavy leather boots of the kind that our foot soldiers wore, thickly soled with several layers of cured and toughened bullhide then studded with heavy metal hobnails made in his own forge; the upper portions were bound and sandalled up to just below his knees, and beneath them he wore heavy stockings of the same thick, dark-grey wool, their tops turned down to cover the boot tops.

At that point, he became aware that I was watching him and turned to look at me, one eyebrow raised in curiosity, but at precisely the same moment Ambrose straightened up from his first scrutiny of the drawings and called to me to come and look at them.

They were very fine, although some of them were scarcely comprehensible to me, and I found myself surprised at the precision of Joseph's penmanship.

"These are excellent, Joseph, but why are there two sets?"

He grunted and sniffed, then put down his cup before answering. "For comparison. We'll use but one of them; the plain set. The other, showing Excalibur as it is, we'll burn as soon as we are all satisfied the main one is correct." He left the fire and crossed to where we stood, holding his cup in one hand while he pointed out details of the drawings with the other. As he stood close by my side I detected the odour of the smithy on his clothes, a nostalgic mixture of forge smoke and something I could only think of as "the iron smell" that transported me immediately to my boyhood. Joseph spoke with the authority of the craftsman as his hand moved swiftly across the drawings. "Here you have Excalibur as it is, and I swear, by all the gods, I've never seen a thing so wondrous fine. I knew it had been made, by Publius Varrus and my father, but the making of it was all I had heard of. My father spoke of it with pride, but now I know he also spoke with great reserve, because he never mentioned the beauty of the thing, or its greatness, or the size or colour of it. I knew it was longer than a short-sword, but I thought of it in those days as something resembling a spatha, but finer, with a blade an arm's length long. Nothing, no imaginings of mine, could have prepared me for the actual sight of it—the sheer size and splendour of the thing. I mean, from what my father did say from time to time, I knew this wondrous sword had no blemishes, but I could never have imagined what he truly meant by calling it flawless. Its beauty is unnatural. . . ." He paused, shaking his head again in amazement.

"Anyway, here are the dimensions of the thing, this list along the edge, as exactly as I could measure them. The angle of the taper, two ways, length and thickness. The length of the tang—it has a triple tang, did you know that?" He checked himself, glancing at me. "Of course you did—it was you who showed me how and why. Anyway, as you know, one piece of that tang, the central strip, looks like a normal tang, but the other two are bent at right angles, to form the bracing—skeleton might be a better word—for the poured cross-hilt, here. Then there is the length and the thickness of the cross-hilt itself, the length and diameter of the hilt, the size of the pommel, and of course, in the case of Excalibur itself, the binding and securing of the covering on the hilt—silver and gold wire intertwined above this blackish, rough material that I guess to be some kind of leather." He stopped speaking and moved around the table to where he could face both of us.

"That brings me to the reason for making two sets of drawings. I could have used Excalibur itself to highlight the differences in the two, but in the preparation for this meeting, I chose to make two sets of drawings, so we will be comparing like to like. Look here."

His index finger swooped to touch on the drawing of the ornately carved and decorated bar of Excalibur's cross-hilt. "This workmanship is superb. Unique and pure Celtic. Loops and twining branches, thorns and leaves, with every detail perfect. Whoever did this was a master. But I see no need to have anything resembling that on the new sword. A plain crossbar is all we need for that one—a functional guard against accidental dismemberment, as I remember you described it, Ambrose. Plain, simple, straight bar of metal—fundamentally an abnormal, lateral extension of the standard boss with no adornments at all, that's what's called for here.

"Same thing with the hilt and the pommel. We'll pour the whole thing, of course, so the pommel will be poured as part of the mould and it won't look anything like the cockleshell on the real one. But there's a problem there, perhaps minor, although it could be major. Either of you have any idea what I'm talking about?"

I glanced at Ambrose, and both of us shook our heads. "What is it?" I asked.

"Weight, and perhaps balance, since the one affects the other. Weight is the one that concerns me. We've weighed the sword, as it is, but I've no idea of the individual weights of the various elements—the blade itself, minus the hilt, for example—but most particularly the weight of the cross-hilt. That is a big, heavy cross bar, functional and solid, built to be a strong protector against other blades, but the decorations on it there are deeply graven, almost as if they were incised, although we know that's not so and they were simply poured into the shaped mould. There's a profusion of them, and it doesn't take a sorcerer's eye to see that. Not an unused thumb pad's width on the whole thing, front and back. Replacing that with a plain bar of iron's going to throw the weight right off, because all those deep grouts between the upraised figures will now be filled with solid metal."

I raised a hand to stop him. "It doesn't have to be a perfect duplicate, Joseph. There's no need for that degree of nicety."

"Isn't there, Master Cay? You told me you required a duplicate. A duplicate is a perfect replica. Besides, if it's too different, the balance is likely to be as ill bestowed as in a drunken man. If this new weapon is to do the job you want it to, then it behooves us to make the damn thing as close as possible to a perfect twin of the original. And we want to get it right the first time, because it will take long months to make, and months again to remake, starting from the basic elements, if it's wrong. That would mean a complete re-start—we can't make modifications to correct errors. D'you take my meaning?"

"Aye, I do, and there's no doubt you're absolutely right. But all we require is a working replica, not necessarily a perfect duplicate. Is your brother capable of doing this?"

Joseph looked squarely at each of us in turn. "I'll tell you true, I would rather make this sword than anything else I could ever think of, and I believe I could make it as easily here as my brother can in Camulod. But common sense says differently. The forges at Camulod, built as they were by Publius Varrus and my father, are well established and the best equipped I've ever seen. Besides that, the iron statue's there, not here, and you, Ambrose, will be returning there tomorrow, so the work could be in hand within the week. Having said all that, I'll state my opinion on my brother. Carol is the only other man in Britain I would trust with such a task."

"Excellent! Then I am satisfied. Have you any other questions? Anything further you wish to discuss?"

"Aye, one thing. The colour of the blade. It's like polished silver, it's so pure. How was that achieved?"

I shook my head. "I don't know, with any kind of certainty. Publius Varrus did not write of that stage of the sword's development. But I have always assumed it worked the same way as the shine on the skystone dagger."

"On the what?"

"The skystone dagger. That was what Publius Varrus called the knife that launched him on the search for his skystone, the mysterious rock that fell from the heavens, the one from which he smelted the metal of the statue we call the Lady of the Lake. His grandfather, Varrus the Elder, had made it from the metal smelted from another, smaller skystone he had found when Publius was a mere child. That was more than a hundred years ago. Publius buried the dagger, eventually, with Caius Britannicus—his parting gesture to his finest friend. Anyway, in his writings Publius Varrus mentioned that he had asked your own father, Equus, how his grandfather had made the metal of the blade shine so brightly, and Equus responded that the brightness was already there, within the metal. They had merely had to polish it to bring it out, and the more they burnished it, the brighter it grew. That is all I can tell you."

"Hmm. Then if you're right, and if the same holds true of the metal in the statue, all we need do to keep it dull is simply to refrain from polishing or burnishing the blade. I've never seen this statue. Does it shine like the sword?"

"No, not at all, and yet it is lighter in colour than all other iron I have seen, and it does not rust—well, I suppose I can't really say that. It has never been exposed to any risk of rust. It has been sitting dry and well maintained in Publius Varrus's own Armoury since the day it was first made. The only time he removed it was when he melted it down to obtain the metal for Excalibur, after which he resculpted it and returned it to its place in the Armoury. Is that important?"

Joseph shrugged. "Only you can answer that. You are the one who will be using the new sword. How important is it to you?"

"It isn't, but I suspect, if our conjectures prove true, that the blade will have a brightness all its own. Even so, we should warn Carol not to make it mirror-bright, like its twin, here. Our purpose in making it is not to draw attention to it—quite the opposite, in fact." I turned to Ambrose. "Will you remember all of this when you speak to Carol, Ambrose, or should I write it down?"

He shook his head. "No need. The drawings are all I will require. I won't forget a word of this discussion or the ones that went before. My head works well, in such matters."

"One more thing I have to ask," Joseph resumed. "Perhaps the most important. How big is this statue, this Lady? I mean, is there enough metal in it to make another sword?"

I gazed at him, speechless and suddenly filled with apprehension. "I have no idea," I said. "I mean, I know how big the statue is now, but I never saw the original, so I have no way of knowing how much metal Varrus took from it to make Excalibur. I've always presumed he took half, but that is sheer presumption. What will we do if there is not enough metal?"

"Well, we will find out early in the proceedings, as soon as we begin to melt it down and turn it into work rods, because we know the number, weight and dimensions of what we require. But by God's bones, we might end up making a scaled-down version, according to what we have to work with. Will that suffice, if it should come to that?"

I shrugged. "I suppose so, but I really can't see that being the case. The statue must be at least three times, perhaps five times or more the weight of Excalibur. I haven't tried to carry it in years, not since I was a boy, but I recall its being very heavy."

"Aye, for a boy." Joseph made a harrumphing sound. "Well, it needs must be twice the weight, at least, for I'll guarantee that half the original weight will be chiseled out and filed away. On the other hand, if you are right and it's five or six times the weight, we may be able to make two of them."

"That would be most unlikely, I should think." I glanced at Ambrose. "What do you think, Ambrose?"

"I'm the last person you should ask. I've seen the statue, but I've never paid much heed to it. It is not the most beautiful sculpture in the world. It is large, though, I remember that." He paused, and then pointed to the set of drawings that I myself had found so strange and incomprehensible. "What are these things, Joseph, these strange symbols?"

Joseph glanced at me and grinned. "Do you know what they mean, Cay?"

When I shook my head, Joseph moved to unwrap the long cloth-wrapped bundle that had clanked so heavily when Ambrose laid it down, and we watched curiously as he extracted a longish, boss-hilted sword, in the style of a Roman cavalry spatha, together with a handful of plain, thin iron rods about the length of his arm, from wrist to shoulder, approximately two handspans. Some of them were round in section, less than the tip of a man's little finger in diameter, others flattened into strips.

Joseph offered the sword, hilt first, to Ambrose. "That is the finest blade I ever made." He nodded towards the iron rods. "Do you know what those are?"

Ambrose smiled, looking from the sword he now held to the rods.

"Joseph, I have a feeling you will be unsurprised when I tell you I have no idea."

"Well, those are working rods. They're the next sword I will make." He reached into the bundle again and brought out a large, shapeless lump of pasty, whitish material with a chalky consistency and placed it beside the rods. "And this is what I'll use to help me achieve that."

Ambrose prodded the lump with the point of the spatha. "And what is that?"

"Birdshit, for the most part—pigeon dung, in fact—mixed with flour, honey, milk and a little olive oil."

I laughed aloud, for a sudden memory of my Uncle Varrus had sprung into my mind, bringing with it a recollection of many long summer afternoons spent with a small scraper and a metal container, scraping pigeon droppings from the dovecote in the Villa Britannicus, for which I was rewarded in a variety of delightful ways. Ambrose glanced at me askance, thinking we were mocking him, and I held up my hands, palms outward, shaking my head to disclaim any complicity in this.

"It's true," Joseph protested. "One of the oldest secrets of the ancient smiths. A paste made of these ingredients, and coated on the iron during heating and forging, hardens the iron." From the expression on his face, Ambrose was still plainly unconvinced and Joseph went on, laughing now, "I wouldn't lie to you in this, Master Ambrose. If you think of that lump there as being made of a hundred equal parts, then forty of those parts will be pigeon shit, twenty-one of them plain, wheaten flour, fourteen of them honey, twenty-three parts milk, and two parts olive oil. That, you'll see if you count them, makes a hundred, and if you think I came up with that out of my head, you give me too much credit. Now these—" He broke off, his hand outstretched towards the thin iron rods, and turned to me again. "May we look again at Excalibur? It will be easier to explain my point if I have it here, to show you what I mean."

I brought out the great sword and handed it to him, and he held it extended in front of him, gripping the hilt in both of his square, strong, smith's hands, his lips pursed in a low whistle of wonder.

"Even now, I can't believe this thing exists. Look at the size of it! Unblemished, absolutely flawless. Until I set eyes on this, I would never have believed such a weapon could be made, let alone made so well. God's bones, I know men who are not as tall as this is long from tip to tip, and so do you! No man, nor no armour in the world, could withstand such a blade." He raised it, straight-armed, until it reared above him to touch the low, vaulted roof above his head, and then he lowered it again swiftly, bringing the cross-hilt close to his face and pointing to the greatest width of the blade as he addressed himself again to Ambrose.

JOSEPH'S DRAWING:
the making of a pattern sword (cross-section)

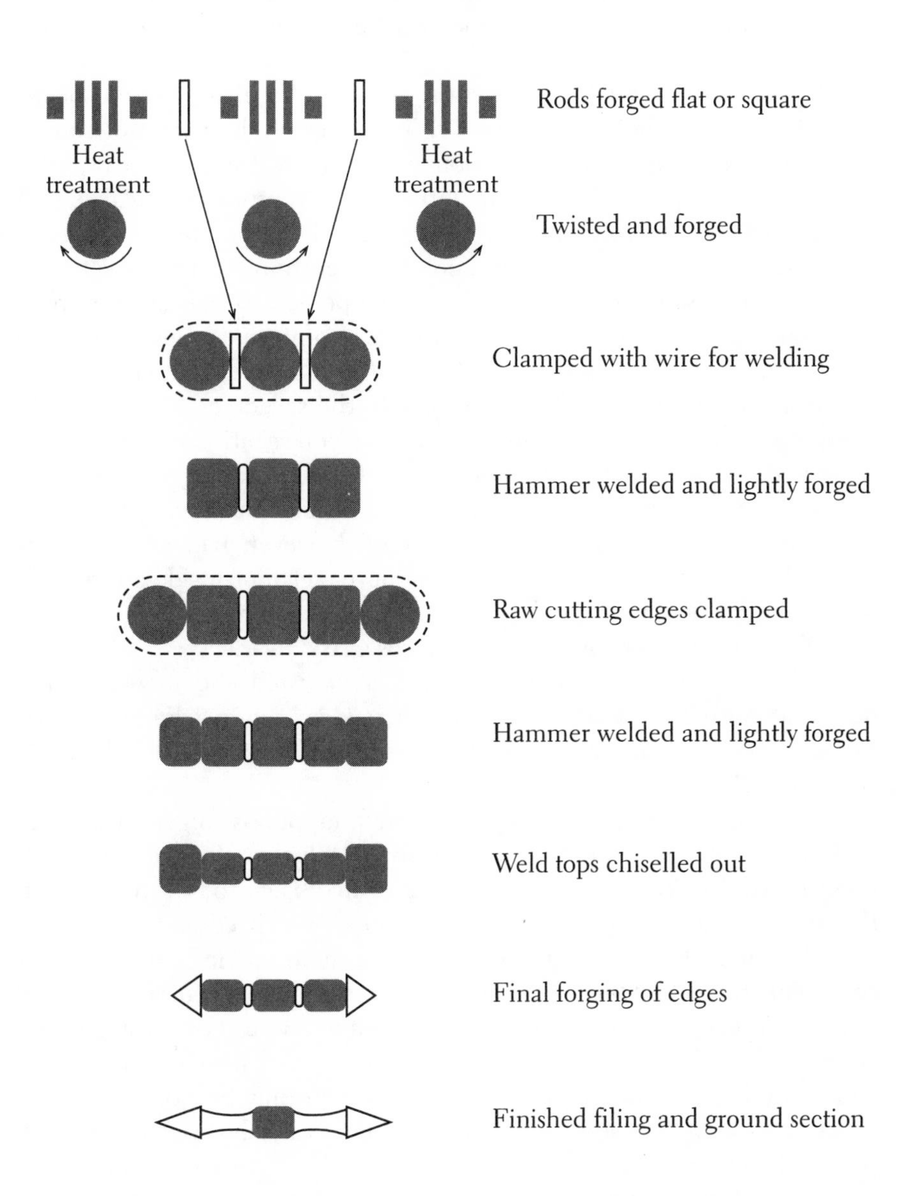

"Look you here, now, at this portion, the thickest and the strongest section. It is, what? three and a half, four fingers wide? Now look here, where the twin blood channels begin, and note the depth to which they sink. Note, too, the patterns in the metal. You see them?"

"Aye, the wavy lines. What causes those?"

"The forging of the sword. Now look here at the parchment and learn a little of the weapon-maker's craft. These marks that mystified you are easily explained." He indicated the strange, stylized markings that had puzzled us.

"If you count, you'll see the entire process of making a sword blade, right there, in ten descending steps. It's an oversimplification, of course, and it gives no indication of the amount of work involved, but to a smith's eye, it's absolutely simple and straightforward. The trick is to realize that you're looking at the thickest part of the blade, the piece I just pointed out to you, just beneath the cross-hilt. Look at the bottom one first. If you were mad enough to saw through the blade at that point, just beneath the cross-guard, and look directly at the sawed-off stump of it, that's what you would see. Then, moving back up to the top one step at a time, you see a reversal of the smithing process, all the way back to the seventeen narrow rods of plain, wrought iron that you started with. Can you see it? Cay, can you?"

I nodded, for what he had described was the missing step between reading Uncle Varrus's observations and notations and seeing them put into effect in very simple terms. Ambrose, however, had never met or known Publius Varrus and had probably never set foot inside a forge. He was staring in perplexity at the drawing. Joseph watched him.

"You have a question, Master Ambrose. Ask away."

"The three large black dots, marked as 'twisted and forged.' What does that mean? I can see the seventeen rods on the first line becoming the flattened and squared pieces on the second, but where did the three come from?"

"Here, here and here," Joseph answered, tapping a finger on the second line. "See, there are three sets of five black rods divided from each other by two whites. Each of those sets of five black rods—three flat in the middle and one square on each flat side—is twisted and forged into a single spiralled rod. We coat each strip of them in the bird dung mixture, bind them together with wire, fire them up, weld one end, just to hold them together, and then clamp that end in a vice. Then, using tongs, we twist the other ends into a spiral. It's tricky, and it takes a long time and many heatings of the metal, because it can only be done when the iron's yellow-hot and soft, and it loses its heat quickly—but in the end, provided you don't do anything stupid, you end up, in each instance, with a single, tightly wound, spiralled rod of layered iron. That's where those markings along the edges of the blade and in the blood channel come from."

He reached over and pulled several pieces of parchment towards him, layering them carefully, one atop the other, so that the deckled edges showed as a succession of tiny steps. "See that, the pretty way the edges flow together? Same thing happens with the iron. You twist five flat straps of metal into a spiral, and you end up with a rod that has twenty grooves running its length—four edges for each strap, you see? Then you heat the whole thing up again and pound it with a smith's hand maul until it's flat again, and you see those markings in the iron, where the edges have been hammer-fused so flat that all they leave are line markings."

"But why go to so much trouble, Joseph? Why not just work with one thick piece of iron in the first place? And why the pigeon dung? I don't follow any of that."

I crossed my arms and leaned my buttocks comfortably against the table as I heard the incomprehension in my brother's voice. I had no urge to interrupt, even though I could have answered his first question, at least. In response, Joseph picked up one of the thin, round rods and casually bent it into a circle shape with his hands, then handed it to Ambrose.

"Wrought iron is too damn soft, in its natural state. Don't ask me why, or why it changes character when you layer it and forge it in multiple strips, because I can't tell you. But I *can* tell you that if you try to twist a single piece of iron into a spiral, sooner or later it will break, and usually sooner than later. So we layer the strips and twist them, and they reinforce each other. As we do that, even before we do it, we coat the individual strips with the heating mixture. I only know it works, and smiths have been using it for hundreds of years because the simple truth is that a spiral rod made that way is harder, and tougher, than an identical rod made the same way, without the mixture.

"Adding the mixture demands an additional degree of care in the heating process. We can't simply coat the rods and thrust them into the coals—the paste would simply burn away. So we smear on the paste, pack the bundles in it, wrap them in cloth and tie them with string. Then we pack the whole thing again, this time in sand, in what we call a gutter trough. That done, we heat the package in a wood fire to orange-red heat for a couple of hours, and then allow everything to cool. Take my word for it, those rods, when the time comes to twist them, are much harder to manipulate than the untreated rods.

"Now, if you look again at the second line, there, you'll see that only two of the sets of rods—the outer sets—are marked for heat treatment. That's because they're the two that need to be hardest. The central piece won't need to do the work of the two outside rods. Its prime function is simply to support the others. The three rods, though, in their upper extensions—about a handspan in each case—will not be welded together. They will form the triple tang on which we'll build the hilt and crossguard. So, there you have it. The secrets of a sword-maker."

"Not all of them." Ambrose was still frowning. "How is the welding done?"

"By heating and forging. We heat the metal to a yellow heat and beat it. In the beating, the components are welded together perfectly."

"Hmm. I didn't know that. There are two more bars here, of a different shading, marked as cutting edges. How do they differ from the black rods?"

Joseph sniffed and sighed, but showed no other sign of impatience with my brother's curiosity. "In two ways, which are really only one. First, it is but one rod, folded almost double and clamped into place along the outer edges of the pre-shaped blade core so that it follows the taper of the blade. Bear in mind what I said earlier—the drawing you are looking at is a section of the blade, through the thickest part of it. The edger is a long rod, at least twice the length of the others, and in the case of this sword we are contemplating, it will be very long indeed, requiring much time to make.

"The second difference is that it will be hardened with the paste treatment, then worked, or forged, for a longer time than the three central rods, since it has to be the strongest, keenest part of the blade. Hence the shading—that indicates the importance of the piece. When it has been added, and welded to the core, and if the smith has done everything with absolute correctness, then nothing remains but long, hard hours and days and weeks of chiselling and final shaping, and filing and polishing, followed by the process of pouring and finishing the hilt. And talking of pouring and finishing, my hot wine is cold and unfinished. Cay, have you more of it?"

"Aye, on the hob there." I paused. "What was that?"

The others stiffened, listening, but there was nothing. Joseph looked at me, frowning.

"What did you hear?"

"I don't know, but . . ." As I spoke, I recognized what I had heard. "The wind has died down. It was the sudden silence that I heard."

Ambrose got up and crossed to the door, opening it and leaning out. Through the open doorway I could see that it was already approaching dusk. He straightened up and closed the door again.

"You're right. The rain has stopped, too. Are we going to eat tonight?"

Joseph barked a laugh. "Aye, but not for another hour or two, at least. It's early yet. That's not the real night you can see out there. The storm clouds have simply eaten the sun. Dinner's nowhere near being ready. I came through the kitchens on my way here. The fires were not even alight yet."

Dinner, a communal affair, was always served in the common mess hall in one of the refurbished barracks blocks just after full darkness had fallen, although that would change as high summer approached. Suddenly, however, the mention of dinner made me realize that I was hungry, and I remembered that I had not eaten since breakfast.

I reached for the jug of wine on the hob by the brazier, pleased with what we had achieved and knowing we had time to finish off the honeyed wine at our leisure. The others accepted a cupful each, and thereafter we sat talking quietly for a spell, replenishing our cups from time to time, enjoying the heat from the fire and the equally welcome heat from the warmed wine. Eventually our conversation died away completely, so that for a long time the only sound in the room was the guttering of the flames in the brazier accompanied by the occasional soft crunching of settling coals, and I found myself dozing contentedly in my chair. Suddenly Ambrose startled me wide awake again by jerking himself to attention, listening.

"What was that?"

"What? I heard nothing."

He glanced at me, then tilted his head backward. "Listen."

We listened, not knowing for what, and then the door shuddered in its frame in concert with the shutters on the windows.

"Damnation!" Joseph rose to his feet and crossed to the door, opening it to look outside, where it was now full night. Two hours at least must have elapsed, I realized, while we sat at our ease before the fire. As the thought occurred to me, the door was torn from Joseph's hand and blown back to slam against the outside wall and a gust of bitterly cold wind whirled into the room, fluttering one unweighted corner of the parchment on the table, extinguishing several candles and making the brazier flare up in a shower of sparks. Joseph leaped outside and in again, pulling the door with him and fastening it securely, after which he turned to look at us in disgust, wiping his hands on his tunic. His hair was tousled and his tunic splattered with heavy raindrops.

"So much for the passing of the storm," he said. "It was regrouping, not retreating."

I saw the woman Tressa at dinner that night and, as had been the case in every instance since I first saw her, once I had noticed her I remained disconcertingly aware of her presence.

Because of the foulness of the weather, there were no absentees from the dining hall on that occasion and the building was crowded, with every table occupied and a mass of children far more noisily in evidence than was normal. I remarked on that to Shelagh when I first arrived with Joseph and Ambrose, and she said it was because the weather had forced the children to remain indoors, depriving them of the opportunity to wear themselves out in their normal fashion and thereby keeping them awake and boisterous when they would normally be ready for their beds.

Ambrose went immediately to sit with Ludmilla and Donuil and Shelagh, where a place had been reserved for him beside his wife and between her and Arthur, Bedwyr, Gwin and young Ghilleadh. I moved with Joseph to sit with Lucanus, Rufio, Dedalus and Mark at a nearby table that was free of children.

Lucanus was in fine fettle that night, and he soon became embroiled in a debate with Dedalus, concerning the relative merits of work horses as opposed to cavalry mounts, that kept all of us vastly entertained. Lucanus, while admiring all living creatures thanks to his calling, had no great love of riding horses, and the discussion was lively and good-naturedly acrimonious, so that eventually others began to drift towards our table, attracted by the hilarity. Soon there was no room for anyone else to sit. Even so, Ambrose arrived after a time and sat himself down beside me, encouraging me with a thrust of his hip to squeeze up closer to Joseph, sitting on my left, and make room for him.

It was at that moment, as I laughingly complained about my brother's rude insistence, that I once again noticed Tressa, bringing a basket of fresh bread loaves to our table. From that moment on I barely paid attention to what was being said around me. My eyes followed her as she moved here and there about the hall fetching and carrying and making sure that supplies of food were replenished as they dwindled. She was not working as a servant, here. It had become traditional for the women to take it in turns to serve the food at night, and those who were sitting to dine tonight, Shelagh included, would serve at other times.

A particularly loud burst of raucous laughter from my companions recalled me, and I looked around to find everyone's eyes on me. My instantaneous reaction was to flush, thinking they had been watching me watching Tressa, but it quickly became apparent that they were all waiting for me to respond to something that had been said while I was distracted.

"Forgive me," I said, shaking my head as if to clear it. "I was somewhere else. Did someone ask me something?"

"Aye," Dedalus said, his big face creased in a huge grin. "I asked you what you're going to ride when that big black horse of yours breaks down, finally, beneath the weight of you." This brought another loud burst of laughter, and I realized that I had truly lost track of their discussion, for I had no idea what they all found so amusing. I took refuge in bluster.

"If you're speaking of Germanicus, Master Dedalus, I'll have you show him more respect. He has borne my weight now for more than a decade without the slightest sign of growing tired."

"Oh, no doubt, no doubt at all, but it's not your mount's redoubtable strength we're talking about here, Master Cay, it's the growing weight of you!"

"What are you saying?" I looked down at my midriff, searching for signs of growing girth that might have escaped me. "Are you saying I am growing fat?"

More hilarity greeted this, and Lucanus leaned forward to look at me from his end of the table. "No, Cay, Ded is but making fun of you, since it's obvious you have not been listening. We were talking about how the armour of our troopers has proliferated since we first began to ride as cavalry. Their armour, and hence their overall weight, has been increasing steadily, while our horses seem to have reached the limit of their growth in recent years. That's when Ded made a remark that you, with your size and the weight of your chain-armour shirt and leggings beneath your cuirass and your greaves, plus all your saddlery and weapons, must one day kill your horse."

I looked around the table, where everyone had fallen quiet. "Well," I said, into the silence, "since death comes to all living things in time, I'll find another like him. Perhaps not his equal, for he has no equal, but akin to him."

"Not here, you won't," Ded growled. "Not down in Ravenglass, or anywhere else outside of Camulod. Our mounts are horses. All else that passes for horseflesh up here is built for midgets, not for cavalry troopers, and most certainly not for giants like you."

I gazed at my large friend, accepting the truth in what he was saying. I had, in fact, no substitute for Germanicus. It was a lack that would have to be soon corrected.

The realization reminded me of another matter that had been bothering me intermittently, each time I thought upon our presence here. Five years, as I had planned, was to be the maximum length of our stay in Mediobogdum. By that time, Arthur would be thirteen, almost ready to assume his role in life. He would also have outgrown his lovely little black-and-white pony. But that was not important now. What was important was that much could happen within five short years, and we were ill prepared, up here in our isolated mountain fort, to deal with any concerted attack that might, somehow, avoid the notice of our Ravenglass neighbours. Now I nodded to Dedalus, concurring in his judgment.

"You're right, of course, and it's too serious a matter to be jesting over. I'll think about some way of changing things."

Dedalus nodded, sober-faced now, and turned his attention to the man opposite him, who had made a comment on some other matter. I turned my back on all of them to speak with Ambrose.

"You recall the conversation we had about an escape route through the valleys at our back, to the great Roman north-south roads?" He nodded. "Well, it has just occurred to me that we might have a requirement to use it as an adit, long before we have a need to use it for escape. You heard what was just said. It makes sense. We will soon need more horses up here, and it's a major task to ferry them on Connor's galleys, in the numbers that we will require."

"How many might that be?"

I shrugged. "I don't know, but we could use a score and more tomorrow, were they available, and it would not hurt us to have some extra manpower on hand, either. Would it be feasible, think you, to send a squadron of troopers up here by road, as escort to a small herd of stock?"

"Stock?" He looked at me askance. "You mean breeding stock?"

"No, riding stock. We've no need to breed any, and we have no pasture to allow it, even did we wish to."

Ambrose was silent for a moment, mulling over what I had said, and as I waited for him to respond, I found myself looking for Tressa again. I found her close by, leaning across to wipe the chin of one of the children at a neighbouring table. As I watched the way her skirts stretched across the curve of her buttocks, Ambrose broke in on my thoughts.

"She's a good-looking one, that, isn't she? She'll be keeping some lucky lad warm on the cool nights. Is she attached?"

"No, not yet. She's one of the newcomers, and single." I saw no point in attempting to deny that I knew who he meant.

"Hmm. Well, it should be interesting to see who wins her, for I'll wager every single soldier in the place will try. Does she interest you?"

"How could she? She's half my age."

He looked at me in surprise, one eyebrow climbing high on his forehead. "What in the name of all the gods at once has that to do with anything? If she is old enough to mount, that's all that should concern you. I have no doubt you're young enough to mount her."

I cut him short. "Enough of that. What were you thinking about after I asked about the horses?"

I saw the hesitation in his eyes as he wondered about my reaction to his mention of the woman, and then his expression altered as he evidently decided to abandon the topic.

"The squadron of troopers. It must be close to two hundred miles from here to Camulod, and that's too far to send a mere forty men to escort a score of prime horses through unknown and hostile territory. They'd have their hands full tending to the stock if anything went wrong, and if they encountered serious opposition on the road, we might lose all of them, horses and men."

I sighed. "It was just a thought. But you're right, it would be folly. We'll have Connor bring a few mounts each time he comes this way. It will take time, but we'll have enough, eventually."

"No, no, no, Cay. You misunderstood me. I was not saying it could not or should not be done. All I meant was that a squadron would be much too small a force. It will require at least two squadrons, supported by a maniple of infantry."

"A maniple? A full hundred and twenty men? You can't mean that, Brother."

"Of course I can. Think about it—our garrison stands at full complement in Camulod today, and we are at peace. Our soldiers need to be challenged. What better training exercise could there be than an expedition to explore the lie of the land and the condition of the people and townships, as well as the roads themselves, between Camulod and here? If they proceed in sufficient strength, they will have no difficulties winning through, and they will have to forage as they go, to feed themselves. I think it's an excellent idea. It will achieve a multiplicity of things, testing both men and officers, challenging them in every way conceivable, and adding invaluable information to our knowledge and understanding of the conditions in the heartland of the country, including the condition of the major roads.

"Camulod has great things to gain from such a venture and, as I see it, little to lose. The men dispatched will see it as a furlough—two months away from garrison duty. I can't see it taking less time than that. They won't be on a route march, but on an information-gathering expedition. We'll send clerks with them, to write down and define the matters they find and explore. And we'll send three squadrons of cavalry, two of them to return while the other one remains with you and returns to Camulod with the next expedition, for once we start this program of discovery, we'll have to maintain it, and I am sure we will wish to. I think you have come up with a superb idea. I'll put it into effect when I reach Camulod, and in fact, I'll head the first expedition myself. I'll wager my largest concern will be in choosing from among the volunteers."

"Excellent! So be it. I'll be looking forward to the first arrivals."

I felt absurdly pleased with myself, and my chest swelled in pleasurable anticipation as I looked about me again, quite openly and brazenly this time, in search of Tressa. As I found her, I saw Shelagh watching me, a tiny smile on her lips. So intent was I on Tressa, however, that the sight of that small, knowing smile did not disturb me nearly as much as it might have. I was euphoric and carefree and unheeding of restraint or common sense. For reasons that I cannot quite define now, even after having thought of them at various times during all the years that have passed since that night, my mind was set upon the straightforward contemplation of an alluring and provocative woman. A woman who, my intellect informed me, would be more accessible than Shelagh and much more amenable to being approached.

I do believe, in fairness to myself, that I might have experienced some short struggle with that strait-laced part of my inner self that had made so much, in recent months and years, of my need to seek and achieve celibacy and self-mastery, but if that was the case, it was a short-lived struggle. I felt young and virile at that moment, charged with a young man's potent imperatives. Then Luke's voice drifted to me from farther down the table, and I resolved to speak with him again, and soon. I turned back to the conversation at the table, and Tressa passed from my sight, but not from my thoughts.

XII

"WELL, BROTHER, WHAT do you think?"

We were standing side by side, huddling half out of the wind and rain beneath the gabled eaves at the eastern end of the roofed stable, across from the barracks block in which I lived. The storm had raged all night unabated. As we watched our companions making their final preparations for the journey into Ravenglass, it was already considerably more than an hour after dawn, although only our minds told us the truth of that. There was little evidence that the sun had, in fact, risen. At that moment we were surrounded by a freakish and impenetrable fog: roiling, billowing masses of low, heavy clouds, churned by the howling wind, obscured everything from view beyond a score of paces in any direction; their density and volume safeguarded them against the fury of the gale, which would otherwise have shredded and scattered them to nothingness.

Ambrose said nothing for long moments, but then, when he did answer me, his response seemed contradictory to his obvious intent.

"I think we must be mad even to be considering leaving for Ravenglass now, in this weather. Even if he arrives on time, Connor will never be able to approach the harbour in a wind like this. He'll be forced to ride out the storm at sea and won't even think about coming inshore until the thing has blown itself out. When that happens, we'll know about it as soon as Connor does, since we are no more than twelve miles inland, and by the time we travel from here to there, he will be approaching anchorage and our reunion will be timely and opportune."

"But . . . ?"

"But what? No buts, Cay. You asked me what I think and I told you—"

"Aye, and I could hear your reservations." I leaned close to him, shouting into the wind that had suddenly swelled to howl around and between us. "You are thinking about the fact that everything is ready now, for departure, and we spent much of last night making it so. And you're influenced by the fact that so many of our people are up and astir already, dressed for the weather and prepared to defy it, cheerfully or otherwise."

The wind dropped away again, leaving me shouting at the top of my voice. Germanicus sidled nervously. I curbed him tight and continued, moderating my tone. "And on top of all that, you're angry at the weather itself, determined not to let it beat you. You don't want to let it push you into a position that you might later see, in your own mind, as weakness."

As I finished speaking my brother turned towards me in mocking disbelief, his mouth hanging open in exaggerated awe. "There you go again," he said. "You and your foreknowledge! How could you possibly know that? How could you know what I was thinking?"

I laughed outright at him and punched him on his mailed arm. "Because I'm going with you, Idiot, and you know as well as I do I've been thinking exactly the same things. I'll wager most of the others have, too. Each one, if you ask him, will probably admit that he has been thinking, longingly, about his warm bed, wishing he had stayed in it this morning instead of dragging himself out here to face a long, cold, wet and windy journey when there's really no need for it."

At this point, protected as we yet were under the stable's roof, everyone and everything was still fairly dry, although tousled and wind-blown. Only Ludmilla and Shelagh were missing, remaining sheltered indoors until it was time to leave. The others, a surprising number, had chosen to escort the Lady Ludmilla and her husband to meet the Eirish galley that would ferry them from Ravenglass back to the coastline close to Camulod. Dedalus, Rufio, Donuil and Lucanus were there, all of them wrapped, like Ambrose and me, in the dense, heavy, horsemen's cloaks of woven and waxed wool that were made to uniform specifications for all troopers by our weavers in Camulod. Arguably the most valuable foul-weather garment any of us owned, these military cloaks were modelled on those worn for hundreds of years by Roman legionaries, but had been redesigned to cover a mounted man warmly and completely, with a heavily draped, ample back that flared out to spread capaciously over the back of a horse, keeping the saddle, and hence the rider's buttocks, dry and protected.

Longinus, Derek's captain of artillery, was also there, but he was out in the roadway, sheltering from the elements for the time being beneath the leather canopy of the wagon that would transport Ludmilla and her belongings. His task in the forest completed, he was returning home to his normal duties and his family today and would ride beneath the driver's canopy on the wagon bench with Lars, Ludmilla's driver for the day.

The remainder of the party consisted of Arthur and Bedwyr, who had been permitted to accompany Arthur's uncle and aunt to bid them farewell. All four boys had sought permission to make the journey, days earlier, but in the interim the brothers Gwin and Ghilleadh had both come down with some form of sniffly sickness that had them, as Donuil aptly described it, flowing from both ends. They would now remain behind, despite their pleas to the contrary. The foulness of the weather would have kept the other two behind as well, had not Lucanus decided they would be better off out in the storm than stuck at home with their wretchedly sick companions.

As I watched the boys, admiring the confidence with which they sat their ponies, swathed in cloaks like ours but made to fit their smaller size, I noticed Dedalus coming towards me. His head was muffled in the cowl of his cape and his helmet made a bulky shape at his waist where he had fastened it to his sword belt by the chin strap.

"Cay, I'm going to go and fetch some coils of heavy rope to take with us. I'll throw them in the back of the wagon. There's ample room. And I think we should take an extra pair of horses along, too." He glanced up at the roof above out heads as though he could see the leaden sky beyond it. "I think we might need them. There will be trees blown down everywhere, and the open roadway might have acted like a tunnel since this storm broke, channelling the wind. The road could be blocked, in places. If it is, we'll need to clear a passage for the wagon."

I glanced at Ambrose. "Ded's right. It could be a nasty journey, but the decision is yours, Brother, and now's the time to make it. Do we go, or stay and wait for the storm to blow itself out?"

Ambrose sighed and drew his cowl further over his head. His helmet, like my own, hung from his saddle bow. My horse Germanicus lifted his tail and made dung, and the warm odour of the fresh droppings mingled with the smells of wet earth and straw and horse sweat all around us.

"We go. Everything is ready, even Ludmilla. I promised Connor we would be there today, waiting for him. Neither of us considered the weather at the time, but a promise is a promise. I'll fetch the women. Tell the others to be ready."

I nodded to Dedalus, who left immediately on his own errand, and then, alerting everyone else to be ready for departure, I pulled myself up into the saddle as Ambrose disappeared through the rain in the direction of the quarters he and Ludmilla had been sharing with Donuil and Shelagh. He returned moments later, accompanied by both women, and a very short time later we were beyond the gates of the fort, filing downward through the gusting rain to where the road led steeply down towards the valley of the Esk and Ravenglass, twelve miles away.

Four times we had to stop between our starting point and Ravenglass, to clear the road of toppled trees or massive, fallen limbs before we could proceed farther. On each occasion the effort of harnessing the extra horses and dragging the dead weight of the shattered wood aside caused us to look at each other and wonder what we were about, subjecting ourselves to such unnecessary punishment on such a day. For some reason, however, attributed much later to some communal form of madness occasioned by the storm, the complaints and wonderings remained unspoken.

We encountered the first and worst of the blockages halfway down the steepest slope from the plateau, in a spot that lay exposed to the worst of the onrushing winds. No mere fallen tree barred our way there, waiting to be dragged aside by newly harnessed, yet-fresh horses. Instead, we found a tangled snarl of interlocked branches and massive boles covering the entire roadway, an insurmountable barrier that made a mockery of our determination and should have driven us back up the hill to safety and shelter in the fort. As we sat cursing the obstruction, however, watching Dedalus explore the tangle for signs of weakness and ways of tearing the mass apart into smaller, more manageable clusters, young Arthur went exploring away from the road and discovered a route by which he thought we might be able to bypass the snarl at the cost of only a modicum of work in cutting down a number of saplings to permit our single wagon to pass.

I went back with him to look at what he had found and discovered that he was right. There was a passage of sorts, a narrow, twisting, open way between the bare rock of the hillside and the overgrown, artificial bank of broken stone created by the debris displaced by the Roman engineers who had first built the road. It was a short bypass, adequate to our purpose, but it was a narrow, dangerous and steep descent—more of a rocky chute than a passage—cluttered in places with stunted, gnarled and ancient trees that would have to be individually removed. I assessed it carefully, then sent Arthur to bring Dedalus to look.

More than two hours later, close to noon, we re-emerged on the road beneath the blockage, soaked through and chilled, despite our celebrated foul-weather cloaks. It had taken all of us to negotiate the narrow descent; even the two women were called upon to leave their shelter and add their weight to that of the men holding the ropes, trying to keep the wagon from breaking away and smashing itself on the rocks all around. We wasted no time in self-congratulation but remounted and continued on our way, nursing our individual miseries. Compared to that episode, the struggles with the three remaining deadfalls were barely worthy of note. Nevertheless, it was approaching dusk on a grey, lowering afternoon before we drew within sight of the fields flanking the last three miles of the eastern approach to Ravenglass, to see the last thing any of us had expected to see.

Arthur and Bedwyr brought the tidings, because they were ranging far ahead of us as usual. They came thundering back through the driving rain, their ponies' ears flattened against their skulls, the boys themselves standing erect in their stirrups and shouting, waving wildly to gain our attention.

"Men! Raiders!"

My mind accepted and absorbed the information instantly, without pause for wonder or curiosity. I sank my spurs into Germanicus's flanks and I was aware, as the big black horse's muscles bunched and uncoiled beneath me, his shod hooves striking sparks from the cobbled road, that my brother and at least two of the others were close behind me. And then I was reining in, dragging Germanicus back, almost to his haunches, as I looked and sought to make sense of what I was seeing through the misty curtain of rain that hampered my vision. Ambrose was beside me now, Donuil, Dedalus and Rufio slightly ahead of me and to my right. Arthur and Bedwyr were behind me, keeping out of my line of sight, I knew, lest I should notice them and send them back to safety with the wagon.

In the distance, barely visible through the driving rain and further obscured from view by the mud that coated them, a score or so of men were making their way in a straggling line across the fields, travelling southward; from our right to our left. Even from where we watched we could see that all of them were too tired for running. Dedalus turned and shouted to me over the noise of the wind.

"They're Eirish, but what are they doing out here?"

Ambrose shouted back, asking the question that was in my mind. "How do you know they are from Eire?"

"Their shields. Donuil, am I right?"

Donuil nodded. "Aye, the shields are Eirish, but the men are not ours. I thought at first they might be Connor's people, since he's expected today, but they're not. They look like Condran's folk, from here. But where have they come from and why would they be coming from the north? There can't be any more than a boatload of them, so they wouldn't be thinking of attacking Ravenglass, even from the rear."

"They're a rabble, too. Let's ride them down."

"No, wait!" I raised my hand, to hold Dedalus back. "You're right, Ded, they do look less than threatening, but let's think for a moment, before we go charging down on them, because Donuil's right, too. Why would they be coming from the north and attacking, in the condition they're in? A mass landing in the north to circumvent the town's harbour walls might make some sense, and Condran might have a leader clever enough or desperate enough to try it, but that would field an army, not a mere boatload."

"It's the storm!" Rufio's head was nodding as he spoke.

"What?"

"The storm! They've been blown ashore, I'll wager, their galley wrecked."

"Damnation! Of course! And they're headed for Ravenglass because they think there's safety there. The town must be under attack from the remainder of their fleet, despite the storm." I stood in my stirrups and looked back to where our solitary wagon sat motionless, some fifty paces behind us.

"Arthur, Bedwyr, back with you to the wagon and make sure that Lars and Longinus keep it well back, away from danger for the sake of the women. Go, now!" As the boys left, unwillingly and showing great disgust, I turned back to the others. "We'll close with them, but keep to the road until we are between them and the town. Once there, we can turn and face them. If they hold the pattern they have now, strung out as they are, we'll be able to roll them up like a strip of parchment. Let's go!"

None of us was ever in the slightest danger. As I had suspected, the sight of five heavily armed and armoured men on massive horses dismayed the bedraggled strangers and extinguished whatever fire might have remained in their hearts. Even before we drew abreast with them, with half the width of the field between them and the road on which we galloped, they faltered and stopped their advance, bunching together as they gaped at us. The wind that had been buffeting all of us for hours stilled abruptly. When we reached the point closest to them I called for the others to halt and ordered them to don their helmets. The mere sight of us sitting there on horseback, facing them and taking the time to throw off our hoods and strap on our heavy helmets, caused them to begin moving backwards, although they faced us still. Rufio's horse reared and whinnied—an angry, impatient sound in the silence of the suddenly windless day.

"How should we do this?" Dedalus asked, his voice sounding preternaturally calm and quiet.

"Line abreast, and not too quickly. Take your speed from me. We'll give them time to absorb the sight of our advance, but bear in mind, all of you, the going will be heavy. Our horses will sink in the mud the moment we leave the road, so be prepared. We'll take the largest group first, those twelve on the right, then veer left and take the next largest and any foolish enough to stand between the two. That should do it. If they choose to fight, so be it. Should they run, however, let them go, don't chase them. I think we might be better occupied in getting to the town without loss of time."

I unhooked the heavy iron flail that hung by its handle from my saddle bow and slipped my hand through the leather loop to grasp the short, thick handle, flexing my wrist against the weight of the weapon and very much aware of the lethal iron ball dangling on the end of its short chain. I glanced along our little line: Rufio on the left, then Dedalus, Ambrose, myself and Donuil. Rufio and Donuil both held spears. I had my flail and Ded and Ambrose both held long cavalry swords. I kneed Germanicus forward, off the road, and as I did so, without any warning, the rain stopped and a glimmer of bright light pierced the cloud cover, so that the sudden cessation of hissing sound and movement gave the entire scene, for a fleeting, transitory moment, an appearance of bright, gleaming, silent unreality. Then we were moving again, the sound of our horses' iron-shod hooves loud on the cobbles of the road before they stepped off into the mud of the field.

The first group we approached, a huddle of twelve men, bunched together even more closely as they watched us coming. But then, when we had halved the distance separating us from them and just before I urged my horse into a canter, when I was beginning to think they might break and run, they split apart and began running awkwardly towards us in a pincer movement, weapons drawn, evidently intent upon surrounding us. As soon as they did so, others who had been watching made shift to join them. I sank my spurs into Germanicus, feeling him surge beneath me.

"They're going to fight! Keep moving, through them and back again. They won't last long."

Nor did they. Three of them died on first contact, two on the spears of my companions and one by my flail, picked up and cast away like a shattered doll, his metal breastplate crushed and ruined by the iron clang of my backhanded, over-arm blow. I had already chosen my next target, but as he saw me look at him and sway my horse towards him, he turned and fled, his feet skidding and sliding in the treacherous, thick mud beneath his feet. I caught up with him in moments, towering above him. I could see his panic in the way he ran, cowering and flinching, cringing from my anticipated blow. Much in me wished to spare his life, to let him go, but there was a clarion need, too, in my mind, to demonstrate that we were here apurpose and were to be reckoned with. Clemency now might—and almost certainly would—be construed as weakness. I swung, hard, whirling the ball high and pulling it over and down and around even harder, backhanded, so that it struck the running man between the shoulders, rising upward, driving the breath and life from him in an audible grunt, smashing his spine and lifting him off his feet to throw him forward, his arms outstretched, to fall sprawling in the mud.

Now I reined in Germanicus, seeing the fleeing Ersemen everywhere. My companions had already stopped and were all watching me. I wheeled my horse and moved back towards the road, and the others fell into place beside and behind me as I passed. All of us knew now what needed to be done; we had to ride to Ravenglass immediately and hope that we were not too late and not too few to help. In the meantime, however, I had another matter to consider, and that concerned the women and boys we had with us. What was I to do with them, now that we had found ourselves so suddenly in a dangerous situation? I had two options available to me, and neither of them was appealing. The first was to leave the women's party here, where they were, while we pressed on towards the town, but that would leave them undefended and totally vulnerable should any other alien force come along this way, and I simply could not consider doing that.

The second option, almost equally beyond consideration, was to take the boys and women with us into Ravenglass, in utter ignorance of what we might find on arriving there. They might all be killed, but in that case, we would all be killed, too, and accompanying them at least we would have some hope of defending them actively against whatever we found in our path. It was no decision worthy of the name. I could only accept the inevitable, and so I stood in my stirrups and waved to Lars in the distant wagon to come now and follow us, and then we were on the move again, all five of us filling the width of the roadway as we rode abreast.

Eyes moving constantly, alert to the danger of entrapment and lurking bowmen, we traversed the short length of forest-lined road between the first of the fields and the outermost edge of the town that had grown up beyond the walls of the harbour fort. At the town itself, we reined our horses to a stop. Nothing moved anywhere, nor was there any sound to be heard except the clatter of one set of hooves from behind us, where Longinus appeared, riding Shelagh's mount, pale-faced and tense with the effort of clinging on to the moving animal. I had no need to ask why he was here; Ravenglass was his home, and his place was there, commanding its artillery. I took hold of his horse's bridle as he clattered up to us and stopped.

"The outer town's deserted." Rufio's voice was rough. "They've all gone inside the walls."

"Aye, but why? I can't see any reason, can you? There's no threat here, no enemy."

Longinus was looking around him as he spoke, as were we all, and it seemed he was right. We were the only people in the outer town. We moved forward, alert for any sign of danger, and as we approached the walls of the fort itself, the missing sounds of the town began to make themselves heard from the safety of the other side. Then I saw movement above and realized that, for the first time since our arrival the previous year, the eastern walls of Ravenglass were manned. The guards were alert, too, but there seemed to be little urgency in their demeanour. They had recognized Longinus immediately, and the outer gates swung open to admit us. Longinus dismounted at once, nodding to me as he handed me the reins of his horse, then made his way swiftly and directly, I had no doubt, to the distant western wall and his beloved catapults.

Relieved that there seemed to be no immediate danger, Ambrose left at once to return and escort Ludmilla, who would, he knew, be concerned about what had been happening, and Donuil accompanied him to rejoin Shelagh for the same reasons. The rest of us, Dedalus, Rufio and I, entered the fort together and went looking for Derek, our ears and minds filled with overheard snatches of conversation and conjectures describing the storm, wrecked galleys and drowned men.

We found Derek up on the western wall overlooking the harbour, and as I mounted the stairs I saw Longinus standing with him, bent forward as he peered down from the battlements. I was surprised to see that there were relatively few defenders up there, but before I could say anything Derek nodded to us and pointed with his thumb in the direction of the wharf beyond the wall.

"The gods were looking after us last night. Look over there."

There have been times in my life when my mind has been swamped and confounded by overwhelming impressions. One of those moments came upon me when I crossed to look down from the battlements into the harbour beneath. What I saw remains with me in images that rear behind my eyes, defying me then and ever since to find words to describe it.

Chaos and madness and unbridled destruction: half and more of the long, seaward-pointing pier of thick oak trunks and planks splintered to ruin, shattered and ruptured amid a nightmarish confusion of sunken, upended and overturned galleys scattered the length and breadth of the harbour; barnacled bottoms pointed skyward, yawing sluggishly in the dying current; shattered keels, broken masts and spars; drifting, torn and severed ropes and frayed, unravelled cables; drowned, bobbing bodies twisting in scores; swirling, scummy broken water, heaving and surging; gleaming, glistening piles and heaps of seaweed everywhere, torn from its roots and cast up by raging waves on to the wharf road along the bottom of the wall; corpses littering the shore and sprawled at the base of the wall where they had been thrown by the same waves' fury; other men scurrying among these, carrying bared blades, looking for signs of life to snuff out; everywhere the signs of overwhelming tragedy and the awful, blasting power of nature's unrestrained rage. And oars everywhere, littering the surface of the sea like impossibly straight, leafless branches, while on the straight upstanding stern of one sundered galley, a scattering of arrows stood in the wood of the planking, the only evidence among the carnage, save for the scurrying scavengers beneath, that men had been involved in dealing death here.

Incapable of speech, I fumbled at my helmet straps and bared my head. Derek stood watching me, saying nothing. Finally, I found something to do. I began to count the shattered galleys. I lost count at fourteen and blew out a deep, sharp breath.

"How many wrecked, do you know?"

He shrugged. "We counted twenty, but there could be more."

"God! And so many bodies. There must be a hundred there, still in the water."

"Aye, but they're the light ones. Those who were wearing armour sank and stayed down."

"Sweet Jesus! What happened? I mean, I know it was the storm, but what could have possessed their leader to allow his boats so close inshore in such conditions? He should have ridden the thing out, safe out at sea."

"Greed possessed him, and a hunger for vengeance. They thought the storm was over, and sought to surprise us in the aftermath. There was a time, last night, when the wind fell and the storm abated and it seemed for a long time to have blown over. We all thought so. It had been raging for the entire day, by then."

I nodded at his words. "Aye, we thought so, too, up in our fort. The wind died down and stillness fell and all was calm for several hours."

Derek was barely listening to me, his eyes staring out to where the low island in the bay interposed itself between the town and the open sea. When he spoke again his voice was low, as though he spoke for his own ears alone.

"It seems now, when I look back on it, as though we were becalmed for a while in a gap between two storms, and when it had moved over and beyond us, the second storm resumed more fiercely than the first had been at its worst. I have never known winds such as those. We lost two men from off the walls here, plucked up and away and blown down into the courtyard. No one can recall such a thing ever happening before." He snorted and spat wetly. "Anyway, thank all the gods, the commander of these people, whoever he might have been, judged the danger past, exactly as we did. He moved inshore in the darkness, preparing to attack us with the dawn, and when the storm returned the high tides took his fleet and dashed it to splinters here." He stepped forward to the wall and leaned out, bracing his hands on the stone parapet. "As I said, I don't know yet how many keels were lost, and we may never know, but I think we need fear little more from the Sons of Condran. Two disastrous visits in succession should destroy their taste for sacking Ravenglass."

He turned now to look closely at me for the first time since my arrival. "You, my friend, are drenched, and blue with cold, and I have been up here all day, since before dawn. Let us go and find a fire somewhere. I doubt your good-brother Connor will arrive today. Born sailor that he is, he probably held his fleet in shelter over there, in the lee of Man."

I looked to where he pointed, and though I could see nothing, I knew he meant the large island that hulked out there beyond the shores of Britain. Though I was no sailor, I had to agree. It seemed the proper thing that Connor, seeing the storm approaching from the west, would have assessed the risks and chosen to seek shelter there on Man, safe in the shadow of the island.

I sighed and cast one last long look around the death-filled bay below and then I turned away, looking down into the town. There stood the two boys, Arthur and Bedwyr, staring up at me, in their own little island of stillness among the throngs bustling around them. Derek had begun to move away and I stopped him, catching at his sleeve. He stopped and half turned, watching curiously as I crooked my index finger and beckoned to the two boys to come up. They turned to each other with incredulous grins visible even from where I stood, and then they began running towards the nearest stairs.

"What are you doing?" Derek's tone was filled with disapproval. "You think this is a sight for boys?"

"No," I responded, watching the boys' heads as they came bounding up the steps. "Not for mere boys. But for future warriors and leaders of men there is a lesson to be learned from this, I think."

Derek grunted disapprovingly but held his peace thereafter. When the boys arrived by my side I took each of them by the shoulder with one hand.

"Listen to me now, both of you. You have it in your hearts to ride to war some day, to fight and to win glory, is that not so?"

"Yes, Cay, when we are old enough," Arthur said, his eyes wide. Bedwyr merely nodded, too full of excitement to say anything.

I nodded, frowning at them. "Aye, when you are old enough." I crouched to kneel on one knee, bringing my eyes level with theirs. "Well, it may be that you will never believe this until you see it for yourselves, but there are some sights that no man ever grows old enough to countenance without pain and fear, and one of them lies now beneath us, there on the outside of the wall. I have decided you should see it. Come now and look."

I led them to the parapet and stood between them, still holding each of them by the shoulder, and I felt the stiffness that came over them as soon as they had seen and begun to absorb what lay down there. I knew it was cruel to do such a thing to them, but it really could not have been better, from my unique point of view as teacher and guide. Even faced with death on such a scale, they were yet distanced from it here on the wall top. Blood and wounds and carnage they could see, but broadly, from afar, washed and diluted by the sea and lacking detail. The glistening entrails and spilled body fluids were too far off to mark, and the foul smells of violent death would yet remain unknown to them for this time, at least. Even so, the spectacle changed and chastened them forever, in the space of brief moments, dispelling for all time the high, laughing excitement of the glory-hungry boy in each of them. When they had seen, and looked their fill, I turned them to me and spoke to them again, aware of the pallor of their cheeks and the tearful distress that filled their eyes.

"As you can see, there is no glory to be found in war, lads. The real truth of it lies there, plain to be seen—death and distress and shame and pity; squalour and filth and madness; wrack and ruin and waste and destruction; a lack of grandness and a disbelieving urge to vomit and to weep with the pity of it all. No man dies well in battle, and none dies gloriously. If you learn nothing else today, learn this: dead men do not win wars. Dead men lose everything, including their dignity, and starting with their lives. Only living men can be victorious. No one—ever—wins in death.

"All of those lifeless men below, littering the water's edge and floating in the waves, are dead because their leader was a fool, criminally lacking in judgment. He endangered all his men and all his fleet by being too rash, and he lost all of them. Had he survived, he should be hanged for his murderous folly, for to command is to bear responsibility for the lives of each and every man in your command. Those lives are yours to spend in winning wars, but you must spend them cautiously, judiciously and with unwillingness, taking great pains to see that none of them, not one, is wasted or uselessly lost. To send men into battle, thus exposing them to death, is the responsibility of leaders, but to squander any one of them without need is murder, plain and simple. Bear that in mind from this time on, and remember these dead hundreds here today, squandered and murdered. Now go, both of you, and find your Aunt Ludmilla. Tell her, and Shelagh, that I am with King Derek and will rejoin them soon. Off with you, now."

Derek had watched all of this in silence, offering no judgment either by his look or bearing, and he had nothing to add as we made our way down from the walls and through the fort to his great house.

XIII

I REMEMBER THAT storm, and that visit to Ravenglass, as marking two events: the beginning of the end of an era in my own life, predicated upon a decision I made while I was there, and the first truly discernible step towards man's estate made by young Arthur Pendragon, in confronting, contemplating and coming to terms with the concentrated death and destruction in that harbour.

Connor appeared, under sails and oars and brightening rays of light from the rising sun, two days after we arrived, confirming Derek's guess that he had anticipated the great storm and sheltered his fleet safely in one of the coves of the large offshore island known as Man. When the weather cleared, he had set out again and on the way had met and engaged the few, straggling survivors of the Sons of Condran's fleet, sinking all of them. He was concerned over the delays and conscious of how little time remained to him to deliver his passengers safely in the south, then turn north-westward again to meet with the remainder of his fleet returning from the north on their way to Eire. Thus, he wasted no time in embarking Ambrose, Ludmilla and all their goods and was soon making his way carefully back out to sea, threading a passage through the wreckage that littered the harbour.

We watched them leave, waving from the battlements until they rounded the bank ahead of us. Then we spent three days assisting Derek's people with the Herculean task of cleaning up the detritus of the storm, salvaging or demolishing the wreckage in the harbour so that it no longer threatened other vessels, and burying those bodies we could find, knowing full well that corpses would wash up on the surrounding beaches for months afterwards.

When all that could be done had been achieved, we made our way back to Mediobogdum beneath sunny skies, surrounded by the singing of a million birds and the lush greens of new, rioting foliage that was bright, in sheltered nooks, with heady, sweetly scented blossom: apple, pear and hawthorn, white and pink.

That homeward journey passed in reflective silence, by and large, each of us dwelling, according to our natures, upon what we *might* have faced on reaching Ravenglass had the storm not briefly gulled our enemies. I found myself recalling it already as a tempest.

We found the tangled mass of ruined trees still in place on the hillside, blocking the steeply sloping road up to our pass. We accepted its enormous presence with stoicism and yet also with vague feelings of surprise to find it all unchanged after a week had passed. Clearing it away, with axes and saws and ropes and teams of horses, and reopening the road would be our highest priority in the days ahead. We passed it by without pausing in our ascent, however, since we had left Lars and the single wagon safe in Ravenglass to await a summons once the way was cleared; it took us but a tiny fraction of a single hour to mount the steep, bypassing defile on horseback, proceeding in single file and grateful that this time we were unhampered by the torrents of cold water that had showered on us from every tree and sapling we had passed beneath on the way down.

I was at pains to ride close beside Lucanus on the most difficult section of the upward slope, for I had noticed some time earlier that he seemed to be in pain and to be making great efforts to disguise the fact: his face was pale and peaked, the lines around his eyes and mouth etched more deeply than I had seen them before. I made no mention of my concern, knowing him to be quick and querulous in denying such things, as though a sickness or infirmity within himself were deadly insult to his physician's craft. Rather than alert him to my suspicions, I merely contented myself to ride close by his side, saying little but prepared to seize him should he begin to fall. Only when we had safely passed the worst of the upward climb did I leave his side, and then I moved directly to where Donuil and Shelagh rode ahead of us, side by side, talking quietly of their own concerns. Warning them not to look back at Luke, I alerted them to my concern and arranged with Shelagh to coax him to his bed as soon as we arrived safely at the fort.

A short time after that, we breasted the last steep gradient and saw the western wall of Mediobogdum bright in the midday sun, above us to our left. Dedalus blew a blast on a coiled, copper horn to announce our arrival, and by the time we turned off the road to approach the main gates, Hector and several others were on the way out to meet us. I felt myself smiling as I saw the welcome on their faces, but the major part of my awareness was concerned with the beckoning plume of shimmering smoke wafting from the flue above the bathhouse furnace. I greeted everyone as required, then hung my helmet and swordbelt from my saddlebow, draped my cloak across the saddle and turned Germanicus over to Donuil, after which I made my way on foot directly to the baths.

The steam room had another occupant when I arrived and I sensed his presence immediately, even though he was invisible among the swirling clouds of steam. The voice of Mark, the young carpenter, answered my greeting. He was standing against the wall when I finally saw him, and he lowered his arms from over his head as I approached, then launched into a series of questions about our journey. Loath to be coaxed into a long and unwelcome chronicle, I forestalled him with an upraised hand, shaking my head and asking his forbearance, pleading weariness and the simple need to stretch out and relax. He shrugged and smiled and nodded, accepting my demurral, and returned to what he had been doing when I entered, raising one arm and reaching behind his head to press the fingers of his hand against his spine between his shoulders while he pushed the elbow backward towards his ear with his other hand. On the point of lying down, I watched him curiously instead, noting his closed eyes and the concentration with which he held his uncomfortable position for a count of perhaps twice ten before changing over and doing the same thing with his other arm. When I asked him what he was doing, he lowered his arms and smiled at me, his face flushing red.

"I'm stretching the muscles of my arms—these ones." He squeezed the massive muscles at the back of his right upper arm with his left hand. "They're stiff and very sore. So are my shoulders and my back muscles—my belly, too, and even my thighs. It's all this felling of trees that does it, swinging an axe from dawn till dusk every day for the past three weeks. Chopping down a healthy oak is like to chopping through a boulder, according to Longinus. He says both will destroy the sharpest axe's edge and bruise any man's muscles, and I believe him." He stopped, turned slightly to brace his left hand against the wall at his back, then raised his right foot, catching it in his right hand and swinging it up behind him so that the long, divided muscles in his thigh sprang into tension. "Crassus, a Roman-trained masseur in the baths at Ravenglass, taught me this technique of stretching aching muscles once they are warm. It's unpleasant at first, but it eases them, relieves the painfulness and stops them from cramping. I've been doing it for months, ever since we arrived here, and it is effective. And it grows easier, too, with repetition."

I was looking at him as he spoke, noticing for the first time the perfect shapeliness of the clean-lined, sharp-etched muscles rippling beneath his skin. He was magnificently made and in the very prime of his young, glowing manhood, smaller than me by almost one third my weight, I guessed, but perfectly proportioned for his size. I glanced down at my own heavily muscled body, seeing the solid thickness of my thighs and calves and my flat belly, innocent of fat, yet lacking the clean, clear muscular delineation that was so striking in young Mark.

"I don't remember you as being quite so—muscular," I said.

He had finished stretching his thighs and was now bent forward, stiff-kneed, his palms flat on the floor. He straightened up easily and grinned at me. "I wasn't—never have been, until I came here and started swinging an axe for hours every day. There, that's all. I'm finished now. A cold plunge and a brisk towelling, and I'll be a new man. You should try it,

Cay—felling trees, I mean. I think you would enjoy what it will do for you."

He picked up a towel from the bench and wrapped it around his waist before he left, and I stretched out again, settling my own folded towel beneath my head and frowning thoughtfully as the first stinging trickles of sweat broke out at my hairline and across my belly. I had grown lax with myself lately, I knew, neglecting my soldier's regimen over the course of the past winter. I would begin the following day, I decided, and spend at least a part of each morning henceforth swinging an axe against solid oak.

No one else came in to mar my solitude. I bathed at leisure, then shrugged naked into my tunic, pulled my sandals over my bare feet, and made my way to my quarters, carrying the remainder of my clothing beneath my arm, bundled into the cuirass I carried like a basket. I was anticipating a pleasurable change into fresh, clean-smelling clothes, but all thought of such things disappeared when I found the woman Tressa in my quarters. She had evidently thrown wide the shutters to air my rooms, and seeing that immediately, I also saw beyond them to where she was working in the shadowed interior with her back to me, wielding a broom.

As soon as I set eyes on her, without pause for thought or any kind of consideration, I spun on my heel and walked hurriedly away, afraid that she might turn and see me there. Even as I did so I was cursing myself for my cowardice, instantly angered at myself for thus cravenly fleeing the sight of a harmless young woman. It would not be accurate simply to say I was surprised and dismayed to find her there in my quarters, although I was—I was actually appalled, and I found the strength of my reaction startling enough to make me question it. When I did, I found conflicting things, strangely hidden deep inside myself, that did not please me greatly. There was no denying that some part of me had hoped to find her there; another part of me, however, a disconcertingly reproving part, had disdained the idea; and yet another large and unsuspecting part of me, the outward-facing part, appeared to me, upon examination, to have been completely unaware of any thought of her.

That latter "truth" was an outright lie, of course, and the fact that it was a lie to myself made it the more annoying. Tressa and her alluring charms, her dimpled smile, her high, proud breasts, lithe waist and swelling thighs, had seldom been out of my thoughts since the night of the storm, when I had watched her so studiously during dinner. Confronting and accepting that, at least, enabled me now to look more closely at the second part of how I felt: the disapproving censure of some other, more carefully concealed part of me. Whence had that sprung, and why so virulently?

Thinking these thoughts, I realized that I was striding along the main street of the fort like a man with a mission, and I forced myself to slow my pace until I was ambling, almost dawdling. Several people passed me, nodding silently in greeting, before I came to the rear gate and walked through to pause on the brink of the chasm where I had hovered a short time before, my arms spread like an eagle on the wind. I found a flat-topped stone outcrop, cushioned with moss, and seated myself where I could look down into the valley beneath and let my thoughts take me where they would.

This ability of mine to take myself to task and thus identify the motives that had prompted me towards a certain course of action was one that I had cultivated over long years of assiduous self-examination. I had begun questioning myself and all my motives in response to a withering criticism from my cousin Uther, who had accused me of being far too smug and all too often self-righteous, judgmental and priggish. Determined, with the arrogance of youth, to change my behaviour from that time forward, I had taught myself to question and examine myself mercilessly, coming eventually to know myself too well ever to gull myself for any length of time.

Now I brought this ability to bear upon the matter of this woman, Tressa, and upon my own very real reaction to her. I stripped myself ruthlessly of false denials and pretenses, and the last scales fell from my eyes so that I accepted what I saw, incontrovertibly, to be true: I found the woman unequivocally attractive, and was resolved to yield to the inevitable and act upon the attraction. I was left, however, with an inner conflict on the matter of celibacy, over which I had spent so many agonizing hours in the past few years. Something deep within me, some niggling voice of conscience, was displeased over that abandonment of what had seemed a glowing ideal. Now, treating the discomfort like some inedible remnant from an otherwise delicious stew, I sat there atop the cliff, beneath the high, stone walls of Mediobogdum, and chewed on it, biting and grinding at the gristly elements of my concern until nothing remained but indigestible fragments that I spat out, one by one.

My desire for celibacy—utterly genuine and heartfelt—had sprung from several sources, each of them entirely comprehensible, if not exactly laudable or logical. My lust for Shelagh was a burden I had carried for years, never satisfied and never justifiable, since it involved perfidy and betrayal to my closest friend. My commitment to chastity on that account had been flawless; celibacy, I hoped, would eventually extend that physical chastity to my unconscious thoughts. My guilt and conflict over my memories—and my two-year loss of memory—of my dead wife, while inexplicable, were nonetheless very real, and some deep-hidden part of me had sought a resolution there in celibacy, too, although I found myself incapable of defining or even delineating why I should be feeling any guilt. And then, apart from Shelagh, the only other woman to whom I had felt an attraction, the lovely Ludmilla, had loved and wed my brother Ambrose. I had no guilt there, and no lustful longings, for which I was intensely grateful. Ludmilla was my sister now, and I thought of her as such, with a fraternal love. And yet, I knew, she, too, had played a role in my attraction to the celibate state: I had dared to begin loving her and had lost her before my feelings had a chance to grow. Celibacy would have removed such a threat forever from my future.

Then had come my terrifying brush with the spectre of leprosy and the foulness of contagion. There was a binding and convincing reason for being celibate! But that had passed, with the arrival and relief of Luke's lost parchment and the shrinking size of what I had assumed to be a leper's lesion.

Amidst all these elements, there had been growing and emerging the love and pride I took in young Arthur Pendragon, and the responsibility I felt for giving him all that lay within my mind and my abilities to give. I had believed that celibacy would empty my mind of all that was profane and leave me free to learn and to teach the boy. And then had come this lovely and attractive young woman Tressa.

My reactions to the merest sight of Tressa had confounded me for a time, but then I had begun to lose my fears of her, recognizing them for what they were: simple fears of rejection and of having grown too old, at forty, to be attractive to a young woman.

Beyond that, I had an illogical fear that the mere admission of being physically attracted to a woman could somehow endow that woman with power over me, and that fear persisted despite the fact that the logical part of me knew it to be untrue—Shelagh was proof of that. I also knew that being attracted by this Tressa woman was a far cry from allowing myself to be besotted by her; I knew my intellect would arm me with the means to keep myself protected from her wiles and knew, besides, that she could be no match for me in such matters. Her speech was slow and simple, her demeanour humble and submissive and her manner deferential and respectful. Her presence, therefore, might be pleasantly distracting, but it could be in no wise threatening, now that I had defined the terms within which I might deal with it.

Having settled my mind to a great degree, I turned again and walked slowly back to my quarters, where I found Tressa working still, setting the place in order against my return. I greeted her calmly, noting the pleasure with which she greeted me, and then attempted to ignore her for the time being, an effort doomed to fail because I was acutely aware of the brightness of the yellow smock she wore, and of her physical proximity.

Once I had assured her that her presence would not disturb me, I seated myself at a small table by one of the windows and busied myself with reading one of Uncle Varrus's large books, while she continued to bustle about, fulfilling the tasks set out for her by Shelagh. In so doing, however, she passed quite close to me on several occasions, and I became acutely aware of how the smell of her filled up the air between us and suffused my breathing. She had a pleasant smell, warm and clean and faintly musky with the suggestion of fresh sweat. I tried to shut it from my consciousness, but the mere awareness of it had awakened in me the realization that I sat there naked, having come from the bathhouse unclothed save for my tunic, and I found myself becoming uncomfortably engorged with lust and blank-minded with helplessness.

Tressa, of course, had no suspicion of the effect her nearness was having on me, and it was that innocence that finally enabled me to overcome my condition and once more achieve a semblance of calm. Once she saw that I was not upset or disgruntled by her presence, she began talking as she worked, prattling on in her soft Cumbrian dialect about innocuous things, and I began to find it subtly pleasant and relaxing to sit there and listen to her voice. As I had suspected from her reaction to my appearance, she had not expected my return so soon. She had been there for only a short time when I arrived, she told me at one point, shouting the words from my sleeping chamber where she was engaged in spreading fresh bedclothes on my cot, but she had almost finished now and would soon be gone, leaving me alone to recover from my journey.

As I half turned to hear her words, which came to me muffled and distorted by the doorway between us, my eyes took in the other table in the room, the main table, and now I noticed that a pile of assorted clothing, all of it mine, lay there beside a covered basket. Curious, I crossed to look more closely at the basket. Its lid opened to reveal a pincushion containing at least a score of various-sized needles and a profusion of small balls of yarn, thread and twine, all mingled with an assortment of bright-hued bits and pieces of cloth. I heard her come back into the room and move towards me, and I turned guiltily, as though she had caught me prying. She seemed unaware of my awkwardness, however, merely glancing at the pile behind me before telling me that when she had finished her first tasks, she had intended mending some of my more ill-used clothing, but that she would now wait until a more convenient time, when I was elsewhere in the fort. She moved towards the table and it suddenly seemed to me that she came looming towards me. Caught flatfooted by this unexpected approach, and incapable of speech, I moved away from her, quickly, stiffly and awkwardly, as though I feared she might attack me, and in doing so I succeeded somehow in overturning her basket, scattering brightly coloured balls of yarn all over the table and onto the floor.

Quick as a kingfisher, without a word of reproach, she bent and began scooping them up, making a lap of her skirts and dropping the balls into it as she reached and stretched to gather them, moving in a scuttling crouch that I found more erotic than erratic, revealing as it did far more of her shape than I was prepared to see. My throat swelled up with excitement and I stood transfixed, aware of a bared ankle and the swell and thrust of legs and buttocks beneath tight-stretched cloth, but incapable of removing my eyes from the sight of the hanging scoop of the bodice of her smock and the full, vibrant breasts exposed there by her posture and activity. Full knowledge of my unconfined condition came flooding back to me as I felt my loins stir and then harden rapidly, and then she caught a foot, somehow, in the fabric of her skirts and wavered, almost overbalancing and lurching close to where my phallus jutted very visibly against my tunic. I spun away from her again and strode into my sleeping chamber, swinging the door safely shut behind me and leaning back against it, hearing the thumping of my heart loud in my ears and wondering if she had seen my blatant and unambiguous arousal.

Months, now, it seemed, I had awaited this moment, only to be undone by the unforeseen clash between my own readiness and unreadiness. The fear of losing the opportunity, of frightening her off by being too importunate, loomed over me like some avenging demon. And then, still overwhelmed by panic moments later, listening with my ear against the door while my heart thudded palpably at my ribs. I heard her leave, pulling the outer door closed behind her. I leaned there, against the door, for a long time, willing my heart to slow down and attempting vainly to empty my mind of the riotous thoughts that swarmed there. When I moved out again, into the main chamber, I knew both pleasure and regret, for although I had succeeded in not alarming Tressa and damaging my own chances, I had yet lost an opportunity that might not be repeated, for Tressa was gone again, safely out of my life for the time being.

Some time after that, when I had regained my equanimity and my sense of humour and proportion, Shelagh knocked loudly at my door and leaned inside, looking at me strangely.

"Are you well?"

"Come in," I said, squinting at her, outlined as she was against the brightness of the afternoon behind her. "What do you mean, am I well? Luke was the one who looked unwell, remember? How is he?"

She stepped inside, leaving the door ajar, and moved to lean beside the window. By now I had shed my old tunic and was dressed completely in fresh clothes. Shelagh, however, was still wearing the travelling clothes she had worn on the journey to and from Ravenglass, a suit of riding leathers fashioned of a long tunic, split to the waist on both sides and worn over soft breeches. It was modelled on my own suit of leathers, which was, in turn, modelled on the clothing worn by Publius Varrus and fashioned for him originally, prior to their wedding, by his wife, Luceiia. At first, upon seeing Shelagh riding like a man, in leather breeches, some people had been scandalized, but she had ignored their outrage, and so inured had everyone become in the interim to seeing her dressed thus that they had now lost all awareness of her sex in this particular respect.

She looked me up and down now with narrowed eyes, her head tilted to one side.

"Lucanus is well. I think he was merely tired from the journey. He's no longer young and, as you know, he never was a horseman. Riding—merely staying in the saddle—is an effort for him and it tires him quickly. As soon as he climbed down from his horse, his colour improved and he became himself again. I tried to coax him to lie down, but he would have none of it. I saw him a short time ago, sitting in the sun talking to Joseph, and he seemed perfectly at ease. How are *you* feeling?"

"Me? How should I be feeling? I'm no different than I was when we rode up here—in prime condition."

"Hmm. Tressa said you seemed unwell, upset."

The moment she spoke the other woman's name, I experienced a flash of revelation. Tressa, on leaving here, had gone directly to Shelagh! Of course she had, I realized now, understanding. Tressa was acting at Shelagh's behest. The knowledge made me thrill, but I was careful to conceal any sign of it from Shelagh. My thoughts and emotions were in a turmoil, but only for a few moments, after which I was in control of myself once more, and, for the first time in my memory, of Shelagh, too. I found myself smiling broadly at my lovely friend, and side-stepping.

"Ah! Tressa," I said. "Well, Tressa was in error. I am not unwell, nor am I upset. But now that you bring her name up, we two should talk of Tressa."

Shelagh shifted slightly, placing herself now directly in front of the window so that she was silhouetted against the brightness of the afternoon. She stood there for long moments looking at me, her head held high and the light behind her preventing me from seeing the look in her eyes. I waited, counting silently to ten before she responded, in a very gentle voice, "Very well then, let us talk of Tressa. What should we discuss?"

What, indeed, should we discuss? More quickly than comprehension could permit, I found myself off-balance. The simplicity and the immediacy of Shelagh's question caught me unprepared, and I realized that I could say nothing in direct response without either betraying, perhaps offensively, my sudden knowledge of what she was about, or sounding both foolish and ungrateful, or, for that matter, without sounding harshly and undeservedly critical of Tressa. I coughed, clearing my throat in an attempt to win myself some time for thought, and then I decided to take refuge in the truth.

"Tressa," I said, suddenly finding it easy to smile. "You set a trap for me, baited with Tressa."

For a fleeting instant, I saw her stiffen, as though in surprise, and then she tossed her head, although her voice, when she resumed, sounded unchanged. "A trap? You make me sound unfriendly, Caius. How would I do that, and why?"

"To lead me astray, perhaps?" I kept my tone light and friendly, part of me afraid she might take offence where none was intended.

"From what?"

"Why, from my resolve to remain sexually unencumbered, what else?"

Again, that fleeting stillness, and then a laugh—high, clear and amused—and all I could see was the black shape of her, all detail lost against the flaring brightness of the sky at her back.

"Unencumbered? You would see a lovely young woman like Tressa as an encumbrance?"

I waited, but she had nothing more to add, and when I was sure of that, I shrugged. "Most men who consider celibacy worthwhile would, Shelagh."

"Ah yes, of course, your celibacy."

"What? What do you mean, 'your celibacy'?"

"Just what I said, and with a heavy hint of scorn. Celibacy, in any man, is an admission of failure to live as the gods intended—but in you, my dearest friend, it is ludicrous." She straightened up, abruptly, and moved away from the window, so that I could see her face again, and I felt a surge of relief. Now she laughed aloud and moved directly to sit at the table where I had sat earlier that day.

"Why are you laughing at me?"

"I'm not." But even as she denied it, her laughter continued, although I knew it as the laughter of a friend, containing nothing demeaning. "Come, come here and sit with me." I moved to sit across from her on the other chair and she sat still for a space of heartbeats, smiling now and shaking her head fondly. "You have the gift we share to thank for this, dear Cay, for I admit I brought Tressa to you deliberately. I saw her, in a dream one night, and saw you with her, smiling." She held up her hand. "Now, don't ask me, for I cannot say whether the dream was prophesy or no, but it was clear, and unmistakable, and wholesome. So I acted upon it."

"Whether I would or not?"

"No, for I knew you would. You need to." She shook her head, briefly and impatiently, and puffed an errant wing of hair out of her eyes. "Caius, this talk of celibacy is absurd, coming from you, and I care not for your careful, self-serving reasons. You are no celibate!" She made the word sound like catamite. "Aye, you'd have me believe you would be celibate! At least, your responsible mind would be, with its love of logic, and that I believe. But what of your other parts—even the other part of your mind, that which purges itself in dreams of women who may or may not be faceless? That purging, that effusion of your seed, is evidence that there is life in you, Caius, demanding to be lived. To deny it, in the face of your god, or mine, or those of anyone else, must be a sin, man! Look at me, now, don't turn your face away."

I looked back to her but said nothing and her eyes narrowed.

"Is it the girl? You find her displeasing?"

I shook my head. "No, not at all. She is most pleasant, and she is clean and wholesome."

"What, then? There's something wrong, somewhere. Where is her lack?"

"She has none, that I can see. None physical."

"And none mental, either. Have you spoken with her?"

I felt my eyebrows rise in surprise. "Of course I have. I spoke with her today. She prattled on for the longest time about the things she was doing."

"No, not like that. She was nervous and afraid of you, I suspect. Have you spoken with her, Cay? Have you conversed with her?"

"On what topic?"

She sighed explosively and threw up her hands in a gesture of resignation. "On anything, man! Caius, you could talk with that girl about anything you have in your mind at any time. Don't be gulled by what you think of—being a man—as her simpleness or her untutored, Cumbrian speech. That young woman is the most gifted seamstress I have ever known, and she has a mind as good as mine or Ludmilla's or any other woman you could think of—and that means it's as good as any man's in a hundred." She slumped back then in her chair, looking at me wide-eyed and shaking her head very gently from side to side as though in wonderment at my ignorance.

"What is it, Shelagh?" I asked. "You have something to tell me, I think."

"I do. Do you remember this?" She dropped her hands into her lap and spread the fingers of each over one of her leather-covered thighs, on either side of where the front of her tunic hung down between them. I gazed at them in confusion, my heart suddenly pounding in my breast.

"Remember what?" The tension in my voice was unmistakable—dense and sexual.

"The body beneath these clothes, the one we decided together long since, and for the very best of reasons, that you may never have. In all the years since then, we have never done a thing of which we need ever be ashamed in the eyes of anyone."

I swallowed the lump in my throat. "Aye, I know all that, so what are you saying to me, Shelagh?"

"That I know how much the wanting can hurt, Cay, despite the fact of a husband whom I love and who loves me and who can satisfy my wanting. It grieves me, and has done so now for years, to know that you have no surcease for yours, other than random dreams."

Her voice faded away and a long silence ensued. Eventually I nodded.

"I see. And so you chose Tressa as my plaything?"

"I chose Tressa, you foolish man, but not as a plaything. I chose her for *you*. And I chose her with great care."

I smiled. "How so? You dreamed her, you said."

"True, I dreamed of her first. But dreams are dreams and life is real—you of all people know that as well as I do—and so I examined the woman very carefully before I made a move. Every part of her—her youth, her health, her background and her character—I sieved for imperfections, and, save one, found none. She is perfect for you, Cay."

"But I have no wish to marry, Shelagh. If I can't have you, I'll have no one." I said nothing of the fact that I had sworn an oath to myself after Cassandra's death that I would never take another woman as my wife. I saw no need to mention that, and I had had no thought of Tressa as a wife.

"There speaks a fool, so those words can't be yours. I said nothing of marriage. Finding you a wife was far from my mind."

"That may be true, Shelagh, but it disregards my own notions of responsibility. To return to the gift we share, I too, have seen things. No dream, but a vision, of a kind. That's why I fled from her today."

"What? What did you see?"

"A thing that frightened me. Today, as I stood over her—she was gathering up her balls of yarn that I had knocked to the floor—I saw an image of her, big with child, gravid and threatening. My child. That was the end of it, then and there."

"Pah! That was nothing. A last-moment flash of conscience and self-chastisement."

I gazed at her in surprise. "You say so? Then it was as effective as it could have been. I'll have no more of it, because she will end up with child, if I lay hand on her, and that is a complication of which I have no slightest need. I would not father bastards, so her pregnancy would mean my taking her to wife, and that, with no adverse reflection on Tressa, simply cannot be. My role in life is clear, clean and decided long since—Arthur Pendragon, first, last and always. So trust my judgment and let be, Shelagh."

"She is barren."

"What?" Her words almost drove the breath from me, and I felt my mouth gape with shock. Shelagh was smiling again, though still gently.

"Tressa is barren. That was the single imperfection that I found in her. Her husband put her out a year and more ago and took another wife, who had already borne him two fat sons while he was wed to Tressa, thus proving that the fault lay in Tressa and not in him. Since then, Tressa has lived solely on her ability to wield a needle better than any other in Ravenglass. So you see, her need for comforting and succour is as great as yours."

"By the Christ, Shelagh, you confound me." I sagged back in my chair, completely at a loss. "You have been conspiring to alter my very life!"

"Aye, my dear, but only with myself. Not even Tressa knows what I have been thinking." She was completely uncontrite, smiling at me. "Think of it, Cay—think about what a nod of the head could mean to you: companionship, a ready wit to keep you agile and alert, a clever woman's mind around you with a pleasant smile and a willing, cheerful bedmate on cold, dark nights . . . even on warm, dark nights. All those you need, Caius Merlyn Britannicus, and all of them are there in young Tressa. And no fear of siring children." She paused, blinking, and her smile faded to soberness. "Even the boy would benefit from such a case, for Tressa's need to mother is fierce and strong." Then, in a quieter voice, she added, "Think you I would advise you lightly in this, Cay? Or wrongly? Or that I would bestow those blessings I covet on someone unworthy?"

I stood up slowly, my mind spinning as I saw the implications here. But before I could find the words with which to respond to such an amazing series of statements, questions and revelations, the door swung open and Dedalus strode in. He almost skidded to a halt when he saw my expression and then Shelagh, sitting opposite me.

"Now, by the Christ! Forgive me, Merlyn—Cay, I mean—for charging in like this without a knock or bidding. I had no thought you might be occupied. Shelagh, your pardon, I'll—"

"Please, Dedalus, enough!" Shelagh rose to her feet, cutting him off with a smile and an upraised palm. "Our talk is done and I was about to leave." She smiled at me. "Think on what I have said, Cay, and consider it at length. There is no need for haste, in any direction. When you are ready to talk further, come and see me." She nodded again to Dedalus and left us with a smile.

Dedalus stepped to the window to watch her walk by, then turned to me. "Again, your pardon, Cay. I entered without thinking."

I barely heard what he said—my mind still reeling with the portent of Shelagh's last pronouncements—but I realized I was being uncivil, so I shook myself mentally and forced my attention to rest on my new visitor.

"What was that? No, no, no. Think no more of it, Ded. You know my door is always open to you. As Shelagh said, our talk was over. We were but making conversation when you arrived. What's that you have there?"

He carried two long pieces of wood clutched beneath one arm. He moved to a chair and seated himself, laying one end of them on the floor and leaning them against his leg as he launched into a long description of what they were and how he had found them. But he might as well have been speaking Attic Greek, for all that I absorbed of what he said, because my mind remained fixed upon what had just passed between Shelagh and me—the deafening knowledge that Tressa was barren! My face must have portrayed a certain interest, nonetheless, because Dedalus kept talking. But as he droned on, his tone changed from a mere accompaniment to my confusion into an annoyance, and eventually I jerked my hand upward in a peremptory gesture of restraint. He stopped speaking immediately.

"Ded, my friend, I must ask you to forgive me, but I have barely heard a word of what you have been saying. My head is filled with other matters."

He sat frowning at me, clearly concerned for me.

"Are you all right, Cay? Is something wrong?"

I shook my head, finding the ability to smile, albeit ruefully. "No, Ded, there's nothing wrong . . . nothing that can be changed, at any rate. It's simply . . . I have too much on my mind—too many things, all small enough but all demanding redress. Shelagh's contribution, though among the least of them, was simply one more complication than I had thought to face at this particular time. Your input then, my friend, has come as surfeit. Can you excuse my lack of courtesy?"

"Tchah! What lack of courtesy?" He rose to his feet, smiling. "I was the one who thrust myself in here without thought. I was but passing by, on my way to meet with Mark, when I thought to show you these things that I have found." He hefted them into the air, catching them beneath his arm again. "But they are solid, as you see, so they won't dry up and disappear. Deal with the problems on your mind, and when you're ready, I won't be hard to find. Can I help you with anything?" I shook my head, wordlessly, and he shrugged and made his way to the door. "I'll leave you to it, then, until later."

When he had gone I stood staring at the door, my mind in some kind of stasis, empty of all intelligible thought. But then the image of Tressa came back to me, to be replaced immediately by Shelagh's smiling face and the sound of her voice. I moved to sit in my most comfortable chair, allowing my calamitous thoughts to swirl and surge around in my mind. They were, however, too disturbing and too turbulent to be dealt with sitting still, and soon I was pacing my floor from one end to the other, tracing and retracing the same path as I grappled with the welter of my feelings and emotions. Finally, I stopped before the window where Shelagh had stood and leaned out into the still-bright afternoon. All at once I was aware of what it was that had been troubling me about Shelagh's declaration: it contained an inconsistency, so frail as to be almost nebulous, yet tantalizingly present, demanding recognition.

Shelagh had chosen Tressa as a mistress for me, and some inner, disapproving part of me was slightly scandalized by that. She had searched diligently, by her own admission, and had chosen carefully, selecting

Tressa over all others. Then, her choice made in secrecy, she had implemented her design and I had refused the offered prize. Only then, in the face of that refusal, had she acknowledged her intent and her manipulation of events for my personal and private benefit. It was, in one evident sense, the gesture of a true and loyal friend, selfless and generous and noble-hearted. And yet . . . and yet, it was flawed.

I could not marry Tressa, for a myriad reasons including my own oath never to take a wife. Shelagh, however, even though she knew nothing of that oath, had not sought to find a wife for me. Instead, she had found a potentially willing mistress who would never be a threat, either to my destiny with Arthur, or to that dear place, that shrine sacred to my long-dead Cassandra, shared now by her memory and by Shelagh herself, in my deepest heart. Most particularly, however, the woman she had taken such pains to find could never tie me to her in the future through the bonds of children.

I knew beyond a doubt that Shelagh had laboured well on my behalf, but now I knew also that she had laboured not quite selflessly or self-effacingly. That physicality which she might not provide herself she had provided otherwise; but the strangely passive secret, amorous, excitement-filled attraction to each other that we shared, on the other hand, she had safeguarded wholly, in her role as panderer. . . . As the full realization of what had passed here flooded through me—Shelagh's tacit, even unconscious acknowledgment of the love she held for me—I found myself smiling again, broadly this time, and filling my lungs with the aromatic air of late afternoon as I bounded out of my quarters and made my way towards Mark's carpentry shop, feeling like a boy released from his lessons.

Dedalus was still there when I arrived, as was Lucanus, the latter sitting on an upturned barrel in the yard fronting Mark's workshop. They were talking of furnishings with Mark, admiring the matching patterns of the close-grained boards in a table he was making. They were all pleased to see me, and when the greetings were all done I turned to Dedalus.

"Now I can concentrate on what you wanted to discuss. You brought some things to show me. Do you still have them?"

"Aye," he murmured, grinning, then crossed to where they were propped against a wall. He picked both pieces up, hefted them one in each hand, then passed one to me. I held it close to my eyes and dug at it with my thumbnail. It was carefully sawed, heavy, dense-grained oak, unplaned but squared on all sides to the width of four fingers. I lowered one end to the floor and the other reached up to my sternum. The second piece, which Ded still held, appeared to be identical.

"It's oak, and seasoned," I said. "Where did you get it?"

He grinned again. "Above the furnace in the bathhouse. Mark, here, was looking for a place to dry some lumber, months ago, when I first repaired the hypocaust system. He didn't need much room at the time, but he required it to be hot and dry and weatherproof, and I knew there was adequate space beneath the bathhouse floor, perfect for his needs. I told him about it, and then forgot about it afterward, but he has been using the space ever since. I went in there today, about an hour before I passed by your place, and found these and a hundred or so others just like them. Mark used them for making bed-legs, when he was building our cots." He saw the incomprehension in my eyes as I glanced towards Mark, who was standing listening, a half-smile on his lips. "Don't you see it, Cay?" I could hear the excitement now in Ded's voice. "It's prime oak, oven-dried and cured, heavier and stronger than ash. We can turn and taper them on Mark's lathe and make ourselves some real, practical staves of the kind we've been discussing—long practice swords, all of a uniform size."

Mark's lathe was his greatest pride, a wonderful machine that enabled him to transform plain, squared lumber into glowing, rounded, exquisitely turned things of beauty. In the flash of a moment, I saw the squared baulk of timber in my hand transformed into a thick dowel, a tapered practice sword.

"By God you're right, Ded!"

"I know I'm right. I'm just glad I went down into the furnace room today, for it would never have occurred to me that we had such perfect material at hand, already cured and seasoned. But what think you, will oak serve as well as ash?"

"Aye, and better, would be my guess." I looked to Mark for confirmation and he nodded mutely, his smile widening.

"I believe it might," he drawled, "but I don't know what use you intend for them, or how much abuse they'll take. If they break, we can always make more, out of ash."

I hoisted the heavy length of wood and caught it at the midpoint. "The Roman practice swords were ash. Our British ones will be of oak. How long to make them?"

Mark looked to Dedalus, who shrugged his huge shoulders. "Like making swords, I would guess. We'll make two as experimental models and then refine them as necessary until they'll do what we require of them." He could no longer contain the smile of delight that broke across his face. "You approve of them, then?"

"I do, and heartily."

"Good, then I'll bring them back to you when they're ready to be used. How long will that be, Mark?"

The young carpenter shrugged. "I can see it's important to you, and this tabletop is finished, for today at least. I can start on them now, if you like. You'll have to show me exactly what you want me to do with them—the length and angle of the taper. I'll need an hour to set the first one on the lathe, but after that, we can begin immediately. If all goes well, they should be ready by this time tomorrow."

Dedalus stood on tiptoe and stretched his arms above his head. "Then what are we waiting for? To work, young Marcus!"

As he stretched, I grinned and launched the heavy length of wood at his midriff. He whipped his arms down just in time to catch it and whirl it, one-handed, up beneath his armpit, as though it were a centurion's cudgel of vine wood, dried and weightless. Then he snapped a flawless Roman centurion's salute, executed a smart about-face and marched into the gloom of the workshop.

I moved to sit on a low stump beside Lucanus's much higher barrel, looking up at him where he sat smiling gently at Ded's antics.

"How are you feeling, Luke? You looked a bit pale and shaky earlier, on the way up the hill."

"Aye, I must admit there was a time back there when I felt that horse would be the death of me. There is something about the rocking motion of a horse that never fails to nauseate me. How you people can stomach it I'll never know."

I sat for a moment, bemused, blinking at him and wondering how he could remain unaware that he alone experienced any rocking motion on a horse. The side-to-side motion to which he referred was born solely of his own execrable horsemanship. Lucanus had never mastered the art of relaxing on a horse's back; he held himself rigid at all times, so that instead of melding with the motion of the animal and riding almost as a part of it, he was forever at odds with it, clinging grimly and in constant discomfort to his precarious perch on its broad back. His failure to see that and to adjust his seat was incomprehensible to me, because I had started riding when I was so young that I had never known, nor I could not remember, any such rocking motion.

"So you felt better when you were on solid ground again?"

"Again, as ever. I vastly prefer riding on a wagon. There's so much more in one of those to hang on to."

I grunted a laugh and shook my head. "What are you going to do now?"

"Now, at this moment? I had thought to move inside and watch young Mark at work, but if you have something other than that in mind, I'll gladly go with you."

"Would you enjoy a stroll around the walls?"

He eyed me shrewdly. "With you? Of course I would. Help me down, would you? I hoisted myself up, but it looks to be a long way down there for bones like mine."

I grasped one hand and helped him down from his barrel and we made our way directly to the nearest wall, the northern one that fronted the chasm behind the fort. When we reached it we turned to our right and began to walk briskly around the intervallum, the circuit road that followed the interior of the walls. I plunged directly into what I wanted to say to him, the excitement in me brimming over uncontrollably.

"Luke, I have something to ask you."

"Ask away," he replied, but then he stopped again and turned to face me, alerted perhaps by something in my tone, and his face underwent a sudden change to dismay. "Oh, Aesculapius," he said, almost groaning. "There's that look that reeks of celibacy. Not today, Merlyn, I beg you. I would rather run and try to jump over these walls than talk of celibacy on such a wondrous afternoon."

"No, please listen to me, Luke. You might actually enjoy what I have to say."

One eyebrow climbed high on his forehead. "Oh, you think so, do you?"

"Aye, I do. I have decided, conclusively, that celibacy is not for me."

Lucanus threw back his head and raised both hands outward to shoulder height, then revolved slowly in a complete turn, his eyes closed and a look of ecstasy upon his thin, ascetic features. I heard a strange, thin sound issue from his nostrils and increase in volume until it was a ringing, high-pitched hum. Then, as I watched in amazement, never having seen him do anything remotely like this in all the years I had known him, he opened his lips and sang the note, unaltered, holding it high and pure in pitch until the breath in his lungs ran out, after which he took another breath and sang in a monotone, holding the last syllable until his breath ran out again, "Thanks be to all the gods of medicine and all their ideas of enlightenment. . . ."

I had not moved throughout this strange performance, not knowing whether to laugh or help him to lie down, and I saw amazement mirroring my own on the faces of the four workmen close enough to hear and see what was going on. Now Luke gazed at me fiercely.

"How did you come to this wondrous decision, and why? Who is she?"

"Tressa," I replied, keeping my voice low, for his ears alone. Until the moment the word passed my lips, I would not have believed I'd ever say it.

"Then blessed be the bounteous Tressa, and I shall rejoice to see you smug and smiling, sated and uxorious in future."

"Uxorious? I am not speaking here of marriage, Luke."

"Nor should you be, my boy, at this stage, but you are speaking of sanity and freshening gale winds of sound good sense. Come, let us walk, for I find the thought of speech on celibacy has suddenly become much less oppressive. I have words to say to you, now that you appear disposed to hear them."

And so we walked, back and forth beneath the stone walls of the ancient fort, and my old friend held me close, my arm tucked firmly beneath his as he spoke of his own agonizing over the requests I had made of him in the recent and not-so-recent past. He had felt all along, he said, that I was in error with my wishes on the matter of celibacy. I had been fleeing towards it, he believed, and he knew well that flight from life was no way to achieve the condition which I thought I desired so profoundly. He had come to believe, to be convinced, that I was determined to launch myself along a road that must surely lead me to failure and frustration, and so he had avoided the topic to the best of his ability.

Now that I had decided to abandon my unrealistic wishes, he informed me, he could hope that I might find far more satisfaction in the little he could teach me of the celibate way of life, for he was prepared, much more so than before, to teach me what he knew of the philosophy that underlay the discipline.

I was surprised to hear him say these things, and I asked him to explain. He reminded me that my original thought had been to learn self-mastery in celibacy, hoping to use that same self-mastery to aid me in my teaching of Arthur. There was nothing arcane in self-mastery, per se, Lucanus said. That was a matter of pure discipline, and I was already close to being adept in the skill, simply by virtue of the life that I had led. Gaining the arcane lore of the magi who had mastered asceticism and self-denial was an exercise in a further discipline that lay beyond mere sexual self-denial, and that lore, he declared, was superfluous, something of which I had no need at all. My gifts, he swore, my own abilities, already lay in my possession; all I required to make the best and finest use of them was equanimity and peace of mind, both of which lay securely rooted in self-confidence. When I had once decided who and what I was, and had accepted and embraced my role in life, he was convinced all those gifts and abilities would be unleashed and would flourish.

Just beyond the halfway point of our circuit of the walls, ahead of us and rushing towards us, a group of noisy children approached, milling around like fallen leaves in a high wind. We stopped to allow them to swirl by us in a babble of high, excited voices, parting around us and ignoring us as though we were invisible. Lucanus turned to watch them recede into the distance and then walked for a long time in a silence I had no desire or need to break.

"Do you know, Caius," he eventually said, "I can't remember ever having run like that, although I suppose I must have. I was a child once, you know."

"So long ago, my friend, that you cannot recall being one?"

"Oh, I remember well enough. . . . Some parts of it at least. The happy parts, mainly, but those seemed very few. Do you remember your boyhood?"

"Aye, vividly, and with pleasure. Uther and I enjoyed a childhood shared by few, filled with the joy of being who we were. We spent every autumn and winter in Roman Camulod, and every spring and summer in Celtic Cambria, although the bruises that we gathered were the same in both places."

"Aye, and they were plentiful, I'll warrant. But speaking of bruises, what is happening with that blemish on your chest? Have you been exposing it to healing air, as I suggested?"

"Aye, I have, but not apurpose, now that I think of it. Since the arrival of your scroll and your assurance that the mark is not what I once feared it was, I've lost awareness of it. But I have been going bare-chested recently, thanks to the clement weather."

Lucanus stopped and turned to face me. "Let's have a look at it. Undo your tyings."

I was wearing only a simple tunic, slashed at the neck and tied with a decorative cord, and I undid it, pushing the material aside to bare my right breast. Lucanus peered at it and sniffed. "Aye, as I thought, it seems to be receding. I remember it as being larger. It will be gone within the month, I'd wager."

He moved on and I walked beside him, adjusting my tunic as he murmured something about the pleasantness of the day.

At that point, seeing that we had completed our circuit of the walls and come close to our living quarters, where a throng of people were milling about, he stopped and turned to face me squarely, reaching out to grasp me by the shoulder and demonstrating that his grip was younger and stronger than his thin face might suggest. In perfect seriousness, he told me that my decision was absolutely the right one to make, and then he went on to embarrass me by saying that he considered me to be the finest man that he had ever known, including my own father, and that he could think of no one better equipped than me to face the task I had set myself.

The boy Arthur would be a king, he said, under my guidance, but given that guidance and the attributes we knew the lad to possess, he believed implicitly that Arthur Pendragon would grow to be a king whose like had never lived in Britain. Not an emperor like Alexander, but a king, conquering no new lands but nurturing and strengthening his own, and gaining for himself a name and reputation that would never die, no matter what came after him.

When he stopped speaking, Luke's eyes were awash with unshed tears, and I had to swallow hard to subdue the lump thickening in my own throat. Thereafter, we were silent until we parted before his door. There was no more to say.

That night, when all our new colonists were gathered at dinner, I crossed to where young Tressa sat among the other newcomers from Ravenglass and sat down beside her. My advent, unprecedented though it was, seemed to provoke no comment, and Tressa betrayed no sign of nervousness or curiosity. She simply welcomed me and then spent the entire mealtime talking pleasantly of general trivia with the others, a conversation in which I joined without reservation. I enjoyed myself thoroughly.

When the meal was over and the gathering broke up, I walked with her out into the evening air, which held a chill and the promise of a late frost. She shivered and clasped her arms over her breast; I unfolded my cloak, which I was carrying over my arm, and draped it about her. She stopped, surprised, and favoured me with a lingering, speculative glance.

"Don't be upset, Master Cay, but what are you about?"

I smiled at her. "What do you think I am about, Tressa?"

She shook her head slowly, smiling faintly in return. "I know not. How could I? This is the first time you have ever paid any heed to me at all, and today you almost ran away from me, I thought. But suddenly now you're sitting with me, looking at me, talking to me, and now wrapping me in your fine cloak."

I realized that I had lost all awareness of what I had thought of in the past as her alien speech patterns. Her voice sounded perfectly normal to me now. I nodded. "I almost did run away from you today, but I have had time and opportunity to think since then. Will you forgive me?"

"Forgive you?" She laughed, a delightful, gurgling sound, deep in her chest. "Why, what have you done that should require forgiveness? I've noticed nothing."

"Well, I have been afraid of you, for one thing."

"What?" She stiffened. "Why would you say a thing like that, Master Cay? Are you making sport of me? If 'tis so, and I think it must be, then I shall leave you now, for I have done nothing to warrant that."

"Shh! Hush." I raised my hand gently as though to touch her mouth and she stilled instantly, watching me from wide eyes. I laid my fingers softly against her cheek and touched the cushion of her lips with the pad of my thumb. "I had no thought to mock you, lass. I spoke the truth, I was afraid of you, foolishly, because I was afraid of me and how I wanted to respond to you . . . to the way you make me feel." I leaned closer to her, stooping my head to gaze into her eyes. "Do you have any notion of how you make me feel?"

Even had she been blind, the tone of my voice would have told her the answer to that question. She nodded, hesitantly, speaking past my thumb which remained in place, hovering lightly over her mouth. "I—I think so, now."

"And does that displease you?"

"No . . . But—"

"But what?"

"What would you of me now, now that I know?"

I felt her warm breath against the pad of my thumb and smiled again, amazed at how much ease I felt in such an unfamiliar situation. I might have known this girl for years, and her face was filling all my vision, occluding Shelagh and even my dear wife Cassandra with the magic power of her nearness.

"What would I of you now? What would you give? I'll ask you for your friendship and your warmth, your smiles and laughter and your ready tongue."

She had not moved, or made any effort to remove her cheek from contact with my fingers. Now, as I paused, she turned her head infinitesimally, increasing the pressure of her cheek against my hand almost imperceptibly.

"And?" she whispered.

"And, should you care to bestow anything at all on me, I'll ask you for your companionship, your softness and your self, Tressa."

"What else, Master Cay?" Her voice was the merest whisper.

I became aware that others were moving about us, but I did not care. I brushed my thumb across her lips, feeling them move and alter their shape, and then I pulled slightly downward, folding her lower lip outward until I felt the moist warmth of soft underlip against my skin.

"I'd have you stop calling me Master Cay. My name is Cay, plain Cay, to all my friends. And I would—will ask you for a kiss. . . ."

"Come." In less than a blink, she had me firmly by the hand, leading me away from the area of the dining hall. "People were starting in to listen," she said eventually, when we were well removed from everyone, but her hand retained its hold on mine. "Have you a fire in your rooms?"

"Aye, if it's still alight. I built it up before I left, but the wood we're burning nowadays is dry and burns up quickly."

"And have you wine, that we might spice?"

"I have."

"Then go you and prepare it. I must fetch my work-basket."

"How so? I had no thought of asking you to sew for me, seated before my fire . . . not tonight."

She grinned and squeezed my fingers, and even in the moonlight I could see her eyes dancing. "Nor had I thought to sew for you tonight. I cannot sew and hold a cup of heated wine, nor anything else that's warm and spillable." The ambiguity of that brought my entire heart up into my mouth, but she had moved on. "But I must have my basket, for I'd not like to leave it unattended for too long. It contains my very life, all of my tools and treasures."

I felt my blood grow thicker and a pulse began to beat quite palpably in my right temple. "But you left it behind you to go to dinner."

"Aye, I did, but without risk—everyone else was dining, too. Now they will all be back, save me, and the temptation to invade my basket during the night might be too strong for . . . certain people. I find it foolish to hold out temptation when I would suffer by having someone yield to it. . . ." She was still smiling, looking up at me, her head cocked to one side. "Don't you think that wise?" I nodded, suddenly struck mute. I saw her eyes watching my Adam's apple, seeing my nervousness, and then she nodded, too, and her voice sank to a whisper. "Good, then I shall go and fetch it, and when I return, you may have your kiss in return for allowing me to share your fire and wine." She turned to leave, but I stayed her with tightening fingers.

"And what of sharing my bed, Tressa?"

She grinned, her eyes alight in the moonlight with wicked mischief. "Now there is a temptation worth the offering, *and* the yielding. Why do you think I felt the need to bring my basket? Go you and build the fire up, now."

I found the fire still smouldering, and after I had lighted several of my beeswax candles from the tallow lamp I had left burning, I stirred it back to life, adding new kindling first, and then stout logs. Then I filled an earthen pot with wine and placed it upon the metal hob over the flames, adding a generous pinch of the last remnants of the precious spices brought to Luceiia Varrus from beyond the seas in years gone by. Too little of this mixture of dried and crushed exotic essences remained then to permit profligacy in the use of it, for it was literally irreplaceable, and I used it only on the most important and celebratory of occasions. I had shared some of it with Ambrose and with Joseph no more than a week before, and this night, I had no doubt, was to be one deserving even more celebration.

I was still working on the preparation of the infusion when Tressa knocked gently and entered, wearing her own long cloak now, over mine, and carrying her precious basket. She stopped inside the door, laid her basket on the floor and pulled the door closed behind her, barring it securely. She then hung my cloak and her own on the pegs on the wall. I had closed and barred the shutters before going out.

"The wine will be ready directly," I said. "Have you tasted it before?"

"Yes, several times. Shelagh made it for me."

"Ah! It's Shelagh's wine you've had, mixed with her fiery honey. This is quite different, prepared with spices from the eastern Empire, whereas Shelagh's mix is made from herbs and simples gathered here in Britain—or in Eire. You may not like this potion."

She came directly to where I stood by the brazier and stood gazing down at the liquid that was beginning to simmer gently in the pot. The parting in her long, rich, dark-brown hair shone pearly white, clean. She raised her head to look at me, no trace of shyness or false coyness in her face. "Your kiss," she said, tilting her head up to me.

I have never forgotten the wonder of that kiss, the first of countless thousands that I was to share with her. I had to stoop to reach her mouth, and I did so hesitantly, quite unsure of how, or if, I ought to touch her with my hands. The result was that I touched her with my lips alone that time, no other contact occurring between our bodies. My awareness of the flaring heat of the fire against my bare leg vanished instantly in the sensation of that first contact with her mouth, banished by the amazing softness of her cushioned lips and the resilience with which they adjusted to the shape and pressure of my own.

She was as tentative as I, in those first moments, gentle and hesitant, unsure, yet both of us gained strength and confidence with every heartbeat and the steady, infinitesimal increase of pressure as our lips and mouths expanded with the pleasure and excitement of the kiss. I moved my head, sideways, and she responded equally, and suddenly the moistness of her lower underlip sent surges of ecstatic intimacy racing through my brain, so that I caught my breath and opened my own mouth to her, sucking her lower lip, full and succulent, entirely into my mouth. She stiffened and her arm came up quickly to clasp my neck, pulling me close, and then my hands were filled with her, the divided column of her back in one, the cup of her soft belly filling the other as her breasts cushioned my ribs. I felt myself grow dizzy with desire and then she was pulling away from me, catching her breath and sweeping the disordered hair back from her forehead.

"Tend to the wine, Master Cay. I must tend to me." Her voice was shaky, breathless.

"I told you, my name's Cay, no Master here."

She exhaled in an emphatic puff. "I know it is, and those who know *me* well may call me Tress, not Tressa . . . but right then, at that moment, you felt like a master." She looked about her. "Now! Wine, if it please you."

As I bent to remove the clay pot carefully from the hob, she moved away, into my sleeping chamber, and I heard her moving purposefully about in there. I poured wine into two cups and replaced the pot, swinging the hob away so that it did not rest directly over the coals. Just as I thought to ask her what she was about, she came back into the main room, her arms filled with the cured animal skins I used as bedding when I went campaigning. As I stood there watching her, a steaming cup in each hand, she dropped the double armload on the floor before the fire and spread them out with her feet and hands, making a double layer. That done, she brought a low stool from against the wall and placed it to one side, after which she lowered herself to sit on the skins and reached for a cup, smiling up at me.

"Now, come and sit down, plain Cay, and drink with me while we enjoy the firelight."

The mere use of the term "plain Cay" reminded me that she alone, of all Derek's folk, was aware of my real identity. I was glad she knew that

I was Merlyn of Camulod, although I remembered being upset when I found that Shelagh had told her. Now it seemed absolutely natural that she should have been informed. Grinning, I sat as bidden, and she tasted my spiced wine, raising her eyebrows high with simulated rapture at the surprising tang of it.

"What is it?"

"Nectar. We call it 'sweet flames.' It's supposed to be an aphrodisiac."

She raised herself higher on an elbow. "A what? Aphrodisiac? What does that mean?"

I sipped, deliberately slurping noisily. "A love potion to promote desire and to extend performance."

"Ooh . . ." Her eyes went round with wonder and mischief. "And does it work? Will I regret the drinking of it?"

"I don't know, lass. Do you think you might?"

"Only if it fails us." She started to laugh, softly at first and then more unrestrainedly, and eventually I found myself laughing helplessly with her, filled with elation and a feeling of release and great relief, so that years fell away from me. We rolled about on the bed she had prepared for us, spilling more than the occasional drop of wine. And soon we had drunk the pot dry, talking and laughing all the while and taking delight in the learning of each other, free of constraint. And as we talked and laughed and took delight, we kissed; and as we kissed, we ventured further, so that soon our clothes were cast aside and we lay intertwined, exulting in the newfound beauty of each other, uncaring if the aphrodisiac were real or not. We had no need of it. And I fed the fire from time to time. And when the sun came up it found us still awake, rejoicing together at the advent of a time that stretched and stretched ahead of us without a care.

PART TWO

MEDIOBOGDUM

XIV

In the late summer of that first full year of our residence, the first overland expedition from Camulod arrived with our new supply of horses, making their way, to the great excitement of everyone in the fort, over the high saddle of the pass above and to the east of us.

Anticipating that they might be arriving some day soon, I had begun posting guards on the peak above the pass several weeks earlier, and so the horn announcing their arrival had sounded as soon as they came into view, permitting us ample time to assemble our own small force and change into our military trappings, seldom used in those peaceful days of building, to welcome the newcomers appropriately.

A stirring sight they made, too, their weapons and armour and equipment flashing in the westering sun as they wound their way down from the heights to our gates, a journey of some third of an hour. They moved in what seemed like an endless file, four wide. Two squadrons of cavalry rode front and rear, with the foot soldiers and extra horses in place between them, the latter haltered and strung together in sets of four, with the outer horse on each rank, alternating right and left, being ridden by a trooper.

Ambrose rode at the head of them all, beneath my own great, black-and-white standard with the silver bear, which had become the standard of Camulod. Watching his approach from my vantage point on our fort's south-east tower, I felt my heartbeat quicken and my breath speed up in a very strange fashion. It was like watching myself ride towards me, which was in fact, as I had to remind myself, precisely the effect Ambrose was looking to achieve. In the eyes of the people, he rode as Merlyn of Camulod, and even I might have been convinced to believe it. The effect on young Arthur and his three friends, however, was far more salutary.

Arthur had always been smitten by the heroic aspects of Uncle Ambrose, as he called him. On this occasion the boy was actually struck dumb by the splendour of the Camulodian approach. I have no doubt the reasons for his reaction were many and mixed. It might have been occasioned by the fact that we ourselves had been away from Camulod for more than a year by then. It might also have been augmented by the fact that we seldom wore armour nowadays in Mediobogdum, and were more akin to farmers and artisans—in appearance and dress at least—than to soldiers and warriors. Then again, it might have been due to the simple apparition of a large, disciplined force of regimented, heavily armed men and horses in a place where we had grown accustomed to seeing the native warriors going about on foot, or on shaggy ponies, individually.

Whatever the reasons, when the vanguard of the Camulodian troops arrived and Ambrose himself sat smiling down at us, immense in his high-crested Roman helmet and heavy, shimmering and highly polished plate armour, flanked by his three senior troop commanders, young Arthur walked forward alone, wordlessly, his eyes shining, his hands held out to relieve Ambrose of his heavy shield. My brother grunted, looking down at the boy, and then swung easily down from his high saddle, passing the shield to him with one hand and reaching out to ruffle his hair with the other; he paused, then, the gesture incomplete, and changed his mind, contenting himself with gripping Arthur cordially by one shoulder before moving directly to embrace me.

"He's too big to be greeted as a child now," he whispered as we hugged each other. I said nothing, stepping back to clear the way for the others at my back to move forward.

When all the introductions had been completed, Ambrose released his three troop commanders to supervise the settling of their men and horses on the flat parade area outside the eastern gate, where the infantry that had accompanied them were already laying out their tents and gear in the traditional Roman style. A group of us moved into the fort and up onto the eastern wall, where we could see what was going on. From that viewpoint, it was Lucanus who observed that this old fort had never seen such a gathering of military might before. At its most active time, shortly after it was built, it might have held five or six hundred men, although we had strong grounds to doubt that it had ever been so fully garrisoned, but it had never seen more than a hundred heavy cavalry mounts at once. As Lucanus pointed this out, Derek, who had been staying with us for a week at that time, stood silent, his arms folded on his chest, his bearded chin resting on the gorget of his leather breastplate as he stared at the horse camp that now filled the parade ground. This was, I knew, the first time he had actually seen any hint of the kind of peacetime force that Camulod could field, and he was impressed, aware that this was merely a patrol dispatched several months earlier and barely missed in Camulod.

When I had told him, at the time of Ambrose's departure months earlier, that we would be having visitors by land from Camulod, the king had been perturbed, fearing that such an open use of the rear road to Ravenglass might point the way for others afterwards, but he had been mollified when I pointed out that the reason for the visit was to leave a defensive garrison of cavalry behind, and that it would be relieved and replaced by newcomers on a regular, twice-yearly basis. The reality of having a solid, well-trained garrison to guard his back had made light of his fears of invasion from that direction.

Finally, once Ambrose had satisfied himself that all was well in hand and that the troops would have no difficulties settling in, I managed to take him aside and sequester him in the steam room of our bathhouse, having first made sure that we would not be disturbed. There, after he had enjoyed the first flush of pleasure at being able to relax and cleanse himself of the soil of his long journey, I was able to question him about his passage from the south, developments in Camulod and most particularly about the matter foremost in my mind: the new sword that was to be forged from the Lady of the Lake.

He set my mind at ease on the latter question immediately. My concerns about the sufficiency of metal in the statue had been unfounded, he said, because it had quickly become apparent, upon a cursory examination of the rough-sculpted form, that Publius Varrus could only have used about one third of the total mass of the Lady for the making of Excalibur. Joseph and Carol together had developed the formula that led to this conclusion: Excalibur, when finished, would have weighed approximately half as much as it did on first being forged. The difference in weight would have been shed in filing, trimming and chiselling the metal into its final shape and size. The surprising and welcome news, then, was that there ought to be enough metal remaining in the statue of the Lady to fashion *two* identical swords, if such was my wish.

That gave me pause. Was it my wish to have two duplicate Excaliburs?

The question was no sooner asked than answered. These swords were representations, not duplicates; they would be practice swords and, as such, would be subjected to much overuse and great indignities. Better to have two of them, therefore—particularly since Excalibur could then remain concealed. That resolved, my next question concerned the length of time it would take to make both. Ambrose's response was an eloquent shrug of his shoulders. He would not return to Camulod until the start of winter, he pointed out, and until he did, Carol would make no start upon the second piece. The first might well be complete by then, but even so, it would remain in Camulod until the following spring.

I had to content myself with that, and for a long time we spoke little more of things political, since all Ambrose now wanted to do was bathe and steam and close his eyes and mind to everything except the pleasure of the moist heat as it leached away his tired and aching stiffness. That process, however, had no deleterious effect on his ability to talk about his own home life and his family in Camulod. Ludmilla had borne him beautiful twin daughters, one radiant blonde and the other raven-haired, late in the summer of the previous year, and their father was enraptured with them, entirely unimpressed by the prevalent opinion that daughters were a burden to a man. He had named them Luceiia and Octavia, in honour of the Britannican ancestors whom he had discovered only after meeting me in Verulamium years earlier, and I believe he could have talked of them happily in his sleep.

Ludmilla was thriving, he reported, and had sent her love to all of us, but most especially to her beloved mentor Lucanus. She had assumed overall responsibility for the medical welfare of the Colony on Luke's departure, at his insistence, and under her supervision all matters of health and hygiene in Camulod were carefully policed and well-maintained. Her staff had grown with the arrival of a young surgeon who had been trained by the military in Antioch, and who had made his way to Camulod purely on the strength of stories about Luke that he had heard in his travels in south Britain. There, having met Ludmilla and no doubt tested her abilities in his own way, he'd decided to settle and practise his skills in Luke's superbly built Infirmary.

From there, our conversation drifted pleasantly to other topics, all of them quite trivial and all of them making me slightly nostalgic for the life and folk of Camulod. By the time Ambrose began to bestir himself and show any inclination to talk seriously again of "important" matters, I had already decided it would be selfish of me to keep his tidings from the others, and equally inconsiderate to keep the pleasures of the baths from my brother's troopers. And so we dressed and left the bathhouse to those who were no less in need of its seductive joys than he had been.

Within the hour, we had assembled the remainder of our initial group, including Donuil and Shelagh, and made our way outside the fort to sit informally in a casual grouping at the top of the chasm that guarded our rear, and there Ambrose told us all the details of his journey from the south. Arthur, of course, was there with his three bosom friends, Bedwyr, Gwin and Ghilleadh, the four of them perched, still as stone pillars, fearful that they might be dismissed. Everyone ignored them, and they eventually settled down to listen.

My brother brought surprising but welcome tidings. The towns he had passed through in his journey, having lain abandoned and neglected for years, were now being inhabited again—not in any highly organized fashion, he reported, but there were definite signs of revitalization. Glevum and Aquae Sulis, in particular, he said, each had populations now of several hundred people, although the new citizens, rather than living in the indefensible Roman ruins, preferred to dwell on the outskirts of the towns, finding security in rapid access to the safety of the deep forest in case of attack. The bridge outside Glevum, over the Severn River, had been repaired and reinforced and was once more, as it had always been, a natural gathering point for people from north and south of the river wishing to trade. Elsewhere, too, he told us, along the great Roman road the people were now calling the Foss Way, because of the wide ditches or *fossae* that lined it on both sides, small centres were springing up where natural routes crossed the high road. People were organizing themselves again in small communities, looking to their own defences, planting crops and even clearing new ground in many places, because that section of the land, at least, was relatively peaceful and unplagued by war. No Saxon hordes had penetrated this far north and west, to date, and raids from Eire were now few and far between. I had little doubt, on hearing that, that thanks were due there to our alliance with Athol's Scots, and to the damage done to the Sons of Condran in the past year.

Ambrose and his troopers had been welcomed everywhere, once the realization had spread ahead of them—magically, it seemed—that they were not intent on pillage and raiding. The sight of strongly armed and disciplined warriors who posed no threat, and their promise to return that way again regularly in the future, had put new heart into people all along the great road, which, he informed us in response to a question from Dedalus, was surprisingly in superb condition, still almost free of weeds and erosion. I smiled at Ded when he asked his question, knowing he was remembering our comrade Benedict and his prediction, on returning from Eire a decade earlier, about trees destroying the roads in Britain, given time. Ambrose went on to talk of the force he had brought with him: three squadrons of cavalry, each forty strong, and a full Roman maniple of infantry consisting of ten twelve-man squads.

Ambrose turned to me directly, saying he had thought to leave four squads of infantry with us, in addition to the squadron of cavalry we had discussed. Could we feed such numbers? I looked to Derek, silently inviting him to speak, since his would ultimately be the task of feeding them. We had no fields of crops, up here on our plateau, and all our food, save wild meat and freshwater fish, was grown by Derek's folk and traded to us in return for our help in their fields and in the forest, plus our commitment to assist them should the need arise to defend their town. Derek thought for several moments and then shrugged, smiling slightly. Forty-eight trained warriors and their officers, he admitted, might be an asset worth making the occasional sacrifice to keep and feed.

Ambrose smiled and nodded. Our new garrison would remain with us, he said, for five months, at the end of which they would be relieved by an incoming complement of troops, and this would go on, twice each year, for as long as we had need of such strength.

From there, Ambrose broadened his discourse to include such tidings as he had from other places. Cornwall was quiet and apparently mending itself, he said, with no news of war or trouble coming out of there, and no news of Peter Ironhair. Ironhair had been reported as living there some time before, and we knew with certainty that his attack on Arthur had been launched from Cornwall, but reports of his presence there had remained unconfirmed and Camulod had received no significant word of his whereabouts. I set that piece of information aside, for later consideration.

Cambria, too, was at peace, with Dergyll ap Griffyd's rule continuing in strength and amity. But word had come out of the north, brought by Connor's ships, of an army being assembled in the far north-east, beyond the ancient Wall, in the lands of a king called Crandal, of whom I had never heard. He intended to raid southward into Northumbria, which would bring his forces into conflict with Vortigern and his Danish mercenaries. None of us hearing Ambrose doubted that the invaders would be stopped in Northumbria. Hengist's Danes would keep them occupied and make them wish they had remained in their northern lands. No news had come to Camulod of Vortigern or Hengist, so Ambrose presumed they both were flourishing. Otherwise, he believed young Horsa's warriors, free of his father Hengist's iron rule, would have come spilling south and west.

With such a willing audience hanging on his every utterance, Ambrose could easily have talked for far longer than he did, I suspect, but he had other matters to concern him and so had to take his leave of his listeners as the afternoon was wearing on towards twilight. His troops were new here, he pointed out, unused to the fort and their new quarters, and he owed it to them to make sure that they were disposed as well as they could be, and that the arrangements were well in hand to feed them all their first meal here in Mediobogdum. As he strode off, leaving the rest of us to wonder at the tidings he had brought to us, Arthur and the other three lads trotted at his heels like well-trained dogs.

Shortly after that, I found my own reasons for leaving and made my way to my quarters, where I sat in the gathering darkness for some time, mulling over everything I had heard that day.

The foremost thing on my mind as I sat there was the matter of the new practice swords. The how and why of using them had plagued me for some time, although I had then considered only having one, plus Excalibur itself. Ostensibly, Arthur would use the new weapon to learn the skills he would require to use Excalibur to best effect. However, the matter was more thorny than that, and the difficulty lay in the danger of employing any such weapon without accidental harm to the user, be he novice or expert. A weapon that could cut through iron, as these could, would make short work of any flesh and bone that came against its edge, so I must make sure, from the outset of our planning, that I became familiar with the tricks and techniques and tendencies inherent in these blades long before young Arthur ever handled one of them.

As though they were fresh written in my mind, I recalled the words with which Publius Varrus had described the damage to his forearm from the very first of the long-bladed swords Equus had made. Equus and he had discovered immediately that the new, long blades, when used against each other, behaved as no blades ever had behaved before, their tempered-metal tongues rebounding and leaping from each other with a hungry power fed to new extremes by the length of the arc of their swing. And those swords, I knew, had been mere tempered iron, lacking the magical essence—the mysterious skystone metal—that gave Excalibur its fearsome strength and edges. Excalibur's cross-guard would, I knew, discount some of that danger, stopping a glancing, sliding blow to the forearm, but I could not rely on that alone to safeguard the boy.

Now that we were to have two replicas, however, the way became simpler, and I decided to include Dedalus, Rufio and Donuil in the exploratory training program with the new weapons. Among the four of us, we would be able to determine the properties of the new blades and the expectations their users should and should not have of them. The boys, in the meantime, could be set to work learning the heft and mastery of the new wooden training staves, strengthening their young limbs to hard usage as they did so. Then, as we four adults devised the ways and means of best using the new, keen blades in combat, we would pass on those knacks to the boys, teaching them variations in the ways they swung their staves, so they would learn to use the new, long swords before they ever knew the swords existed. I relaxed then, having formulated that design, feeling in my heart that it was right.

Later that night, long after everyone was well abed, Ambrose, who had spread his bedroll on the floor of my quarters for the night, woke me up to go with him to inspect the guard, since this was the first night of the new order in Mediobogdum and I ought to make myself familiar with the routine right from the outset. It was a beautiful summer night with a cloudless, starry sky, and I sucked the night air deep into my chest with great enjoyment as we walked the full length of the parapets of Mediobogdum, talking to each guard we met and finding all of them alert and watchful. Then, from the fort itself, we made our way out onto the parade ground, which had been transformed in the space of one afternoon into another heavily guarded armed camp.

The young officer of the guard there was a man unknown to me and barely out of his boyhood. I found out that his name was Decius Falvo and that his father had been one of my companions on my expedition to Eire. Ambrose regarded young Decius as one of his most promising infantry commanders and I was unsurprised, because his father, whom I had always known simply as Falvo, was one of the finest and most thoroughly dedicated soldiers I had ever had the privilege of knowing. Decius told us that he had mounted an outlying guard high above us, on the peak above the pass, and that there was a wide and well-worn path up to the place, attesting to the fact that the Romans had used it as a lookout point long centuries before.

Ambrose turned and looked at me. "Feel like a climb? We can't inspect the inner guard and leave the outlying ones neglected."

We were challenged and identified ourselves long before we reached the top of the steep path up to the peak. There a cluster of four men stood on duty, peering out and down from the heights into the blackness of utter night, unrelieved by a single spark of light. Above our heads, in brilliant contrast, the sky was a mass of twinkling stars and a crescent, newborn moon hung just above the topmost peak of the high fells to the north-east.

Ambrose and I stood side by side, gazing outward, neither of us feeling the need to speak. The experience of simply being there made me feel powerful and privileged. I turned to look down to where the fort lay hidden in the darkness of the plateau beneath us, and it seemed strange to me that, apart from the dull glow of several sunken fires, I saw no sign of life or movement where I knew large numbers of people slept. The corollary—that there might be an army on the other side of us, similarly shrouded—seemed too commonplace to mention. A short time later, having had a few words to pass the time of night with each of the sentinels, we were on our way back down to the camp beneath.

When we arrived back at the front of the fort itself, in plain sight of the guard stationed at the main gates, Ambrose stopped by the smouldering remains of a fire and began to stir it back to life, feeding it with kindling until the first flames sprang up, then piling heavier fuel on top. Avoiding the heaviest drift of the smoke, I seated myself on a nearby log, and presently he pulled another log close to mine. We had had little opportunity to speak on our inspection tour, since all our attention had been given to negotiating narrow, rock-strewn pathways in the darkness.

We talked for a time then about Tressa, and about my relationship with her, and I was absolutely open with my brother. He was curious, of course, and evidently did not want to pry, but I was so happy in my life with Tress that I told him everything in my mind, and he listened and was glad for me. I spoke at length about Arthur and Tress and the relationship—not really surprising, given a modicum of thought and consideration—that had sprung into life between them, based upon mutual trust and liking and their shared human need: his for a mother and hers for a child.

At that point, while I was speaking of that particular need, Ambrose interrupted me to ask after Turga, who had been the boy's companion and nurse since infancy, saving his life first as a wet nurse and then remaining with him, protective as a lioness, after he was weaned. Seeing the frown between his brows as he asked the question, I knew what had prompted it and I was happy to be able to tell Ambrose that Turga had blossomed in the intervening years, turning into a bright, attractive woman very different to the mute and half-sane wreck she had been when

I first found her in the ruins of her home in war-torn Cornwall, surrounded by her slaughtered family. She had known men, occasionally, but had never taken another mate, nor had she produced any further children of her own, but somehow, unobtrusively and perhaps without even wishing to, she had assumed responsibility for a brood of four—Arthur and his three bosom friends. No one, including the boys' parents, could quite explain how it had come about, but Turga had simply ended up as general caretaker of all four boys, living in the same quarters as Donuil and Shelagh, and apparently existing simply to keep the boys clean and well-fed. And one fortunate aspect of that development had been that, with her own responsibilities expanded to the care of the four boys, rather than simply Arthur, Turga had adjusted easily and without jealousy to the relationship that sprang up between Arthur and Tressa, seeing and appreciating that it was very different to the relationship she herself had with boy and that Tressa was no threat to her in any way. Perhaps as the result of that, the three of us, Tressa, Arthur and I had created a family for ourselves in the short space of several months, strange though that might have appeared to be in the eyes of others. Lovers though we were, openly and unashamedly, Tress and I continued to live apart. Similarly, Arthur continued to sleep in the home of his friends Gwin and Ghilleadh, as he had always done, being cared for by Turga and deferring to Shelagh in all things as his adoptive mother. And yet somehow, Arthur and Tress and I had become a solid, tightly interdependent familial unit, sharing our lives, our strengths and weaknesses, our beliefs and our ideas, without stinting, and blessed in being able to do so without the internal jealousies and strife that seemed to mar so many other people's family lives.

When I had finished talking of my love, we sat in companionable silence for a little while, and then Ambrose turned our conversation again to young Arthur.

"The boy looks well," he said. "He's growing tall, as we expected he would, and he shows signs of having shoulders as broad as yours and mine. He's skinny, though, don't you think?"

"He's a growing boy, Ambrose, and that's normal. I was that way at his age, weren't you? All the food he ingests—and he eats like a horse—is used to push him up to his full height. Once he's achieved that, he'll grow in breadth and weight."

Ambrose glanced at me, his eyes twinkling. "You sound like Lucanus."

"And so I should. Those were Luke's very words to me, when I said the same foolish thing to him, bare months ago. The boy will grow upward, first, and then fill out. In the meantime, our task is to make sure he stays as strong as he can be."

"And how do we do that?"

"He's almost ten, now, as I said, and in the past year his education has undergone a shift in direction—less book study, less indoor theorizing, more practical training in weaponry and soldiery. He and his friends have been working with the new training swords, ever since you left for Camulod last time with Connor—" I broke off as his eyes crinkled into a broad smile. "What is it?"

"Nothing, really. I remember the weight of those things, that's all. Are you still making them from solid oak? Those boys should hardly be able to lift them, let alone swing them."

I nodded. "Aye, well, that's true. For the time being, they're using lighter shafts suited to their strength, and using them two-handed, treating them most of the time as spear shafts. But that is changing, and the boys are growing stronger every day as they build up the muscles in their arms and shoulders. Dedalus and Rufio are sharing responsibility for training them, and as our two most able experts on the new weapons, they are hard taskmasters. Wait you, till you see. I promise you, you'll be surprised."

My brother nodded and changed the subject. "There's one more thing I wanted to discuss with you. It's for your ears alone, I think, although what you choose to do with the information is your concern."

I turned to face him squarely, alerted by something in his tone. "What is it?"

"Arthur may have a brother in Cornwall."

"What?" I sat blinking at him, unable to accept the import of what I had heard him say. He shrugged, holding my gaze, content to allow me to think through what he had said. "That's not possible," I said finally. "Uther and Ygraine are both dead since his birth."

"Cay, your mother has been dead since your birth and yet you and I are brothers."

"We had different mothers."

"Precisely so."

I sat staring at him as the full import of what he had said began to sink home to me. "Sweet, gentle Jesus! Are you telling me that Uther sired a child on another woman before he died?"

"No, I'm telling you that I have heard a report—a rumour, and no more than that—that Uther lay, initially, with one of Ygraine's women, before he entered into his liaison with the Queen herself. I have no knowledge of the truth of it, the story simply came to me by chance, overheard as a soldiers' legend, like the tale of your magic in the empty room, that Uther had rutted wondrously amidst Queen Ygraine's women. You know how soldiers are. They give their heroes, and dead heroes in particular, attributes and personalities that would defy the gods. The word is, among some of the men, that Uther plowed a broad furrow in Cornwall and fathered bastards by the score."

"Well, that's not difficult to believe. Uther's appetites were legendary in that respect, and most of his men almost destroyed themselves seeking to outdo him. Rape and venery are part of war and part of the payments soldiers take for risking their lives. Given how long that war dragged on, Cornwall must be full of bastards sired by Uther's men, and I've no doubt my cousin did his share of repopulating the countryside after his armies emptied it."

"Aye, no doubt." Ambrose leaned forward and pushed at a burning log with his foot, thrusting it closer to the heart of the fire. "But one of those bastards he sired may be of noble blood on both sides of the tryst, and that could breed a challenge to young Arthur, in time to come. The rumour says that the woman involved was one of the Queen's ladies, sent to Lot's court by her brother, a king called Crandal."

The name surprised me, for in the space of a single day, never having heard it before, I had now heard it twice. Ambrose told me that this man was a king among the Painted People north of the Great Wall and that his name had spread far and wide in recent years because of his conquests. Apparently the man was no mere warrior but a champion and a hero to his people. He had never been beaten in battle and had conquered all the lands that lay around his own, so that his domain now extended the length and breadth of eastern Caledonia, from the Wall to the edge of the high mountains in the north and west.

I sat listening in silence, aware only of Ambrose's voice and the crackling of the fire, until he had finished. When his voice tailed off, though, I was still dissatisfied.

"So why did you bring up his name now?"

He looked at me in surprise. "Why? Because now, it appears, he is preparing to strike southward, into Britain below the Wall. But this matter of his sister makes the business more immediate to us. I didn't want to mention the woman's involvement today, when we were speaking earlier, because the boy was present."

"Hmm." It was my turn now to stare into the fire, thinking deeply. "So where is this woman now?"

Ambrose shook his head. "I know nothing of her. In the tale I heard, she left to have her child elsewhere, once it was known that the Queen had taken up with Uther."

"She was banished?"

"No, apparently not. From what I heard, she had lain with Uther at the Queen's instigation, as a ploy to win favours for her mistress. That she was quickened was . . . unfortunate—unplanned but not disastrous. It was only later that the Queen herself became involved with Uther."

"Damnation! So this story could be true? There could be another heir to Uther's kingdom?"

"Aye, and a firstborn one, at that. Bastard though he be, he's no more so than Arthur."

"So where is he?"

Ambrose shook his head slowly. "Who knows? He could be anywhere, concealed like our own boy for his own safety. But bear in mind, Caius, I heard only a rumour. It may be total fabrication."

"Aye, and it may equally be true." We sat quiet thereafter, each of us with his own thoughts, until I said, "What if it *is* true?"

Now Ambrose roused himself and stretched. "What if it is? All that would change in our design is that Arthur might conceivably lose the Pendragon mountain kingdom in Cambria. True, it's his patrimony, but its loss would not be totally unbearable. He'd still have Camulod and all its strength, and the kinship of the Eirish Scots, and his claim to Cornwall. Sufficient there to keep a lad of Arthur's mettle on his toes for fifty years or so. Anyway, there's little profit to be had from fretting over it. If this boy is out there, somewhere, he will come forward, sooner or later, to declare himself—and when he does, he won't have Uther's Seal to wear on his right hand, nor Uther's armour on his back, nor Uther's Camulodian cousins on his side. Have you spoken to Derek yet about regaining Uther's armour?"

"Aye, several times. I believe he'll give it to the boy when the right time comes, but he'll do it through me. He has no wish for the child to know or even to be curious about who killed his father. He keeps the armour well maintained, though. I've seen it. It's free of rust and the leather harness is supple and well oiled. . . ." I sat gazing into the fire for a while, then expelled my breath loudly and stood up.

"You're right, Brother, there's little to be gained by agonizing over a child who might never have been sired or, if he was, might well have died in infancy. If he's still alive, and dangerous to us, we'll find out soon enough. But we won't discover anything tonight. Let's go to bed."

Ambrose remained with us in Mediobogdum for only two weeks on that occasion, at the end of which he returned to Camulod by the same route. But from the first day of that visit, young Arthur threw himself more wholeheartedly than ever into his training, working ceaselessly with the wooden practice swords and driving his companions to equal his own efforts. Remembering the sight of his Uncle Ambrose riding down from the high pass at the head of his troops, Arthur would take no rest from that time on until he had ensured that he, too, would one day make such a commanding appearance at the head of his own men. I was well content with that and drove him the harder because of it, deriving pleasure from the speed with which he absorbed everything to which I set him, and from the satisfying way his lean, narrow frame soon began to fill out and grow visibly stronger.

I find it strange that I seem to have lacunae in my memories of that brief, happy time. Few coherent images linger in my consciousness of the passage of time in the period of years that followed; the summers and the winters, springs and autumns blended into a timeless, almost unheeding idyll during which we were unthreatened by the world outside and utterly uncaring of its affairs. To some extent, my inattention was attributable to the luxurious novelty of my life with Tressa. Perhaps the truth might be served better by phrasing that last observation as "the luxurious novelty of having Tress in my life," for I have no wish to suggest that we two settled in together to enjoy a life of conjugal bliss; that would be far from the truth. We did, however, grow quickly into a close friendship that was cemented by the sexual intimacy we enjoyed openly and without subterfuge.

Of course, there were events that took place during those years that do stand out, but all of those were self-contained, brief ruptures in the fabric of our daily lives—many of them pleasant, others less so. Marriages were made among our folk and Derek's, and children were born, and some of those—very few, thanks to our good Lucanus—died in infancy. One of our number, a newcomer from Ravenglass, ventured outside the north gate late one night, far gone in drink, and fell over the abyss to his death, taking with him the companion who had walked with him hoping to lead him safely home.

Ambrose himself returned as often as he could, at least once a year, as did Connor from Eire. I recall quite clearly that on his third visit, or it might even have been his fourth, Ambrose astonished us all by telling us that Camulod had garrisoned the abandoned town of Lindinis, or Ilchester as it was being called nowadays, the closest settlement to our Colony on the great road south to Isca. His announcement created a furore of questioning and debate upon the wisdom of such a thing.

Ambrose sat back throughout the entire chorus, smiling to himself and simply allowing us to vent our outrage and disbelief, his eyes ranging from face to face as he listened. Ilchester, he was informed, as if he did not know, had degenerated quickly after the legions left, becoming a dreary, squalid, dreadful place of ruins and desolation. It was entirely unsuited as a garrison station for Camulod's troopers. It was too far away from Camulod itself and would be practically indefensible in the event of attack from north or south. The road itself offered an enemy direct access to the walls. What was the Council thinking of, initiating such a thing, and had they no concern at all for the morale of the troopers stationed there in such a place?

I had noted the smile on my brother's face from the outset, and so had contributed nothing to the general storm of disapproval, preferring to wait and hear what he would say when it had blown itself out. Dedalus, too, I noticed, sat in silence, and it amazed me that none of the others seemed aware of that. His was the voice that should have roared above all the rest, and yet its silence went unheeded. Eventually, however, the noise subsided and the few individual voices that still muttered tailed self-consciously away into a lengthy silence that no one seemed inclined to break. I caught my brother's eye and leaned forward.

"Aren't you sorry you mentioned that?"

"No," he replied, his smile growing wider. "I expected it and I enjoyed it."

"Then you have a response?"

Ambrose looked about him. "Of course, and I'll give it gladly, although I may not be able to address every point that was raised here." He paused. "First, let me say that Lindinis, or Ilchester, whichever you prefer, is a vastly altered place from the desolate slum you knew. The ruins are all gone, leaving a wide, cleared space all around the fort. The walls stand high and strong, far higher than they were before, three earth-filled tiers of them, faced with new palisades of logs. Inside the walls, the houses are all rebuilt and full of people—the garrison and their families. We have new earthen walls reaching to new heights, new parapets and towers housing artillery, and a broad, deep, triple ditch surrounding all, crossed by three separate bridges that are raised and lowered from gate-towers by the garrison. The town is virtually impregnable today, even from the open road, and morale there is very high. In the space of a year, incredible as it might seem to you who knew it years ago, Ilchester has become a sought-after post." He stopped, and looked around from face to face.

"Now, why did we do it? Why did we go to such great lengths to redeem a lost town, thirty and more miles from our home base?"

Hector spoke up. "Overcrowding. It was bound to come to that."

"Precisely, Hector—overcrowding." Ambrose turned his gaze back on the others. "You were all there at home the year following the Great Winter. You know how hard we worked to build new quarters for the intake of soldiers we enlisted that year to fill the ranks left empty by the wars in Cornwall, and if you think upon it, you'll recall how much talk there was of reallocation of our arable lands for crops to feed them all. Years have passed since then, and each of them has seen a new intake of soldiers, because soldiers are our lifeblood.

"None of us can ever afford to forget the reason for Camulod's founding. It was survival! Survival in the face of catastrophe and invasion by aliens. That survival involves military readiness—not simply the will to fight but the strength to fight and win, and that strength is our garrison. The moment we allow our garrison to weaken in any way, we might as well lie down and die, because our survival will be at an end." Again he paused, letting his listeners agree to that before he hammered home his next point.

"But soldiers have to eat, my friends, and even though Camulod is blessed in being wondrously fertile, there are limits to what the land can produce. We were aware more than a year ago that we had begun to approach those limits, but that is when one of our councillors, Lucius Varo, put forward the suggestion in Council that we should reclaim the fields that lay fallow around the town of Ilchester.

"The idea seemed sound, if logistically difficult, and so a scouting expedition was dispatched to look into the matter. I commanded that expedition, and my report was enthusiastic, because I saw a double opportunity present itself: a new source of food, combined with an end to overcrowding. Besides that, I recognized that the reclamation and refurbishment of the old fort would give our soldiers something new to occupy them when they were not training for war—something useful, and something permanent in which they could take pride. I had obtained some documents, a year or two before that, detailing the construction of a highly sophisticated fort in Gaul, and I decided we should have a similar construction here in Britain. It took a year to build, with more than a thousand men labouring on it every day, but it was completed months ago, before the winter set in, and it is magnificent. Thomas Atribatus, the fourth generation of his name in Camulod, commands the garrison, and Lucius Varo himself is installed as civil governor, representing the Council and responsible for the farming operations in the surrounding area. Our new *castella* is not made of stone, so it won't stand forever, but it will serve our needs for the next hundred years."

There was more discussion after that, but the fire had gone out of our objections in the light of Ambrose's clear and dispassionate comments.

I find it curious that I can recall instants like this, across the gulf of decades, with great clarity, and yet there are others that are lost forever in my mind. Letters arrived from Germanus in Gaul, and swords and weaponry arrived from Camulod; soldiers arrived and stayed, and were relieved and left; and life went tilting onward.

I revelled in the novelty of becoming a working member of a small, close-knit and happy community. I was a warrior first and foremost, nonetheless, and I never lost sight of that. I trained and drilled for several hours every day, with the boys and away from them, pitting myself against Dedalus, Rufio, Donuil and others daily as I had done throughout my life, keeping my muscles hard and supple and my military skills well honed.

I know now that I was completely at peace in those days, for only the second time in my life, savouring and loving the challenge of hard, daily work in the forest and the daily bliss of coming home at last to the warmth of Tressa's company. And as I luxuriated in the happiness of my new life, years slipped by inexorably and invisibly.

Thinking back on that time earlier today, I found myself smiling to remember that, of all the people who might have recalled me to the realities of life and the passing years, it was Derek who shook me from my daze. It had been a blazing hot summer, and on that particular day, distracted by the heat, I had been unable to concentrate on any of the tasks I had assigned myself. Instead, I saddled up Germanicus and made my way out of the fort and down into the valley towards Ravenglass itself. I had no particular purpose in mind at the time; I was simply being lazy and indulging myself.

Truth to tell, I was feeling rather neglected and sorry for myself, because Tress had no time for me, and my other close companions were all involved elsewhere. Tress was cloistered with Shelagh and three other women, hard at work indoors, adding the finishing touches to an ornate and quite magnificent robe on which they had been working, under Tressa's guidance, for many months. The garment was to be a gift for Salindra, the second, very young and hugely pregnant wife of Derek's eldest son. She was expected to give birth at any moment, and Tressa was concerned that after all the weeks and months of work that had gone into her endeavour, the birth might yet occur before the robe was finished. I had visited the stone tower room in which they were all slaving over the thing, apparently sewing by feel, rather than by sight, in the cool semi-darkness.

Lucanus had been absent for more than a week, on affairs of his own in Ravenglass, and I did not expect him back for at least several more days. He had recently become concerned over the scarcity of certain medicaments he prized highly, and had determined to spend time with the captains and crews of the various vessels that called into Ravenglass, in the hope that he might be able to enlist their support and find ways and means of replenishing his stores. Rufio, Donuil and Dedalus were down there, too, involved in other matters concerning stores and supplies, all of those far more mundane than Luke's. In the interests of education, they had taken the boys with them as supernumerary quartermasters. Consequently, alone and at loose ends, I made my way down from our plateau and through the forest towards the town and, I hoped, some convivial company.

On emerging from the forest road and into the fields lining the last few miles to the town, I found myself thinking again of the spot to which Derek had led me that first day when I had arrived in Ravenglass. Soon I had threaded my way through the massive agglomeration of loose stones and boulders that lined the outside edges of the fields and was angling Germanicus up the densely treed slope beyond it, towards the elevated site on the far side of the crest, where Derek and I had sat and talked.

The place was exactly as I remembered it, a natural throne overlooking the enclosed, forested valley beneath and the shimmering sea in the western distance. I dismounted and made myself comfortable in the spot Derek had occupied, finding it opulently padded with moss and perfectly positioned to provide the best view of the prospect far beneath. I sat there for the next half hour, gazing out to sea and thinking about nothing in particular, before I was alerted by the unmistakable sounds of someone mounting the trail towards me. My sense of logic told me it must be Derek, but I rose immediately to my feet and took cover nonetheless, concealing myself among the trees until I could see the newcomer.

It was indeed Derek and as soon as I recognized him I stepped out of my concealment, calling his name. He was surprised to find me there but not displeased, and I was glad to see the welcome in his smile, for it had occurred to me somewhat belatedly that he might be as jealous of his seclusion on this secret spot as I had been of my own in my little hidden valley close to Camulod. If he was put out, however, he gave no indication of displeasure, and after having traded greetings and civilities, he settled down in his own preferred spot and waved me down to join him. Thereafter we indulged ourselves in talk of such trivialities as the uncommon weather and the progress of crops and work projects. Within the month, he reminded me, it would be time to begin gathering in what looked to be a prime crop of grain and vegetables, and we talked for a time about how my own people, including our soldiers, should be distributed among his in order to share the task equitably and bring in the harvest as quickly as possible. Then for a while we simply sat there, basking in the afternoon sunlight and dozing shamelessly, lulled by the heavy droning of bees, the darting flight of blue, red and green dragonflies and the buoyant, fluttering dance of butterflies. One of the latter, a brilliant thing of brown and white and red, landed on Derek's outstretched leg and sat there twitching, alternately opening and closing its magnificent wings to the sun's caress.

Derek glanced at me to see whether I had noticed it and then grunted, "You ever see one of these things being born?"

I nodded. "A few times. It's a miraculous thing to watch, isn't it?"

"Aye, it is that, although I've seen it but once. How did you see it the first time, can you recall?"

I smiled. "I had to be shown it, otherwise I would never have noticed it, or even thought to look. I had a teacher called Daffyd, a Druid who found a place, one year when I was a mere boy, where several of the cocoons had been secured to a stone wall. He watched them closely, and when he gauged that they were ready to split, he brought me to the place and made me watch." The memory filled me with pleasure and I laughed aloud. "It took a long time—almost an entire day, as I recall—and he wouldn't tell me what we were waiting for. I had convinced myself that he had merely found a new and malicious way of keeping me from my games, making me sit motionless, peering at a brown and highly polished but utterly lifeless, uninteresting thing. It looked like some kind of insect, I could see, but it was undeniably dead.

"I remember I suffered the boredom stoically, at first, but then as the day drew on I grew more and more disgusted and fidgety—so much so that he eventually decided to forego the pleasure he had thought to win from my surprise, and told me what we had come there to see. It seemed utterly outlandish and impossible that a large, hairy caterpillar could have enclosed itself within that tiny thing—a chrysalis, he called it, and now that I think of it, I'd like to ask him where he heard that word, for it's Greek, the only Greek word I ever heard him use. Anyway, the caterpillar part was bad enough, but it seemed even more impossible that out of it would come a butterfly. And then it happened! The casing began to move, and to split, and out crawled a shaky little thing that unfolded to become a butterfly. I've never seen anything as lovely or as moving as the way its wings unfurled and dried. Why are you smiling?"

Derek shook his head very slightly. "Simply remembering how I felt, too. It shook me to the bottom of my being, and I was man full grown when I saw it. It was after I first met you, in fact, during Lot's wars. I was hiding, being hunted by some of your cousin Uther's people, and they were right on top of me. I was huddled against a rock and this thing, whatever you called it, was right in front of my face. It began to split open and I couldn't believe what I was seeing. I mean, it was so close to my face, and so ugly looking I was disgusted. My flesh crawled and I wanted to vomit. But I could hear the voices of the people who were searching for me—they were almost within arm's reach, and I didn't dare move. And then the damn thing crawled out and stretched and spread its wings, and they seemed to dry out, and it was the most beautiful thing I've ever seen. When it finally flew away, leaving the empty shell behind, I felt as if I had been robbed. I've never forgotten it, and I've never seen it again, but it taught me that sometimes things more glorious than you could imagine can crawl out from places that amaze you."

I said nothing, and after a moment, he continued. "But I don't think I'd go so far as to believe the damn things start out as creepy-crawlies . . . caterpillars. That sounds like it came from someone who'd had too much mead. I mean, think about it. You don't really believe that, do you? Butterflies come from eggs—strange-looking eggs, but eggs, nonetheless. Birds do, too—they break the shell and crawl out, feathers, wings and all. But the eggs are laid by birds. You don't hear anyone saying that things like worms wrap themselves in eggshell and then come out as birds. That's ridiculous."

I was grinning at him. "I wouldn't argue with you, Derek, but butterflies aren't birds, and that is what happens. It's called metamorphosis."

"What?"

"Metamorphosis. Another Greek word. It means a change of form. The butterfly lays eggs that hatch into caterpillars. The caterpillars then grow to full size and spin themselves a complete covering of some kind of material they produce in the way spiders spin webs. They wrap themselves completely in that covering and go to sleep for a long time, and when they wake up again and emerge from their covering, they're butterflies."

"Horseshit!"

I threw up my hands, laughing. "Fine! I won't argue with you, because there's no way for me to prove it, but it's the truth, I swear."

He favoured me with a long, considering look that dripped scepticism, then sat silent for a long time, so that when he spoke again his words took me by surprise.

"Like that boy of yours, young Arthur."

I turned my head to look at him. "I don't follow you."

"Meta-what-you-called-it . . . He's changing into something very different."

"What d'you mean? You've lost me."

"He's changing. Arthur. Changing quickly. Growing up. He battered half the life out of my Droc this morning, right outside my door. Cracked his skull, I think, and broke a few bones belonging to Droc's cronies, too."

"By the Christ! Are you serious?"

"Of course I'm serious. Mind you, they deserved it, and probably more than they got. I had to lay down the law to the young louts, in terms they couldn't misunderstand. But Droc didn't hear me. He was unconscious when I arrived. Good thing Lucanus was in the town. He took him away and wrapped him in bandages from head to shoulders."

I was stunned. "I find that difficult to believe. Droc is twice the size of Arthur and years older. How could young Arthur have beaten him so badly? He's a mere child."

Derek began to scoff, then stopped, looking at me in disbelief. "A mere child? When did you last see him?"

"Who, Arthur? A few days ago, the morning he left for Ravenglass."

"Then you saw a different boy from the one I saw. I'm talking about young Arthur Pendragon."

"I know you are. So am I."

"Then one of us has ailing eyesight, and it's not me. Let me ask you again, in different words: When did you last *look* at him?"

I gazed back at him, considering his rephrased question. When had I last looked at Arthur closely, analytically? I did so now in my mind, focusing on how he had appeared to me that last morning, and I saw immediately that I had been less than judicious in my assessment of the boy. He was no mere child; Derek was correct. Arthur had stopped being a child long before today, but I had failed to note, to really register, the change.

In truth, at thirteen, nigh on fourteen, Arthur was almost as tall as the tallest among us—myself and Derek. He was still slight, of course—still gangling and unformed—but he was strong and well made, with ever-widening shoulders and the merest suggestion of dark fuzz beginning to appear on his chin and cheeks. I visualized his hands, long and slender yet filled with strength, with tapering, blunt fingers and thick wrists, corded and muscled with the constant exercise of swinging the wooden practice swords. Then I thought of his smooth, tanned face with its piercing, tawny-yellow eyes, sharply planed cheekbones above a wide, laughing mouth with perfect, brilliant teeth, the whole head framed in long, dark-brown hair shot through with golden streaks and set on a thick, strong neck and shoulders that already showed the sloping musculature that would grow and thicken into massive manhood. Arthur Pendragon was growing up very quickly, I realized. I nodded, pursing my lips and sniffing to acknowledge that Derek had the right of things.

"Tell me what happened."

Derek reached into his tunic and produced a long, thin-bladed knife and a length of hollow reed on which he had evidently been working, carving it into a whistle.

"Well, on one level, two boys had a grudge fight. It happens all the time. But one of the boys isn't really a boy any longer, and he's a bully, to boot. Unfortunately, he's my son, and I'm not proud of that, but I've taken my boot to his arse often enough to convince myself that beating him won't change him. Perhaps what happened to him this morning will have more effect than I've had. We'll see." He began marking the reed, preparing to cut notches along the top of it.

"Was he bullying Arthur?"

"No, no." He held the reed up to his eye, squinting along the length of it. "He'd tried that, apparently, but couldn't make it work. No, he was bullying the little one, Ghilly, and his cronies were helping him. They beat the little fellow up quite badly. I wasn't there, you understand, but I got to the bottom of it after I'd been summoned by one of the women who saw what was going on. Anyway, as I pieced it together afterward, they were knocking the young lad around when Arthur came riding into the town, and they stopped as soon as they saw him—not because they were afraid of him but because they wanted to see what he would do.

"Turns out that they'd been trying to win some kind of superiority over Arthur for months, but he wouldn't fight, no matter what they did. Simply ignored them. They tried intimidation, and they tried insulting him, and they tried jostling him. One of them even walked up to the lad on one occasion and punched him in the face. Arthur simply took it and ignored them—wouldn't react, wouldn't fight. They couldn't understand that and they couldn't overcome it and it drove them to wilder and wilder extremes. They knew he wasn't afraid of them, because he never tried to avoid them, but they could not provoke him into fighting. Until today. One of them had the bright idea of taking out their spite on little Ghilly, guessing that they might get a reaction from Arthur that way.

"Well, they did, and it was more than they expected. Arthur saw

Ghilly lying on the ground, bleeding. He helped him up and led him away. Never said a word to anyone or looked at a single one of Droc's people. But no sooner was he out of sight than he came back, this time carrying one of those fighting sticks of yours. He walked straight up to Droc and his group and said, 'Very well, I'm here,' and then he let loose. Dropped three of them before any of them realized he had come to fight, and once they did realize what was happening, they couldn't do a thing against him, even though they're all bigger than he is. I've never seen him use that stick, but according to what I heard this morning he makes it do magic."

I was smiling broadly. "How many of them were there?"

"Eight, and he walked up to them as though he were the only person in the street. Not a care, not a flicker of hesitation. And he beat all of them, including Droc, my fearless son, may the gods protect his useless, brainless bulk. Arthur didn't break his head, by the way, he merely tripped him. Droc fell head first into a wall. He does that kind of thing very well. What are you looking so pleased about?"

"Am I? I suppose I am. It pleases me that the boy can be so . . . mature. Mature enough to avoid fighting when he thought it unnecessary or unwise, and also mature enough on the other hand to fight without hesitation against bigger, older boys—and thrash them—when he felt it necessary. But now I have to leave you here and go and find Dedalus and Rufio. I've matters to discuss with them."

"Concerning the boy."

"Aye, and his education. Clearly it's time to move him along."

"Along to where?"

"Towards manhood."

Derek grinned and shook his head, turning his attention to his whistle. "He'll get there soon enough, my friend. But I suppose if you feel you have to speed him along, then that's what you must do."

I spoke at length with Dedalus and Rufio that afternoon before I returned to the fort, and later that evening and long into the night, I discussed my plans for the next stage of the boy's education with Donuil and Shelagh, and with Tressa, whose opinion I had long since come to value and respect. The first step in the next stage must be Arthur's alone, I told them. It was a crucial step, and I had to be assured of his readiness. I saw no place there for any distractions occasioned by the presence of his friends, although I had little doubt that they would soon follow him into formal weapons training, as they followed him in all things.

Arthur appeared at the door of my quarters before mid-morning, smiling diffidently and clearly wondering why he had been summoned here alone.

"Tress told me to come and see you."

"I know, I asked her to send you over. Come in."

He stepped into the room, looking around him, a half-smile on his face, his eyes resting only briefly on the oaken practice sword that stood propped against the table where I sat.

"Have I done something wrong?"

"Why would you ask that?"

His smile grew wider, but lost none of its uncertainty. "Why wouldn't I? You haven't sent for me like this for ages, and the last time it was because I'd stayed out late, after curfew."

"That's right, I'd forgotten. No, you're not in trouble, so sit down."

He sat, his face clearing quickly, and waited for me to continue. I sat looking at him for a few moments longer.

"Derek told me yesterday you were fighting with his son."

"Oh, Droc. Yes."

"You thrashed him."

He looked uncomfortable. "Yes."

"You used your practice sword. How?"

"What?"

"How did you use the stick, one- or two-handed?"

"Er . . . I'm not sure. Both ways, I think. Didn't have time to think about it."

"Hmm. Where is it now?"

"Outside, on my saddle."

"Fetch it, then, and come with me. I have my wagon outside."

He harnessed his mount to the tail of the wagon and climbed up onto the bench beside me. I slapped the reins and sat silent as we plodded through the fort to the eastern gate, heading towards the drilling ground beyond. When we reached the stone hut by the gate-tower, where we kept our leather practice armour, I motioned to him to jump off and put some on. I was already wearing heavy, toughened bullhide armour, including the arm-protectors that we had made to protect us from shoulder to wrist. He leaped down and disappeared into the tower, and I carried on through the gate without waiting for him.

I stopped the wagon close by the ramp leading up to the parade ground on the flattened knoll overlooking the fort and jumped down, swinging my heavy weapon and loosening my arm and shoulder muscles as I made my way up the ramp. A short time later I heard him running to catch up to me, but I reached the top of the ramp ahead of him and turned to point my weapon two-handed at him.

"Exercises first."

He stopped, facing me, not even out of breath, then held his weapon horizontally towards me, both hands gripping the ornately carved hilt end, and closed his eyes, concentrating. Then he drew a deep, steady breath and launched into the exercise program we had devised, first to loosen, and then to strengthen our arm and wrist movements.

I simply stood and watched him, saying nothing and missing nothing of his performance. I was uncomfortably aware that I had last watched him do this a full six months before and that I had been lax since then in looking to my charge, lulled by the placid sameness of our day-to-day life. I had known he was training hard, and I had known he was doing well, thanks to Dedalus and Rufio, who worked with him daily and kept me informed of his progress, but I had had no concept of how much the boy had learned and improved. Six months earlier his performance had been impressive, but now it was spectacular.

His eyes remained closed in concentration, and the stick-club weapon in his hand whirled faster and faster until its movements became a sustained blur, impossible to follow as he spun it two-handed, then one-handed, then from left grip to right, over and beneath and down and up and around until the final snap, when he spun on one leg, stepped forward with the other and brought the shaft flashing down to stop abruptly where it had begun, parallel to the ground, in a blow that, had the weapon been edged, would have split an enemy in two. When he opened his eyes again to look at me, his face expressionless, I had to collect myself.

"Impressive," I said, tonelessly. "Dedalus and Rufio told me you had improved. Now, apart from exercises and attacks on unarmed boys, can you use the thing effectively when someone else is pitted against you?"

His teeth flashed in a brilliant smile and I found myself surprised once again, in spite of their familiarity, by his radiant, wholesome good looks. "Shall I try?"

Well, he tried, and I had my hands full trying to beat him. His strength and resilience took me completely by surprise, and the fury of his attack made me forget within moments that I was pitted against a boy, "a mere child" as I had called him the previous day. He backed me up soon after we began by deflecting one of my blows and stepping inside it, forcing me to leap backward to safeguard my ribs. Once he had me on the retreat, he kept me there, reacting to his whirlwind attacks from every direction, so that I had no time to develop attacks of my own. Finally I gulled him by leaping back from one of his blows and allowing the impetus of his missed swing to take him sideways, opening his right flank to my attack. I threw myself back towards him, and I pressed home my advantage as though I were fighting Ded or Rufio, no thought in my mind of decreasing my drive because of his youth or lesser strength. I forced him to take one pace backward, then another, and then a third, which brought him to the steep edge of the slope beyond the drill ground. There I caught his whirling blade high on my own, stepped in close and smashed him with my chest, pushing him over the edge to where he slipped and fell to one knee.

I grounded my weapon immediately, deeply grateful for the opportunity to do so, and held out my hand to help him back to the level field, where he stood watching me, clearly prepared to continue. I had to force myself to breath evenly, when I wanted to pant and puff like the old man I felt myself to be. Eventually, when I was sure I could control my voice, I spoke.

"Good. Now I think you're ready for the next stage."

He simply stared at me expectantly, knowing that this was an important moment but with no idea of how it was or what it might involve.

We had had the two new Camulodian swords by then for several years, and in all that time none but myself, Dedalus, Rufio, Lucanus, Shelagh and Donuil had seen them; Shelagh and Luke only because they had been there when the swords arrived. It had seemed safer to all of us, from the beginning, to keep their existence secret, and we had been extremely conscious of the need for care in how we handled and transported the weapons, and in where and how we actually used them. In use, as we had discovered that first day, they rang with a clarion sound that was unique and astonishing and audible from great distances, and so we had been at pains to find a practice spot that was unlikely to be discovered by curiosity-seekers, such as inquisitive young boys, attracted by the ringing of the pure iron blades.

That we had found the place very quickly was due more to sheer, blind fortune than to any form of scientific questing: Dedalus had almost fallen headlong into it on the morning of the day the swords arrived. It was little more than a deep cleft in the rock face below the escarpment on which the fort was built, but it had high, vertical walls that contained the noise we made and a level, grassy floor that was both wide enough and long enough to suit our purposes perfectly. To reach it, however, involved almost an hour of travel from the fort itself, first down the road to the valley below, then along the accumulated scree at the bottom of the cliff face to where a dense clump of hawthorn concealed the narrow entrance to the cleft.

We kept the swords there, in situ, most of the time. When they had to be transported to and from the fort, we moved them in plain sight, wrapped in cloth in the bottom of the wagon, which was normally full of tools and pieces of equipment. No one had ever paid the slightest attention to them.

Now I led Arthur back to the wagon and hauled the long, cloth-wrapped bundle from the wagon bed, unwrapping the swords and handing one of them to him, hilt first. He was speechless, entranced by the lethal beauty of the weapon in his hands. It was far from being the first sword he had ever held, but it was the most fearsome. For almost two full years now, he and Gwin, Bedwyr and Ghilly had been working with Roman short-swords, traditional gladia made decades earlier by Publius Varrus.

All four boys were adept in their use, having learned the basic disciplines of cut, stab and thrust in the traditional manner, "fighting" a solid practice post sunk in the ground and working from behind the shelter of a heavy infantry shield. That training was the practical reason for the daily use of the wooden staff Arthur now used so effectively: the heavy ash or oak staves were designed to be twice the weight of the swords they represented, so that when a warrior held a real sword in a real conflict, the weight of the weapon would seem negligible compared to what he was accustomed to.

As I stood watching him, Arthur raised his eyes from the sword he held, looking first at me, then turning his eyes to where the four practice posts were sunk into the earth at one end of the parade ground.

"No," I said, knowing what he was thinking. "Not that. Practice posts are useless for these swords. The weapons are too long, their arc too big. Cavalry swords require and demand an entirely different technique, and that's what you'll be learning from now on. You've been learning it already, for the past few years."

He gazed now for long moments at the weapon he held, the lower third of its blade resting on his open left palm, and then he looked me in the eye. "This isn't like any of the cavalry swords I've seen before. Where did it come from?"

"From Camulod," I replied. "Carol made it, and it is a cavalry sword, just like the others, yet very different. It's longer, heavier and above all sharper and more dangerous. You'll find there's more discipline attached to the use of this sword than to any other. All the rules apply that apply to other swords you've used, but there are new, additional rules that apply to these particular weapons. Ded and Rufio will continue to be your teachers, and from time to time I'll be working with you, and so will Donuil."

He was hefting the sword as I spoke, looking at the blade that stretched out from his fists.

"One other thing should be obvious. You won't be using this in quite as many ways as you use your staff. The only time you'll use it two-handed is when both hands are on the hilt. Try closing your fist over any part of that blade and you'll lose your fingers. Now, let's see those exercises again, using the sword."

He went through the entire sequence of exercises again, very slowly at first as he adjusted to the novelty of the feel and heft of the new sword, then with increasing confidence, until I could no longer see the hesitations where he had eliminated moves that involved catching the end of his weapon in his left hand to block a downward chop or deliver a full torso thrust. He did not say much, but it was evident that he was fascinated by the task that now lay ahead of him: the mastery of this new sword. I resisted the temptation to cross blades with him then and there; there would be time aplenty for that in the days ahead.

That same afternoon, I instructed Mark to set up four practice horses—Arthur, as I had known he would be, had been most insistent that his friends be permitted to enter on this new phase of training with him. His reasons for insisting, however, had pleased me greatly. What point was there, he had asked me, in his graduating to the next phase of his training alone? Without the shared participation and the assistance of his friends, he would have a more difficult and trying time mastering the new techniques, and their friendship might suffer because of it. With their equal involvement, however, the effort would be lessened by a factor of four, since they could all work together. Even Ghilly, he pointed out, who was not yet twelve, had earned the right to move ahead and would not let either his youth or his lack of muscle hold him back from taking his rightful place among the four. I had listened, shrugged and agreed with him.

The practice horses were made of short, massive logs mounted on wooden legs. They resembled ludicrous sawhorses big enough to accommodate a saddle with stirrups and reins and a bridle. I had discussed their construction some time before with Mark, and so he was able to erect them quickly at the far end of the parade ground, close by the upright posts we used for short-sword practice—now that the boys were to be taught the use of the new swords, there was no further need for secrecy or concealment. Mark and the two men he had conscripted to help him hoisted the last of the awkward structures into place before sunset, using a tripod and pole block and tackle. The "horses" were far from elegant or graceful, but they were adequate and functional, and I saw the rightness of them when I went out to examine them at Mark's summons.

In the gathering dusk of evening, just before dinner that same night, I took the four boys out to see the new structures, and in order to mark the occasion in their minds as being of more than normal significance, I had Dedalus, Donuil and Rufio accompany us. There, once the four boys had clambered up onto the stationary devices and their initial exuberance had worn down, we informed them that in this place, mounted on these saddled forms, they would learn most of what they needed to know to use these new weapons. They would learn to use them on foot, too, I pointed out, but not as much and not as often. Like the ball-and-chain flail invented by Uther Pendragon, these long swords were primarily cavalry weapons.

Thereafter, we entered a period when the bell-like ringing of skystone iron could be heard coming from the parade ground at all hours of the day. We had four students and four teachers and only two of the swords, and so we worked out a roster which ensured that each student would work regularly with each teacher. Much of what we four teachers had developed was new, common to all and suited to the properties of the swords, but each had acquired small tricks and idiosyncrasies of his own, naturally suited to his individual fighting techniques.

Eventually, and very soon after the initial excitement and novelty of the new weapons had begun to abate, Arthur's inquisitive mind and his natural sense of justice brought him to my quarters with questions. Why were the four Camulod boys the only ones to be learning the new techniques? That was simply answered. There were no more than two swords and a finite number of hours in the day. Then why were there only two swords? Could Joseph not make more, since these weapons were so obviously superior to anything else in existence?

To answer that one, I had to tell him that the swords were made from the statue Publius Varrus had smelted from the skystone, his Lady of the Lake. He was thoroughly familiar with the tale, of course, but only with the early part of it. He had no idea that Excalibur existed, and I was determined that he should not yet learn about it, even though I was utterly convinced he was the one destined to use the sword. Publius Varrus had entrusted me with the secret of Excalibur, and it was one I had guarded well. Arthur would see it and own it one day, but not until he was ready, and right now he was still a boy.

He listened to what I had to say about the two new swords and the uniqueness of the metal from which they were made, and when I fell silent he nodded slowly, obviously not quite convinced of the correctness of my logic. I watched him.

"What's the matter? You wish to say something more? Speak out."

He shrugged. "Well, Merlyn, I understand what you mean, but it still doesn't seem right to me that Gwin and Bedwyr and Ghilly and I should be the only ones to learn to fight with new weapons. What about my other friends? This makes it look as though we are . . . different, better somehow, more privileged."

"You are." He blinked at me and I plucked at my lower lip. "These other friends of yours, are you referring to the other boys living here in Mediobogdum, or are you including those in Ravenglass? Remember that the Romans lost the world because they taught the barbarians the Roman way of war. Would you want Droc and his cronies learning how to beat you more thoroughly than they can now?"

"I didn't mean them!"

"No, I assumed that, but where do you draw the line? Are we to tell King Derek that we don't wish to teach his son anything? He hasn't asked us to, prior to this, but if you start giving lessons to all your friends who are his people, he'll have every right to demand that his sons share the learning."

That quieted him, and I stared at the top of his head as he gazed at his feet, thinking the matter through.

"Look, Arthur," I said then, taking pity on him. "There is one thing you have to bear in mind. You are the central and sole focus of all of these activities. You are Arthur Pendragon, great-grandson of Publius Varrus and King Ullic Pendragon, great-great-nephew of Caius Britannicus, founder of Camulod. You are the son of Uther Pendragon and the rightful heir to Cambria, and on your mother's side you have a claim to kingship of the Hibernian Scots. The day will come when you may have to fight for one or all of those birthrights. That day will find you well prepared, indeed uniquely prepared, if we continue as we are. Gwin and Ghilly and Bedwyr train with you because they are your closest friends and have been since your infancy. Some day, they'll be your commanders, weapons in and of themselves, and therefore they are worthy of being taught what they must know to perform their tasks and achieve what you will require of them. Do you hear and understand what I am saying to you now?"

"Yes, Merlyn, I do." He nodded his head with conviction, his great, golden eyes wide and solemn. "But I would at least like my friends to learn the fighting sticks."

I laughed, a short bark. "Then you'll have to teach them, because none of us who are already teaching you have the time. Are you prepared to do that? D'you think you are capable of doing it?"

He looked at me calmly, his eyes level and filled with confidence. "Yes, I do, if you'll permit it."

I shrugged, smiling. "I wouldn't think of stopping you. I'll have Mark issue the staves you'll need. How many of your friends would like to learn now, today?"

"Seven." He did not even have to count.

"Fine. You'll have seven staves, tomorrow or the day after, depending on when Mark has time to turn them on his lathe. Now run away and let me back to work."

It took little longer than a week for me to become used to the sight of him and his three satellites drilling their less-privileged friends in the uses of the wooden staves the others had envied for so long. I thought at first it might be a passing thing—that all of them, including Arthur and his three trainers, would soon grow tired of the discipline required and the daily grind of practice in addition to their normal round of chores and tasks. But such was not the case, and I watched with ever-increasing admiration as the seven novices grew more and more proficient. Their numbers swelled to thirteen and then to seventeen, and all the time Arthur was indefatigable in his attention to them.

It occurs to me again now, as it has so many times in the years that have elapsed, that the stature young Arthur achieved was due as much to what lay inside him as it was to the external, dictatorial forces that shaped his behaviour. He was to meet many powerful men—kings and princes, chiefs and warlords—in the time that lay ahead of him, and he was to see and evaluate for himself an entire spectrum of examples of how and how not to mould men, train armies, conduct campaigns, make laws and govern peoples and territories. He carried within him, however, from his earliest boyhood, a natural sense of rightness and the fitness of certain things, allied with an innate regard for justice, as opposed to power and privilege, that set him above all others of his time and made ordinary men love him.

Time and again I witnessed it during his boyhood, as in the instinctive and immediate sharing of his four ponies with his three bosom friends—an offer made in ignorance of the fact that this had been precisely the intent of the gift-giver, Connor—and again in this matter of sharing his knowledge and his fighting skills with his less-privileged friends. The task involved great inconvenience and sacrifice of personal time and freedom for him, yet it would never have occurred to him not to do it. He saw it as a natural obligation, to be taken in stride and accomplished to the best of his abilities, and he would spend long, additional hours on balmy summer afternoons when he might have been fishing or riding, instructing any of the boys who were having difficulty in mastering the tricks they were learning. I watched quietly, as did Ded and the others, and took pride in his dedication and his apparent selflessness, but yet, for all my pride, I must admit it never occurred to me that I was watching the evolution of anything amazing.

I saw and admired the conscientious young man; I overlooked the future warrior, champion and king completely.

VERY SOON AFTER the installation of the wooden horses, the slow-passing, idyllic days of the previous years-long interlude began to seem like an impossible dream. Time, once again, dictated a steady, marching beat. The harvest, which began less than a month after Arthur's first session with the new swords, introduced the new order with a slow and stately roll of drums. Everyone—our own people and the folk of Ravenglass—worked together to a clearly defined plan.

Within the week, however, the steady rhythm of the drum beat gave way to a stuttering, irregular staccato as the weather broke without warning and a succession of heavy storms crashed down about us, each more savage than the last. The early storms of the first few days were greeted philosophically, but as their frequency and intensity grew greater, every other task in Ravenglass was abandoned so that every able-bodied person could work in the fields to salvage the crop before it was utterly ruined. Nursing mothers carried their babies swaddled on their backs as they wrestled with stooks or flailed the grain on the thrashing floors, and old people of both sexes, many of whom had done no hard labour for years, worked as crews on the wagons and grain sleds or spent their time tending the horses and oxen, without whose strength the grain could not have been transported. The weather worsened steadily, bringing torrential rains and high winds every day for almost three weeks, so that eventually we had to abandon almost a full quarter of what should have been a prime harvest to rot where it lay, utterly waterlogged and ruined.

Harvest time also brought a brief visit from Connor, who, accompanied by little Feargus, had sought shelter from the terrible storms at sea. He brought tidings to accompany the bleak outlook that this ugly month had spawned. War had broken out again in Eire, and the pagan, north-western tribes called the Children of Gar were now in possession of the major part of Athol's former kingdom on the east coast. They had not yet taken all of it, Connor reported, but that was due only to the fact that one tiny portion on the coast itself was defended by a rear guard garrison of warriors, the last of Athol's clan to remain in Eire.

The women, children and old people had now all been successfully transported to the clan's new territories in the islands off the coast of Caledonia. The ferocious, last-ditch campaign was being fought only because the remaining defenders literally had their backs to the sea and nowhere to go. They were to have been evacuated as quickly as vessels could be brought in to transport them, but the logistics involved were intricate. Surrounded and heavily outnumbered as they were, the Scots had to stand fast. Even with galleys available to them, none could simply sail away, abandoning their less-fortunate comrades, so no withdrawal was possible until sufficient galleys had been assembled to take the entire army off in one night.

That assembly had been close to complete when Connor and Feargus had sailed, a few weeks previously, carrying the last cargo of young cattle and livestock across to Liam Twistback in the south, and by this time, Connor was confident, the operation should have been completed and the race of Scots should have been completely removed from Eire, which they had already ceased to think of as home. In consequence, he and his men were now travelling directly to the north, where Connor would henceforth base his fleet with his brother Brander's, in his clan's new territories.

The storms abated, eventually, and fine weather returned. Connor set sail for the northern isles, and within days of his departure the autumn column arrived by road from Camulod, under the command of three of our old friends, Benedict, Philip and Falvo, all of whom had travelled with us to Eire a decade earlier. They, too, had taken the brunt of the weather god's displeasure, and their troops presented a spectacle very different from all those that had come before. No glorious panoply here; these soldiers had been on the open road for almost a month, sleeping in one-man legionaries' tents of leather the entire time. Many of them were practically unfit for duty, suffering from chronic exposure to malignant conditions and rife with chills, aches, pains, congestion, fevers and ulcerated abrasions caused by the chafing of cold, wet armour.

Poor old Lucanus went to work the moment they arrived, and we saw little of him for the ensuing few days. Shortly after our arrival in Mediobogdum, he had designated one entire building as his Infirmary, and he lived there, in the senior centurion's quarters at the western end of the block. Luke seldom ventured out, even to eat. His meals were taken to him where he sat with one patient or another, touching them, talking to them and willing them back to health.

The sight of our three old comrades was like a draught of heady wine for Dedalus, Rufio and me, and the celebration of their arrival was a major event, although a highly exclusive one, since none but the six of us attended. Only the next day, when the fumes had cleared from my head and my skull had ceased reverberating like a brazen cymbal with each beat of my heart, did Benedict hand me the letter he carried from my brother.

I had asked him the previous day what had kept Ambrose from us, and he had merely shrugged and said that Ambrose now felt he should no longer keep the challenge of the long journey to Ravenglass to himself; that it was time others shared the responsibility and honour. I had accepted that. The letter, however, threw a different light on things. I made my way outside the rear gate to where I could sit undisturbed and broke the seal on my brother's letter, hearing his voice in my mind as I read aloud what he had written:

Ambrose Ambrosianus
to Caius Merlyn Britannicus:

Greetings, Brother
I have received word out of Cornwall, brought for your attention by a Druid of those parts, that there has again been great strife in that unfortunate region. Kings and princes, including that Dumnoric who won prominence after the death of Gulrhys Lot, have gone down in death, and the land is fought over and laid waste by a large number of warring factions. One of the warlords involved is your old enemy Ironhair, of whom we had hoped to hear no more. Alas, having resurfaced, he has won a degree of preeminence and seems bent, according to this report, upon the total destruction of all his challengers. In a reversal of roles, it appears he is now assisted by Carthac, whom we know to be a depraved monster of a man, the mere sight of whom strikes terror into their enemies.

I inquired of the Druid why this should be so, and his response brought back to me the tales you told of this Carthac's descent into dementia after a head injury received in his youth. It would appear now that his depravity is such that he is no longer worthy of being considered human. He has gigantic strength and he kills for the sheer pleasure of spilling blood and causing pain. I am told his prowess in battle is extraordinary and his presence in a fight is the equal of ten normal men. That may be greatly exaggerated, but nonetheless it bespeaks great strength and power. His blood lust is insatiable, they say, and does not abate once free of the battlefield. This Carthac loves to kill by slow torture and has been known to do so merely to while away some evening hours, choosing victims at random, even from among his own army.

The primary horror, however, and the greatest cause for the fear and awe the monstrous being causes, is his cannibalism. He roasts the flesh of his victims and eats it, and he wears necklaces of human ears about his neck and shoulders. Everyone walks in terror of him, save for Ironhair, to whom the creature seems devoted. Our Druid friend came here seeking your assistance for the

> people of that land, and mistook me for you. He was greatly disappointed not to find you here and begged me to pass on this word to you, and to wish you well. His name is Tumac, and he says he knew you well, once, long ago.

Tumac! I released the bottom of the tightly rolled scroll, allowing it to spring back into place, rose to my feet and began pacing agitatedly. Tumac had been the second, and the younger, of the two students apprenticed to my old teacher Daffyd the Druid. They were mere children when I first knew them, and years younger than me. Long before I knew I had a brother called Ambrose, Tumac and Mod had been as dear to me as siblings. Daffyd had been viciously slain by this same Carthac for his loyalty to me, and Mod, the elder student of the two, had been speared and left for dead at the same time, vainly trying to assist and protect his tutor.

The unexpected sight of Tumac's name in this letter dispelled any doubt I might have had about the truth of the report on Carthac's madness and atrocities. Cannibal and murderer by torture! Why had someone not put an end to him long before now? He was but a man, despite his fearsome reputation, and even a mad dog would be long since dead for lesser sins than those of which he stood accused.

I had no doubt his appalling ferocity might inspire terror in any individual man, but I remembered Dergyll's description of how, when Carthac's boyhood excesses had become too grim to suffer, his companions had banded together to get rid of him, abducting him by force and thrashing him savagely, then abandoning him high in the hills with dire warnings of what would happen to him should he ever dare return to afflict them again. That had been effective in deterring him then. Perhaps his dementia had progressed too far in the interim to be checked, but I found myself wondering why someone had not simply killed him, from concealment, with a well-aimed arrow.

Deeply agitated by these thoughts, and shaken by the depths of the feelings of revulsion, anger and disgust they stirred in me, I forced myself to breathe deeply and made a determined attempt to empty my mind of Carthac and of Ironhair. I walked the length of the escarpment behind the rear gate several times, staring down at the carpet of tree tops far beneath and forcing myself to keep my mind empty of anything except what I could see with my eyes. Then, when my unruly thoughts had settled down and I felt calm enough to read again, I returned to the letter, settling myself again on the rock that had become my favoured seat.

> Caius, I have no idea how these tidings will affect you, but I suspect you will be much disturbed by what you are reading here. If that is so, rest easy. Cornwall is as far from your new home as

it is possible to go in west Britain, and Tumac says that Ironhair's ambition is to rule as king in Cornwall. I see no reason to doubt the rightness of that, and it follows naturally that, as an upstart king, usurping power in Cornwall, Ironhair can pose no threat to you in Ravenglass, where no one knows your true identity. Nonetheless, forewarned is forearmed. Ironhair yet lives, and now we know where.

Otherwise, all is quiet here in Camulod. I have no word of how things are developing in Vortigern's domain. Optimist I may be, but I choose to accept the silence as confirmation that the king is well and Hengist still has power upon his son Horsa. Dergyll reigns on in Cambria, and he and I have met several times in the past few years. He is an amiable fellow and seems to rule his folk with benevolence and wisdom over and above his iron hand. He asked me to wish you well, wherever you might be.

Greetings, too, from Owain of the Caves, who continues to instruct our bowmen in the art of the great Celtic bow. He assumed responsibility, a few years ago, for two unwed sisters here in Camulod who had lost their only brother to the wasting sickness several years prior to that, and since then he has kept both of them pregnant and seemingly well content. He spoke warmly of you when last we met and asked me to pass on his good wishes when next I saw you. I was surprised that he should know anything of your whereabouts, or that you and I should be meeting each other, but then I realized that with the passage of so many of our people between here and Ravenglass, it would be impossible to keep the secret close. I treated his approach with circumspection, nevertheless, and made sure to betray nothing, even though he is an old friend of yours. He made no mention of our boy, so I believe his wishes may be taken at face value.

I hope you enjoyed the sight of Falvo, Benedict and Philip coming down the hill towards your gates. Ludmilla sends her love to all of you. Be well.

Ambrose

Ambrose's comments on Owain of the Caves troubled me almost as much as his tidings of Ironhair and Carthac, and the fact that I should be troubled by such a seemingly insignificant thing increased my uneasiness. So to rid myself of the ridiculous sense of wrongness where no wrongness ought to be, I took great pains to think the entire thing through logically, seeking the non sequitur that must be there. I found the answer in what was perhaps the most innocuous line of the text: "I . . . made sure to betray nothing, even though he is an old friend of yours. . . ."

The inconsistency was one of allusion rather than fact. Owain was one of a group of Uther's Celtic captains who had eventually made their way to Camulod after deciding they could no longer stay in Cambria with Uther dead. They had all been Uther's friends as well as followers, utterly loyal to him, and upon their return from the wars against Lot of Cornwall, mere weeks after Uther's death, they had found themselves, collectively, unable or unwilling to cast their lot so soon in favour of one or any of the contenders for Uther's vacant kingship. Unfortunately, each of the contending warlords had construed such neutrality to entail hostility, and the group had become *personae non gratae* in their own homeland.

After four of their number had been murdered individually by stealth, leaving only fourteen of them alive, they decided to come down out of the mountains and offer their allegiance to me, and I was glad to accept both it and them. They had been my companions and comrades in arms for years by that time, and that association breeds strong ties. But there was only one of them, Huw Strongarm, son of the bowyer Cymric who made the first longbow of yew, whom I would think of calling a real friend. Though Owain and I had marched and camped together, and had fought in several engagements together, and I knew that Uther trusted him as he did all the others, he had been one of Uther's men and no more than that to me. And yet, I thought, he might have harboured more friendly feelings for me, in the most casual way, just as I had held amity for him without conscious volition.

I would have dismissed the question then and thought no more of it, save that one matter had been plaguing me for years: someone had betrayed young Arthur's security to Peter Ironhair and smoothed the way for Ironhair's assassins to steal into Camulod and attempt the life of the boy. In that attack, which was undone only by Shelagh's quick thinking and her mastery of her deadly throwing-knives, Hector's wife had been violated and murdered and Arthur and the other children had barely escaped with their lives. Someone we knew, some trusted person within Camulod, had betrayed our trust and remained concealed. That knowledge had sown fear and suspicion among us, who had never known distrust prior to then, and had resulted in my flight—for it was nothing less—with the boy in tow, from Camulod to Mediobogdum.

And now Owain of the Caves, who had been in Cambria when Ironhair was fighting there to install Carthac as the region's king, and who had been in Camulod at the time of the invidious attempt on Arthur's life, was asking questions of our whereabouts and calling me an old and valued friend. I knew that I was probably inferring too much from what Ambrose had written, but the fact remained that someone in Camulod was steeped in treachery and in the pay of Ironhair. Owain had mentioned nothing of the boy. Nor had he need to. In finding me, he would have found Arthur. And now, with Ambrose's acknowledgment that our presence here in Ravenglass was no secret today in Camulod, I was forced to accept the inevitable corollary: the traitor might or might not be Owain of the Caves, but if the betrayer was still in Camulod, and I must assume he or she was, then the boy was no longer absolutely safe here, and there was nothing I could do to change that, short of fleeing again, this time to the Caledonian Isles.

Unsure of precisely how to proceed, since my suspicions were purely personal and very probably unfounded, I yet sat down and wrote to Ambrose at length, telling him of my reactions to his letter and asking him to keep an eye and an ear open and attentive to Owain of the Caves from that time on, taking note of how inquisitive he might appear to be about me. When I had written it, I read it over and again, then sealed it and dispatched it back to Camulod with the returning troops whose tour here in the north-west was over.

That done, I led the newly arrived officers to Ravenglass within the week and presented them to Derek, inviting him to visit the fort, where we would introduce him formally to the new garrison. He welcomed our three friends and their junior officers magnificently, mounting a banquet in their honour the night we arrived and arranging for them to tour the entire area around the town—inspecting it from a military, defensive perspective—the following morning.

On returning from the tour, while the others were sampling the best brews of the town's hostelries, I took Derek aside and told him about Ambrose's letter, my suspicions about Owain and my consequent fears for Arthur's safety here in Ravenglass and for the security of Camulod itself. He made no attempt to make light of my concerns; he listened gravely to all I had to say and then attempted to put my mind at ease.

There had been few strangers in Ravenglass for several years, he pointed out, since the death of Liam Condranson and the expulsion of his followers. Most of the traffic passing through the port nowadays was local, made up mainly of fishermen, with the only heavy ships and galleys being those of our Eirish friends and other peaceful clans trading from further north along the coast. Barely one visitor in any score was a stranger nowadays, and he promised to make sure from this day on that every unknown person coming through was watched by his people at all times.

Greatly reassured by his level-headed reaction to my worries, I thanked him and sat back, aware that he was staring at me and plainly had more to say.

"What?" I asked him. "You have a question? Spit it out."

"When will you be leaving?"

"What?" His question was simple and straightforward, but it surprised me so much that its immediate meaning was beyond me.

"When will you be leaving, you and your people? Don't tell me you haven't been thinking about it. You've been here now for more than six years. That's how long you said you'd stay, when first you came: five or six years, until the boy was grown. He's grown."

"I haven't been thinking about it. And the boy's not grown—not quite."

"Horseshit. For all intents and purposes your boy's a man. He's almost fifteen. If he hasn't started tupping the wenches already, it's only because Shelagh keeps him on a tight leash and an early curfew. But curfews are for evading and leashes were made to be slipped. Short of iron bars across the doors and windows, nothing's going to keep the boy inside at night if he wants to be outside, baying at the moon. Personally, I'd wager he's had more than a few of my young women spread-eagled ere now. God knows there's few around here that would fight him off. He's too good-looking by half."

I simply sat and stared at him, hearing the truth in his words. Arthur, I knew, was almost through his transition from boyhood to manhood, but I had never really thought of him until now as being sexually awakened. As soon as Derek spoke the words I saw the extent of my own blindness, and I asked myself how I could think of myself as being attuned to Arthur's needs and yet remain completely unaware of this. Tress, I knew, must be aware of it, but she had said nothing of it to me. I resolved to ask her about it that very night, then made shift to empty my mind of that and to focus my thoughts upon Derek's surprising question.

"Where do you think we would go, if we were to leave?"

"Go?" His eyes widened in mock surprise. "Well, let's think about that. . . . Camulod? Would that be a good starting point? Or Cornwall? Or Cambria, perhaps?"

Ignoring the heavy sarcasm, I shook my head.

"Derek, you may not believe it, but it's been years since I've thought about leaving here."

"Then you should be ashamed. You're spending too much time with your head between Tressa's legs, my friend—your thoughts are focused on the wrong end of things. Boudicca's buttocks, man! You've spoken of your mighty destiny so much to me that even I believe in it now—I, Derek of Ravenglass! And now you tell me you've abandoned and forgotten it? Is that supposed to make me feel happy?"

I waved my hands to cut him short. "No, no, no. That's not what I meant at all, Derek. I haven't forgotten any of—"

"Then what's wrong with you? You brought the lad up here to save his life and to train him. He's trained, Merlyn, and he's full-grown. Now he needs to be refined. He'll grow bigger and he'll grow older, but if he does either here, in Ravenglass, then the world will be passing him by. He needs to go out there now, into the world, and learn how it functions. He has nothing more to learn here, I swear to you, other than the arts of spreading female legs, and he can do that anywhere. Now he needs to travel, to see other regions, to meet other men and form his own judgments by which he'll stand or fall. He needs to meet strangers and fight with them or turn them into friends and even followers. You've talked long in the past of how he will rule Camulod, one day. That day is nigh, my friend. Time to go meet it."

I drew a deep breath and thought about the rightness of what he had said. I felt ashamed of myself. I had never lost sight of what he described, but what I had lost sight of—willfully—was the closeness of the departure point for the next stage of our venture. Now I saw that I had grown too comfortable here in Derek's north-west haven, had grown too soft, mentally, in my tranquil life with Tress. I rose to my feet and gulped down the remaining wine I had been savouring.

"You're right, my friend," I said. "I've lingered here too long and the world is unfolding elsewhere. There's a monster in Cornwall who needs to be put down, and his master's as mad a dog as he is. Arthur needs to ride to war."

Derek looked intently at me. "Who's the monster in Cornwall?"

I told him briefly about Carthac and Ironhair, and when I had finished he sat up straight.

"It's going to be quiet around here, once you people leave."

"Aye, it will be, I suppose. But what about the garrison? Will their absence henceforth cause problems for you?"

"How should it? This town's almost impregnable. It stood intact for hundreds of years before your garrison arrived, and it'll continue to do so long after they are gone."

I felt my eyebrow rising at that. "Impregnable? I seem to recall a certain acquaintance of mine—the king of Ravenglass, I believe he called himself—pleading with me and my friends, a few years ago, to stay close by and help him fend off an attack his people could not repulse alone."

Derek was completely unaffected by my sarcasm. "That was different, and you know it. We had been at peace for a long time, unsuspecting of treachery, and we had an entire Erse fleet inward bound with no thought of hesitating, or scouting the land, or taking any preliminary measures. They came to conquer and they thought their treacherous whoreson of an admiral already had us beaten. I needed Connor's men up on my battlements to be seen in their numbers. It was a simple message to go away and stay away."

I nodded, acceding the truth of that, then looked him in the eye. My thoughts drifted back to the day we'd landed in Ravenglass, and everything that had passed between us since then. "I'll miss you, my friend."

"No you won't. I'm coming with you. That is, if you'll have me. I'm old bones, but not much more so than you, and I can still carry a shield and swing a sword or an axe. Will you?"

"Will I have you?" I was amazed. "Of course I'll have you, and gladly, but when first we came to Ravenglass you said you hoped you'd never have to swing a sword again. You'd had your fill of war and slaughter."

"Aye, and I believed every word of it, at that time. But now I've changed my mind. I'm coming with you."

"What about your people?"

"What about them? Let my sons look after them. They're only waiting for me to die, anyway, watching me grow fat and closer to an apoplexy. They huddle like a flock of crows, watching and waiting so they can squabble over the pickings. We'll let them squabble early, then, and sort the matter out among themselves. Besides, I want to see this boy of yours ride into battle, and I want to see this Camulod of yours, as well, to see if it really rivals Rome itself."

I grinned at him and held out my hand. "So do I, Derek, so do I."

I took my leave of Derek and went to collect the others who had accompanied me into the town, and within the hour, we were on our way back up to Mediobogdum, a laughing, light-hearted group made up of Donuil, Lucanus, Dedalus, Rufio, Philip, Falvo, Benedict and me. When I judged the time was right, about halfway through the journey, when the ceaseless bantering had abated slightly, I told them of my thoughts and my decision to leave for Camulod in the spring, and then asked them to say nothing to anyone else until we could convene the whole populace of the fort at one time. The decision to return to Camulod was mine, I emphasized, and would not be binding on any of our group who might wish to remain when the garrison and serving officers returned to Camulod. None would, I thought, but everyone deserved the right to have the choice.

Once home, I stabled Germanicus and left my companions bantering among themselves as I made my way to find Tress. We were home much earlier than expected, and she met me at the entrance to my quarters, wide-eyed with alarm, one hand held up to her mouth.

"Cay, what's wrong?"

"Nothing, there's nothing wrong, my love. Calm yourself." I went directly to her, taking her into my arms. "Something came up, in Ravenglass, that's all, something unforeseen, and we decided to return immediately. Tomorrow, I must call a meeting of all our people and talk to them."

She leaned back into the support of my arm, cocking her head at me. "What was it that came up? What happened?"

"Nothing really happened, I merely had a long overdue talk with Derek, that's all. He made me see that I've been dangerously close to wasting time here."

Her frown was instantaneous. "What? Wasting time, how?"

"By being indecisive. Avoiding the inevitable. Now I have to leave. We have to leave. To return to Camulod. It's past time—Hey!"

She had spun away from me as I said the words, ripping herself out of my arms, her entire body rigid with displeasure and disapproval. I stood blinking at her, aware that she was hurt and angry but incapable of guessing why. And then, being male, I asked the male question: "What's wrong, Tress?"

"Nothing." The chill in her voice would have blighted ripening fruit.

I felt anger stir in my own breast. "That's ridiculous! Something is so far wrong you look as though you might never recover, but I'll be damned if I know what it is. What did I say to cause that? I said we're leaving, that's all."

She withered me with a sidelong look, and when she spoke I heard, for the first time in years, the burr of her local idiom in the acid of her tone "That's all? That is *all?* After five, almost six years, you decide to leave, on the strength of one conversation, and that is all? Well, you'll pardon me, I hope, if I overreacted. We'll all regret the loss of you, I'm sure."

Suddenly, blindingly, I saw the cause of her anger and stepped towards her again. "Tress, I said *we* are leaving. Us. You and me. I meant you first of all, with me, and then young Arthur and all the others. I'd have no place in Camulod today without you by my side. I made the error of assuming that you'd come with me and so forgot to ask you if you would. Will you?"

She was staring at me, great tears trembling on her lashes. "What?" she asked, her voice faltering.

"Will you come with me, to Camulod?"

"You'd want me there, among all those grand people?"

I laughed then. "*Want* you? Are you mad? And what's this nonsense about grand people? The place they live in is grand, I'll swear to that, but they are all very ordinary. . . . Well quite extraordinary, some of them . . . but there's no reason for you to have any fears on that account. You're more than equal to any of them. Of course I want you there, beside me as my wife, mistress or concubine. As any one of those, yes, I want you, although I hope you'll be there as my wife and remain my mistress and my wanton concubine."

She frowned again, her eyes filling up with some thought I could not decipher.

"What's this about being your wife? Why would you say such a thing? Years you've known me now, and ne'er a word about being wife or husband has passed between us. No need for such a thing with us, I believed, as you did, too."

"Aye," I agreed, shrugging my shoulders. "But that's changed now—" In truth, it had changed but that moment, with the sudden, flaring fear that she might not come with me. My former vow never to wed had been reviewed in that flash of time and rejected as foolish.

"How, changed? And why so quickly?" Her eyes were flashing sparks. "Is what we have not good enough for Camulod? Will all your mighty friends be shocked to find you living with a common woman who is not your wife?"

"Gods, will you listen to the woman? Tressa! That's not what I meant at all! I meant only that I have grown to love you too dearly to wish to continue without being your husband. If I cannot have you with me, then, God protect me, I have no wish for Camulod. I want you there as my true friend and companion, guide, confidante and counsellor. Yes, again, to all of those. But as a female intimate who lies with me and then goes home to sleep alone, no, that I will abjure from this time forth." I reached out and gathered her into my arms, feeling the uncertainty with which she let herself be pulled. "There's a place already prepared for you in Camulod, my love," I whispered into her hair. "A place filled with light and love and airiness in which you will spread your wings and glow like the most precious-coloured butterfly. A place of honour, in the house of my Great-uncle Varrus and my Great-aunt Luceiia, and it entails being my openly professed lover and my spouse and my true friend. Will you take it?"

She leaned back in the crook of my elbow for long moments, looking up at me with tears trembling on her lashes, and then her arm swept up and her hand cupped the back of my neck and she drew me down to her mouth, and then, for a long spell, there was nothing that I need to write about or that any other needs to know. I met with all our folk the following day and told them of my thoughts and my decision, taking great pains to let them know that I considered none of them to be bound by my wishes. They had accompanied me from the south long years before and since then had created a new home here on this harsh mountain plateau, forging friendships and alliances with Derek's folk in the town beneath and with those of Derek's folk who had come up to live with us in Mediobogdum. Any who wished to remain behind when we left for Camulod, come spring, would do so with my fullest blessing and support, and any of the people there from Ravenglass who wished to come to Camulod would be equally welcome.

When I had finished speaking there was a long silence, broken finally by a loud and prolonged belch from Dedalus. As the laughter died away, he said, "Well, having rid ourselves of that foul air, we had best apply ourselves to bethinking what we have to take with us when we leave. Winter will soon be down about our ears, and when it's gone we'll be too close to leaving to have time to spend rooting around for things we've missed. My proposal is, we draw an inventory from the stores, tally up everything we own and have, and decide then what we must leave behind. Derek's folk will be glad to have anything we choose not to take, and that could amount to many wagonloads of goods. Who are our scribes and clerks? Let them go first to work, and then the rest of us will improve on what they have to say.

"But first, Cay, if you're sure you want to leave in the new year, you ought to send word in advance to Camulod, now, before the first snowfall. Otherwise Ambrose will know nothing and will send out the relief column to come up here. We might miss them on the way, if they're patrolling."

And so the work began. Within the week a mounted party of ten men went spurring south to Camulod, bearing a letter from me to my brother, explaining what was in my mind and telling him that we would be beneath the walls of Camulod within a month of the last snow's disappearance from our northern hills. Systematically, we set about dismantling the home we had created for ourselves in Mediobogdum. Two hundred years it had sat empty ere we came, and after we had gone it might be yet two hundred more before another came to live in it.

Tress began to pack up all the objects that surrounded our life together, secure in knowing that we would be travelling side by side and that she need have no fear of being abandoned. Nothing was actually moved away from where it would normally be found, but I began to note that every article, every utensil, every stick and piece of furniture was marked with a twist of coloured yarn. I said nothing, content to leave the marshalling to her, but I found it interesting to compare the various items that were marked with the same colours. I felt sure there must be logic and reason behind the patterning, but it escaped me utterly.

Arthur found me, one dull and cloudy afternoon not long after that, engrossed, for the first time in years, in a meticulous inspection of the contents of the larger of the two wooden, iron-bound chests that had belonged to Caspar and Memnon, the long-dead warlocks who had brought about my father's death and plunged us into the first battles of our war with Gulrhys Lot of Cornwall. I had kept the heavy, solidly constructed boxes close to me, always locked, ever since they had first come into my possession, years before the boy was born.

Always I had told myself that I would learn the secrets of their tightly wrapped and carefully preserved contents, and in the early days of owning them I had, in fact, tested many of them and formed some hazy notions of the uses for which several might have been intended. As far as I had been able to discern, however, every single item contained in those chests had but one purpose: the infliction of death by means unknown and unconscionable to the soldier warrior. The forms of death within these two receptacles, meticulously ordered in nested trays and laid out in some bewildering symmetry of malevolence, represented an abundance, an entire spectrum of chaos that lay far beyond the intent or understanding of ordinary, sometimes violent men.

Each of the two chests contained several layers of trays, varying in depth, but each carefully fitted as a cover for the one directly beneath it, and all of them equipped with long, looping thong handles to permit their removal. As far as I could see, all of the evil deaths of political assassination, of sorcery, of necromancy and of ruin sown among mankind for the sheer pleasure of creating terror and chaos were represented in this unique collection. There was nothing in either chest, that I could find, that embodied anything other than grief and pain and agony and despair. And so I had soon abandoned any study of them.

Not daring to accept the risk of having them fall into other hands, I was nonetheless unable to destroy them. I had not yet explored them fully; indeed, I had not even looked at all the contents of the second, smaller, chest. My better judgment told me there was no such thing as good in either of them, but until I knew that to be absolutely true, I would remain incapable of simply destroying them.

My renewed interest in the chests had sprung from Tress's personal coding of our goods with coloured yarn. Within the seeming chaos of her coloured threads, I knew, there was a clear and flawless pattern, discernible to her, and that thought had led me to renewed thoughts of the warlocks' chests. A similar pattern, I suspected, must lie waiting to be deciphered among the neatly wrapped packages in their trays and compartments. Everything within them spoke of care and order.

"What are you doing, Cay? Oh, your pardon—may I come in?"

I waved to Arthur to enter and then sat back on my stool with a short, violent sigh, looking at the ordered disorder I had strewn about me. The contents of the two topmost trays of the larger box lay spread out on my left and on my right, arranged beside the empty trays themselves. The third tray, consisting of twelve compartments, four across by three down, all a handsbreadth deep and each containing a clay bottle of some kind, lay exposed within the chest. Several thoughts flashed through my mind as I heard the boy's voice, the foremost among them that I should banish him with the rough edge of my tongue before he could see what I was doing. I abandoned the idea even before it formed.

"Pull a stool over here and sit beside me, and don't touch anything else."

He did as I said and then sat there, bent slightly forward, his bright, gold-flecked eyes flicking over everything that could be seen within and outside the chest. I held my peace, waiting for him to speak, but he said nothing for a long time. Finally he glanced at each of the empty trays on the floor.

"Trays upon trays. There must be others beneath that one there, still in the chest?"

"Aye, there are. How many would you estimate?"

His eyes flicked back to the two empty trays. "Which one of those was uppermost?"

"That one." I nodded towards the one on my left.

"Hmm. Then they grow deeper as they nest deeper, so I would say there might be three more, the same depth as the one still in there. No more than that and probably fewer—one or two. Is the other one the same?" He was gazing now at the second, smaller chest.

"More or less," I answered him. "Different contents, but the same overall effect, I imagine. I find enough to occupy me here, in the larger one."

"What's the overall effect you mentioned? What's in them?"

"Death, and a dilemma."

He glanced sideways at me, his eyes wide with surprise. "What do you mean?"

I turned to face him. "Do you recall the story of my father's death?"

He nodded. "He was murdered in his bed by sorcerers. What were their names . . . ?" His eyes were distant, seeking recall. "Caspar, that was one of them, and Memnon."

"Aye, those were the names. Caspar and Memnon. Sorcerers, as you say. I think of them as warlocks."

"What's the difference?"

"Very little on the surface, I suspect. To my mind, however, a sorcerer is one who seeks to use things magical, supernatural, to influence the world of men. Whether they do it for good or ill matters little and depends upon the sorcerer himself, or herself. But since I do not believe in magic or the supernatural, I find sorcerers to be pitiable, laughable and usually harmless, once they've been exposed as being impotent."

"Woman can be sorcerers?" He sounded surprised, and I laughed at him.

"Arthur, women can be anything that men can be, except fathers. You'll find that out very soon now."

He was not to be distracted from his main interest this time.

"Tell me then, if sorcerers are pitiable, what makes the difference between them and warlocks?"

"Warlocks are an altogether different form of being, Arthur—at least they are in my estimation. The difference is no more than a matter of degree, in some respects, but in others—very important others—it is a matter of great moment. You should understand, of course, that that's no more than my own, personal opinion and I could be wrong. Nevertheless, I have thought about it long and often. Warlocks are real and frightening. They seek, and exercise, powers that normal men cannot credit, let alone understand. And in contrast to those others whom I think of as sorcerers, warlocks deal only in evil. They use physical magics like these things you see here: a hundred forms of poison, each one causing death. Warlocks bring death in their train. They deal only in evil and in ruin for the people they encounter." I had surprised myself, never having put these feelings into words before.

The boy sat staring at me. "Well," he said at length, "that's the death part. What's the dilemma? The death I can understand, if all those packages and boxes and those vials contain the poisons you spoke of. Do they? Every one of them?"

"Near enough. I don't know every use of every thing that's there, but all of those I have identified are carriers of death in one form or another, most of them agonizing."

"Will you show me?"

"Partially. I'll show you those I have identified, but I will not demonstrate their venom for your amusement. You'll have to take my word for that."

"And you say you haven't yet examined everything in the boxes? How can that be? Aren't you curious? I would have had them all out and examined by now. How can you be so . . . disciplined? You're amazing, Merlyn."

"You must call me Cay, remember?"

He threw me a glance of pure irritation. "Yes, I remember, but we're here alone, and you've always been Merlyn to me." He ducked his head. "That one slipped out. I'll try not to let it happen again. But you still haven't told me what your dilemma is, regarding these . . . things. Is there a name for them?"

"I think of them as nostrums, but that's not accurate, for nostrums are medicaments, whereas these are malignancies. As to the dilemma they present . . ." I smiled at him, a weary smile completely lacking in amusement. "Can you not guess?" I did not wait for his response. "I don't know whether to destroy them or to study them further."

"You should study them, of course. But how would you destroy them, even if you wanted to?"

"Some I would burn—most of them, in fact. Others I might bury, or dilute to nothingness."

He inched his stool closer to the chest. "Show them to me, please."

Item by item, then, I showed him the various substances I had identified in the larger chest, beginning with the glazed clay boxes, with tight-fitting lids, that contained the noxious, greenish paste that brought awful, burning death to anyone cut by a weapon coated in its residue. This was the venom, I explained, that Lot's warriors had smeared on their arrowheads when they ambushed his father's troops in Cornwall, and which I had used to execute the warlock Caspar, slitting his brow with one of those same arrowheads.

Arthur listened closely, eyes wide with fascination as I moved on to unwrap and expose other items with which I had become slightly familiar during my first few weeks of study long years before. Among them were the tightly wrapped linen strips containing the deadly, envenomed thorns with which Caspar had thought to make me keep my distance from my threatened Aunt Luceiia. The notes which I had made at the time of my first investigations were still there, folded on the topmost tray of the larger box, and I consulted them as I went on, remembering the thrill with which I had first ventured into these mysteries, and detailing my own discoveries about them for Arthur's understanding. I showed him all of those I had defined to any depth at all, and those I had set aside as having properties which I had not yet identified.

Watching his reaction, it was easy to recall my own fascination with the astonishing array of nostrums spread before us now. I remembered my amazement at the range of colours—every colour I had ever seen and many I had never seen before—and the textures and materials that had emerged from all the many wrappings and containers held within the compartments of each tray: glass phials and stoppered tubes of weird and wonderful proportions held dozens of crystalline mixtures and unknown powders; small boxes and containers made of wood, or clay or sometimes waxed papyrus, held strange pastes and crushed mixtures of things that had been ground down by mortar and pestle; others contained unguents and oily substances that seemed to me to have been rendered over fire; rolled tubes of bark and others made of leather protected bunches of varied grasses and dried leaves and twigs, and there were tiny, cunningly made boxes filled with dried berries, seeds and nuts.

I reached out and picked up one handspan-long tube made from the bark of some exotic tree and tied with a leather thong. It held a single twist of long, dried, yellow grass, folded upon itself time and again and bound, in turn, with a loop of its own stuff.

"This," I said. "I have no idea what it might be, and it looks innocuous enough, but I suspect, from the care with which it has been wrapped, that it has more than casually lethal properties."

He nodded. "What would you do with it?"

I shrugged. "Who knows? Cut it up into tiny flakes and sprinkle it in someone's food? Boil it in water to extract its juices? Set it alight to give off lethal smoke? I've no idea. But judging from the materials with which it is surrounded, all of which are highly toxic—and I know that, before you ask, because I fed small amounts of each of them to animals and they all died—I would hesitate to think that this particular grass might have some therapeutic quality. There's little fear that I would bind a wound with it, for example.

"There is my dilemma, in miniature. If I wished to destroy this grass, this single substance, how would I go about it, safely? Can't burn it, because I might inhale the smoke and die convulsed. Nor can I bury it without wondering if something might dig it up and eat it. Can't scatter it upon the wind, in conscience. And yet it is no more than a twist of grass, only one element of what these chests contain." I paused, remembering. "But here's something else that will interest you, and it is the single, most convincing reason I have found for not destroying everything that's here, because it's the one and only thing I've found in here that is not poisonous, and I've tested it quite thoroughly. It is, nevertheless, lethal."

I dug into the lowest layer of the open chest, removing the remaining trays one by one, and finally brought out the most fascinating substance I had found in the entire collection. It was contained in a rather large, flat wooden box, the largest of all the boxes in the chests, that was tightly bound with twine. I undid the twine and removed the lid to reveal a blackish, granular powder, knowing it would fail, utterly, to impress Arthur visually. The powder was odourless and practically tasteless save for a saline, brackish tang. I knew it to be non-poisonous, since I had tested it by feeding it to three rabbits, none of which had suffered any ill effects. This powder, I had long since discovered, would not dissolve in water, but when I had thrown it on the fire, thinking it useless, it had frightened me near to death by flaring up with an appalling, flashing hiss and throwing off great clouds of dense, black, bitter smoke which had made me splutter and cough but had done me no other harm. Recovering from my first terror, I had made other tests and found this mixture to be the most volatile and dangerous material I had ever experienced, igniting even with the heat of a stray spark. What purpose it might serve lay far beyond my ken, but I suspected it must be dire. I had attempted to visualize the conflagration should an errant spark once fall into the box, and my spirit had quailed at the horror. In consequence, I treated the substance, which I thought of as "fire powder," with great care and circumspection.

Now I took a generous pinch of it between two fingers and my thumb and wrapped it tightly in a twist of cloth. I made sure to close the box carefully, then handed the twist to Arthur.

"Here, there's nothing more to see of it than you have seen. It has no taste, no odour, no particular colour apart from black and brown, and no use that I could find for it. It does not dissolve in water, nor in wine, and it's not poisonous. Throw it in the fire, there, behind you."

He turned and did as I had bidden, watching to see what would happen. The twist landed on some unburned coals and lay there, beginning to smoulder at the ends. He turned to look at me and I waved him back to the fire, and his eyes returned to the smouldering cloth just as the powder inside it ignited. There came a sudden, concussive *whuff* of sound, a blinding glare of blazing light, and then thick clouds of black, evil-smelling smoke, shot through with whirling sparks, boiled up and belched outward from the brazier. I had been expecting it, but even I was taken aback by the ferocity of the reaction.

Arthur leaped to his feet in terror, the colour fleeing from his face as he fought against the panic that urged him to run and hide. He teetered there for a long moment, poised between flight and acceptance, and then he suddenly dropped to his knees, grasping a piece of kindling from beside the brazier and using it to brush a number of fierce-burning embers towards the hearth before they could set the entire room alight. I rushed to help him, horrified by the sight of so many burning patches on the rug Tressa herself had woven for me. Between the two of us, we somehow cleared everything before any noticeable damage had been inflicted, and then we both sat back on our haunches, puffing and laughing nervously.

"Well," said Arthur, "that's two things you can't burn without risk: the yellow grass and the black powder. What is it, Cay? Do you have any idea?"

I shook my head. "None. It looks like crushed charcoal, doesn't it? But it's not like any charcoal I've ever seen before."

"It burns so quickly, that's the frightening thing about it. No warning of any kind, just *whoosh!* and it's gone. Have you ever heard of anything like it?"

"Absolutely not, but the warlocks who brought it here were from the distant reaches of the Empire. Their names were Egyptian, but I suspect they came from even farther afield than that, perhaps from beyond the eastern borders, where the people are said to be yellow of skin. I'd wager that even if they were not from those parts, they'd been to them. Anyway, now that you have seen how this powder works, what do you think I ought to do with it?"

He shook his head and then smiled. "Use it to frighten people? It works very well for that."

I laughed with him and then rose to my feet and placed the box of powder back into its space at the bottom of the chest, after which I allowed him to help me in repacking everything else I had unearthed. As I was locking the padlocks, he stood off to one side, watching me.

"These things are very dangerous, Cay."

"Aye, they are that, but they're safe enough in there, for now, so long as I have the only keys to the boxes. There's only one of each. I haven't looked inside these things in years, but now I know I have to go through everything they contain, meticulously, and try to discover what each item is, and what might be done with it. I could never bring myself simply to destroy them without trying to discover what they are. D'you understand that?"

"Of course I do. They represent knowledge. Though you might not, there are people somewhere who know all the uses of them, and knowledge is power."

Knowledge is power. I smiled, hearing him quote the words I had said to him so many times.

"There were people, once, who knew the uses of them, Arthur, but they are dead. Perhaps they took their knowledge with them into their graves. We may never discover what these things are."

"You will. If you apply yourself, the way you're always telling me to apply myself, you'll answer all your own questions. All you need do is work at it."

I grinned, dropping my keys into my scrip. "You are impertinent, but I hope you are also right. Come, let's find Tress before she finds us and sees what we almost did to her handsome rug."

Tress, I knew, was visiting Shelagh, and as we walked towards Shelagh and Donuil's quarters I placed my hand casually on Arthur's shoulder, gauging his height as I always did. In the past few years he had shot up so that, where once I walked with my elbow only slightly bent to hold him, I now had to raise my hand almost to the level of my own shoulder.

"It will rain tonight," I said.

He looked up at the lowering clouds and grunted, his lack of interest apparent in his next question. "Cay, will you take me some day to see Stonehenge?"

"Stonehenge? Yes, of course, if you want me to. What made you think of that?"

"I was thinking of the lichen Grandfather Varrus noticed on the standing stones, the day he first waited with Great-uncle Caius to meet my Grandfather Ullic. It was a cloudy day then, too, like today. I was thinking, too, about knowledge and its power. When I first read that tale, I didn't know what lichen was, and so I asked Lucanus and he showed me some. I'd seen it before, but I'd thought it was just dirt and grime and that the colours in the patches were accidental. Lucanus told me lichen are living plants, just like moss. Today I see lichen everywhere. But if Grandfather Varrus had not written those words, I would never have known."

He half turned and squinted up at me, something else on his mind. "Grandfather Varrus had his books, and your Grandfather Britannicus had his, and I know you have writings set down by your father, my Uncle Picus. I've read all of them and I've learned much from them, but all of them have left me feeling . . . I don't know what the correct word is . . . incomplete? I feel as though I am still learning, still being exposed to the thoughts of my elders, and you are my most recent elder. Will you write down your thoughts some day?"

I found myself wanting to grin, self-conscious, yet amused and flattered. "I don't know, Arthur. I had not thought that far ahead. I have the task of caring for the books now, but I hadn't thought of adding to them. I haven't had time, to tell the truth. Of what should I write?"

"Of your life! About Camulod, and Ravenglass, and Eire. And of my father Uther, and Cornwall. If no one had written down the early tale of how the Colony was founded, none of us would remember. This is an important task, Cay. Someday I will write my life's tale down, for my own sons and grandsons, just as Grandfather did."

I grinned at him and squeezed the back of his neck, feeling the hard column of young muscle. "Should you live so long," I teased him, "I'll keep you mindful of that promise."

Ah, the dreadful things we say in jest!

There was one more item contained in those chests that was not maleficent, and I found it the following day. I mention it now because, insignificant and quaint as it seemed at the time, it yet became one of the two most powerful items contained in that evil collection.

I found it at the very bottom of the second chest, carefully wrapped in soft and supple, beautifully tanned leather. On first opening it, handling the package with great care, I regarded it with sheer horror, unable to bring myself to touch it. It was a human face, eyeless, but miraculously preserved and complete with full head and facial hair, and my flesh crawled at the visualization of how it had been achieved. It had apparently been removed intact from a living skull, then treated somehow, to maintain the colour and the texture of the skin, and lovingly wrapped in the leather covering.

Only after I had stared at it aghast for several endless moments did I begin to discern that it was not what I had taken it to be, and even then it took me a long time to gather up the strength I needed to be able to reach out and touch the thing. As soon as I did touch it, however, my fingertips informed my still-doubting mind that they were touching wax of some strange kind. It was a mask, and it was made up of two parts, but it was unlike any mask I had ever known.

The hair was real enough, but it had been applied with great artifice to a foundation of the finest, open-weave cloth, which I soon recognized as a precious, diaphanous stuff from Asia Minor much prized by my Aunt Luceiia. The mask itself had been made up of many tiny layers of this delicate material, obviously laid over a real human face and coated, piece by piece, with some kind of glue or fine paste. I could clearly see the outlines of the integrated parts when I held the thing with its back towards a bright light. Then, once the outlines of the face had been achieved, the outer surface had been coated with some kind of pliable yet hardened wax, and the magician who constructed the wonder had shaped and painted the outer coating to resemble life itself.

The upper piece fitted over the eyes and nose, completely covering the wearer's own features, and the attached wig, of long, coarse, dark-brown hair sown into a soft, thin cap of the same material as the mask itself, fell in ringlets to cover the wearer's own hair entirely. The upper edges of the eye holes were covered by thick, fierce brows, but the lower edges were so thin as to be almost insubstantial, fitting against the lower lids and sagging downwards into deep, utterly realistic bags of seeming flesh on either side of a thick, jutting, pock-marked nose. From visible pores in the skin of the cheeks, just below the pouches beneath the eyes, the hairs of a long, unkempt beard sprouted wildly, blending into a long, dark-stained moustache.

The second, lower part was similarly made, but fully bearded, fitting the bottom part of the face from just beneath the ears and covering the jaws and chin, ending just beneath the wearer's lips. I realized immediately that this part would have to be applied first, and the upper part must fit over it. I also realized that, wondrous as it was, the mask would be usable only by the person for whom it had been made, or by someone who very closely resembled him, facially. It was unyielding in its main structure, made to fit only the cheekbones on which it had been moulded. And naturally, having discovered that, I held it up to my own face.

Expecting to feel the hard edges of ridges that would not conform to my own bone structure, I felt instead a tenuous, quite unidentifiable comfort, which quickly flared into a surge of something approaching superstitious terror as I realized the thing had snugged completely and alarmingly onto the contours of my face, coating my features like a second, cool and omnipresent skin. It fit me perfectly, and on realizing that, I instinctively released my grip on the thing so that it should have fallen. Instead, it remained in place, its fabric warming to the feel of my own skin and nestling so thoroughly against it that the mask felt weightless and insubstantial.

The awareness of how unlikely such a fit must be set my heart hammering and raised the small hairs on my neck. My mind threw up a score of reasons for the impossibility of such a thing. How could this possibly have occurred? Of the hundreds of men I knew, none other, save my brother Ambrose, could have matched the facial contours of this mask so perfectly. Whose mask had it been? I knew immediately it could have belonged originally to neither Casper nor Memnon, the two warlocks. Their faces had both been utterly different from mine and from this mask. Memnon was facially disfigured, with grossly protuberant eyes on different levels. My memory seemed to indicate that Caspar might, possibly, have been able to wear it. But it had not been made for Caspar's face. His cheeks had been too flat, his nose too long, his eyebrows too prominent and his chin too regressive. Whose face, then, could have been the model for its creation, and why should I, of all men, end up in possession of the thing? Did it possess some frightful portent? Had some god arranged for it to fall into my hands? Or might God Himself have meant me to possess it for some purpose of His own? It fit me perfectly, defying all the odds of probability, and the knowledge of that shook me to my depths, so that, flaring with excitement, I went searching for a mirror for the first time in my life.

I quickly found that the mask would not stay in place indefinitely without the pressure of my hand, and once I had accepted that I went back to the source—the tray in the chest—looking for whatever means Caspar had used to keep the thing in place on his face. There, in the bottom of the tray, I found a tiny flask of liquid that was astoundingly adhesive, sticking my fingertips together instantly, yet not so firmly that I could not pull them apart with a degree of ease. I also found several small, round boxes of waxed papyrus that contained pastes of varying colours, clearly cosmetics intended for use in the final preparation of the disguise.

I locked my door and amused myself for several hours in front of Aunt Luceiia's silver mirror, marvelling at the completeness and complexity of the changes I effected in myself. Then, irked by the painful tenderness caused by the adhesive, I packed everything carefully away, and made my way to the bathhouse.

XVI

ONCE AGAIN, THE secrets of the warlocks' chests were driven from my mind by more pressing events that demanded my attention. I would think of that late autumn, forever after, as the Autumn of the Beasts.

First came the wolves, driven to descend on us, Lucanus believed, as the result of some sickness that had decimated their normal prey. It seemed to me he must be right, for there were very few deer around that year, and one could ride for an entire day through the forest without encountering any of the hares, rabbits or squirrels that normally abounded in the woodlands.

Wolves, like bears and other large animals in the wild, generally take pains to avoid contact with humans. That particular year, however, the wolves came closer to our fort at Mediobogdum, and in greater numbers, than they ever had before without the spur of winter starvation to impel them. The sound of their howling, just beyond our walls, became a nightly commonplace from the late summer onward, and after the loss of several of our animals, we were forced to move all our livestock into the safety of the fort each evening before the sun went down. We were completely unprepared, however, to be attacked and plundered in full daylight.

Shelagh had begun raising swine the first year after our arrival, and her herd had prospered. She had quickly acquired buyers for as many prime yearling pigs as she wished to sell, but from her father she had inherited a keen eye for healthy traits in beasts and she always managed to retain the best of each litter as future breeding stock. Because she now owned a dozen prime sows, she had constructed a large and spacious pen to hold them, close to the bathhouse and its plenteous water, but far enough removed so that the stink of the proliferating farrows would be bearable to people coming and going from the baths. At night the animals were brought inside the fort and penned again in another enclosure built against the north wall, as far away from our habitation as they could be.

On one late and lovely afternoon, when the trees had almost lost their golden cloaks completely, a pack of wolves, desperate with hunger, braved the nearness of men and attacked the swine pens.

The alarm was raised immediately, of course, although the squealing of terrified pigs would have brought us running even had no one seen what was happening. Within moments of the first outbreak of noise, more than a score of men, all armed, converged upon the vicinity of the swine pens. I was one of the first to arrive, having been on my way to the bathhouse, but because of that, I was one of the few who arrived unarmed. Dedalus came running next, from another direction, carrying a spear, his longbow and a quiver of arrows slung across his back. Seeing me without a weapon, he threw me the spear and unslung his bow, nocking an arrow even before we had seen any targets.

The noise was appalling, and among the demented squealing of the pigs we could hear what we took to be the snarling of dogs. The dogs were wolves, and they were swarming everywhere, attacking with awe-inspiring ferocity. I counted fourteen of them before I gave up and began to concentrate on reaching them and beating them off, only to discover that the latter was easier to think about than to achieve. These wolves betrayed not the slightest inclination to slink off as they normally would when challenged by men. Instead, they turned on us and attacked us without hesitation. One huge animal leaped directly at me, fangs flashing, and it was by the merest chance that I was able to drop to one knee and fling up my spear point in time to pierce his hurtling body; even then the dead weight of him threw me over backwards.

I scrambled to my feet again, wrenching out the spear point, and saw another gaunt form writhing on the turf ahead of me, skewered by an arrow. Dedalus had positioned himself to my left, on a little knoll, and was drawing and shooting methodically, bringing down wolf after wolf, not bothering to kill each one since he knew that there were enough of us to finish off the ones he wounded. And then Hector, on my right, went down beneath two animals, one of which had sunk its fangs in the wrist of his sword arm.

I was in easy throwing distance but dared not throw, for I might have killed Hector as easily as either of the wolves. Rufio saved Hector's life by leaping to his side and swinging a massive axe I had never seen before. With two enormous blows he destroyed both animals and then leaped forward, over Hector, to confront another that was slinking forward, belly down, towards the fallen man. When he landed in front of it, the beast warned him away with flashing fangs, growling and slavering, but Rufio was already swinging and the edge of his axe caught the wolf on the shoulder, cleaving it and hurling it to Rufio's left, where I pinned it to the ground with my spear.

The battle seemed to last for ages, but it must really have been only a very short time before the first wolf fled, yipping and yowling, and the others followed it to safety. Even then, however, they withdrew only a short way before stopping to turn and snarl at us again from what they took to be a safe distance. The Celtic longbow that Dedalus held, however, was lethal at far greater distances than that, and he killed four more of the animals before the surviving beasts realized how vulnerable they yet were and fled, pursued by two more of Ded's deadly arrows.

We found twelve dead wolves in and around the pens, and opinions varied as to whether seven or nine had escaped the slaughter. We also found five dead yearling pigs and two so severely savaged that we had to kill them. None of the fearsome sow matrons had been injured. We dined communally on pork for the ensuing week.

And then, a mere ten days after the wolf attack, Rufio's horse came home alone in the middle of the day, lathered with sweat, its eyes rolling in terror partly caused, I had no doubt, by the unaccustomed flapping of its saddle's empty stirrups. My mind immediately filled with visions of the surviving wolves from the previous week's escapade, and I was the first one to horse, although Arthur and his three friends and every other man then in the fort were close behind me. Once we had left the fort and reached the road, however, there was no way to tell which direction to take; the ground was too hard and stony to show any sign of passage. I reined my horse in hard and waved the others down, and we returned immediately to the fort, where we summoned the garrison from the camp and organized search parties.

No one had any knowledge of what Rufio's intentions had been when he rode out that day. He would not have ridden down into Ravenglass, we knew. We had a rule, informal but observed, that no one was to ride to Ravenglass without reporting his or her intentions—primarily to avoid causing concern should the journey require an overnight stay, but also because there was always someone who required something from the town and was unable to go there personally to collect it. We also knew he would not have crossed the saddleback pass into the next valley, since there was no conceivable reason for anyone to go there. But that was all we knew. He might have gone up the flank of the hill to the south-west, towards the places where we were working in the stone quarry and the forest; or he might have gone down into the forested valley beneath, in the hopes of finding deer or other game.

We had eighty bodies available for the search, half of them infantry. I sent forty men on foot down into the valley and took the remainder with me up onto the south-west flank of the mountain above us. Less than six hours of daylight were left to us, and we searched until the gathering dusk became too thick to deal with, so that we arrived back at the fort long after dark, making our way slowly and with great difficulty down the rock-strewn hillsides towards the beacon fires that our friends had lit around the walls of the fort. In all our minds and hearts, we hoped that the other party had found Rufio, but they had not returned, so our hopes were quickly dashed. Sure enough, when they eventually straggled home exhausted, they had seen no sign of our friend.

That night, one of the few occasions when Tress actually slept beneath my roof instead of returning to her own quarters, I frightened her by snapping awake and bolting upright in bed, shouting something that I did not remember and which she failed to understand. She sprang up immediately and threw her arms about me, clutching me tightly to her warm bareness as she made shushing, soothing noises. Eventually, when I relaxed and subsided to lie on my back, staring at the ceiling, she remained leaning over me, her soft breasts cushioned against me.

"What was it?" she asked, eventually, her voice the merest whisper.

"A dream." I could see her clearly, outlined in the light of the full moon that shone through the open window of my bedchamber. "Rufio. I saw Rufio." The effort of saying the words was enormous, for I had no wish to articulate them. The prospect of admitting my dream, even to myself, appalled me, for I had foreseen the deaths of far too many of my friends in former years, in dreams just like this one. I had thought that far behind me nowadays, for it had been years since the last occurrence of the frightening phenomenon, in Eire, where a dream had shown me the murder of one of Donuil's brothers.

There was a pause the length of several heartbeats, and then, "Where was he?" No hint of surprise or disbelief.

I swallowed, hard, trying to moisten my dry mouth. "In a hollow, a clearing, among trees on a hillside . . . a rock face behind him . . ."

"Was he alive?" When I said nothing, she grasped my shoulder and shook it. "Cay! Was Rufio alive?"

I tried to pull away from her embrace, but she clung to me. "How would I know that? It was a dream, Tress, nothing more."

"No!" She pulled me closer to her, hissing with urgency. "It was one of *your* dreams, Cay, and I know about your dreams. Now think hard, before the veil closes. Did you see anything else? Was Rufio alive?"

I resisted asking her how she came to know about my dreams, drawing comfort instead from the way she evidently had no doubt of my abilities, and forced myself to concentrate on the image that had brought me shouting from my sleep. Closing my eyes, I sought to breathe deeply and evenly, emptying my mind of everything that might distract me. Tress seemed to be aware of what I was doing and remained silent, looking down on me, braced on one elbow. Somehow, it seemed as though a mist swirled in my mind, and then it began to settle and the vision came back to me, hazy and indistinct, but real and discernible.

"He's masked in blood, unmoving . . . no telling whether he's alive or dead. . . . Helmet's missing. . . . Blood everywhere—on the grass, on the stones . . . He's lodged between two trees . . . moss on the trunks, and blood on the moss. I can see where his fingers have clawed the moss from the bark. . . ." As I described it, the image shifted, as though my eyes had adjusted, and I saw something else, half-hidden in the shadows among the surrounding trees. My mind rebelled in disbelief, and the scene faded back into mist, leaving me staring wide-eyed at the dark ceiling. I held my breath for a long time, struggling with my thoughts, and then expelled the air from my lungs, allowing myself to relax. "That's all. It's gone. That's all I saw."

"Hmm . . ." She released me and swung away, out of the bed. I watched her naked form as she moved across to the door into my main room. "Come, Cay, I'll rekindle the fire. Get dressed, and hurry."

"What? Why? What good will it do to sit up by the fire? We don't know where he is, Tress."

"We might. Or we will. Put on your clothes."

I rolled out of bed and went to the bowl on the night stand, where I threw cold water on my face before beginning to dress myself, fumbling in the darkness for the clothes I had shed with abandon when I realized that Tress would not leave that night. By the time I had shrugged into them and crossed into the other room, Tress had candles, lit and the fire was alive again, flames licking hungrily at the new fuel she had piled on the freshly stirred coals.

She herself was still naked, crouched over the fire with her arms out to the heat. I crossed directly to her side and caressed the smooth, warm bareness of her, loving the firm softness beneath my hands. There was no thought of such matters in Tress's head, however, and she pushed me away, motioning me towards one of the two chairs flanking the fire as she ran lightly back into the bedchamber and emerged moments later wrapping a woollen blanket about her. She sat then in the chair opposite me and stared at me, wide-eyed and expectant.

"What?" I asked her. "What is it? You obviously expect me to say something significant." She made no reply. "Well, I have nothing to say, that I'm aware of. You'll have to prompt me."

"Rufio. We know where he is."

"No, we do not, Tress. It was dream, and I saw no signposts."

"Of course you did, you silly man. We don't know exactly where he is, that's true enough, but we know more than we did earlier today."

"How so?"

"Because you saw him lying in a hollow, in a clearing on a hillside. Is that not so? And he was lodged against two trees, with moss on their trunks, that he had scraped away."

"So?"

"Ach! Cay, that tells us much, or it tells *me* much. There was a rock face by him, too. That tells us more."

"I don't follow you, Tress."

She shook her head sharply, to silence me.

"He was lodged between two trees, you said, with a rock face behind him. How did you know he was on a hillside? And how was he positioned between these trees?"

I blinked, thinking back. "The ground sloped down, sharply. He was on his back, his head hanging backward, down the hill. The trees were close together, almost touching—perhaps a fork, two trunks of the same tree. His spine was arched over them. He had tried to push himself outward. That's when he clawed at the moss."

"So the moss was towards his head."

"Yes."

"And the rock face you saw. Where was it? You said behind him, but was it to his right or left?"

Again I sought the memory of my vision. "On his left, running parallel to where he lay."

"Aha! You looked in the wrong places."

I looked at her with a measure of scorn. "That makes as much sense as my dream."

"I know it does, even though you do not. Think about it, Cay! Moss grows mainly on the northern side of trees—every child learns that on first entering the woods—and it grows thickest on the very northern side. You saw Rufio lying with his feet pointing south between two northern-facing trees, his head hanging downhill to the north, with a cliff face on his left, his east side, facing west. That means he's on the hillside below the pass, where you didn't search, low down, in the river valley."

"How do you know he is low down?" I was convinced she was right.

"Because the moss was thick on the tree trunks. There's no thick moss on the trees on the high slopes."

I nodded, acknowledging my own short-sightedness, then shrugged.

"What," she asked immediately. "What's wrong?"

"Nothing, Tress, nothing really. I admire the way you make sense of my vision, but it was only a dream, and it was incomplete."

"How incomplete? I don't understand."

"I didn't tell you all of it, and the part I withheld makes nonsense of the whole thing."

She sat up straight, the blanket falling away from her shoulders, waiting for me to continue.

"I saw a man called Peter Ironhair just beyond the clearing, watching me."

"Peter Ironhair?" She was frowning. "You mean the ironsmith who tried to kill Arthur in Camulod, and then ran off to Cambria and thence to Cornwall?"

I sat staring at her. "You know," I said, eventually, "I find myself amazed by how much you know of things I've never told you."

"Shelagh has told me everything about you. I know everything there is to know." She stood up and crossed to where I sat, then settled into my lap, placing her right arm around my shoulders and wriggling until she was comfortable. The fire in the brazier snapped and spat sparks onto the stone flagging of the fireplace. When she was settled, she pulled my head down towards her breast and spoke into my ear.

"You know, Caius Merlyn Britannicus—" She paused, then leaned forward, blowing the warmth of her breath against my ear. "You know I love you, do you not?" She waited for an answer and I nodded, mutely. "Well," she continued, "know this, too. I believe in you, and in your gifts, which you think are some kind of curse. I believe that you have the gift of prophecy. What was it Master Lucanus called it? Foreknowledge. Is that the word?" She waited for an answer, and I nodded, again. "Well then, I believe in your power of foreknowledge, and I believe you have seen Rufio, lying hurt, perhaps dead—the gods forbid—in a place unsearched till now. Tomorrow, therefore, you must go down into the valley and along the cliffs until you reach the downfall of the fell behind us here, to the east."

"And what if he's not there? Not only will I appear to be a fool, but I might well have destroyed any chance of finding the real place where he is lying, at least in time to save his life."

"He will be there." She took my right hand in her left and slipped it between the folds of her blanket to lie between her breasts. "You feel that? My heart beating? My knowledge that you're right is as sure as the beating of my heart." She released my hand, but left it where it was, to behave as it would while she continued talking.

"As for the face of Master Ironhair, that is as far beyond me as it is beyond you. Shelagh told me you sometimes fail to understand all that you see. Is that true?"

"Aye, too frequently."

"Then this is one of those times. But remember what you saw—Ironhair's face where simple reason tells us it could never be. The meaning will come clear to you one of these days, and when it does, you'll know what to do. In the meantime, however, you have to find Rufio."

She paused, leaning out and away from me to squint at my reflection in the light of the fire. "You're still not sure, are you?" I shook my head slowly and she continued. "Very well, here's what to do. Send out the search parties tomorrow, exactly as you had planned to do, to cover the territories you selected earlier tonight, but go by yourself, with several of the men you trust most and who know you best, and search the area you dreamed about."

"Dedalus," I said. "And Donuil. Luke's too old for the kind of terrain we'll be covering, and Philip. Falvo and Benedict should remain with their troops. But they're Rufio's closest friends."

"Then take them with you. They have officers beneath them they can trust, and the troops will all be split up, anyway. Take Rufio's friends with you. Shelagh won't stay behind, either, when one of the men she thinks of as her own is lost. Take her and the four boys. One of you will find him."

"So be it." I pulled her to me and kissed her long and deeply, overflowing with relief and determination, and soon we returned to bed, as impatient for each other as we were for the night to recede.

It was, in fact, Shelagh who found Rufio, in precisely the circumstances I had dreamed, at the farthest end of the valley beneath our escarpment, in an area that I would never have thought even to penetrate, let alone search. And, as Fortune would have it, Shelagh was accompanied by Lucanus, who had refused to remain behind in Mediobogdum, claiming that Rufio would have great need of his skills if he was still alive. I was far beneath them with Arthur and Bedwyr, almost on the valley floor, when they made their discovery, but their cries reached the ears of Dedalus on the slope between them and us, and young Bedwyr's keen ears picked up Ded's bellowing in the distance above our heads.

I knew the clearing, immediately, as the site of my dream. Shelagh and Luke were on their knees beside Rufio, working quickly and with great concentration. Dedalus stood over them, his face a picture of anguish and anger, and beside him Gwin and young Ghilly gazed in pop-eyed horror at the ministrations being performed nearby.

"How is he?" I called, dismounting hurriedly.

"He's alive, but barely," Ded answered.

I turned towards Arthur and Bedwyr, both of whom were preparing to dismount, and ordered them to stay where they were, then I made my way forward to where I could see Rufio. *Black and white,* I thought immediately, my memory taking me back to the day when I rode into the carnage of the scene at my cousin Uther's last battle. Then, as now, the white had been the pallor of dead flesh and the black the ugliness of dried and crusted blood. Rufio appeared dead, despite Ded's statement to the contrary.

Luke had already removed Rufio's armour, slicing through the leather straps that held it in place with a sharp knife, then cutting away the clothing beneath to lay bare the awful wounds that marred our friend's shockingly pale flesh. I had suspected an accident of some kind, perhaps even an attack, but nothing had prepared me for the sight of Rufio's wounds. He had been savaged, not merely wounded; his flesh lay open at the left shoulder, scored in great, parallel gashes, two of which extended all along his upper arm, and his face was invisible beneath a mask of dried blood that plastered his hair flat against his head so that it seemed to be a polished black skull.

"What in the name of God—"

"It was a bear. Look at that." Ded nodded towards something on the ground almost by my feet and I looked down to see an enormous black paw, tipped with claws longer than my fingers. It had been severed cleanly at what would have been the wrist on a human limb. Mute with disbelief, I looked from it to Rufio. Dedalus read my mind.

"Rufe must have brought one of the two new swords with him. I know of nothing else that could have taken off a thing like that."

I looked all around, but saw nothing. "Where is it now, then?"

"Stuck in the beast, I'd think. Nothing else would explain why it left him here without eating him."

I sucked in a great breath, to settle both my stomach and my mind. Dedalus was right. Lacking a paw, the beast should have been sufficiently enraged to destroy Rufio utterly. Only a greater wound, and greater pain, could have driven it off before it killed him.

I was aware of Lucanus issuing orders to the others who had arrived, and somewhere in the back of my mind I knew that he was telling them to build a litter in which to carry Rufio back to the fort, or at least out of the woods to where Luke could have space to do what must be done to cleanse and bind those dreadful wounds. My thoughts, however, were bound up in what lay before me.

"We have to find it," I said.

"What, the sword or the bear?"

"Both. The one we need, the other we need dead."

"Aye, granted. But I'm not going up against that thing, wounded as it is, without a score of spears around me."

"It should be dead by this time."

"Aye, and so should Rufe, but he's alive."

"You're right." I turned towards the boys. "Arthur, take young Ghilly with you and Bedwyr and find the nearest search party. Tell them we've found Rufio, but that we need assistance to track and kill a wounded bear—a very large bear. We need men with spears, as many as you can find and not less than a score. Tell whoever you find in charge to send someone back to the fort with word to call off the other searchers in the hills above the fort, and to have the Infirmary prepared with fresh bedding and bandages and boiling water. Lucanus always requires large quantities of boiled water. Go now, quickly, then lead the others back to join us here. We'll be waiting for you. And be careful! We don't know where that bear might be. If you hear it, or see it, stay well clear of it. Go!"

The boys were gone in a matter of moments, and shortly thereafter Luke and Shelagh left, too, walking one on either side of the litter and each holding one of the ends of a leather strap, Rufio's swordbelt, which they had passed beneath the centre of the bier, ready to take up the strain should any of the four bearers, Donuil, Philip, Falvo and Benedict, slip or lose their balance on the treacherous hillside.

Ded and I watched them leave, then turned our attention to the blood-soaked ground around us, looking for the trail of blood left by the departing bear. It was not hard to find, and from the wide swath of blood-smeared destruction leading off downhill into the woods it soon became obvious that the animal had charged away, blinded with pain and fury and bafflement, into the heart of the forest. We went no farther than ten paces along the trail before we turned back to wait for the others, and for the next hour we stood close together, seldom speaking and staring tensely into the silent forest all around us. I found myself looking for the tree that had concealed Ironhair in my dream, but I failed to find it.

"What about him?"

"Who?"

"Ironhair. You said his name."

I wasn't aware that I had spoken. "I dreamed of him last night, that he was here."

Ded turned slowly to look at me. "Ironhair was here, in your dream, with Rufe? D'you mean that?"

I shrugged. "No, not with Rufe—farther back, among the trees. It was but part of the dream, a nonsensical part."

"Hmm." For a long time I thought he would say no more than that solitary grunt, but then he continued. "I don't know anything much about this power of yours, Merlyn, but it seems to me that no part of it can be nonsense when so much of it is potent. If you dreamed of Ironhair being here, then in some way he must have been here."

"Tress thinks the same. She believes the meaning of it will become clear to me, eventually."

"What was that?"

I cocked my head, wishing for the hundredth time in my life that I had the sharp hearing of my brother Ambrose. "I didn't hear anything."

"I did. There it is again. It's the others, finally."

Sure enough, moments later, I heard the first sounds of our approaching reinforcements making their way up the hillside to where we waited.

As soon as they arrived—Philip and some forty of his infantry, with Arthur and Bedwyr in the lead on horseback—we split them up into groups of six and led them into the forest, following the clear-marked blood trail of the wounded beast. Those of us who had been mounted left our mounts tethered in the clearing, safely distanced from the bloodied area where we had found Rufio. Philip walked by my side at the point of the hunt. The others, seven groups of six, spread out behind us, each successive pair of groups farther out on the flanks of those ahead, so that we formed a sweep that would have been a hundred paces wide, had we been able to proceed in order. The steeply pitched hillside, however, densely treed as it was, made any kind of orderly progress impossible.

"What's that?" Philip had seen something, and I turned immediately to see where he pointed. I saw the gleam of metal in a thicket that our quarry had charged through, and we had found our missing sword. From the streaks of blood on the blade and the increased profusion of blood on the grass all around, it was clear that the cross-hilt had snagged in the bushes and been wrenched free as the bear passed on.

"It has to be dead," Philip muttered. "It must be. This blood's been here since yesterday and there's too much of it around for the thing to have survived. And look, when the sword came out of the wound, it must have split it wide open. Look how the blood is so much thicker here, beyond the point where we found the sword." He glanced at me. "Don't you agree?"

I nodded, and he raised his voice, shouting to his men. "Stay sharp! The animal's close by. Logic says it must be dead, but until we've skinned the carcass, take nothing for granted."

We found it less than fifty paces farther up the hill, and it had been dead for a long time. It was enormous, humpbacked—fully as large as the behemoth I had faced outside the walls of Athol's fort in Eire—and it was ancient. One of its eyes had been lost in some long-ago battle, and its thick, matted old coat, where we could see it beneath the blood that clotted it, was criss-crossed with long-healed scars and battle wounds. Its coat was hoary, almost silver with age; only its three remaining paws were still black as night.

I stood there, gazing at it as the others crowded around, exclaiming with awe. Where they saw size and incredible strength, however, I saw only mystery and enigma. I saw Ironhair, plainly, in the colour of the great beast's coat, and yet I wondered, still, at my own translation. Had I seen the bear, early in my dream, and its colour made me think of Ironhair? Or was there some other, supernatural connection? Did this bear, somehow, represent Ironhair, or the threat of Ironhair? I had no way of knowing. I had never been a believer in the supernatural, and I was loath to begin to give any credence to the matter then, at that stage of my life.

One of Philip's men had a long skinning knife and was stropping it against the tautened end of his belt as he stood gazing down at the dead animal.

"Well," Philip asked. "What do you think?"

The man grunted and leaned down, grasping a handful of the animal's thick coat and tugging at it. "Nah, this thing's been dead for almost a full day. My guess is it'll be a waste of time to skin it, though it's a pity. Too late to cure the hide—it's too far gone. The hair'll fall right off it, now, no matter what you do." He glanced up again, at Philip. "I'll go ahead, though, if you want me to."

Philip looked to me, and I shook my head.

"He's right. It's too far gone by now. Leave it to rot, and let's go home."

We turned and left it there, with its three fearsome sets of claws, and as we made our way back down to where we had tethered our horses, the talk among the men was all of Rufio and his chances for survival. My mind, however, was filled with Peter Ironhair.

The final and most astonishing incident in the Autumn of the Beasts occurred the very next day. Even now, recalling it once more as I have so frequently in the years that have elapsed, the memory of it fills me with wonder and even religious awe.

Much of what people regard as Fortune, whether good or ill, depends upon the recipient's being in a particular place at a specific time. I once saw a horseman killed by a lightning bolt that struck a tree beneath which he was passing. The impact of the bolt shattered the tree and he was killed by a falling limb. I had been watching his progress, for he was one of my men, on his way to me with a message, and afterwards it became clear to me that his death occurred by the merest, most random chance. His horse's gait brought him to that place at that time. Had his mount been travelling more slowly, he would have survived, but his chosen speed brought him beneath the tree at the precise moment when the lightning struck, and his horse was still rearing in terror when the limb fell.

We had begun to quarry the friable local stone from an exposed hill face above the fort the previous summer, using the material we dug out to make repairs on the most dilapidated stretches of the fort's wall and several of the corner towers. The local stone fractured easily, splitting naturally into long slabs that varied in length and width but maintained a uniform thickness, anywhere from a thumb's length to a handsbreadth in size. The entire fort of Mediobogdum had been built of this stone, save only for the main gateposts, which were of quarried red sandstone blocks shipped down to Ravenglass from farther up the coast.

The work of refurbishment, small in scale though it was, was not strictly necessary to our welfare but had been undertaken for one excellent and self-evident reason: the garrison soldiers tended to grow bored up here on our rocky platform, miles away from Ravenglass, and the hard labour of their compulsory daily stint in the quarry kept them out of mischief and in good physical shape. Rome's legions had built the great Wall of Hadrian across the north of Britain centuries before for precisely the same purposes.

Benedict's garrison troops were now the third such body to be employed in our quarry, and the scope of the work had been extended to accommodate the increased manpower made available by the additional infantry contingent. Our other communal workplace, in the forest where we had set up our timber-felling operations, lay about half a mile downhill and to the west of the quarry.

My recent decision to leave Mediobogdum in the spring had called the need for all such labour into question, but I had insisted that it be continued, reasoning that we might return here some day in the future, and that the work of repairing the walls and trimming, shaping and dry-stacking the timber baulks we had cut would fend off boredom during the winter ahead. No one questioned my decision, and the work continued in both locations.

On the day when the events I am about to describe took place, I had ridden up to the quarry with Benedict and Philip, simply to review the situation up there and to pass the time of day with our troopers, from the viewpoint of keeping up morale. It was a fine day, with the definite snap of the first, mild frosts of autumn in the air. Philip became involved in a technical discussion with the overseer of the quarry, an engineer from his own company, concerning the effects of frost on lines of cleavage or something equally incomprehensible to us, so Benedict and I left him to it and set out to stroll together down the half-mile-long stretch of open hillside to the forest clearing, where the rest of our work parties were sawing lumber. We left our horses at the quarry and walked.

We talked about Rufio and his condition. Lucanus's extraordinary skills had given us hope that our old friend might survive a series of wounds that ought to have killed him. No one was yet making any wagers on Rufe's chances either way, but everyone was convinced that his carefully cozened survival had been little short of miraculous. His right arm and shoulder had been badly mangled, the flesh shredded from the bones by the bear's razor-sharp claws, and he had four enormous puncture wounds in his left shoulder, two in front and two behind, where the animal's monstrous canine fangs had sought to crunch clean through him. His right femur had been broken cleanly, and several of his ribs crushed, but his skull appeared to be intact and the only other wound he had incurred was a deep, clean slash, probably caused by a claw, on his right thigh.

Luke's own prognosis was cautiously optimistic. His major concern was the danger of putrefaction in the bite marks and claw cuts, but he had cleaned the wounds thoroughly and carefully, making liberal use of powerful astringents that, he assured me, Rufio would have been unable to bear had he been conscious at the time of their application. If Rufe could pass the next few days without developing a fever, Lucanus now believed he would probably survive, although he might never swing a sword again.

As we walked away from Philip and the others, picking our way carefully among the stones that littered the sloping ground, Benedict began reminiscing about some of the exploits that had kept Rufio consistently in conflict with his superiors—of whom I had been the senior—in earlier times. I was half listening to him, smiling as I remembered some of my own experiences with Rufio's antics and trying to avoid falling on the loose stones underfoot, when Benedict suddenly stopped walking and raised one hand to press it against my chest, stopping me, too.

"Hey," he said. "Look at this."

I turned to look where he was looking and for a few moments, before some inner alarm began clanging in my breast, I did not know what to make of what I was seeing. I know that the events that followed occurred very quickly, but each time I relive them in my mind, and I do so frequently, everything seems to happen very, very slowly.

We were not yet out of the small quarry. The cut itself was at our back, with one steep face—the cliff that had attracted us to begin quarrying here—directly to our left; the short, mountain grass, scattered with shrubs, resumed again some twenty paces below the point we had reached. There was an animal, a small fox, trotting up the hill directly towards us, its tongue lolling sideways from its mouth as it approached. My first thought was that it had somehow failed to see us, for foxes are timid creatures that avoid any contact with mankind, but I quickly dismissed that idea, since the beast was staring directly at us.

"Tame little bugger, isn't he?"

Benedict's question chilled me abruptly, for no truly wild animal is tame. I looked again, much more sharply now. The fox had halved the distance between us and I could hear it growling as it came, its pace unvarying, directly for us. I looked again at its open mouth and lolling tongue and saw thick, ropy saliva slavering from its jaws.

"No, Ben, it's not tame, it's mad—rabid! It's attacking and if it bites one of us, we're dead. Quick, up the cliff. Move!"

Benedict stood there, hesitating, his hand starting to move towards the hilt of his short-sword, but I punched him on the arm then grabbed him, propelling him in front of me towards the cliff face. "Climb, dammit! You'll need both hands. Get up there!"

I was less than half a pace behind him as he reached the base of the cliff and began scrambling upward, scrabbling for handholds. I scooped up a large flake of stone. The fox was still coming directly towards us, no more than twenty paces distant. I hurled the stone, but the animal gave no sign of having seen it. Belatedly I remembered the long cavalry sword hanging between my shoulder blades. No time now to unhook it, unsheathe it and prepare myself. I launched myself at the cliff after Benedict.

"It might follow us up, if it's strong enough to climb! If it does, be ready to kill it when it reaches the top. Don't try to stab it—cut the damn thing in two!"

The cliff we were scaling was perhaps fifteen paces high at this point, sloping steeply and not difficult to climb, either for us or for the fox.

"Whoreson's coming up," Benedict gasped.

"Let it come! Keep climbing."

I grasped an outcrop of rock and it broke off in my hand just as I was hauling my whole weight up on it.

I knew instinctively that I would fall. And I knew, too, without looking, that the rabid animal was immediately beneath me. For a long moment I hung there, clawing at the cliff before I toppled. Somehow I twisted around as I fell, to slither down on my back, jarring myself painfully during my descent.

Then several things happened simultaneously: the point of my sword lodged in the cliff face, ripping its retaining hook from the ring between my shoulders. The fox suddenly appeared level with my eyes, slashing at me. I jerked my arm away from the thick rope of saliva that looped itself the length of my forearm, away from the gnashing teeth. And I swept the beast's front legs from under it, so that it fell with me, end over end.

I landed at the bottom on my feet, hard, hands at my back, catapulted myself forward into a rolling dive and slammed my shoulder against a large stone. Then I was on my feet again, running, looking back over my shoulder. The fox was already coming after me.

Vaguely aware of voices shouting above and beyond me, I threw myself headlong over the uneven ground. I may have managed a score or more long, bounding paces before my ankle twisted on an outcrop and sent me sprawling, slamming down hard. Slightly stunned, I whipped myself around, onto my elbows and backside to face my fate.

The fox was leaping for my throat, yellow teeth bared, when the shadow glided over me. There was a mighty slamming of bodies together, like a fist striking flesh, and an enormous eagle hung just above the ground before me, gripping the limp body of the fox in its powerful talons.

For a moment, the bird hung there, stationary before my eyes, its huge wings measuring strong, steady beats. Slowly, firmly, it stroked the air, its pinions nearly brushing the ground, holding it and its prey aloft. Three, four long, deep strokes gradually propelled the two upward, further into the eagle's own element, away from the earth. Each ensuing beat drew them higher, hauled them deliberately forward and away from me, above the trees.

I pushed myself to my knees, panting, and then to my feet to watch each surge of those mighty wings. My salvation, the magnificence of the eagle, the miracle of its intervention transfixed me. I strained to follow the bird's unhurried progress, watching it rise higher and higher above my head, in great, soaring circles, until it appeared to be the size of a tiny sparrow. And then it released the fox, and I watched the animal fall to earth and heard it smash among the rocks behind me moments later. The eagle was now a mere speck against the blue firmament, moving away, towards the distant Fells.

What had brought this eagle to this place at this precise moment? Perhaps God truly did watch over the lives of individual men, as the Church taught. Had the eagle been sent expressly to save me? The sane, rational part of me rejected the notion as nonsense, yet I could not help but wonder whether I had been spared for some specific purpose.

The arrival of my friends interrupted my reverie. They were as full of wonder as I was at what they had seen, so I said nothing and pondered all these things in my heart.

Late that afternoon, during the general discussion before dinner, when everyone had gathered around the big fire outside the main gates, Shelagh and Donuil came to where I sat with my arm about Tress's waist.

"It's a beautiful evening, Cay. Why don't we go for a stroll?"

Her tone was anything but casual, and I looked from her to Donuil, and then to Tress, who had already moved away from me and was standing, pulling her shawl tight across her arms and shoulders. Clearly, they had something to say to me that they wanted no one else to overhear. I simply nodded, saying nothing, and stood up to join them. We made our way down towards the road, Shelagh and Tress chatting animatedly between themselves and Donuil and I strolling in comfortable silence.

When we were a good hundred paces from the nearest of our neighbours, Shelagh moved next to me, linking her arm through mine.

"What's this about?" I asked her. She tilted her head back and looked up at me in wide-eyed, exaggerated innocence, but I cut her off before she could form any kind of reply. "Don't throw that wide-eyed look at me, Shelagh, I know you too well. You and this innocent-looking woman here, not to mention my good friend and sometime adjutant, have words to say to me and you've plotted this, to get me here alone with the three of you, so that I'm the only one who doesn't know what's going on. So talk. What's this about?"

She grinned, but then her expression grew serious immediately.

"Dreams, Caius, what else?"

"Go on."

She ran the tip of her tongue across her teeth, making her upper lip bulge out as her tongue moved, then she made a "tutting" sound and plunged ahead.

"Do you remember the first dream you and I discussed?"

I nodded. "Of course I do. It was in Eire, the first night we really met, when your father and the others went off to look for the fellow Rud, who had disappeared in the forest. . . ."

Shelagh had been terrified that I would expose her secret—that she too had prophetic dreams—and that she would be banished from her home and people for sorcery. It had been difficult to convince her that her secret was safe in my keeping, but once I had done so, she had told me everything, without reservation.

She had dreamed about a bear, a boar and a dragon that battled. Only the bear survived. It rode on the back of a white bull and it met another bear. All three then fought among themselves in a ring of wolves. The first bear was badly wounded and thought to die, until a great eagle rode in on a broadening beam of light. The eagle attacked the wolves and scattered them. It killed the dominant wolf and ripped the coat from its back, exposing the crimson scales of a dragon beneath. Finally, Shelagh saw me, watching from the shadows, and saw the crimson dragon settled on my breast and the eagle come and sit on my shoulder.

I recounted this to Shelagh, speaking straightforwardly, omitting nothing, and when I was finished no one rushed to break the silence.

"Hmm," Shelagh said, eventually. "Your remembrance is surprisingly complete after ten years."

I smiled as I contradicted her. "Nothing surprising there at all. You were the only person I had ever met who dreamed like me, and your dream was about me. Of course I remembered every detail. But why would you ask me about it now?"

I saw that I had really surprised her now. "You really have to ask me that? Can it be possible you see no connection between that dream and what happened today?"

I fought to keep my face clear of expression, not wishing to hurt her by seeming to scoff at her, for in truth, even now, I could see no connection. The eagle in her dream had slain a giant wolf. Mine had killed a tiny fox. "I can see that you do," was all I said.

"Of course I do, and so should you. But you should know, too, that the dream came back to me, two nights ago, and this time it was different."

I frowned, wondering where she was going with this, the civilized, sceptical Roman within me—the fearful cynic who shied back from recognizing potency in dreams—warring with the superstitious but unwillingly credulous Celt. I kept silent, however, seeing the tension in her and knowing she had more to say but would not speak it until I asked her to. "How, different, then—and how different?"

She paused, watching me closely, then continued. "I have never forgotten that dream, Cay. It seemed too . . . portentous . . . too important to disregard, and in the years that have gone by since then, I've made some sense of parts of it, at least."

"How so? I never have made sense of it, save for the obvious—but then, I have not thought of it in years."

She said nothing for a count of five heartbeats, then cocked her head to one side. " 'Save for the obvious,' you said. What was obvious?"

"I was. The bear is my emblem—Camulod's emblem, if you like, as the dragon was Uther's and therefore Cambria's. Together, Camulod and Cambria destroyed Lot, the boar of Cornwall. That much was obvious. But the ring of wolves and their giant leader? There, I confess, I lost the track, other than knowing that the wolves are enemies and encirclement by such threatens destruction. . . . The white bull means nothing to me, either. Nor does the eagle, other than that it signified the Roman legions, long since gone and never to return."

Shelagh nodded her head, glancing at Donuil and Tressa, both of whom were listening closely. "I've seen more, since yesterday—found more to understand—than before."

"Like what? Tell me, now that you have me ready to hear."

"Well, the white bull, and perhaps the eagle."

I thought of the forces allied to and opposed to my own, considering their emblems, and suddenly much became clear to me. "Of course! How blind can I be? The eagle is from the Pendragon! Their War Chief wears the eagle-crowned helmet. I remember Uther's grandfather, Ullic Pendragon, wearing that emblem."

"Aye, but it's more than that, Caius. Many of the Pendragon Celts are warriors, who worship the white bull of Mithras, the warrior's god. No—" She raised her hand to silence me before I could protest. "Mithras was not a Roman god. The Roman soldiers worshipped him, but Mithras was ancient before Rome was built, and he has had many names throughout the ages. But by them all, he is the white bull god."

"Wait you now." I accepted her words on Mithras completely, but I still had doubts. "I'm growing confused. How can the Pendragon be both bull and eagle, in your dream?"

"I did not say they were. You said that. I think the eagle in my dream is young Arthur. Listen, now, to how my dream the other night was different. In it, the bear and the dragon fought and killed the boar, but only the bear survived. If we accept what you call the obvious, then that must be immutable, for Lot and Uther are both dead. The bear then rode upon a white bull's back to meet another creature, something like a bear, that was yet not a bear . . . something far more fearsome and savage, as though a bear had mated with a wolf, or some other dire beast. It was a . . ." She hesitated, seeking a word that she did not possess.

"A chimera," I said.

"A what?"

"A monstrous, mythical creature, fashioned of different parts of savage beasts."

"Aye, then it was a . . . chimera."

"And what befell when these things met?"

Shelagh raised her chin and met my eye.

"They fought in the ring of wolves, among waterfalls of blood . . . and when the fight was over, the bear was sorely wounded. He thought to die alone, but then a sudden darkness descended, and with it, launched from the shoulders of the bull on a broadening beam of light, came the eagle to save him, and the . . . the chimera withdrew, and all the wolves were scattered."

I nodded, swallowing an urge to grin at the awestruck expression with which Donuil was staring at his wife. Instead of smiling, I made my voice more jocular than I had meant to.

"And so the bear recovered. So I live?"

But Shelagh had no smile for her response. "No, Cay. The bear did not recover. It fell dead. And yet I saw it rise again from within itself—one form supine and dead, the other, identical, rising from it whole and alive, to walk away. But as it went, it changed before my eyes into a dragon with bright-gleaming scales. And then there you were, as in my former dream, the dragon on your breast, the eagle on your shoulder, and yourself fading away into the gathering darkness. . . ."

"I see," I muttered eventually, although in fact I saw nothing. Any meaning that she might have expected me to draw from what she had told me was completely obscure to me. "So what you are telling me is that your dream would make of me some Christ figure, rising from the dead?"

She shook her head, not in denial, but in acknowledgment of her ignorance, and for a time we all stood silent.

It was Donuil who spoke next, his pragmatic sensibilities unmoved by all this talk of dreams and omens. "We'd better head back. They're getting ready to serve the food, and I'm famished. If we're late, we'll be likely to go hungry."

"Hardly that," Shelagh replied, turning to smile up at her hulking husband. "What you really mean is that if we're late, someone else will be ahead of you in reaching the prime cuts." She looked back at me. "Anyway, that's what I wanted you to know. My dream was different the second time, and although I don't know the significance of all the changes, I do know, deep inside, that they are important. And the similarities between parts of that dream and what happened to you today are too striking to ignore. Your emblem has always been the bear. The danger you faced today wasn't from wolves, but it was from a rabid canine creature, and the eagle saved your life, destroying the creature in the process. That is not coincidence, Cay."

"Then what is it, Shelagh? Magic?"

She squinted up at me, cocking her head to one side, then shrugged one shoulder. "It might be. Who am I to know or even you?"

"It doesn't matter," Tress said, speaking for the first time. "What it is, I mean—magic or not. Something has changed, and it's clear to me that you're the victorious one, Cay, since the eagle saved your life. What it really means will become clear in time."

"You, too?" I smiled at her. "Ah, well. I'll take your combined word for that. And I'll heed your warning, Donuil, for I'm half starved, too. Let's eat."

It would be years before I learned that Horsa called his savage Danes his Sea-Wolves and took pride in being their Wolf King. That knowledge alone, had we possessed it then, would have gone far towards explaining the chimera in Shelagh's dream. But had we known it then, it might also have terrified and awed us to the point at which we would have become impotent to act the way some power had ordained we must.

By the time we entered the dining hall many of our companions had already filled their platters and seated themselves at the long tables with their food. We crossed directly to the serving tables and mingled with the people there, and Tress and I ended up being separated from Donuil and Shelagh. I helped myself to a broad, wooden platter and laid a large, thick slice of fresh-baked bread on it, completely covering the flat surface. One of the women serving us that night—a red-cheeked, smiling matron in her late thirties whose name was Monica—waved me forward and sliced a succulent, dripping slab of beef, marbled with fat, from the huge roasted hindquarter in front of her. She placed it on top of my bread and then poured a thick, steaming gravy of onions, greens and salted beef juice drippings over the whole, more than doubling the weight in my hand. I thanked her and moved away, looking over my shoulder to make sure that Tress was behind me. Most of the places at the closest tables were already filled, and Tress nodded to one in the far corner, where Hector sat by himself. We made our way to join him, and for a time thereafter none of us spoke, each intent on the business of eating.

Finally, when I could eat no more, I pushed my platter aside and sat back to look about me. The first person I saw was young Arthur, seated at a table on my left in the row ahead of mine, deep in conversation with a brightly attractive young woman who sat close beside him on the bench. As soon as I saw them there, heads close together, talking with that feverish intensity that full-grown adults seldom seem able to duplicate, my discussion with Derek sprang back full-blown into my mind. I had to fight the urge to go and join the two young people immediately, so eager was I to listen to all they had to say to each other. Of course I gave no outward sign of my interest, but merely sat back, focusing my gaze on them and watching intently. I was aware that Tress was deep in conversation now with Hector, to my right, but I had no idea what they were discussing. Tress, I knew, could tell me in an instant who the young girl was, but for the time being, at least, I preferred to make my own observations.

From the way the girl sat staring wide-eyed into Arthur's face, I could tell that she was entranced and enraptured with the lad. He, however, had his back to me, so I could form no real impression of his reaction to her. From the way his head hovered close to hers, though, I could guess that her admiration was being returned in full measure.

Arthur said something humorous, for the girl broke out into a clear, tinkling laugh that carried clearly to where I sat. Then she scooted even closer to him, grasping him by the right biceps to gain additional leverage as she pressed herself against his side. As she did so, another girl, this one a pretty, fair-haired thing with an open, laughing, wholesome-looking face, approached their table and seated herself on Arthur's other side. The first girl stiffened noticeably, tossing her hair, and sat there rigid while Arthur spoke to the newcomer, turning his head towards her so that I could see his expression. He spoke easily and graciously, although I could not hear what he was saying, but while his head was turned away from the companion at his back, she leaned forward, peering over his shoulder and piercing the other girl with a look that ought to have thrown her to the floor. The new girl ignored this hostility completely, leaning close and saying something in a whisper to Arthur, who remained blissfully oblivious to the tension resonating in the air about him.

"Rena and Stella," Tress's voice said in my ear. "They're at each other's throats over him nowadays. I wonder which one he'll choose tonight?"

I snapped my head around to look at her. "What d'you mean, tonight? Are you saying he chose one of them *last* night?"

She laughed aloud, looking at me askance. "I don't know. He may have. The gods all know he could have. The girls buzz around him like bees around honey, and so they should. He's a fine young man."

"He is a boy." I knew, even as I spoke the words, that I should have kept silent.

Tress reached over in front of me and gathered up my discarded platter, laying it atop her own, and for several moments I thought she would say no more. But then she turned more fully towards me.

"He is a boy fully intent on reaching manhood as quickly as he can. As you must have been, at his age. Don't tell me you disapprove? Would you prefer him to be lifeless and unattractive, distasteful to women, like Derek's Droc?"

I shrugged, feeling foolish. "I hadn't noticed it till now, that's all I meant. Who are the girls?"

"I told you, Rena and Stella. They are from Ravenglass, like all the other girls in Mediobogdum."

"Aye," I grunted. "But whose girls are they, and what do they do around here?"

Tress was grinning now. "They live and grow, like all young people. Stella, the fair-haired one, works with her mother, Rhea, who works with me. She'll be a good needleworker one day, that girl, and she has a good head on her shoulders, although it's turned askew right now whenever Arthur comes around. Rena is the daughter of Longinus."

"Longinus? Is she, by God? And why have I not seen her here before?"

"Because, my love, you've not had eyes for it. You notice only those with whom you have some pressing business."

"Hmm!" I sat silent for a while, staring again at Arthur and the two young rivals for his attention. If he was aware of any tension between them, he gave no indication, and shortly afterward all three rose and left the hall. I watched them as they went out, and then I turned back to Tress.

"How long has this been going on, this thing with the girls? Does Shelagh know about it?"

Tress laughed. "Of course! Think you Shelagh is blind? Everyone knows, Cay. There's no secret to it."

"And does she permit it?"

Tress raised her eyebrows in amazement. "Permit it? How would she stop it? As well try to turn the tide by disapproving of its progress. That's a silly thing to ask."

"So she permits it."

"Permits what, Cay? The boy is growing, awakening to himself. Shelagh has no more ways of stopping that than you have. But acknowledgment is not encouragement. She keeps young Arthur on a short, tight rein at night. Other than that, there is nothing she can do."

I shook my head. "And I had not seen it until now."

Tress bent forward and kissed my cheek, caressing my chin lovingly as she did so. "I told you, love, it had no importance to you then, so you paid no attention."

I would in future, I swore to myself, and for the remainder of that night I spent my time wondering where Arthur was and what he was doing.

XVII

It STARTED TO rain in the week that followed the incident of the eagle and the fox, and for the following fourteen days our entire world was wet and dank and grey, with thick banks of fog and mist roiling up from the valley beneath us like displaced clouds, seeking reunion with the lowering clouds above. The forested hillsides around us faded into shifting shrouds of textured blackness, and we lost sight completely of the high Fells that overlooked our mountain perch.

It was impossible to be out of doors and dry at the same time. Everything we wore became waterlogged, doubled in weight and smelled of dampness. Exposed wrists and necks and knees grew red and chapped from the constant, chilly friction of moisture-laden hems and, in the case of the garrison soldiers, the chafing, unyielding edges of cold, wet armour. Not once in that entire period did the sun break through the overcast. From time to time, every few days, the skies above us would lighten slightly, as though to hint at brightness struggling to break through, but such intervals were always short-lived; the layers of cloud between us and the promise of new light would always grow heavier again, and more dense.

Our people became dispirited with the lack of brightness, the late, leaden dawns and the early, depressing nightfalls. Even the horses, cattle and swine huddled miserably beneath any shelter they could find, too listless to forage for food, depending upon us to bring them oats and fodder. Occasionally, we would hear thunder rolling somewhere in the distance, but no lightning flashed. We grew inured to the heavy, dull silence that pressed down on us, broken only by the constant patter and hiss and the unending, listless drip of falling water.

And then, late in the afternoon of the fourteenth dreary day, I emerged from one of the buildings and looked up to see a hint of yellow, filtered brightness on the hillside above us to the south. I waited there, almost stoically, for the phenomenon to fade. Instead, it grew stronger, and the dull yellow effulgence strengthened and spread outward, hazily illuminating a large stretch of tree-covered hillside. The sky above was still grey, but it was the lightest grey I had seen now in weeks, so I leaned my shoulder against the doorpost and lingered there, feeling a tiny thrill of anticipation fluttering in my chest.

Then, through an unseen break in the clouds, a quartet of sunbeams lanced down to splash real light on the distant trees, bringing the late-autumn colours into startling prominence. Still I remained, fascinated to see the sunbeams thicken and spread outward, joined by others now and melding together so that, all at once, the entire hillside opposite me was awash in light, reflecting and refracting flashes of colour and dazzling glare. When the clouds began to break apart, bright blue patches appeared where before there had been nothing but dull, impenetrable greyness. A sudden brilliance blinded me, as sunlight reflected from a puddle on the ground in the roadway outside the building where I stood, and I knew, finally, that the weather had broken. I considered going back into the room I had just left and telling the others the good news, but then I decided to leave them to the pleasure of discovering it for themselves, and I walked away towards my own quarters, whistling merrily.

The brief period of warm days that followed was summer's last song. After that, the evening temperatures plummeted, and the mornings crackled with thick hoarfrost that sometimes lingered until noon. A few, errant snowflakes drifted down on us from time to time, and the people of our little commune threw themselves urgently into a tempestuous flurry of last-minute preparations for the long winter months ahead. We men piled up vast supplies of fuel for the furnaces and fires, while the women cleaned and aired our living and communal quarters, scrubbing the concrete floors and covering them with fresh, dried rushes brought up months earlier from the wetlands below. In addition to these tasks, men laboured alongside women in drying, salting, smoking and curing the last of our meats for storage: pork, wild boar meat, venison, poultry and small game—though little of that, that year—beef and fish, both saltwater and fresh. The fat salvaged from the butchering was rendered down in vats to give us oil for cooking and for mixing with lye to prepare soap. The last yield of berries, wild apples, plums and nuts were gathered in and carefully preserved, and several late-arriving wagonloads of bagged corn, millet and mixed grain from the fields around Ravenglass had to be husked and ground into meal and flour. Some vegetables—turnips and cabbages and kale—we had grown ourselves in the few tiny patches of arable land we had been able to identify close by the fort, and these, too, had to be collected and stored in cool, well-ventilated storage rooms. The granaries and warehouses of the old Roman Horrea were still intact, after hundreds of years, and we made full use of them, so that before the first snow fell, towards the end of December, all our work was complete and we felt confident about facing the winter.

I was one of the very few in Mediobogdum who knew that almost a hundred years before, the Emperor Constantine, assuming the role of an apostle, had decreed December 25th, the date of the ancient Roman festival of Saturnalia, to be the proven birth date of the Christ. None had argued against him, despot that he was, and despite a widespread conviction that the "proof" on which the imperial decree was based smacked tangibly of political contrivance and expedience, what had been a pagan celebration from time immemorial was Christianized and sanctified, made respectable and sacred almost overnight. The smug churchmen had won a double victory: they had nullified a godless reminder of ancient times and evil ways, and asserted their superiority, and that of their religion, over all the people of the Roman world, by creating a festival of Christian worship at a time when all the world prepared for festivities in any case. But to all those old enough to remember their elders talking of what they could recall of what had been before, December was still the time of Saturnalia, when hard-working folk celebrated together their successful efforts to bring in their harvests and prepare for winter.

Our Saturnalia that year was swelled by the presence of six unexpected guests, emissaries from Camulod, bearing letters from home for me and several of the others. They had descended from the saddleback of the high pass in the opening flurries of the first serious snowfall, thankful to have made the long and hazardous journey so late in the year without serious mishap. Their arrival itself warned me that the letter they bore for me from Ambrose must contain grave tidings, and so I excused myself from the company to read it in the privacy of my own quarters. It was substantial, and I read it with steadily increasing apprehension, noting curiously that it contained no opening salutation naming me.

> Brother:
> I hope this finds you in good health, although I fear it will do nothing for your peace of mind, reflecting my concerns as it must. I know its arrival, overland so late in the year, will have filled you with distress already, fearing that all is not as it should be here in Camulod. Let me put your mind at rest at once on that. Camulod, per se, is well. We have our problems, as ever, but most of them are concerned with growth, and adjustment to the demands generated by that. I shall deal with that at greater length later in the course of this. For the moment, however, put your mind at ease over Camulod. All things here are as they ought to be.
>
> Elsewhere, however, matters are more troubled and degenerating rapidly. The hour is late here, as I write, and that will enforce brevity upon me, since I must find time for sleep and be abroad before dawn. Come morning, I will be leading a column of our best cavalry to Dergyll ap Griffyd's stronghold in Cambria, travelling quickly even though we are too late before we leave.
>
> Dergyll is dead. The how and why of that will become clear as you read on.

Peter Ironhair has reappeared, after long years of silence. Early, imperfect tidings of his new endeavours came to us some months ago, shortly before the last relief column left to go to you.

You should know that I took steps to strengthen our position the moment I first heard Ironhair's name resurface. I bullied the Council into approving a further intake of recruits, the largest ever since the Colony was founded. I called for a conscription of two thousand men, half immediately and the remainder within the year. There are no concerns over our ability to train and equip them; that is the simple part. The major concern arises over housing and feeding them. This is a grave and genuine concern, as you already know, since each thousand newcomers equates to fifteen hundred or more mouths to feed, once one has acknowledged the dependents who arrive with them. Some of the new recruits will bring in wives and children, while others have close family obligations that preclude their entering our service alone. Some of them, those few who are not utterly raw recruits, we will post out to Ilchester, to the garrison there, but Ilchester, large as it is, is at capacity and we dare not spread our people there beyond the walls. The space around the walls is kept strategically clear, and any houses there would be too vulnerable to attack. The new intake will all be fed and housed, one way or another, nonetheless, and should we be forced into war, our numbers will be reduced again more quickly than we might wish. The dilemma never seems to change, and the answers to the problems of today provide the challenge we must face tomorrow. But the point I sought to make was that our combined forces will now be close to ten thousand men.

In the meantime, since Benedict's arrival in the north-west, your latest letter has arrived, announcing your intention of returning here early next year, when the snows have cleared. The information, and your resolved intent, both gladdened me. We need you here. Let me speak clearly and with brevity, for there is much to tell.

It would appear your suspicions concerning Owain of the Caves were not without foundation, for the man has disappeared, and rumours have come home to us that he has found a place for himself with Ironhair in Cornwall. He knew of our suspicions, I fear. Although he said no word about it to anyone, several of the people I had set to keep a casual eye on his activities all reported to me that he had become aware of their scrutiny. He finally walked out of the gates one day more than a month ago and has not been seen since—not in our lands, at least. I have no proof that he is in Cornwall, but I believe the reports I have heard, precisely because they confirm your suspicions.

Cornwall has been in chaos for more than a year now, torn apart between competing warlords, the most disgusting of whom is Ironhair's demented creature, Carthac. It would seem now that the war there is over and all opposition to the joint overlordship of Ironhair and Carthac has been either subdued or exterminated. Last month, Carthac led an expedition by sea from Cornwall into Cambria, landing near the old Roman town of Venta Silurum, called Caerwent by the local Celts. From there they began raiding inland and westward, burning and wreaking havoc, and threatening Dergyll's fort at Cardiff. Dergyll summoned his warriors and led an army out against them, meeting them close to his own fort, and in the course of the fight came face to face with his relative Carthac, who had set out to find him and kill him. Word has come to us, along with a plea for assistance, that that is exactly what happened. Carthac, in what has been described to me as a gargantuan feat of arms, hewed his way almost alone through Dergyll's chosen guard and killed the king, beheading and dismembering him after he was dead, then cutting out and eating Dergyll's heart in front of all his men.

As you might guess, the sight was too much for the Cambrian host. They ran from the battlefield and dispersed immediately, fleeing in all directions from Carthac's pursuing furies.

Cymberic, Dergyll's eldest son, managed to rally some of them eventually, but finding themselves safe, the survivors then refused to return and outface the inhuman invader, whom they believe to be accursed by their gods and therefore answerable to no living being, god or man. Cymberic has now sent delegates to Camulod, requesting our assistance in regaining his father's kingdom, and I believe that, since it is Arthur's kingdom in truth, we have no other recourse than to offer what we can. If Ironhair and Carthac are to be brought to battle by Camulodian arms—and I can see no means of avoiding that conclusion—then I would rather have it happen otherwhere than in the lands of Camulod.

Yet that is not all. Word has come to me from the other side of the country that Hengist, too, is dead, unnaturally, in Northumbria, and the territories there are plunged in war also. No tidings have yet come to me of Vortigern, and so I fear the worst, there, too. That information, and the lack of it in sufficiency, concerns me even more than this of Cornwall and Cambria. The enemy here in the west is known to us. In the north-east, however, our potential foe is alien, with many differences in beliefs and ways that are completely unknown to our people here, the first and most important being that they fight very differently from us, as you are well aware, and I am concerned that they might come spilling inland, clear across Britain, to do us mischief.

Therefore, dear Brother, waste no time in setting out once the snows have melted. If Connor reappears before you leave, come south with him and leave your men to take the slower route by road. We need you here. I need you here. Everything is as you left it, in good condition and prospering, but who knows how long that may last, with threats from West and East?

I wait to embrace you and see your smile again.

A

When I had read the letter for the third time, I called one of the guards and sent him to find Lucanus, Donuil, Dedalus, Benedict, Philip and Falvo and summon them to join me.

Lucanus was the first to arrive, as I had expected, since his Infirmary was in the block next to my own quarters, and Rufio, who was progressing better than anyone had expected, was his only resident at the time. But the Lucanus who appeared in my doorway was not the presence I had looked for. He looked dreadful, pallid and haggard, his eyes red-rimmed and bloodshot, and he stopped in the doorway, swaying slightly and reaching out to steady himself against the door post.

I leaped to my feet and rushed to take his arm, shocked at his appearance, but he pushed me away, frowning and muttering something about merely having caught a cold. I held his elbow as he moved to a chair, nevertheless, then moved quickly to pour him a cup of wine from the flagon I had ready. He accepted it graciously enough and sipped deeply at it before sighing and placing it on a small table I had moved close to him.

I watched him closely, trying to hide my concern over the way he looked, for I knew he would resent any sign of solicitousness from me. I had remarked before, on the few occasions when I had seen him in less than perfect health, that Lucanus had no patience with his own humanity and simply refused to be sick like any other person. He seemed to take any sign of sickness in himself as a slight upon his own abilities as a physician, and that was the only vanity I ever saw in him. On this occasion, however, he was evidently ill and lacked the strength even to resent the plainness of the fact.

When he picked up his wine again I noticed that his hand was trembling so violently that he almost spilled his drink. I stood gnawing on the inside of my mouth, wondering what to do and how to do it without drawing down his ire. I resolved that, when this meeting reached an end, I would commit him to the care of Tress and Shelagh. He could bark and roar at them, and they would ignore him as casually as they did Donuil and me. Now he was staring down into his cup and I looked down at him, seeing the pallor of his scalp shining through the sparseness of his hair. My old friend had grown frighteningly aged, too suddenly, and was all at once too physically frail. Always a tall, lean figure, he was stooped now, and gaunt, his frame emaciated and his movements tentative and slow. Yet mere weeks earlier, when I had thought him far too frail to journey out to look for Rufio, he had surprised me first by stubbornly refusing to remain behind and then by travelling as quickly as the others in his party, showing no sign of weakness or infirmity.

I told him he looked sick and should be in his bed, not here, and I started to order him away there and then, but he growled at me again, something unintelligible. Then he collected himself and apologized, admitting that he had caught a chill some nights earlier and that it had lodged in his head and chest. He was not vomiting, he told me, nor were his bowels loose. He merely suffered from some inflammation of the joints, a heavy, rheumy cough and a congestion in his head that affected his eyes, making them tear over constantly and depriving him of the ability to read. I informed him that I was going to send Shelagh and Tress to visit him, and to feed him some medicinal broths, and he muttered and grumbled but made no great commotion.

From that point, having won my concession, I thought it better to change the topic, and so we discussed Rufe's progress as we waited for the others to assemble. As each one joined us, he listened for a spell and then asked questions, so that poor Luke had to repeat himself several times. Eventually, everyone was present and each held a cup of wine and withheld from questioning me. They all knew about the letter I had received, of course, and all were curious, but they held their peace. I said nothing until everyone was assembled, at which point I read the letter aloud and invited their reaction and comments.

They were understandably slow to respond, mulling over the tidings and weighing the portent, each from his own viewpoint. Dedalus, as usual, was the first to speak, and he asked me if I would read the letter for them again.

Even after the second reading, no one had much of anything to say. Ambrose had said it all and no amount of wishing or analysis could change the content or alter the way matters stood.

Philip spoke up. "If Connor does appear before we leave, will you do as Ambrose suggests and sail back aboard his galley?"

"Aye, I think that makes good sense. I'll take my original party with me, too, leaving you and your troops to return the way you came. If things are as bad, or become as bad as Ambrose thinks they might, then the sooner we're back in Camulod, the better it will be for everyone concerned." I stopped, seeing doubt in his eyes. "You disagree with that?"

He shrugged, shaking his head. "No, not at all. On the surface, it makes good sense, as you say. I was but thinking of what Ambrose said about Carthac invading Cambria. There could be a fleet of Cornish galleys between here and the coast off Camulod, so your safety might depend on the number of vessels Connor brings back with him. We've no idea of the number of galleys Carthac has, but if his fleet is large enough to move an army, it's large enough to cause you grief on your way south. You might be safer on the road."

I glanced at Dedalus, who nodded, and then I looked to Donuil.

"What think you, Donuil?"

"Philip's right. If Connor brings a strong contingent with him, and I think he will have no less than he's been bringing for the past few years, then we ought to be safe enough. But he'll be shipping no more cattle from the south now. This latest shipment was the last. So he might not bring a strong escort. He might not come at all, in fact. I'm sure my father will have work enough for him to do in the north." He paused then, throwing up his hands. "But who knows what will happen? My advice would be to make a decision about when you'll go, but you can't even do that until we see how fierce or mild the winter will be. If there's no snow, or little of it, you'll be able to leave early, and if you leave early enough, you'll be halfway to Camulod before Connor drops anchor here. If your departure and his arrival coincide, on the other hand, then you can make up your mind which way to go when you see how strong his fleet is. But that's months away, so any decision we seek to arrive at now will be futile."

"Aye," I agreed. "Futile, premature and foolish. So be it, we'll have to wait and see. But one thing has changed, since we first discussed returning. We now face the certainty of war, on at least one front. Even if the threat from the north-east does not materialize, Cambria will not be put to rest until Carthac and Ironhair have been stamped out. I want this winter to be spent in training for war. I don't care if the snow reaches the roof tops, we'll find some place to train our men and keep them in fighting trim. And the same applies to the four boys. They might well see their first campaign before the summer comes, so I want their training stepped up and intensified in every area."

"Rufio should be able to help there." Lucanus had not spoken since I began reading the letter aloud, and now his words brought every head around to look at him. He nodded, sniffing gently and dabbing at his weepy eyes with a square of cloth. "He will be well enough to move around within the month, and that is when he'll need something to do, to keep him occupied. His right shoulder will take months longer to knit, and he may not be able to walk much for the immediate future, but his mind is as active as ever and he needs to be kept from boredom. The boys should serve that purpose."

The assembly, in full agreement, dispersed shortly afterward.

* * *

I did not dream of the death of Lucanus, although that night, when Tress woke me from a deep sleep, raising the alarm, I leaped up in bed with a terror that I had previously known only in connection with my horrifying, prophetic visions.

Luke's health had failed completely in the days and weeks that followed his last meeting with his friends in my quarters. The cough that racked him had grown worse and he had started spitting up blood, as though something had broken loose deep within him. The flesh fell from his bones, so that he withered almost visibly from day to day, and he had grown fevered, alternating between burning temperatures that brought the sweat pouring from his every pore and agued, shivering chills that made him shudder uncontrollably, tossing and turning wildly in delirium.

He had been strong enough to feed himself at first, for several weeks, and had chafed constantly about being kept abed by Shelagh, Tress and the other women of our small community, but as his sickness persisted he grew weaker and the trembling in his hands grew more pronounced, so that by the time the first heavy snow fell he was incapable of spooning broth unaided and his meals were fed to him, with great patience and greater love, by whomever of his friends was present when mealtimes arrived.

Soon even that arrangement became impractical, when he lost the ability to chew or even swallow voluntarily, and it was Shelagh who evolved a system, adapted from the way she had fed orphaned lambs at home in Eire, of feeding him with watered honey and warm milk through an elongated teat made, like a sausage, from the tight-sewn gut of a slain sheep, one end of which she stretched and tied over the neck of a bottle. When it became clear, eventually, that he was incapable of digesting even milk, his diet shrank to watered honey, and we knew that our brave and wonderful Lucanus was doomed.

I was distraught and refused, for the longest time, to accept the evidence that lay before me. I became so obsessive in my blind belief that he must survive that I savaged anyone who seemed, to my eyes, to be too pessimistic concerning his chances. So intractable did I become that my other friends soon chose to stay away from me, rather than risk earning the rough edge of my tongue. Only Tress and Shelagh seemed to have endless patience with my despair, and it was they who carried me to bed the night my old friend died.

I had been awake for three whole days and nights—and they had, too, save that they relieved each other—sleeping only fitfully in a narrow, wooden chair beside Luke's cot. When my body betrayed me and I fell from the chair to the floor without waking up, they carried me between them to another bed close by Luke's and covered me. A short time later, Shelagh went to rest, leaving poor Tress to keep watch, and Tress, too, fell victim to Morpheus.

When she woke me, she was wild-eyed and terrified, and the sight of her terror brought out my own. Lucanus was gone, she cried, out into the snow, barefoot. I can remember thinking, as I threw my cloak over my shoulders, that he had been abducted. He could not possibly have had the strength to walk unaided. Shelagh was awake by this time, grim-faced and filled with resolve, and I sent her to rouse the others. Then, with Tress close behind me, I ran out into the whirling snow and followed the clear imprints of Lucanus's bare feet.

I followed them for more than seventy paces, to the open flight of steps that led up to the high wall's parapet, and there I found him, huddled where he had fallen sideways from the treacherous, snow-covered steps. Donuil and Benedict, the first to emerge after us, found me by the sound of my howls of grief. It was they who carried the still form between them, back into the futile warmth of the Infirmary, where he had spent so many hours and days tending the ills of others.

I have seen and known far, far too many deaths in my long life, and everyone I loved has gone before me, but only one other death in all the years affected me so deeply and so grievously as that, the tragic ending of my closest, oldest friend.

By the time we came to bury Lucanus, I had managed to bring my grief under control and was able to perform the funeral rites with something approaching dignity. On the day of the ceremony, I visited his bier alone to say my last farewell, and I wept as I stood over him, my hand touching the cold hands crossed upon his breast. The widow's peak of his hair was perfect in its symmetry, but the flesh of his face had already fallen in upon itself, settling tightly over the skeletal bones of his cheeks and jaws, and it came to me that this presence I was facing contained nothing of my dear friend and companion, the man whose empathy had healed a score of thousand wounds and bruises. This corpse had nothing in it of the kindly face that laughed so warmly, although rarely enough to make the sight a joy to behold. Where had that warmth and kindness gone, so suddenly?

I can recall speaking to his corpse, but I have no idea what I said to him. I know I was almost overwhelmed several times by the realization that I would never again speak to him or hear his voice. God, how I wanted to honour him in some majestic, all-embracing way! I thought about burning him, as we had my father, in honour of his enormous contributions, not just to us alone in Mediobogdum, but to the generations of Colonists and soldiers he had tended to in Camulod. In the end, however, we interred him on the threshold of his Infirmary and covered him with a simple slab of the local stone, inscribed by our stonemason with a representation of the caduceus of which he had always been so proud and the plain, simple name LUCANUS.

As our masons laid the stone in place and levelled it, I saw the tears streaming down Arthur's cheeks, and I laid my hand on his shoulder, drawing him aside. He walked with me a way, then stopped and looked back at the grave. The snow around it had been tramped into slush by all our feet, but it was still snowing lightly, and the stone stood out stark and black, against the pale ground.

"It's so ugly," the boy said, more to himself than to me.

"Aye, it is, lad," I said softly, knowing he meant the grave and not the stone. "But it's the common fate of all mankind. We all go there, eventually."

He turned on me, angry. "Why, Merlyn? Why should we?"

I had no good answer for him.

"Why must we go into the grave?" he continued. "It's too . . . final, too utter!"

I found myself frowning at him. "What d'you mean by that? It's inevitable, Arthur. The grave awaits all men and women."

"And most deserve no more. But there are some . . . like Luke . . . who deserve more. Now he is there, in a hole, in the ground. Identifiable. Ended. Finished. He's done! There's no more hope that he will ever again . . . achieve . . ."

"How could he, lad?" I asked softly. "Luke's dead."

"I know that, Merlyn!" He was almost spitting out his words, so great was his frustration. "But that doesn't make it right that he should come to such a public and a final end right here. . . ." His voice failed him and he shook his head tightly, his fists clenched by his sides.

"It's not his death that angers me, Merlyn. It's this visible statement we are making that everything he ever did—all his achievements—have ended here, in a clearly marked hole in the ground. There's no need for that, other than that created by our need to honour him. But his honour is in our hearts and memories. We should enshrine him in our minds, but leave his final resting place obscured from all men's eyes. In the spring we will be gone, and he'll be here alone, forgotten and neglected. When men pass by this way and see his stone, they won't know who he was. They'll walk on him, they'll know nothing of him save that he's dead and he's rotting here! Better to bury him someplace unmarked and secret. Then he would be safe from gawking fools and left alone to live in our memories."

I found that my mouth was hanging open in amazement, not at his eloquence but at the content of his speech. I had never heard any man utter such perfect and incontestible good sense and wisdom, and my own bafflement in the face of such obvious truth left me speechless. But there was nothing I could do at that time. I had a momentary vision of the reaction of the others, were I to walk forward and uproot the stone prepared so lovingly to mark Lucanus's grave.

To cover my confusion, I reached out and placed my arm about young Arthur's shoulders, with no notion that, years later, I would recall those words of his and act upon them on his own behalf. Instead, and perhaps foolishly, in retrospect, I looked for a way to break his train of thought and take his mind off on another track. I turned him to face me directly and grasped him by the shoulders.

"Listen to me, Arthur! Where a man rests after his death is unimportant. His importance lies in his life and what he did with it. Luke's life was exemplary. He was, I think, the finest man I've ever known, apart from my own blood. In all things that he did, he was a giant among men, the very soul of wisdom, of compassion and of strength. He stood for the nobility of ordinary, commonplace people. If you seek to emulate him in that aspect alone—in knowing who you are and what you stand for, and perfecting that—then you will live a fine and honourable life.

"Luke's task was to be a surgeon, the very finest surgeon he could be, and he was proud of that. He trained in the finest school on earth, in Alexandria, and then in the Corps of Legionary Surgeons, and he devoted five decades of his seven to serving his fellow men and women. A fine life. A fine record. As you say, he will continue to live long in the minds of those of us fortunate enough to have known him. So face him now, and make your last farewell as it ought to be. Then come and walk with me for a while. After that we will visit Rufio. He'll be despondent over having missed this farewell to our old friend."

I followed him as he turned back to the graveside. There he stood for several moments with his head bowed. I walked slowly towards the parade ground. Arthur caught up to me and walked beside me, and as we went I spoke at length, and he listened.

"May God rest his soul, as befits the soul of one who has done all that was asked of him and all that he asked of himself. His task is done. Mine is ongoing, and yours is about to start." I glanced sideways at him, to make sure he was paying attention. His eyes were looking directly into mine. "Your task is to be a leader of men—a warrior and perhaps even a king some day, in your father's land." I stopped walking, forcing him to look at me again.

"Beginning in the spring, your school will be the field of battle. You'll come to Camulod with me, and you'll ride to war, as a servant and a student, sometimes to me and at others to your Uncle Ambrose. You'll keep our weapons bright and clean and dry. You'll keep our horses fed and clean and dry. You will run errands and fetch and carry messages and orders and dispatches, and you will learn at every turn. And one day, when you have earned the right to do so, you will have messengers and servants and your own armies at your own disposal. This is your real training.

"You have learned much, till now, yet you have not even begun to learn. War is a harsh teacher, Arthur. Its lessons are stark and chastening and its punishments are death and deprivation."

I saw the fire kindle in his eyes. He drew himself up to his full, imposing height, his chest swelling with pride, and I saw a question forming in his eyes.

"Will I have a sword, of my own?"

"Aye, a short-sword at first, purely for self-defence. I will give it to you today. It was made by your own great-grandfather, Publius Varrus, and you will find none finer the length and breadth of this land. It has a matching dagger, perfectly appointed, and a belt to hold the sheaths that house both weapons. But bear in mind at all times henceforth that your primary task in this endeavour will be to learn to follow and obey, not yet to fight. You will obey orders and follow your commander wherever he may lead you.

"In the year ahead of you, you will remain a boy, and yet you'll be expected to comport yourself at all times and in all things as a man. In following, and in obedience, with due attention and observance, you will learn to lead, and to command the honour and respect of the men who will fight with you and for you." I paused, watching the excitement in his eyes dim, and I recalled the bitter chagrin I myself had felt at his age, constrained to ride out with my elders knowing I had not yet earned the right, in their eyes, to fight as a man. The memory bloomed fresh in my mind as though it had been only yesterday. I clenched my fist and laid it against his jaw, nudging him.

"Believe me, lad, although you may not think so now, the time will come soon enough when you will have your own command. Far sooner than you can imagine. Now look at me, eye to eye and man to man." He raised his unique, yellow-flecked eyes to gaze into mine. I felt my throat swell in acknowledgment of his physical beauty and his splendid youth.

"Hear this of me now. I promise you that on the day you take up the burdens of a man, I myself will give you your own sword, and it will be a weapon the like of which men have never seen. These are not idle words, Arthur." I had seen a moment of doubt flickering there in his eyes.

"Yours will be a weapon to set men staring in awe. Not simply your own sword, but one for all the world to marvel at. I promise you that."